"The scenario is going to be a very simple one."

Max continued, "The poor young widow—bravely struggling to support her small daughter—agrees to marry the wealthy prince, and they both live happily ever after. A deeply romantic story. And one guaranteed to bring a tear to the eye of the *most* hardened cynic."

...moments before Amber was fully ...he was saying.

MARY LYONS was born in Toronto, Canada, moving to live permanently in England when she was six, although she still proudly maintains her Canadian citizenship. Having married and raised four children, her life nowadays is relatively peaceful—unlike her earlier years when she worked as a radio announcer, reviewed books and, for a time, lived in a turbulent area of the Middle East. She still enjoys a bit of excitement, combining romance with action, humor and suspense in her books whenever possible.

most in...

It was some m... ...
able to comprehend what he ...

"You must be crazy!" she gasped.

"On the contrary, it makes perfect sense. My daughter clearly needs a father. And I'm *quite* determined that she's going to have one."

Books by Mary Lyons

HARLEQUIN PRESENTS
1499—DARK AND DANGEROUS
1610—SILVER LADY
1633—LOVE IS THE KEY

MARY LYONS

The Yuletide Bride

Harlequin Books

TORONTO • NEW YORK • LONDON
AMSTERDAM • PARIS • SYDNEY • HAMBURG
STOCKHOLM • ATHENS • TOKYO • MILAN
MADRID • WARSAW • BUDAPEST • AUCKLAND

ISBN 0-373-11781-7

YULETIDE BRIDE

First North American Publication 1995.

Copyright © 1994 by Mary Lyons.

This edition published by arrangement with Harlequin Books S.A.

® and TM are trademarks of the publisher. Trademarks indicated with
® are registered in the United States Patent and Trademark Office, the
Canadian Trade Marks Office and in other countries.

Printed in U.S.A.

CHAPTER ONE

'I'M SORRY to be late,' Amber called out breathlessly as she made her way through the noisy, crowded café, to where her friend was sitting at a small table beside the window.

'There was no need to hurry,' Rose Thomas told her, before ordering a pot of coffee from a passing waitress. 'Sally hasn't arrived yet. If I know her, she's probably spending a fortune in one of the dress shops. *And* busy catching up on all the latest scandal, of course!'

'I expect you're right,' Amber grinned. Their friend Sally, the wife of a wealthy and highly respected lawyer, was affectionately known amongst her friends as being both a shop-aholic, and an avid collector of local news and gossip. 'But, as far as I'm concerned,' she added, sighing with relief as she lowered her carrier bags and parcels down on to the floor, 'trying to do any ordinary, everyday shopping during the run-up to Christmas, is nothing but sheer murder.'

'Don't I know it!' Rose agreed with a rueful laugh. 'Even though it's only Thursday, the supermarket was packed as tight as a tin of sardines, and I didn't manage to buy half the things on my shopping list. Since my dreaded mother-in-law is threatening to descend on us for the Christmas holidays, I was just wondering if I could ask you to make me a large plum pudding? And maybe some sponge cakes to keep in the freezer just in case of any unexpected visitors?'

'No problem—all orders gratefully received!' Amber grinned as she pulled out a chair and sat down.

'That'll be wonderful,' Rose sighed with relief. 'By the way, how is your business doing?'

'Well, it looks as though I'm going to be very busy in the kitchen, since I've now got lots of orders from the local shops for Christmas cakes, puddings and mince pies. Unfortunately, the paying-guest side of the business isn't doing so well. Bookings are down, and we don't have anyone staying with us at the moment. On top of which...' she hesitated for a moment. 'I don't want anyone else to know just yet, because I'm still trying to summon up enough courage to break the bad news to my mother. However, after a really awful interview with the bank manager, I've finally had to face the hard, financial facts of life and put my house on the market.'

'You don't mean...?'

Amber nodded. 'Yes, I'm afraid so. I've seen Mr Glover, the house agent, and the Hall is going to be advertised for sale as from the beginning of next week.'

'Oh, no! I'm *so* sorry,' Rose exclaimed, gazing at her friend with deep concern and sympathy. Since they'd both been born and raised in the same small, riverside market town of Elmbridge, she was well aware of the misfortunes suffered in the past by Amber's family; the public scandal and disgrace surrounding the crash of her father's large business empire, swiftly followed by his death and her mother's complete mental breakdown. It seemed so desperately unfair, Rose told herself, that after all the trials and tribulations which she'd so bravely confronted in the past, her friend should now be having to face yet even more problems.

'Oh, well—it's not exactly the end of the world. The Hall is far too large for us, and the heating bills are astronomical,' Amber pointed out, attempting to put a brave face on what was, in reality, a disastrous family situation.

'But where will you go?' Rose asked anxiously as the waitress brought a tray to their table. 'Have you found anywhere else to live?'

Amber sighed. 'No, not yet. I'm hoping to buy a small cottage, not too far away from Elmbridge. Mainly, of course, because I don't want to take Lucy away from either her school, or her friends.'

'I'll keep my ear to the ground, and let you know the moment I hear of anything,' Rose assured her earnestly. However, as she poured them both a cup of coffee, she couldn't help worrying about how her friend would manage to cope with life in a small cottage.

She'd been away at college when Amber, at the age of eighteen, had married Clive Stanhope, a very wealthy if somewhat wild young man, who'd owned Elmbridge Hall, an ancient Tudor mansion and by far the largest house in the district. Clive's wedding to Amber—the once rich, but by then penniless only child of a disgraced businessman—followed by the birth of a daughter only six months after their marriage, had provided plenty of ammunition for gossip

in the small town. However, Amber had subsequently
won everyone's admiration by the way she'd coped
after her husband's fatal car accident, a year later,
when it became known that Clive had apparently been
a compulsive gambler, and all the land was heavily
mortgaged. In fact, after everything had been sold to
meet a mountain of debts, the young widow had been
left with nothing but Elmbridge Hall.

Over the past few years, Rose had looked forward
to a time when her friend would meet the right man
and live happily ever after. With thick shoulder-length
straight hair, a glorious shade of deep golden brown,
and large green eyes set above a warm generous
mouth, Amber was a very beautiful woman. Certainly Philip Jackson, the young local doctor, seemed
to think so. But, despite all her matchmaking efforts,
Rose couldn't understand why her friend—who was
also a loving mother and superb cook—appeared to
be so reluctant to get married again. But now . . . well,
surely Amber would see the sense in marrying a man
who had so much to offer her?

'I saw Philip Jackson the other day. He tells me
that he's going to his parents' home in Cumberland
for Christmas.'

'Oh, yes?' Amber murmured, eyeing her friend
warily.

'Well, I was just wondering if . . . er . . . if he's asked
you and Lucy to join him?'

'For Heaven's sake—don't you *ever* give up?'
Amber groaned, shaking her head in mock exasperation. 'I thought you'd promised to stop trying to
marry me off to all the single men in town?'

'Yes, well...' Rose's cheeks reddened slightly. 'I really don't mean to interfere in your life. But it's almost seven years since Clive died. And it's as clear as daylight to me—especially after hearing the sad news about the sale of your house—that what you *really* need is a husband.'

'I hope you're not suggesting that I should marry Philip—or anyone else, for that matter—merely to provide a way out of my difficulties?' Amber demanded bluntly.

'No—of course, I'm not,' Rose protested, waving a hand dismissively in the air. 'But surely this is the perfect time to think seriously about your future?'

'Oh, come on, Rose! We're not just talking about me. There's Lucy to consider, as well. It's not everyone who'd want to take on a little seven-year-old girl— not to mention my scatty mother.'

'I know your mother can be a problem 'at times,' Rose agreed, well aware that Violet Grant, who'd never really recovered from the trauma of her husband's sudden death, was an extra and often tiresome burden for the young widow's slim shoulders to carry. 'But Philip is clearly mad about you, and you can't deny that he'd be a really good choice of stepfather for Lucy. On top of which, I happen to think that you'd make a *marvellous* doctor's wife.'

Amber smiled and shook her head. 'Thanks for the vote of confidence! I know you mean well, and that what you're saying probably makes sense, but... OK, OK, I promise to give the matter some thought,' she added hurriedly as her old friend seemed determined to press the point. 'Now, tell me—is your mother-in-law going to be staying for the *whole* of the Christmas holidays?' she asked, firmly changing the subject. Unfortunately, there was no way she could tell Rose the truth; that having already made one marriage of convenience—although Clive Stanhope had been a very kind, generous-hearted man—she was desperately wary of entering into such an arrangement ever again.

To be fair, her friend did have a point about Lucy. Ever since Clive had died, when her daughter was just under a year old, she had done her best to be both mother and father to the little girl. That she hadn't always succeeded in properly fulfilling the two, very different roles over the past seven years, was a fact of which Amber was becoming daily more aware. So, maybe Rose was right? Maybe she ought to stop shilly-shallying, and force herself to take the practical, sensible decision to marry Philip Jackson?

A highly respected doctor, who'd recently joined a local practice, Philip was a genuinely nice and considerate man. The fact that he also had a private income, lived in a large house all on his own and was reasonably good-looking, with fair hair and kind brown eyes, made him the obvious candidate as far as her friends were concerned. But, while she was very fond of Philip, she wasn't in love with him. And having once experienced the intense, tempestuous drive of overwhelming emotion and desire, it seemed quite wrong to settle for second best.

' . . . so, the old dragon is bound to make Christmas a misery for all of us, and . . . *Good Heavens*! It looks as if Sally really *has* been spending a fortune!'

Startled by Rose's sudden exclamation, and guiltily aware that while she'd been buried deep in thought, she'd missed most of what her friend had been saying, Amber looked up to see a petite blonde woman making her way towards them, her progress impeded by the enormous amount of parcels she was carrying.

'Hi, darlings! I'm sorry to be so late,' she cried. 'I've never known the shops to be so crowded. But I know you'll both forgive me when I tell you some absolutely *riveting* news!'

'I don't know why you aren't running your own gossip column in the local newspaper!' Rose mocked as she and Amber exchanged a quick grin with one another.

'Oh, don't be so stuffy,' Sally laughed good-naturedly, placing her shopping on an adjacent chair as she sat down to join them. 'Besides, this isn't a rumour—it's the genuine truth, which everyone will know about sooner or later,' she added before turning to Amber. 'Do you remember Lady Parker? The mega-rich old woman that lived near you, and who died in a big fire at her house well over a year ago?'

Amber nodded. 'I never actually met the old lady, because she'd been a recluse for many years. Apparently the house was burned to the ground.'

'Right. Well, my dear husband was in charge of her affairs, and it seems that she always refused to make a will,' Sally continued excitedly. 'So, it took John simply *ages* to track down her only living relative. However, he's now finally succeeded, and Lady Parker's ten thousand acres—plus goodness knows how much extra money in stocks and shares, has all been inherited by...''Mad Max''!'

'*What*?' Rose gasped in astonishment. 'You don't mean...? Not...not the old vicar's son—Max Warner?'

'Yes!' Sally beamed at her friends, delighted at the expression of shock and surprise on their faces. Amber, in particular, appeared to be totally stunned.

'I just *knew* that you'd both be amazed to hear about the return of our old school heart-throb,' she continued happily. 'Of course, it's been years since the Reverend Augustus Warner died, so I suppose that it's not surprising that we'd forgotten all about his son. When John first told me about the return of ''Mad Max'', I could hardly believe my ears!'

'He certainly deserved that nickname!' Rose laughed. 'I remember him as a wild tearaway—with a simply *terrible* reputation for breaking girls' hearts. All the same...' she paused, staring into space with a dreamy expression on her face. 'Max really *was* diabolically attractive, wasn't he?'

'Absolutely scrumptious!' Sally agreed with a grin. 'In fact, with his curly black hair and those twinkling, wicked blue eyes, the effect on our young teenage hearts was completely *lethal*!'

'Mmm...' Rose gave a sheepish grin. 'After he kissed me at my sixteenth birthday party, I can remember being madly in love with Max for a whole year.'

'Weren't we all?' her friend sighed heavily. 'Of course, Amber is two years younger than either of us, and so probably won't recall any of the completely crazy things he used to get up to. Do you remember that huge black motorbike of his? And the really *ferocious* competition amongst us girls, as to who could wangle a ride behind him on the pillion seat?'

'Oh, yes! One of the highlights of my teens was when he once took me down the motorway at well over a hundred miles an hour.' Cheeks flushed, Rose shook her head at her own folly. 'I was absolutely scared to death, of course. But it was worth it. I reckoned I was the envy of everyone at school for at least two whole weeks!'

Sally giggled. 'You certainly were. I can remember Cynthia Henderson, for instance, collapsing into a jealous fit of raving hysterics—right in the middle of school assembly!'

'It's all very well to talk about old school days, but where's Max been all these years?' Rose asked. 'I know he was very clever. And, despite fooling around, he passed his school exams with flying colours before gaining a scholarship to university. But his father, old Reverend Warner, died while I was away training to be a nurse—and I've never heard anything about Max from that day to this.'

'Nor had anyone else,' Sally agreed. 'In fact, my dear husband had almost given up the search for him. And then...when he was invited to a very grand, fundraising dinner in London a few weeks ago, he discovered that Max Warner was the principal guest speaker!'

'Good Heavens!'

'We all thought that Max had dropped off the edge of the world, didn't we? But not a bit of it!' Sally gave a loud peal of laughter. 'It seems he had an uncle in America. So, when his father died eight years ago, Max went off to the States to make his fortune. He's now returned to England as the terrifically successful, managing director of a huge, high-powered public company. *And* he's made an appointment to see John sometime soon, here in Elmbridge. *How about that*!'

While her friends were chatting excitedly together, exchanging news of a long-lost old school friend, Amber had been sitting rigidly still, her mind dazed and reeling, as though she'd been hit on the back of her head by a heavy sandbag. Even Sally's sudden shriek of horror hardly managed to penetrate her stunned brain.

'Oh, help—just look at the time!' Sally quickly jumped up from the table. 'I should have been at the hairdresser's at least ten minutes ago!'

'What an extraordinary piece of news about Max Warner,' Rose mused as Sally bustled out of the café, before catching sight of her friend's chalk-white face and dazed, stricken expression.

'*Amber*! What on earth's wrong? Are you all right?'

'Yes, I...' She took a deep breath and tried to pull herself together. 'Really, I'm fine,' she shakily informed Rose, who was gazing at her with deep concern.

'You've been trying to do too much,' her friend pointed out firmly. 'Having to cope with your mother is enough to try the patience of a saint! And running that huge old house...'

'I'm sorry...I have to go. I really must get home...there's so much cooking to do....' Amber muttered breathlessly as she swiftly gathered up her parcels.

'You don't look at all well. I hope you're not going down with flu?' Her friend gazed with concern at Amber's pale face and trembling figure. 'If you're not feeling too good, there's no need to worry about picking up Emily from school tomorrow. I can easily put off my trip to London.'

'No... don't do that. I'm fine. I've just got a lot to do today—that's all,' she assured Rose, before hurriedly making her way out of the café.

Dazed and shivering with nervous tension, Amber sat huddled in the front seat of her ancient Land Rover, staring blindly at the wind-rippled, dark water of the wide river estuary. Completely shattered by Sally's news, she'd known that there was no way she was in a fit state to drive the five miles back to Elmbridge Hall. Not when it had taken her several fumbled attempts to even place her key in the ignition. But since she couldn't continue sitting in the town car park, either, she'd cautiously made her way down to the quayside which was, as she'd hoped, completely deserted at this time of year.

She ought to have *known* that this was likely to happen sooner or later, Amber told herself grimly, wrapping her arms tightly about her trembling figure. What a blind, stupid fool she had been—living in a fool's paradise for the past eight years. While she'd had no idea that Lady Parker was his grandmother, she *should* have realised that Max Warner must eventually return—like the prodigal son—to his old home town of Elmbridge.

Suddenly feeling in need of some fresh air, Amber opened the door and stepped down from the Land Rover. Walking slowly up and down over the frosty cobblestones, she desperately tried to clear her mind, to try and work out what she was going to do. But it was proving difficult to think clearly when her mind seemed to be filled with memories of the past.

A much-loved and only child of wealthy parents, Amber had always been protected from the harsh facts of life. But the catastrophic events surrounding the collapse of her father's business empire, during the long hot summer of her eighteenth birthday, had shattered and destroyed for ever the safe, secure world of her childhood. Shocked and bewildered by the newspaper headlines trumpeting 'Financial Scandal!' and 'Millions Lost by Suffolk Businessman!' she'd been totally ill-equipped to deal with either the devastating news of her father's bankruptcy, or his sudden death from a fatal heart attack. And when her mother—unable to face the prospect of either being shunned by her former friends, or the total reverse of the family fortunes—had collapsed and been placed by the family doctor in a local psychiatric nursing home, Amber had found herself standing completely alone amidst the ashes of her previous existence.

Maybe if, during that tense and anxious time, there had been someone with whom she could have discussed her problems, her life might have turned out differently. But with no close relations other than an elderly aunt in London, and all her school friends either away on holiday—or prevented by their cautious parents from associating with the child of a man who had, reportedly, been involved in crooked financial dealings—her only relief from the mounting stress and strain had been to take long, solitary walks through the deserted meadows edging the river-bank near her home. And there it was that Max had found her, one hot afternoon in late August, weeping with despair and deep unhappiness.

Despite an early teenage crush on the wickedly glamorous Max Warner, she'd seen nothing of him during the past five years. However, it had seemed the most natural thing in the world when he'd put his strong arms about her trembling figure.

'How could I have forgotten those wonderful, sparkling green eyes?' he'd said, smiling lazily down at her as wiped away her tears. 'I always knew that you'd grow up to become a real beauty.'

'Have I really...?' she'd gasped, her cheeks flushing hectically beneath his warm, engaging smile as he gently brushed the long, damp tendrils of hair from her wide brow, before lowering his dark head to softly kiss her trembling lips.

Miraculously, it seemed that Max—unlike so many of her family's friends and acquaintances—did not hold her personally responsible for her father's misdeeds. And as they'd walked slowly back to her house, whose contents were now mostly in packing cases for despatch to the local saleroom, she realised that he, too, was suffering from the sudden loss of a parent. Completely immersed in her own problems, Amber had only been dimly aware of the Reverend Warner's recent death from a massive stroke, resulting in Max's urgent recall from America, where he'd just completed his postgraduate degree at the Harvard Business School. However, when he confessed to the misery and desolation of being now alone in large empty rooms of the vicarage, or his deep regret at not having been closer to his father, saying, 'I was pretty wild as a teenager, and there's no doubt he must have found me a considerable pain in the neck,' she was easily able to understand Max's thoughts and feelings at such an unhappy time.

If *only* she hadn't been quite so young and innocent! Amber squirmed with embarrassment as she now gazed back down the years at her youthful self. With her head stuffed full of romantic fantasies, her dazed mind reeling beneath the assault of those glittering blue eyes and his overwhelming sensual attraction, it was no wonder that—like some modern-day Cinderella—she'd immediately fallen head over heels in love with her very own Prince Charming. But if Max found her obvious adoration a nuisance, he gave no indication of doing so, as day after day he joined her for long walks along the deserted river-bank. So, it was perhaps inevitable that, having tripped and fallen over a log hidden in the thick grass, she should have found herself clasped in his arms, fervently responding to the fiercely determined possession of his lips and body.

It wasn't for lack of trying, of course. But, over the past eight years, Amber had never been able to fool herself into believing that Max was totally to blame for what happened. Pathetically ignorant of lovemaking as she was, the feverish impetus of her desire had been every bit as strong as his, her ardent and passionate response clearly overpowering any scruples he may have had.

It had always seemed to Amber as if the next few weeks had been an all too brief, halcyon period of enchantment and rapture. Neither the deep sadness of her father's death, nor her increasing worries about her mother's mental condition, had seemed to disturb their mutual ecstasy and euphoric happiness, or the uncontrollable desire that exploded between them each and every time they were able to be alone with one another.

Unfortunately, there was nothing they could do to prevent the harsh, cruel light of reality from eventually breaking through their cloud of happiness. Both the fast-approaching sale of her family home, and the offer to Max of a job in his uncle's large firm in America, meant that they would soon have to part.

Starry-eyed with joy when he placed a small gold ring on her finger, vowing that they would be married just as soon as he was well established in his new career, Amber had never doubted Max's total sincerity. 'My uncle's offering me a good salary, with a partnership in the near future. So, it won't be long before we can be together for ever and ever,' he'd pledged, clasping her tightly in his arms before leaving for the airport. 'Just promise that you'll wait for me?'

'Of course I will,' she told him fervently, blinking rapidly in order to prevent the weak tears from running down her cheeks as she waved him goodbye.

And she *had* waited. Waiting, alone in the empty house through the long autumn days, while her father's creditors checked that all her family's precious possessions had been sold; waiting, while her mother who, if not yet ready to leave the hospital, was showing definite signs of improvement. Until, well over two months after his departure, her increasing apprehension that she might be pregnant hardened into certainty, and she realised that she was in deep and desperate trouble....

A sudden, freezing gust of wind cut into her memories of that intensely unhappy time, bringing her sharply back to her present-day problems—and the questions raised by the fear of Max's return. However, by the time she found herself driving back home, Amber had managed to regain a small measure of self-control.

She couldn't, of course, pretend that Max's return was likely to be anything other than a major disaster. On the other hand, to have found herself in such a blind panic, feeling sick and shivering like a leaf at the mere sound of his name, wasn't going to achieve anything, either. Leaving her own desperate worry and fears about Lucy aside, it was plainly quite ridiculous of her to have been so overcome with sheer terror. Max may have inherited Lady Parker's large estate—but so what? If, as Sally had said, he was enjoying such a successful career in London, and only visiting Elmbridge to meet his grandmother's lawyer, there was very little likelihood of his ever returning to live permanently in the area. Besides...all this frantic shock and worry could well prove to be completely unfounded. It was more than likely that such an attractive, vital man would be married by now, and have completely forgotten all about their very brief, secret love affair.

As she made her way up the drive, she was comforted by the familiar sight of the ancient mansion with its warm red brick and mullioned windows, which, despite its imminent sale, seemed at the moment to offer a place of refuge and safety.

An American guest had once referred enthusiastically to Elmbridge Hall as a 'Medieval Gem'. He may have been right, Amber thought wryly as she carried her shopping into the house, but he should try living here in the winter! Which was yet another reason for selling this huge, rambling old house, she reminded herself grimly, only too well aware of the astonomically high bills for coal and electricity, which would be due for payment in the new year.

'Hello, dear. Are you going out shopping?' her mother murmured, wandering into the hall and casting an approving glance at her daughter's old tweed coat, over a matching skirt and green, polo-necked sweater, the same colour as her eyes.

Stifling a sigh, Amber explained that, far from going anywhere, she had just returned with the shopping—before once again reminding the older woman of the large note pad and pencil beside the telephone.

'Mother! Do *please* try and concentrate,' she added, as Violet Grant drifted about the hall, idly touching up a flower decoration here, and straightening an oil painting there. 'I've got a huge order for plum puddings. So, I'm going to shut myself away in the kitchen until it's time to collect Lucy from school. As I won't be able to hear the phone here in the hall, I'm relying on you to take down any bookings. It's *very* important that you write down the correct names and the exact dates they want to stay with us—OK?'

'There's no need to worry, dear.' Violet Grant gave her daughter an injured look. 'You know that I always do my best to welcome your friends to the house.'

Amber closed her eyes for a moment, mentally counting up to ten. While she loved her mother very dearly, there was no doubt that even her seven-year-old daughter, Lucy, seemed to have a stronger grasp on reality than poor Violet. Unfortunately, the older woman seemed incapable of understanding either the family's dire need for hard cash, or the necessity of accurately recording all telephone messages.

A child of wealthy parents, and much indulged by her rich husband, Violet's butterfly mind had never been able to fully accept their changed circumstances. Even though it was now a long time since all the scandal and newspaper headlines, which had surrounded both the crash of her husband's business empire and his subsequent fatal heart attack, Violet continued to live in a private world of her own.

Four years ago, when Amber had first floated the idea of taking in paying guests, her mother had been distraught.

'You must have taken leave of your senses!' Violet had gasped in horror, before collapsing down on to a chair. 'To think that I should live to see my own daughter running a . . . a *boarding-house!*'

'Oh, come on, Mother—it's hardly the end of the world!' Amber had retorted with exasperation. While she felt sorry for the older woman, she nevertheless knew that they both had to face up to the harsh facts of life. 'When poor Clive died, he left us with nothing but this house and a huge pile of debts. We've sold everything we can, and now that Lucy is growing up, she's going to be needing clothes and toys, and lots of other things that we simply can't afford at the moment. The house is our only asset, which is why I've decided to take in paying guests. However, if you can think of an alternative plan of action—I'll be glad to hear it!'

Not able to come up with a viable course of action, it seemed the only way Violet Grant could cope with their changed status was to completely close her mind to what she called the 'sordid, financial aspects' of Amber's business. However, by insisting on treating those who came to the house as personal guests of her daughter—charmingly welcoming everyone as if they were old family friends—Violet had, in many ways, proved to be a considerable asset.

But that state of affairs was now coming to an end, Amber quickly reminded herself as she made her way to the kitchen, feeling distinctly guilty at not yet having found the courage to tell her mother about the forthcoming sale of the Hall. She was deeply ashamed of being such a coward—but dreaded having to face the hysterical scenes that were bound to follow such bad news.

All the same... she told herself some time later as she moistened the heavy, dried-fruit pudding mixture with a hefty dose of brandy, she *really* couldn't put off telling her mother the truth for much longer. As for the question of Max's return—well, the sooner she put it out of her mind, the better. After all, no one had any idea of what had happened during that long, hot summer over eight years ago. So, there was no reason why the episode shouldn't remain firmly buried in the mists of time.

Continuing to sternly lecture herself throughout the rest of the day and most of the next, Amber had gradually managed to recover her usual good sense and equilibrium. Being busily occupied in trying to catch up with all her orders for home-made Christmas produce was proving to be a positive advantage, since she simply didn't have time to think about anything other than the job in hand. Only abandoning the kitchen to collect Lucy and her friend, Emily Thomas, from school, she was delighted when they decided that it would be fun to explore the contents of some of her mother's old trunks up in the attic. There was nothing that Lucy liked more than dressing up in Violet's old clothes—a fact that Amber welcomed, since it meant that the little girls were happily occupied while she made another batch of mince pies for the freezer.

Busily absorbed by her work in the kitchen, she was startled when one of the row of old-fashioned bells began ringing high on the wall above her head.

Glancing up, she noted with surprise that there was obviously someone at the front door. Certainly Rose, on a shopping trip to Cambridge, wouldn't be collecting Emily for another hour at least—and she couldn't think of anyone else likely to be calling at this time of day. However, as the bell was given yet another impatient ring, she realised that she was going to have to go and answer it.

Wondering who on earth it could be, Amber didn't bother to remove her messy apron as she hurried down the dark corridor, through the green baize door, which separated the kitchen quarters from the rest of the house, and across the stone floor of the large hall.

'OK, OK, I'm coming!' she muttered under her breath as someone began banging loudly on the old oak door.

'I'm sorry to keep you waiting . . .' she began as she opened the door. And then, almost reeling with shock, she found herself frantically clutching the large brass door handle for support. With the blood draining from her face, her dazed and confused mind seemed barely able to comprehend the evidence of her own eyes. Because there—standing casually on the doorstep beside Mr Glover, the house agent—was the tall dark figure of Max Warner!

CHAPTER TWO

JABBING a fork into the iron-hard frosty ground, Amber tried to ignore the bitterly cold wind gusting through the large kitchen garden. Saving money by growing their own fruits and vegetables was all very well, but having to dig up leeks and parsnips in the middle of winter wasn't exactly one of her favourite pastimes.

On the other hand, she'd always found that there was nothing like a bout of hard digging or hoeing to put any problems she might have in their correct perspective. Unfortunately, it didn't seem to be working at the moment, Amber told herself gloomily, pausing for a moment to brush a lock of golden brown hair from her troubled green eyes.

What on earth was she going to do? It was a question that she had been asking herself, with increasing desperation, ever since she'd discovered Max Warner—together with the house agent, Mr Glover—standing on her front doorstep. Even now, two weeks later, there seemed nothing she could do to calm her tense, edgy body, while her brain appeared to be frozen rigid with fright. In fact, with her nerves at screaming point, she wasn't able to think about *anything*, other than Max's sudden reappearance in her life—which had to be one of the most catastrophic and potentially disastrous twists of fate she'd ever experienced!

She'd hardly been able to believe the evidence of her own eyes. Almost paralytic with shock, the breath driven from her body as if from a hard blow to the solar plexus, it had taken her some moments to realise that it truly *was* Max, and not an evil figment of her overheated imagination.

'Good afternoon, Mrs Stanhope. It was very good of you to agree to see my client at such short notice,' the estate agent had murmured pompously, his voice seeming to be coming from somewhere far away. 'I...er...I hope you haven't forgotten our appointment?' he added hesitantly, gazing with apprehension at the young woman, who was staring silently at both him and Mr Warner in such a wide-eyed, unnerving manner.

'An appointment...?' Amber echoed helplessly, her mind in a chaotic whirl as she stared past him to where a sleek, glossy black sports car was parked beside Mr Glover's vehicle on the gravelled drive outside the house. 'I don't understand. Do...do you mean you want to see over the house?'

'Yes, of course.' Mr Glover gave a nervous laugh, clearly wondering if the young widow was entirely 'all there'. 'I made the arrangement with your mother this morning, and...'

'Oh, no!' Amber gasped, suddenly realising that her mother was likely to appear on the scene any minute. 'I'm sorry—you can't *possibly* see around the house today. It's *absolutely* out of the question!' she babbled hysterically, glancing nervously behind her as she tried to close the door. 'I haven't yet told my mother, you see. She doesn't realise...she has no idea that the Hall is for sale. You'll just have to go away, and...and maybe come back some other time.'

Unfortunately, Max Warner had quickly taken a firm grip of the situation. Swiftly placing a well-shod foot in the door, he thanked Mr Glover for his services, smoothly informing the estate agent that he was quite capable of coping with the 'delicate' state of affairs at the Hall.

'There's no need to worry or disturb Mrs Grant. I'm quite confident that her daughter will be pleased to give me a personal conducted tour around the house.'

Oh, no, I won't! Amber screamed silently at him as the house agent gave a helpless shrug of his shoulders, walking back down the steps as Max pushed the door open, moving calmly past her trembling figure into the wide, spacious hall.

Completely stunned, Amber could only stare at him with glazed eyes, quite certain that she must be in the midst of some awful nightmare.

'I should have been in touch with you before now,' Max told her quietly. 'But I've been abroad and only recently heard the news.'

'"The news"?' she echoed blankly.

'I merely wanted to say that I was very sorry to learn about Clive's death.'

'Yes...um...it was a long time ago, of course. So much seems to have happened since then,' she muttered with a helpless shrug.

'However, it does seem as though you've done very well for yourself, Amber,' he drawled, glancing around at the old family portraits in their heavy gilt frames and the warm, comfortable effect of copper vases filled with greenery against the highly polished, old oak panelling.

The unexpectedly cynical, scathing note in his deep voice acted as a dash of freezing cold water on her shocked, numb state of mind. Her hackles rising, she was just about to demand an explanation for his sudden appearance—surely he couldn't really be interested in buying the house?—when her mother floated into the hall.

'How nice to see you. Have you come far?' Violet murmured, giving the tall man a welcoming smile.

Amber nearly groaned aloud. This was definitely *not* the time for her mother to be putting on a performance of her 'gracious hostess' routine!

Max took the older woman's outstretched hand and smiled warmly down at her. 'It's some time since we've met. However, I think that you'll probably remember my father, the Reverend Augustus Warner. He was the vicar here at Elmbridge some years ago.'

Violet beamed up at the man towering over her slight frame. 'Of course, I remember him. And you must be Max. The naughty boy who was always in trouble,' she added with a twinkling smile.

'Indeed I was!' he agreed with a grin.

'Well—you've certainly grown since those days! It looks as though you've done very well for yourself,' Violet told him, casting an approving glance over his expensive, obviously hand-tailored, dark grey suit.

'Now—I'm sure that you must have had a long drive. How about a nice cup of tea?'

'Mother! I really don't think...'

'Nonsense, dear,' Violet murmured, ignoring her daughter's husky, strangled protest as she placed a hand on his arm, leading Max towards the large sitting room. 'If he's driven some distance, I'm sure the poor man must be simply dying of thirst.'

'*Mother*...!' Amber whispered urgently, but the older woman clearly had no intention of taking any notice of her desperate plea. As for the 'poor man'— he merely turned his dark head to give her a cool, sardonic smile before accompanying the older woman into the sitting room.

Left standing alone in the hall, Amber could feel her initial shock and dismay rapidly giving way to long-suppressed feelings of rage and anger. How *dare* Max swan back into her life, completely out of the blue like this? Not only intimating that she'd married poor Clive for his money, but with absolutely no appearance of regret—let alone an abject apology for the way he'd treated her in the past.

However, just as she was telling herself fiercely that she'd *never* sell the Hall to Max—not even if he offered her a million pounds—Amber caught sight of herself in a large mirror hanging on the wall.

Nearly fainting with shock and dismay, it was all she could do not to shriek out loud in horror! The woman gazing back at her looked as though she'd been drawn through a knot-hole backwards, her face hot and flushed from the heat of the stove, and her apron covered with smears of flour and mincemeat.

No wonder Max had been looking at her with such a caustic, scathing expression on his handsome face!

Realising that it was far too late to worry about his initial impression, Amber flew back along the corridor into the kitchen. Slinging the kettle on the hot plate of the ancient Aga, and practically throwing a tea tray of cups and saucers together, she ran back to the hall and up the wide curving staircase, taking the steps two at a time as she raced towards her bedroom.

Now, when it was almost too late, the shock waves of Max's unexpected arrival were gradually clearing from her mind. And it was the sharp, sudden awareness of the fresh danger she was facing that lent wings to her feet as she hastily stripped off the grubby, sticky apron and ran into the adjoining bathroom to wash her hands and face. Dragging a brush through her tangled hair, she could feel her heart pounding like a sledgehammer, just as if she'd been doing an exhausting aerobics workout. And it looked as if she was going to need all the agility of just such an exercise, she told herself breathlessly as she desperately tried to pull herself together.

Unless she could put a gag on her mother's garrulous tongue, there was a strong possibility that she was going to find herself in the middle of an utterly *disastrous* situation. The only chink of blue in an otherwise dark, ominous cloud was that she could hear the faint sounds of footsteps and movement overhead—evidence that Lucy and Emily were still playing happily together up in the attic.

Fervently praying that the little girls would stay safely out of sight, Amber quickly checked her appearance in a large, full-length mirror. Unfortunately, there was nothing she could do about her old navy sweater and jeans. Mostly because she couldn't spare the time, but also because she was determined not to let Max think that his sudden, startling manifestation on her doorstep mattered a jot to her one way or another.

Who are you trying to fool? she asked herself with disgust, realising that there was little she could do to disguise the hectic flush on her pale cheeks, or the hunted, wary look in her nervous green eyes. There was nothing for it, but to face the music. Let's hope they're playing my tune, she thought hysterically, her stomach churning with nerves as she quickly left the room.

'Max and I have just been reminiscing about old times,' her mother trilled happily as Amber entered the sitting room carrying the tea tray. 'We really do miss his dear father, don't we?'

'Er...yes, we do,' Amber muttered, trying to stop her hands from shaking as she poured the tea. Carefully avoiding Max's eyes, she chose a seat on the other side of the room, as far away from him as possible.

She'd been very fond of the Reverend Warner, a rather austere and scholarly widower, who'd been the vicar of Elmbridge during the years when she had been growing up. However, it had been obvious that neither he nor the rapid succession of housekeepers at the vicarage had the first notion of how to cope with his motherless son, Max—who'd gained a considerable local reputation as a wild tearaway.

'You'll hardly recognise the town nowadays,' Violet informed him. 'The old Victorian theatre has been turned into a multiple cinema, and there's a hideous new supermarket next to the railway station,' she added, oblivious of her daughter's tense figure as she turned to ask, 'What do they call it, dear?'

'Pick 'n' Pay,' Amber muttered, staring fixedly down at the cup in her trembling hands.

This is absolutely ridiculous! What *am* I doing, making polite conversation as if I've never met this man before...? she asked herself with mounting hysteria, convinced that she'd somehow strayed into a completely mad, unreal world. And why was Max here? Surely he couldn't be seriously interested in buying the Hall—not when Sally had said he was based in London?

For the first time since she'd clapped eyes on him, Amber realised that she knew nothing about Max— or what had happened to him during the past eight years. But obviously, such an attractive man was bound to be married by now, she told herself grimly.

'...isn't that right, dear?'

'What?' Jerked out of her depressing thoughts, Amber gazed at her mother in confusion.

'I was just talking about some of your old friends who are still living in the town,' the older woman murmured, frowning in puzzlement at her daughter, who for some reason was looking strangely pale and nervous, before turning back to their visitor. 'There's Rose Thomas, of course. As it happens, Rose's daughter, Emily, is playing here with Lucy this afternoon, and...'

'I'm sure Max would like another cup of tea,' Amber said quickly.

'No, I'm fine, thank you,' he drawled, lifting the cup to his lips.

Luckily, it seemed as though her swift, hasty interruption had succeeded in turning her mother's thoughts in a new direction as she asked, 'Are you now thinking of coming back to live here in Elmbridge?'

'Well...' he murmured, pausing for a moment as he turned his dark head to gaze at her daughter's suddenly stiff, rigid figure. 'John Fraser and I are still trying to sort out the affairs of my grandmother, who died over a year ago. Unfortunately, following the fire, there's no longer a large house on the estate. So, I'm not entirely sure about my future plans.'

Violet Grant looked at him blankly for a moment before exclaiming, 'Goodness me! I'd quite forgotten that old Lady Parker was your grandmother. She must have been well over ninety.'

'Ninety-two, I believe,' he agreed with a dry smile.

'I hadn't seen anything of her for the past ten years. But it was a shock to hear that she'd died in that terrible fire,' she told him sorrowfully. 'Such a lovely house—what a shame that it's now nothing but a burnt-out ruin. Is it *really* true that Lady Parker cut your mother off without a penny?' Violet added, unable to resist a juicy piece of gossip. 'That she refused to either see or speak to her daughter after she ran away to marry your father?'

Max shrugged his broad shoulders. 'Who knows? I certainly never met my grandmother,' he said briefly, before changing the subject and encouraging the older woman to relate all the changes that had taken place in the town over the past few years.

Once her mother was launched upon the safe, harmless topic of the recent development of Elmbridge, Amber could feel some of her nervous tension draining away. And it gave her a chance to covertly study the man she hadn't seen for such a long time.

Although they'd grown up together, the six-year difference in their ages had seemed the most enormous gap when she'd first entered her teens. Especially as Max had always appeared to be older and more mature than his true age. There had been something about the determined set of his mouth and the glittering blue eyes that had never been young. And, while she'd been too dazed by his sudden reappearance to register more than an instant recognition, she was now able to see that Max appeared to have hardly changed at all.

Although that wasn't strictly true, of course. There was now an austere, almost stern cast to the youthful features she had once known and an unfamiliar bleak and steely glint in his startlingly clear blue eyes. However, it seemed so unfair that, in all other respects, he should still appear to be the same devastatingly attractive man that she remembered only too well.

And then, as he shifted slightly in his seat, the movement of his broad shoulder and the quick, fleeting smile with which he greeted something her mother was saying to him sent a sudden sharp quiver of sexual awareness rippling through her body.

Gritting her teeth, Amber desperately tried to think of something—anything—to prevent herself from re-calling the firmly muscled chest, slim hips and hard thighs lying beneath the dark formal suit he was wearing with such effortless poise and assurance.

Maybe it was a sense of the total injustice of life that lent an extra sharpness to her voice as she found herself saying, 'It's been very nice to see you again, Max. However, I'm sure you must be a busy man, and we really shouldn't take up any more of your valuable time.'

'Really, Amber!' her mother protested with a quick, nervous laugh as her daughter glanced pointedly down at her watch. 'Besides,' she added with a puzzled frown, 'surely dear Max is staying the night with us?'

'Nonsense!' Amber snapped, feeling as though her temper—already on a very short fuse—was about to erupt at any moment. 'Of course he isn't. He...er...he just happened to be in the area, and...'

'No, dear, you're quite wrong. Because, now I come to think about it, it must have been Max's name, which I wrote down this morning.'

'*What*?' Amber's green eyes widened in horror as the older woman vigorously nodded her head. 'But I checked on the note pad in the hall, and there's nothing there—only something about a call from the grocer.'

Violet Grant gave her daughter a slightly guilty, shamefaced smile. 'Yes, well...it looks as if I might have made a slight error,' she admitted airily. 'But I thought the man mentioned Mr Warnock. So, I nat-urally assumed it was something to do with our local grocer. I didn't realise the call was about Max Warner wanting to spend the night with us.'

You idiot—he's only here to view the house! Amber wanted to scream at her mother. But she couldn't. Not when she hadn't yet told the older woman about the proposed sale of the Hall. Oh, Lord! What on earth was she going to do about this increasingly perilous situation?

Unfortunately, Violet Grant—now with the bit firmly between her teeth—appeared to be virtually unstoppable.

'It will be so nice having an old friend staying here with us, here at the Hall,' she told Max. 'I still haven't got used to complete strangers marching through the house. Although our paying guests always say that it's so much nicer and more comfortable than an impersonal hotel,' she confided before turning to Amber. 'There's no problem, dear. After all, we have plenty of rooms available.'

Amber knew that she ought to be thoroughly ashamed of a sudden, overwhelming urge to place her clenched hands tightly about her mother's neck. 'We're...um...we're all booked up,' she lied wildly.

'How can we be?' Violet frowned. 'Only this morning, you were saying that you wished we had some guests for the weekend.'

Amber gritted her teeth. She was just trying to think of some of their regular visitors, who might have arranged to stay at very little notice, when she caught sight of the chilly, mocking gleam in Max's glittering blue eyes.

Her heart sank like a stone as she suddenly realised that he was actually enjoying her discomfiture. Although, what she'd done to deserve his enmity, she had no idea. After all, *he* was the one who'd abandoned her.

'I'd be delighted to stay here at the Hall,' Max drawled, his mouth twisting with sardonic amusement at the expression of consternation and dismay clearly visible on Amber's face. 'Unfortunately...' he added after a long pause, 'I have to return to London tonight. But I'd be very interested to see over this house.' He turned to smile at Violet. 'I understand that it dates from Tudor times, and is one of the oldest houses in Elmbridge.'

The older woman nodded her head. 'Yes, you're quite right, it is. I'm sure Amber would be delighted to show you around.'

Oh, God—he's positively enjoying this! Amber realised, her body almost shaking with tension. Far from being prepared to accept that he wasn't wanted, Max was clearly getting the maximum amount of grim enjoyment from this fraught situation. And time was running out. She *had* to get rid of him—as quickly as possible. But how on earth was she going to do it?

Just as she was coming to the conclusion that the sooner she showed him around the house—keeping well away from the attic, of course—the sooner he'd be gone, her desperate thoughts were interrupted by a loud knock.

'Hello...?' Rose Thomas put her head around the sitting-room door. 'I've just come to fetch Emily. I hope she's been behaving herself?'

'Of course she has.' Amber turned to smile at her friend, momentarily overcome with relief and euphoria at the welcome interruption. But, as she heard the sound of childish laughter only a second or two later, she realised there was nothing she could do to avoid a catastrophic disaster.

'Mummy... Mummy! We've had a really *stupendous* time dressing up in Granny's old clothes!' Lucy called out as she ran full tilt into the sitting room, quickly followed by Emily. 'We looked absolutely *terrific*!'

'I'm sure you did,' Amber managed to gasp, almost frozen with terror as she watched the little girls running excitedly around the room. She had no hope of being able to fool a clever, perceptive man like Max. But Rose, who'd known Lucy since she was a baby...? Would she notice the startling similarity between the two heads of dark, curly hair and sparkling blue eyes?

But her friend clearly hadn't noted anything amiss as she gazed across the room at the tall, dark stranger who was rising to his feet.

'Surely, it can't be...?' Rose exclaimed as the man gave her a broad smile. 'Good Heavens—it really *is* Max Warner!' she laughed, her cheeks pink with excitement as he crossed the room towards her. 'I'd heard that you were now back in the country, but never expected to see you quite so soon. You hardly seem to have changed at all.'

'Since I shudder at the memory of myself as a wild teenager, I sincerely hope that I have, my dear Rose,' Max grinned, taking her hand and lifting it gallantly to his lips.

Despite her fright and panic, Amber felt a flash of indignation at this piece of quite outrageous flattery. Surely plain, calm, sensible Rose *couldn't* be so silly as to fall for such a line? However, as they chattered together, with her friend sparkling beneath the awful man's quite overwhelming charm, it really did seem as if she'd become momentarily transformed into a lovely woman.

You had to hand it to Max—he was a real con artist! she acknowledged grimly as Rose very reluctantly took her leave.

'*Well* . . .!' she exclaimed as Amber accompanied her and Emily across the hall towards the front door. 'When I arrived and saw that glamorous car, it never occurred to me that it might be Max Warner. What a surprise!'

'Yes, it certainly is,' Amber agreed bleakly.

'I don't understand.' Rose frowned. 'If you weren't expecting him—what on earth is he doing here?'

'Don't ask!' she groaned. 'It's all to do with the sale of the house. But everything has become so complicated——' Amber broke off, looking nervously back over her shoulder. 'I . . . I'll give you a ring to-morrow . . . explain everything,' she added, quickly bending down to kiss Emily goodbye, before dashing swiftly back to the sitting room.

Unfortunately, on her return, she discovered that even those few minutes' absence had proved to be fatal.

' . . . of course, Lucy's a very clever little girl,' her mother was saying. 'I'm hoping that she'll be clever enough to get into the local grammar school. But, as she's only seven years old, there's still a few years to go yet,' she added, smiling she patted the glossy, dark curls of the child sitting on her lap.

'But I'm going to be eight years old in June,' Lucy added quickly, jumping to her feet and running over to the tall man leaning elegantly against the mantelpiece. 'How old are you?'

'I'm as old as my face—and just a little older than my teeth,' Max retorted, waving aside her grandmother's protest as he smiled idly down at the small girl.

'That's a *very* clever answer!' Lucy grinned up at the man towering over her small figure. 'Are you going to be staying with us for a while?'

'I'm afraid not,' he murmured, his dark brows creasing into a puzzled frown as he gazed down at the little girl.

'That's a pity, because I really like riddles. My friend, Emily, told me a new one today—and I bet Granny won't know the answer,' she confided, before turning to skip back across the carpet to where Violet was sitting. 'When is a pony not a pony?'

The older woman smiled and shook her head.

'When it's turned into a field!' Lucy shouted before collapsing into a fit of giggles.

Standing frozen in the open doorway, Amber felt as if she were viewing the curtain rise on the last act of a Greek tragedy. Numbly waiting for nemesis to strike, she watched as Max turned his head to look into the large mirror over the mantelpiece. She saw his body becoming taut and rigid, his eyes narrowing to dark points of hard steel as he stared first at himself, and then at the reflection of the small girl on the other side of the room.

Paralysed by panic, and helplessly unable to prevent her whole world from crashing down about her head, Amber's heart thumped wildly in her chest as Max continued to stare blindly into the mirror, his expression grim and forbidding. And then, as if coming to a decision, he turned to cross the room. Murmuring a polite farewell to Violet Grant, he glanced down intently at Lucy for a moment, before striding swiftly towards where she stood in the doorway. Grasping Amber's arm in an iron grip, he barely halted his swift progress as he dragged her after him into the hall, then slammed the door shut behind them.

'*My God*!' he exploded, the sound of his angry voice reverberating loudly in the large, vaulted space of the hall. '*Why* didn't you tell me?'

'Tell you what?' she muttered, helplessly aware that she'd never been any good at telling lies as she felt the hot colour flooding over her pale cheeks. 'I . . . I don't know what you're talking about.'

'Oh, yes, you damn well do!' he retorted harshly, his fingers tightening cruelly on her arm. 'That little girl is obviously *my daughter*—for Heaven's sake!'

'No! No, you're quite . . . er . . . quite wrong. . . .' she whispered, desperately tried to evade his fierce gaze.

'I'm not prepared to listen to any stupid lies, Amber,' he ground out threateningly, before swearing violently under his breath as he glanced down at the slim gold watch on his wrist. 'Unfortunately, I'm already late for another appointment. But if you thought you'd seen the last of me eight years ago—

you were *very* much mistaken!' he growled, the icy-cold menace in his voice sending shivers of fright and terror running down her spine. 'Because, I'll be back just as soon as I can. And that's not a threat—it's a *promise*!'

And she had absolutely no doubt that he would be back, Amber told herself, shivering with cold and nervous exhaustion. Max had very clearly stated his firm intention of seeking her out once again. And there was *nothing* she could do, but wait with ever-mounting despair for his return.

It had seemed, during the past two weeks, as though she was existing in the midst of a living nightmare, never knowing from one moment to the next when or how he would turn up to cast an evil shadow over her life. And while she was normally very busy at this time of year, she'd hardly been able to concentrate on even the simplest task. In fact, with Max's sudden reappearance in her life, she was finding it almost impossible to focus on the present when her mind was so completely filled with memories of the past.

'Mummy...? Where are you?'

'Over here,' Amber called out as her small daughter appeared on the other side of the old walled garden.

'Do hurry up!' Lucy begged, running down the gravel path towards her. 'If we don't go soon, I'll miss my riding lesson.'

Amber grimaced as she glanced down at her watch. 'Sorry, darling, I completely forgot the time.'

'I hope you're going to change out of those old clothes,' Lucy told her, critically viewing her mother's slim figure, clothed in a scruffy pair of jeans beneath a windproof jacket, which had clearly seen better days. 'And you've got some leaves stuck in your hair.'

'Hey—relax! It's Saturday, remember? No one has to get all dressed up at the weekend,' Amber laughed, bending down to allow the little girl to remove the greenery from her thick, golden brown hair.

'I thought you were going to do some Christmas shopping.'

'Oh, yes, you're right. I'd completely forgotten. OK, you win,' she grinned through her hair at her daughter. 'I'll try and find something smarter to wear.'

A self-appointed arbiter of her mother's wardrobe, Lucy had very strong views on what was, and what wasn't, suitable attire for various social functions. However, not having any spare money to spend on clothes, Amber had quite cheerfully stopped worrying about the dictates of fashion a long time ago.

'What *are* you going to wear?' Lucy demanded as she finished removing the straw from her mother's hair.

'Oh, I'll think of something.'

'All my friends say that you're very pretty. When I'm grown up, I'm going to buy you lots and lots of lovely clothes,' Lucy told her solemnly.

'Thank you, darling!' Amber grinned down at her daughter. Although she was only twenty-six and still— if Philip Jackson was to be believed—an attractive woman, she knew that she'd never been half as pretty as Lucy. With her cloud of black curly hair and large, clear blue eyes, the little girl was the spitting image of her father. Which was yet another problem to be faced. Because it wasn't *just* the threat of Max's return that was causing her so much anxiety and distress—there was the added worry of how and when to break the news to her friends. And that was something she was going to have to do sooner rather than later. Because, while Rose had been far too excited by Max's sudden reappearance to notice the startling resemblance between father and daughter, Amber knew that she couldn't rely on her other friends being so blind. And, most important of all—what about Lucy herself? How on earth could she even begin to try and explain to such a young girl the torturous events of the past . . .?

'Oh, do stop day-dreaming, Mummy. *Please* hurry up!' Lucy pleaded, almost dancing with impatience.

'Just give me five minutes to change, and I'll be right with you,' Amber promised, sighing heavily as she picked up the basket full of vegetables before slowly following her daughter back down the garden path.

CHAPTER THREE

'DON'T panic—there are *still* ten shopping days to go before Christmas!'

Momentarily unnerved by the words being hoarsely whispered in her ear, Amber gave a startled yelp, nearly dropping her heavy load of parcels as she spun around to find herself staring up into the twinkling brown eyes of Philip Jackson.

'For Heaven's sake!' she gasped as the young doctor swiftly removed the packages from her arms. 'It's bad enough having to fight one's way through the crowds without you scaring me half to death!'

'I didn't mean to give you a fright,' he grinned. 'But why does everyone seem to be gripped by a "shop till you drop" frenzy at this time of year?'

'I don't know. It's crazy, isn't it?' she agreed as they walked slowly up the street. 'So, just what are *you* doing here, in the middle of town on a Friday morning?' she teased. 'Surely a busy doctor ought to be in his surgery looking after the sick and infirm.'

'I've taken the morning off for some last-minute shopping,' he confessed with a rueful grin, before insisting on leading her into the Market Tavern for a mug of their famous 'Winter Warmer'—hot chocolate with a dash of brandy. 'It will do you good, and you'll still be quite sober enough to drive home,' he assured her when she expressed her doubts about the wisdom of drinking in the middle of the day. 'On the other hand—how about joining me for lunch in one of the local restaurants?'

Amber shook her head. 'I'm sorry, Philip. I can't make it today. Mother's in bed with a heavy cold, and I must get back to keep an eye on her.'

'I'm sorry to hear that. Although I have to say that you don't look too well, either,' the doctor added, glancing with concern at her pale, finely drawn features and the dark shadows beneath her eyes.

'I'm all right,' she shrugged, perfectly well aware—from a despairing glance in her mirror this morning—that she was looking like death warmed up. Just as she knew that part of her present exhausted state of mind wasn't just the worry about Max's return. She was also becoming deeply disturbed about her mother.

Amber had finally been forced to explain to her mother the necessity of selling their home, and Violet Grant's reaction had been every bit as bad as she had feared. Amber still shuddered to recall the wild, hysterical accusations and virtual collapse of the older woman. It was well over a week since her mother had taken to her bed, claiming that she had a bad cold and refusing to leave her room—an action that was now causing her daughter grave concern.

Unfortunately, it was all too reminiscent of Violet's behaviour eight years ago, following the scandal and collapse of her husband's business. And so, while she was trying hard not to overreact to the situation, Amber knew that if her mother continued to avoid facing up to life by hiding in her bedroom, she was going to have to seek some serious medical advice.

'Would you like me to call and have a look at your
mother?' Philip asked.

'No...er...not just at the moment—but I'll be in
touch with you if she gets any worse,' Amber assured
him before quickly changing the subject. 'What are
you doing for Christmas? Are you still planning to
join your family in Cumberland?'

He nodded. 'I only wish that you and Lucy were
coming, too. My parents were really disappointed that
you couldn't make it.'

'I'm sorry—but this is always such a busy time of
the year for me,' she murmured evasively.

She was very fond of Philip and she also liked his
mother and father whom she'd met when they'd
visited their son earlier in the year. However, until
finally making up her mind about whether to accept
his many proposals of marriage, Amber hadn't wanted
to become too involved with his family.

In any case, the idea of marrying *anyone* was just
about the last thing on her mind at the moment. Besides, it would be totally unfair to involve the young
doctor in a nasty local scandal, which was likely to
erupt just as soon as Max Warner carried out his threat
to return.

It was now three weeks since she'd seen Max, and
she still didn't feel able to relax. It was like waiting
for a bomb to go off, she told herself grimly, realising
that there was no way out of the trap in which she
now found herself. Because, even if Max only intended to visit the small town every now and then, it
would be impossible to hide the truth. With her glossy
black curls and large blue eyes, it was going to be

glaringly obvious to all and sundry that Lucy was an absolute carbon copy of her father.

Amber knew that she couldn't put it off any longer. She *must* tell Rose and her other close friends before news of the whole story became public property. But finding the courage to do so seemed completely beyond her at the moment. Even trying to explain what had happened in the past to Philip, for instance—who, like everyone else in the town, believed Lucy to be Clive Stanhope's daughter—was enough to make her break out in a cold sweat.

'...so I'll pick you up at about seven o'clock. OK?'

'Hmm...?' Amber stared blankly up at her companion before realising that she'd been so immersed in her own dark, sombre thoughts that she hadn't heard a word he'd been saying.

Philip gazed at her with a wounded expression in his kind brown eyes. 'I thought we'd arranged, some weeks ago, to go to the buffet supper party in the old Assembly Rooms? I hear the organisers are hoping for a large turnout to raise funds and support the town's protest about the destruction of the old Tide Mill.'

'Oh, I'm sorry—I'd forgotten all about it,' she confessed with a tired, guilty smile. 'Mainly because I've been so busy trying to catch up with all the last-minute orders for Christmas cakes. And, with Lucy away until tomorrow, I've been working flat out in the kitchen,' she added, explaining that Rose Thomas had invited her daughter to join a family trip to London. 'They're staying the night with David Thomas's sister, and Lucy was absolutely ecstatic about the thought of seeing a pantomime *and* visiting a large department store to meet Santa Claus!'

'She'll have a wonderful time,' he agreed with a warm smile. 'But it's a pity Rose will miss the party. No one seems to know who owns the development company, Suffolk Construction. But their plans to pull down the old mill and build a large new marina in the old mill pond certainly seem to have upset just about everyone in the town. Feelings are running pretty high at the moment,' he added with a frown. 'I hope things will soon calm down.'

'So do I,' she agreed, aware that most people in the town were extremely angry and grimly determined to keep the modern developers at bay.

Standing derelict and unused for the past forty years, the ancient Tide Mill was a rare survivor of a bygone age. Unfortunately, both the rapidly expanding tourist trade in the small East Anglian town and the increasingly loud demands for a modern marina by the local sailing fraternity had led to the threatened destruction of this important landmark in the town.

The local outcry against the loss of the mill was mainly due to its ancient, almost unique system of operation. Since it had depended on the river water being trapped in the mill pond at high tide, which was then released to turn the huge wheels when the tide had fallen, the old mill's working hours had been dictated solely by the flow of tidal water entering the river from the North Sea.

As far as Amber knew, there was only one other such mill, farther up the river at Woodbridge, which had been saved from decay some twenty years ago. 'If the inhabitants of that town could raise the money to restore *their* mill, so can *we*!' Rose Thomas had declared stoutly, before quickly calling on the help of her friends and organising strong local resistance to the plans for its demolition.

It was at this point that Amber had found herself in an embarrassing position. Because, the old mill, with its surrounding land and large mill pond, had once been owned by the Stanhope family, who'd leased the property to a succession of millers ever since the sixteenth century. Unfortunately, it was her late husband, Clive, needing money to settle some gambling debts, who had sold the mill to a local builder some time ago.

'Nobody blames you,' Rose had repeatedly assured her, pointing out that it was hardly Amber's fault if the land had changed hands several times over the past few years. 'After all, there's a world of difference between building a few houses on the site— and Suffolk Construction's plans for a glitzy, modern marina!'

If only there was some way to satisfy the yachtsmen without having to destroy such an ancient building, Amber told herself, gathering up her parcels as her companion paid for their drinks. The obvious answer, of course, was to talk the matter over with Suffolk Construction. But, as Philip had pointed out, nobody knew anything about either the development company or its owners.

'Is anything troubling you, Amber?' he asked, noting her shivering with cold as they left the warmth and comfort of the Market Tavern. 'You don't look at all well.'

'I'm perfectly all right. Really, I am,' she told him firmly as he continued to gaze at her with a worried frown. 'I'm just feeling a bit tired, that's all. But I'm quite well enough to attend tonight's party.'

'Well, for goodness' sake, try to make sure you eat properly and get some decent night's sleep. Otherwise, I'm going to insist on taking you down to the surgery for a complete overhaul.'

'OK, OK, anything you say, Doctor,' she grinned, raising a hand in mock surrender.

'By the way, I was very sorry to hear that you've decided to sell the Hall,' he said as they slowly made their way along the High Street, which was thronged with Christmas shoppers. 'David Thomas told me that you're letting him have a look at the old house deeds.'

'Yes . . .' she muttered, feeling guilty at having been so busy that she'd completely forgotten to tell Philip about the forthcoming sale. 'I've lent the huge pile of old documents to David because he's so interested in local history.'

'I wish you didn't have to sell your home,' he told her with a frown. 'You know how I feel about you, Amber. And, although this isn't either the time or the place, you must let me know if there's anything I can do.'

'Yes...yes, of course I will,' she murmured, grateful to be saved from having to say any more as they were momentarily parted by the many passers-by crowding the pavement.

The news that the Hall was now up for sale had obviously become a topic of conversation in Elmbridge. In fact, Amber had been surprised by the amount of people who'd stopped her in the street today, all expressing their regret and sympathy at the loss of her home. Despite all her problems, it was really comforting to know that so many inhabitants of this small provincial town seemed to be genuinely concerned for both her and her family's welfare.

Rose, Sally and her other friends had rallied around, promising to try and find a small cottage to house the family. Unfortunately, there didn't seem to be anything at all suitable on the market at the moment. But as 'Gloomy Glover', the house agent, had so bluntly pointed out, there was no need for her to worry about that, since it was likely to take her some time before she found a buyer for her present home.

'I had hoped that Mr Warner might be interested,' he'd told her before giving a mournful shake of his head. 'But why would a single man—however wealthy he might be—want to saddle himself with such a huge old house? No,' he'd added with a heavy sigh, 'I'm afraid that it will take me a long time to find a buyer for your property, Mrs Stanhope. A very long time indeed.'

Amber hadn't known exactly *what* she felt on learning that Max wasn't a married man. However, the news of his brief visit to Elmbridge—and that he apparently had neither a wife or children—had become a major talking point amongst her friends. Rose, for instance, had been clearly thrilled to meet him again, as well as being highly amused by Sally

Fraser's groans of envy at having missed the opportunity to do so.

'If *only* I hadn't been out when he called to see John! Was he really every bit as handsome as he used to be?' Sally had demanded, almost grinding her teeth with frustration as Rose pretended to give the matter some thought.

'Well...' she'd winked at Amber before turning to give Sally a bland smile, 'on the whole, I think that Max is definitely *more* attractive nowadays. He's still very good-looking, of course. But now that he's become such an obviously sophisticated and successful man, he seems somehow more...er...more sexy—if you know what I mean?'

'Oh, *why* didn't I have the luck to meet him?' Sally wailed before rushing off to spread the news of the handsome prodigal's return.

'Don't say it—I know that I ought to be ashamed of myself!' Rose had laughingly confessed to Amber when they were left alone together. 'But it isn't often that I manage to upstage Sally. And, although *you* don't seem to be very struck by Max Warner, I really must admit—happily married woman that I am—that he definitely made me feel quite weak at the knees!'

Amber, who dearly wished that she'd taken her house deeds to David Thomas's office instead of deciding to leave them with Rose, could only give her friend a weak, sickly smile before rapidly changing the subject.

'Here we are.'

'Hmm...?' she blinked, before realising that she was standing beside her old Land Rover.

'You really should lock your car when you leave it parked in the street like this,' Philip told her sternly as he opened the door and put her parcels on the back seat.

'The locks are useless—they're all rusted away, and I can't afford to fit any new ones,' she explained with a brief, helpless shrug of her shoulders. 'Thank you for that lovely, warming drink—and for carrying my shopping all this way,' she added as he bent down to give her a quick kiss on the cheek before striding off down the street.

Settling down into the driving seat, she turned on the ignition—only to be met by complete silence. Some moments later, having tried everything she knew to try and start her vehicle, Amber gave a deep heartfelt groan before beginning to swear violently under her breath.

'This old wreck should have been thrown on the scrap heap years ago!'

The sound of the deep voice caused Amber, for the second time that day, to give a startled shriek of fright and alarm. Quickly turning her head, she found herself facing the tall, dark-haired man who'd dominated her dreams for the past few weeks.

'*Max*! What on earth are you doing here?' Amber gasped, her face as white as a sheet as she stared glassy-eyed at the tall figure, whose perfectly tailored, black cashmere coat over a sober dark grey suit seemed more appropriate for the City of London than the small market town of Elmbridge.

'It would appear that I am about to have the pleasure of rescuing a damsel in distress,' he drawled coolly.

'Not *this* damsel you aren't!' she snapped nervously.

'Don't be tiresome, Amber. This heap of rust clearly isn't going anywhere. However, since I was on my way to Elmbridge Hall, I'll be able to give you a lift home.' He nodded towards the long black sports car parked beside the pavement a few feet away from the Land Rover.

'Why are you doing this to me?' she wailed, thumping her steering wheel with an angry fist.

'Doing what?' Max gave a harsh, sardonic bark of laughter. 'Is it *my* fault that you're driving around in an ancient vehicle, which should have gone to the great scrapyard in the sky years ago?'

'I meant why...why *here*...in the middle of the High Street?' she ground out through clenched teeth. 'Why couldn't you just telephone and make an appointment to see me? Like any perfectly normal, sane person?'

'Because I became fed up with getting nothing but your damned answerphone,' he retorted, taking no notice of her furious protests as he swiftly transferred her parcels and bags of shopping to his vehicle. 'Jump in—and shut up!' he added grimly, waiting with barely concealed impatience until she did as she was told.

However, Amber had no intention of obeying his last command.

'If you rang when my answerphone was switched on,' she said furiously as the long, low sports car snaked along the country lanes to Elmbridge Hall, 'I can see no reason why you couldn't leave a sensible message like everyone else.'

'If I remember correctly, you run a boarding-house....'

'I most certainly do not! We take in paying guests,' she snapped before realising—with a sinking heart— that she was beginning to sound just like her mother.

'...and I have no intention of allowing complete strangers to listen to my private phone calls,' he told her firmly. 'Incidentally, I don't think much of the prissy message you've put on the machine. Quite frankly, Amber,' he added, his mouth twitching with amusement, 'you sounded like a frightened rabbit!'

'Thank you!' she ground out, furious at the description of her voice—and also with herself for having been so easily outmanoeuvred.

When a friend had offered her a very cheap, second-hand telephone answering system some weeks ago, it had seemed like a gift from heaven. Not only would it cope with her mother's complete inability to take down a simple message, but she'd also hoped that it would help her to avoid any direct contact with Max. So that, when he left a message giving the date and hour of his return, she wouldn't be taken unawares. It had *never* occurred to her that he would refuse to use the damn machine. Didn't he believe in modern technology, or what?

'That's still no excuse for not contacting me in the normal way,' Amber retorted bitterly. 'There was absolutely no need to...to kidnap me like this.'

'Kidnap? Surely I'm doing nothing more than rescuing you from an unfortunate predicament?' he

drawled smoothly before taking a hand off the wheel
to punch some numbers into his car phone.

'I didn't *need* rescuing,' she ground out through
gritted teeth. 'I could easily have sorted out the
problem myself.'

'I very much doubt it,' Max murmured dryly,
forestalling her angry retort as he picked up the phone.

'Ah, Cruickshank—it's Max Warner here. I want
you to ring up the local garage and get them to pick
up an ancient Land Rover, which has broken down
in the High Street. Tell them to give it a thorough
overhaul. Oh, there is just one thing,' he added.
'Please ask them to check the electrical wiring under
the dashboard.'

'Oh, great!' Amber exploded at the end of his call.
'And just *what* am I supposed to use for transport
while my car's being fixed?'

'I'll see that it's returned to you before I leave.'

She gave a shrill, angry laugh. 'If you think that
amount of work can be done in the twinkling of an
eye, you must be off your head! I've never heard of
Mr Cruickshank, but while our local garage is fairly
efficient, they can't perform miracles!'

As the harsh, grating tones of her normally soft
voice seemed to echo loudly within the confines of
the car, Amber forced herself to take a deep breath
and try to calm down. Shouting her head off or
making cutting remarks wasn't going to get her anywhere with this obviously hard-boiled, tough man.

'Just what are you doing here in Elmbridge
anyway?' she asked a few moments later in a quieter
tone of voice.

But, even as she said the words, Amber knew that it was a stupid question. Because, of course, she already knew the answer. However, she was surprised to find, after all the unrelenting stress of the past three weeks, that it was almost a relief to be at last facing the man who'd caused her such overwhelming fear and tension.

She was well aware that it was extremely childish to be so rude and aggressive, or to keep on quarrelling so furiously with Max. But, driven as she was by an almost overwhelming need to hurt and wound him as much as possible, it was also extraordinarily liberating to be able to release some of the long-suppressed, pent-up rage and fury at the way he'd treated her in the past.

'Why am I here...?' He gave a nonchalant shrug of his broad shoulders. 'Surely you can't have forgotten my promise to return?'

'You're quite right—I haven't!'

'In that case, you will be pleased to hear that I'm still interested in looking over your house,' he drawled, coolly ignoring her grim snort of disbelief. 'Particularly since I was able to see very little of the Hall when I called some weeks ago.'

'If you're *so* keen to view the house, why didn't you make an appointment with Mr Glover?'

'When I last visited your house, you were insisting—almost hysterically so, in fact—that Mr Glover should definitely *not* be involved. Do I take it that you have now changed your mind?'

'Yes...no...I mean, it's not a problem any more—not now that my mother knows about the sale,' she muttered defensively.

'I hope she wasn't too upset?'

'Well, she obviously isn't thrilled about the situation,' Amber retorted caustically before adding quickly, 'I'm afraid there's no question of your seeing her today. She's in bed with a heavy cold.'

'I'm sorry to hear that. I hope she gets better soon,' he said as they turned into the driveway leading to Elmbridge Hall. 'Do you have any guests staying with you at the moment?'

'No, as a matter of fact we don't. Why do you ask?' she demanded, turning to glare at his handsome profile with distrust and suspicion.

'I merely wanted to be sure that I wouldn't be causing you any trouble,' he replied smoothly. 'However, from what you say, it seems as if there's no reason why you can't give me a guided tour of the house, hmm?'

After staring at him grimly for a moment, Amber gave a heavy sigh. 'I suppose not,' she muttered as his car came to a halt outside the front door.

Amber knew that it was undoubtedly spineless of her to cave in, despite being quite certain that Max had no real interest in the house. But there seemed no point in continuing to defy this seemingly indomitable man. It was obvious that he was just amusing himself by playing a savage game of cat and mouse, waiting until she was in a total state of nervous exhaustion before pouncing on what he *really* wanted.

And there was no doubt of what that would be, she told herself, suddenly feeling sick with nerves.

However, by the time Max was helping to carry her parcels into the kitchen, she'd managed to partially pull herself together—even if she was finding it difficult to stop shivering, despite the warmth of the room. It was some comfort to realise that with Lucy safely away in London, there was no chance of Max seeing the little girl. And before her daughter returned tomorrow, she'd have plenty of time in which to come up with a plan of action. Although exactly *what* she was going to say or do would depend on Max, of course. But after having been in such a blue funk for the past three weeks, feebly waiting like a condemned woman for the noose to tighten about her neck, it was about time she started using her brain.

It was stupid to be so frightened of this man. She might not have seen him for the past eight years, but he couldn't have changed all that much, surely? Desperately trying to ignore the tight knot of apprehension lying like heavy lead deep in her stomach, she knew that she *must* try to take control of this dire situation.

But Max clearly had no intention of allowing her to gain the initiative.

'What a charming room,' he murmured, gazing around the warm kitchen, dominated by a massive old-fashioned oak dresser and a large, well-scrubbed pine table surrounded by comfortable old chairs. 'In fact, I already feel so much at home, that I think I'll stay here for a night or two.'

'*What*?'

'My dear Amber, there's no need to sound quite so surprised,' he drawled mockingly as she stared at him with glazed, horrified eyes. 'You told me yourself that you frequently have paying guests.'

'Yes ... but ...'

'And, since you also told me a few moments ago that you don't have anyone staying at the moment, I'm quite sure there must be plenty of room.'

'No...no...you can't possibly stay here,' she gasped breathlessly, floundering as she tried to think of a sufficiently good excuse. 'I mean, a single man, on his own ... it really wouldn't be at all ... er ... at all suitable,' she added lamely, waving her hands helplessly in the air.

He raised a dark, sardonic eyebrow. 'Are you telling me that you've *never* had a man staying here on his own?'

'Well ... um ...' she faltered, her voice dying away beneath the intense, mocking gaze of his clear blue eyes.

'How sensible not to try and lie to me. Especially since you always were a shocking liar!' he grinned.

Amber stared blindly at the tall figure calmly removing his dark overcoat, her head beginning to pound with a dull, throbbing ache as she desperately tried to cope with the situation.

It really did look as if it was only a sudden, last-minute idea of Max's to stay here at the Hall. Could it be that he was just teasing her? Trying to pile on the pressure so that she'd weakly agree to whatever it was he wanted? If so ... maybe it *would* be a good idea to show him around the house after all. At least it might give her an opportunity to try and persuade him to go away or stay in a local hotel.

'OK, I'll give you a quick guided tour of the house,' she said grimly, moving towards the door.

However, it soon transpired that her half-formed, confused and hazy ideas for getting rid of Max hadn't a chance of being realised that quickly. As soon as they entered the hall—and almost before she knew what was happening—he had disappeared briefly through the front door, removed an overnight case from his car, and returned to follow her reluctant figure up the wide oak staircase.

'I...I can't really believe that you want to stay here,' she muttered helplessly as she showed him into a guest-room.

'Can't you?' he murmured, placing his case on a nearby chair, and raising an ironic, quizzical dark eyebrow as he gazed about the room, whose delicate antique furniture, long red velvet curtains and large paintings in heavy gilt frames gave an impression of comfortable warmth and luxury.

'No. Just as I can't see any reason why you should want to buy this house,' she retorted, aware that she was sounding strained and brittle as she moved quickly past him to jerkily open one of the large, mullioned windows.

'Maybe now that my grandmother has left me her estate, I feel like settling down here in Elmbridge,' he drawled, strolling across the carpet towards her. 'And, since there is now no longer a house on the land, I might well need somewhere to live, hmm?'

It all sounded very reasonable, but Amber still didn't entirely believe him. And the atmosphere between them suddenly seemed to become tense and claustrophobic.

It had been different while she'd been quarrelling with him in the car. But now, standing so close to his tall, dominant figure, she was starkly aware of the hard, almost aggressively male body beneath the expensively tailored dark suit. How could she have made the mistake of thinking that he hadn't changed? Because this was no longer the youth of twenty-four, with his whole life stretching out before him. Now, as Max turned to gaze down at her with a formidable, enigmatic gleam in his glittering blue eyes, she suddenly realised that she was facing a fully mature and dauntingly powerful man. A man, she instinctively realised, who could prove to be very dangerous indeed.

'If... um ... if you want to look around the house, I'm afraid you're going to have to wait while I provide lunch for my mother,' she told him nervously.

'Ah, yes. I *was* surprised when you appeared to need—in this day and age!—the protection of a chaperon,' he drawled blandly, his eyes gleaming with unconcealed mockery. 'After all, with your mother and daughter living in the house, I'm quite sure that your reputation must be spotless!'

How *could* she have ever imagined that she'd once been wildly in love with this really foul, sarcastic man? Amber asked herself wildly, trying to inch past his tall figure towards the safety of the door.

'My mother isn't at all well,' she muttered, dismayed to find him moving to block her retreat.

'And your daughter...?' he enquired silkily. But when she didn't reply, remaining stubbornly silent as she glared defiantly up at him, the atmosphere in the bedroom suddenly became tense and very frightening. His mouth tightened ominously, a muscle beating in his jaw as his eyes became hard chips of blue ice.

'Don't even *think* of trying to play games with me, Amber!' The harsh, grating anger in his voice cracked like a whiplash in the quiet, still room as his hands came down on her slim shoulders; the strong fingers tightened like cruel talons in her soft flesh, shaking her roughly as though she were a rag doll.

'Let me go!' she cried, gasping with pain as she desperately tried to escape his vicelike grip.

'Only when you understand that it's pointless to defy me!' he snarled, his voice heavy with menace. '*I want to see my daughter.*'

'You can't...' she gasped, prevented from saying any more as she found herself trapped within a fierce, iron-like embrace, roughly forced against his hard body, a hand firmly gripping her chin and forcing her head up towards him. She had only a brief, fleeting glimpse of the raging anger in his steely blue eyes before his mouth possessed her lips with harsh, deliberate intent.

The bruising, relentless pressure seemed unending, forcing her lips apart as her helpless protest became an inaudible moan. Twisting and wriggling as she might, there seemed nothing she could do to escape. And then, the hand pressing her so firmly towards him began slowly sliding down over the curves of her body, the punishing torture of his mouth subtly changing, becoming soft and tender as his lips moved sensuously over hers, arousing a response she was helpless to control.

A treacherous warmth invaded her trembling body pressed so closely to his hard, muscular thighs, the soft seduction of his lips and tongue having a disastrous effect on her long-dormant emotions. Bemused as she was by the burning heat flooding her mind and body, she was still capable of realising that he was deliberately using his undoubted sexual expertise as a weapon, callously forcing her to acknowledge his mastery of her emotions. But it was eight long, long years since a man had kissed her like this, and trapped in a dense mist of raging desire, she was helplessly unable to prevent her body from hungrily responding to the tide of passion sweeping through her veins.

It seemed an age before Max finally raised his dark head, looking down at her flushed cheeks as she slowly opened her eyes.

Mentally paralysed for a moment, she gazed up at him in confusion, dazed and bewildered by his assault on her long-dormant senses. But as the harsh, cold facts of life finally broke through the miasma in her stunned mind, she gave a horrified sob as she tore herself from his arms. Fighting to control her ragged breathing, she stared at him in utter consternation.

What *had* she been doing? Panting as if she'd just run a mile, and totally appalled to find herself still quivering with sexual hunger, Amber almost collapsed with shame. How *could* she still be attracted to a man who, not content with callously abandoning her all those years ago, was now clearly intent on asserting his parental rights to her daughter? There was only one possible conclusion: she must be stark, raving mad!

Max's face was taut and strained, pale beneath his tan, his blue eyes glittering like steel chips. And while he, too, appeared to be breathing roughly, he seemed to have no difficulty in finding his voice.

'That was a mistake—and not one I have any intention of repeating,' he told her grimly. 'At the risk of sounding tedious, I'll repeat what I said a few moments ago. I want to see my daughter.'

'Well, that's just too bad—because she's not here!' Amber retorted savagely.

A moment later, she could almost sense the blood draining from her face, suddenly feeling quite sick as she realised that she'd just made a really terrible, *terrible* mistake. Because, if she'd ever hoped to deny the fact that Max was Lucy's father, she had now thrown away any chance of doing so.

CHAPTER FOUR

How *could* she have been such a fool?

Practically throwing the bread tins into the hot stove and loudly slamming the oven door shut did nothing to soothe Amber's fury with herself at having been such an idiot.

There was little comfort to be gained in realising that it wasn't entirely her fault; she'd been so emotionally shattered by Max's kiss that she hadn't even known whether it was night or day—let alone been capable of withstanding a tough cross-examination. Unfortunately, once she'd made the colossal mistake of telling him that Lucy was away from home, there had been nothing she could do to repair the damage.

If only she could have taken refuge upstairs in the privacy of her own bedroom, giving way to tears of overwhelming rage and anger—both with Max and herself. Unfortunately, with her mother's lunch to prepare, she had no choice in the matter. But there seemed nothing she could do to stop her hands shaking, her knees knocking together like castanets as she recalled Max's swift stride over the faded bedroom carpet, his hard blue eyes staring intently down at her trembling figure.

It had been no contest. He hadn't even needed to raise his voice. Once she'd glimpsed the flush of anger beneath his tanned skin, a pulse beating in his formidable jawline and the cruel, tight-lipped expression on his face, she'd immediately caved in.

'I'm telling you the truth. I...I really wasn't lying,' she had assured him quickly, her eyes sliding nervously away from his hard, steely gaze. 'Lucy really *isn't* here at the moment.'

'I'm pleased to hear that you've decided to be sensible, and that there's at least one battle I won't have to fight,' he'd grated, his words accurately confirming her own dismayed thoughts. 'So, where exactly *is* my daughter?'

'She...she's in London, with Rose Thomas's family,' Amber had muttered helplessly, being forced to explain that Lucy wasn't due to arrive back home until tomorrow, before Max had allowed her to leave the room.

Leaning wearily against the warm stove, Amber desperately tried to pummel her mentally weary brain into some sort of clear, cohesive thought. But it seemed an almost impossible task. She couldn't seem to banish from her mind the images of Max's sensual mouth poised above her own, her body still quivering in response to the erotic seduction of his lips and hands.

Oh, help! What on earth was she going to do? she moaned silently, knowing that there was virtually no chance of her being able to stop Max seeing Lucy tomorrow. And then, what? Would he insist on telling the little girl that he was her father?

Almost whimpering at the thought of her small daughter's safe, secure world being smashed to pieces,

Amber knew that there was nothing she could do to prevent it happening. However, there was no evading the harsh fact that, having been without a father all her life, Lucy might well be thrilled to discover she was the daughter of such a handsome, successful man. A man who could easily, for instance, buy his child anything her heart desired—even the pony, which the little girl had been wistfully hankering after for the past two years.

However, according to Mr Glover, Max wasn't a married man. So, without an established family of his own, it seemed unlikely that he was seriously intending to drag Lucy away to live with him in London—or wherever he was living at the moment. Even if he attempted to do such a thing, she was certain that the law must be on her side. Surely no judge would agree to a child being torn away from her natural mother? But since his claim to be interested in buying this house was obviously a total red herring, she *must* try to work out exactly why Max was here and what he hoped to achieve.

Unfortunately, and however much Amber tried, she could only come to one conclusion. It looked as if Max not only wanted to see the little girl, but he was also going to tell Lucy that he was her real, long-lost father.

But that wasn't all. While Amber was ashamed to be so pathetically small-minded, she dreaded the thought of Lucy's illegitimacy becoming widely known. Even thinking about all the hullabaloo and juicy, scandalous gossip—which was bound to run like wildfire around the small town—was enough to make her feel faint and dizzy.

'Ah, there you are,' Max said, almost causing her to jump out of her skin with nerves as he silently entered the room. 'I was just wondering where you'd got to.'

'This kitchen is strictly off limits to paying guests,' she informed him stonily, noting that he'd removed his suit jacket and tie, and was now wearing a black, V-necked cashmere sweater over the open-necked shirt, whose white collar only seemed to emphasise his deep tan and the firm muscular cords of his strong neck.

'But that restriction hardly applies to me,' he drawled coolly. 'Especially since we've established the fact that I'm now practically one of the family.'

Amber glared at him, desperately clamping her lips together in an effort to suppress an extremely rude reply.

Life was so damned unfair! Surely, if there was *any* justice in the world, this wretched man would have come to a sticky end a long time ago. But it seemed her friend, Rose, had, alas, been quite right. Instead of succumbing to a richly deserved and malignant fate, he was now obviously very rich, highly successful— and even *more* devastatingly attractive than ever.

'I'm told that you're a wonderful cook,' he murmured, his eyes flicking over her slender figure before glancing at the large pan of soup bubbling on the stove. 'And I must say, that smells absolutely delicious,' he added, with such an engaging smile that her heart almost missed a heat.

'Get lost, you smooth bastard!' Amber muttered under her breath as she turned away, reaching up for an apron hanging beside the stove.

'What did you say?'

'Oh . . . er . . . nothing,' she mumbled, determinedly keeping her back to him, her face flushed with anger, and she mentally cursed her fumbling fingers, suddenly all thumbs as she attempted to tie the apron strings into a bow.

'What are you giving your mother for lunch?' he enquired, moving across the room to lean casually against the large oak dresser.

Amber shrugged, taking the bread out of the oven before placing a tray on the table. 'I can't think why you're interested. However, if you *must* know—my mother's having freshly baked bread with home-made leek and potato soup, followed by apple pie and cream. I *do* hope the menu meets with your approval?' she added sarcastically.

'It most certainly does. I hope you've got enough for me, too.'

'*What* . . .?'

'I had to leave London at the crack of dawn this morning. Which means that I haven't had a thing to eat all day.'

'Talk about damn cheek!' she gasped, almost unable to believe that she'd heard him correctly. 'First you kidnap me in broad daylight, then you invite yourself to stay in this house, assault me upstairs in the bedroom, and now...' She waved a wooden spoon wildly in the air. 'Now you're calmly expecting me to serve you lunch!'

'Come on, Amber!' he grinned wolfishly at her. 'That kiss was hardly what I would call an "assault". In fact, I was amazed to discover just how enthusiastically you responded to...'

'I did nothing of the sort!' she snapped furiously, her cheeks burning with embarrassment. 'I was just taken by surprise, that's all.'

'Oh, really?' he drawled, a clear note of disbelief in his voice, before adding firmly, 'I suggest that we both do our best to forget the whole unfortunate episode.'

'Yes...well, that seems a good idea,' she muttered, carefully avoiding his eye as she laid the cutlery on her mother's tray.

'However, I wasn't kidding,' he told her with a disarming smile. 'I really am extremely hungry.' When she remained stubbornly silent, he added plaintively, 'Surely you can't refuse to feed a starving man?'

'Oh, no? I wouldn't like to bet on it,' she retorted grimly.

You really had to hand it to Max, she told herself, not knowing whether to burst into tears or scream with hysterical laughter. His capacity for sheer, brass nerve was *totally* amazing! And since he was also clearly intending to make her present life as difficult as possible, this whole ghastly situation was rapidly becoming a complete farce.

Astonishingly, she found herself giving a dry, ironic bark of grim laughter. 'Oh...all right. I'll give you lunch. But only because at least one of us ought to behave like a civilised human being,' she told him coldly before carrying the tray upstairs to her mother.

Unfortunately, Violet Grant was feeling fretful, one minute saying that she wasn't hungry, and the next demanding to know why her daughter was late with her meal.

Determined not to let the older woman know about Max's visit—not too difficult, since her mother's rooms were in a separate wing at the side of the house—Amber was forced to spend some considerable time trying to calm her mother down and make her more comfortable. All to no avail.

'If only dear Clive were still alive. *He* would never have agreed to sell this house,' Violet muttered in a querulous tone of voice. 'Clive was such a kind, generous man. I hope you realise just how lucky you were to be married to him,' she added peevishly. 'Husbands like that don't grow on trees, you know.'

'No, I know they don't,' Amber agreed quietly, refusing to be drawn into a silly quarrel as she tried to coax the older woman to drink her soup.

While her mother's grouchy remarks were entirely out of character, and solely due to her acute depression about the sale of their house, she had to admit that Violet was right. Clive had indeed proved to be an exceptionally kind and generous husband. Not that she had ever dreamed of marrying him all those years ago when she'd been so madly in love with Max Warner.

Amber could still recall with remorseless clarity her feelings of overwhelming fear and panic when a London doctor had confirmed that she was expecting a baby. With the family house sold to pay her father's creditors and her mother still in hospital, she'd been staying with her aunt, who lived in a gloomy old house in Kensington. But urgently needing to earn some money to feed and clothe herself, she'd been lucky enough to find a temporary Christmas job in the Men's Gifts section of a world-famous department store.

It had been a long time before Amber forced herself to accept the hard, brutal truth that Max was never going to get in touch with her. And even longer to come to terms with the bitter pain and humiliation of his cruel desertion. Having always known about Max's wild reputation as a breaker of hearts, she knew that she had only herself to blame for having been so starry-eyed. So high on cloud nine, that while she'd given him her future address and phone number in London, she had no idea of where to contact him in America.

Where could she go? What *was* she going to do? Day after day, the questions seemed to pound away like sledgehammers in her brain. There was no way she could tell her aged spinster aunt about the baby. Nor could she bring herself to consider terminating the pregnancy. In fact, during her long working hours, it seemed as if she was merely existing on autopilot, smiling blankly at her customers while all the time her mind was in a ferment as she desperately tried to think of a solution to her problem. And then, one day, she found herself selling some cuff-links and a tie to an old friend from her childhood.

The orphan grandson of a wealthy landowner, Clive Stanhope had been raised at Elmbridge Hall before being sent away to boarding-school on the death of his grandfather. Although Amber had only met him briefly since he'd inherited the Hall and its large estate, he seemed delighted to see her again, and insisted on taking her out to dinner.

Clive had proved to be a warm and amusing companion, managing to lift her dismal spirits by making her laugh. Discovering that they had many interests in common, he'd also been very kind and sympathetic about her father's death and her mother's hospitalisation. So much so, in fact, that she was astounded to find herself telling him about her pregnancy and her desperate worries about the future.

'There's a simple answer to that problem,' he'd told her cheerfully, tossing back a large glass of wine. 'The solution is to marry me—and we can then both live happily ever after!'

Convinced that he was joking, she'd laughed at such a ridiculous idea. But after listening to Clive's explanation of just how lonely he found his grandfather's huge old house, and his aimless existence, which seemed to revolve around drink and gambling, she found herself feeling very sorry for the supposedly lucky, rich young man.

'To tell the truth, Amber, I seem to have made a complete and utter mess of my life so far. But at least I've still got enough sense to know that I must try to pull myself together. And if I had someone like you by my side—someone to help turn that draughty old house into a home—I'm quite sure that I could straighten myself out.'

Despite her protests that she couldn't possibly agree to such a mad suggestion, Clive had pointed out that his proposal of marriage would solve many of her urgent problems. 'The only money you've got is what you can earn, right? So, what happens when the baby arrives? Will you give him or her up for adoption? Or are you planning to try to live on what little you can dig out of the Social Services? Because you only have to read the newspapers to know what a nightmare scenario that can be!

'And what about your mother?' he continued. 'She's not likely to be happy living in a small, cramped apartment—even if you could afford to pay the rent. And while you haven't told me the name of your lover, I imagine you must still be in love with him. So, I would hardly expect you to leap into bed with me,' he'd grinned.

'Quite honestly, Amber, I don't see any reason why two people—who happen to be good friends— shouldn't come together for their mutual benefit. Give yourself time to think about it,' he'd urged before driving her home to her aunt's depressingly gloomy house.

Amber had spent sleepless nights trying to think what to do for the best. But, in the end, it was the desperate need to place a roof over both her mother's and the baby's head that had finally made up her mind. Clive had been delighted at her agreement to marry him, suggesting a quiet register-office wedding in London before their returning to live in Elmbridge.

There had been some gossip, of course, but when Lucy was born, most people seemed pleased that the once hopelessly wild Clive Stanhope had finally settled down and become a sensible, down-to-earth family man. For her part, Amber had been deeply grateful to Clive, both for looking after her and the baby, and his patience with her mother, who'd come to live with them on leaving hospital. 'I'm very fond of your mother even if she's sometimes as nutty as a fruit cake!' he'd laughed. 'In fact, as far as I can see, we've got years and years of happiness in front of us.'

And so they might have had, if Clive hadn't died in a car accident when Lucy was barely a year old. It had been such a deeply unhappy and worrying time that Amber had barely been able to mourn the loss of poor Clive. All her energies had been consumed in the struggle to survive the horrendous financial problems resulting from his premature death. And although she'd managed to keep going for the past seven years, it now seemed dreadfully ironic that Max should have come back when, for the second time in her life, she was about to lose the roof over her head. Surely, if there was any justice in the world, she ought to be free of the man who'd caused her so much pain and torment all those years ago?

But as she carried her mother's tray downstairs, she knew that life was never particularly fair or easy. And she couldn't help wondering if she'd always known, deep in her heart, that their brief love affair had been just a dream within a dream. That the sense of having found a secret measure of time—with the rest of the world fading into a grey mist about the sunlit, radiant figures of Max and herself—had been nothing more than a foolish delusion.

If so, she'd certainly paid in the past for such folly in torment and heartache. And now, it seemed, she

was going to have to pay yet again. Because, with
Max's return, there seemed absolutely nothing she
could do to prevent her whole world from being
smashed to smithereens.

Feeling sick and queasy with nervous tension,
Amber stared down at the food in front of her, unable
to do more than push it around her plate. Unlike Max,
who'd demolished a large bowl of soup, together with
umpteen slices of fresh brown bread and butter, before
finally wolfing down two large helpings of apple pie
and cream.

'That was wonderful! As my father, who liked to
quote from the Bible, would have said: "A good
woman's price is far above rubies",' he grinned,
leaning back in his chair as she rose to clear the plates
from the table.

'Since your wild, teenage behaviour meant that no
housekeeper ever stayed at the vicarage for more than
a few weeks, I'm not at all surprised that it was one
of your father's favourite quotations,' she retorted
sourly. 'Do you want some coffee?'

'Yes, please,' he said before giving a rueful shake
of his head. 'You're quite right, of course. Poor old
Dad. I really was pretty appalling in those days, wasn't
I?'

'Yes, you certainly were.' Tearing her eyes away
from his dynamically masculine figure, she tried to
control her nervously trembling hands as she scooped
freshly ground coffee into a jug before placing the
heavy steel kettle on the stove. 'In fact,' she added
waspishly, 'I can't see that you've altered in any way.'

He rose slowly to his feet. 'Now, that's where you're quite wrong. Believe me, Amber, it would be a *grave* mistake to think that I'm still the poor, deluded young fool that you once knew,' he drawled, a threatening note of menace underlying his words. 'I can assure you that a great deal of water has passed under the bridge since then.'

'Yes, I'm sure it has,' she muttered before taking a deep breath and forcing herself to turn and face him. 'Look—why don't we cut out all this nonsense and get straight to the point?' she demanded. 'I want to know why it's taken you over three weeks to return here to Elmbridge. And *exactly* what is it you want from me?'

He stared at her in silence for a moment before giving a shrug of his broad shoulders. 'I couldn't return here before now because I've been away in America on business. And we'll come to what I want in a moment. But before doing so—I'd be interested in hearing the answer to a minor question, which has been puzzling me for some time.'

'And that is . . .?'

'It's ancient history now, of course. But I've often wondered if Clive Stanhope ever found out that you'd been two-timing him with me all those years ago?'

Amber's jaw dropped as she gazed at him in astonishment. Having steeled herself to face yet another interrogation, together with ruthless demands for access to her small daughter, she was now feeling totally bewildered and confused. Two-timing him . . . with Clive? What on earth was he talking about?

Viewing the girl who was staring at him with dazed, stunned eyes, Max gave another wry shrug of his shoulders. 'It's merely an academic question now, of course, since the guy is dead. But what I've never been able to understand, Amber...' he paused, his lips twisting sardonically as he raised a dark eyebrow, 'is why you were also having an affair with Clive—of all people!'

'You never liked him, did you?'

Max shook his head as her bitter retort seemed to echo around the quiet room. 'No. You're quite right, I didn't,' he agreed slowly. 'I was, of course, genuinely very sorry to hear about his fatal accident. However, to tell the truth, I'd always regarded Clive as basically a spoiled brat—a weak personality with far too much money for his own good. But you clearly thought otherwise, hmm?'

'Yes, I most certainly did! Because, as far as I'm concerned, Clive was one of the nicest men I've ever known,' she retorted furiously. 'He may have gone slightly off the rails when he was younger, and I'd have to admit that he was always fairly hopeless with money. But Clive was basically a sweet, kind-hearted and generous man who was very, *very* good to me,' she added vehemently as Max walked slowly towards her.

He gave a scornful laugh. 'Since you're now living such a comfortable, easy life in one of the largest houses in the district—the sale of which is likely to make you a wealthy woman—it certainly seems that Clive *was* very good to you. Very good indeed!'

'How *dare* you insinuate that I married poor Clive for his money. You...you know absolutely *nothing* about my way of life,' she cried, almost choking with rage and fury.

But when he gave yet another caustic laugh of sheer disbelief, something seemed to snap in Amber's brain. Almost without knowing what she was doing, and intent only on removing that contemptuous, scathing expression from his face, her hand flashed up to slap him hard on the cheek.

There was a long, deathly silence, broken only by the sound of Max's sharp intake of breath as he stared down at her, his blue eyes as hard and cold as ice.

'That was a *very* stupid thing to do,' he grated harshly.

'I...I'm not sorry. It serves you right for being so despicable,' Amber gasped, backing nervously away from his tall, rigidly angry figure, her retreat abruptly halted as she felt her spine jar against the hard steel edge of the sink unit.

'You can't bear to face the truth, can you?' he snarled, raising his hands to clasp hold of her slim shoulders, and staring down into her defiant, angry green eyes. 'And the truth, as we both know, is that you're nothing but a money-grubbing, two-timing bitch!'

'My God, that's rich!' she cried. 'Especially from you, of all people! ''First he loved her—then he left her'' was *your* theme song, remember?' she ground out bitterly, trying without success to escape from the tall figure looming over her. 'Only, in *my* case, you left me holding the baby. So, if you really want to see a lousy, rotten, two-timing bastard, why not take a good look at yourself in the mirror?'

There was a long silence as the aggression seemed to drain away from Max's stiff, rigid figure, his face pale and strained as he stared intently down at her, his dark brows drawn together in a deep frown.

'Are you seriously trying to tell me...?'

'I wouldn't dream of trying to tell you *anything*. You're the one who claims to know it all,' she snapped nervously as he leaned forward, raising his hands to slowly and deliberately wind his fingers through her golden brown hair.

'I certainly once thought that I knew you,' he murmured.

Amber stiffened, warning bells jangling loudly in her brain as she noted the oddly thick, husky note in his voice. Oh, Heavens! she told herself wildly. She *must* get away from this highly dangerous man—and as quickly as possible.

'Yes, well, we all make mistakes,' she muttered breathlessly, trying to wriggle out from beneath his long, tall figure. But Amber realised that she'd left it too late as she felt his fingers tightening in her hair, holding her firmly imprisoned against him.

Desperately trying to maintain the force of her anger and fury, she was dismayed to find it swiftly draining away. Her senses seemed bemused by the enticing masculine scent of his cologne, while tremors of sensual excitement were rippling through her body in response to the warmth of the long, muscular thighs touching her own.

Despite knowing—who better?—that Max was a cold-hearted Casanova with all the morals of an alley cat, she couldn't seem to control a treacherous weakness from invading her quivering limbs. Time seemed suspended as she felt a hand moving slowly down her back to clasp her tightly about the waist, hot shivers gripping her stomach as he pulled her even closer to his hard, firm body, whose rapidly pounding heart seemed to be beating in unison with her own.

'No!' she gasped, struggling helplessly within the iron strength of his embrace as his dark head came slowly and inexorably down towards her, his mouth possessing her lips in a kiss of such burning intensity that desire seemed to explode like a firework inside her.

Helplessly trying to cling on to reality, she could feel it quickly slipping away in a mist of rising passion. She was only aware of a feverish, long-denied hunger—a compulsive need to respond to the fiercely invasive heat of his tongue, and the erotic touch of the hands sweeping down over her hips, fiercely pulling her soft body even closer to his tall, muscular frame. And it seemed as if she was caught up in a sudden frenzy of desire, moaning helplessly as she raised her arms to clasp him tightly about the neck, convulsively burying her fingers in his dark, curly hair.

'Amber...!' She hardly heard the deep, ragged groan as his lips left hers, feathering down her neck to seek the softly scented hollow at the base of her throat. As he raised a hand to caress the soft curve of her breast, his fingers brushed over the hard firm peak, causing a fierce shaft of pleasure to flash through her trembling figure. Trapped in a dizzy haze of scorching excitement, it was only when she became aware of the increasingly loud, strident whistle from the kettle she'd placed on the stove that cold reality began to break through the thick mist of passion and desire.

'Ignore it!' Max grunted impatiently as she began struggling to release herself from his embrace. But the magic, enchanted spell that he'd woven was now utterly destroyed, and with a sob she tore herself from his arms.

Shaking as if in the grip of a raging fever, her trembling legs almost gave way beneath her as she staggered across the room to the stove. Making sure that she had the safety of the kitchen table between them, she fought to control her ragged breathing, staring at Max in horror and dismay.

What on earth was happening to her? This was the *second* time that she'd found herself in his arms—and in the space of less than two hours. It was almost unbelievable! But unfortunately, and despite his total betrayal of her in the past, it looked as if she was *still* pathetically susceptible to Max's fatal, dark attraction—an attraction that, as she now bitterly reminded herself, had already caused her untold suffering and torment.

'I...I thought you said earlier, upstairs in the bedroom, that you weren't going to make that sort of "mistake", ever again,' she accused him bleakly.

'Yes, I believe I did say something of the sort,' he agreed with a mocking smile.

'So...?' she demanded indignantly.

He gave a careless shrug of his broad shoulders. 'It looks as though I must have changed my mind, doesn't it?'

'Well, you can just change your mind right back again,' she ground out furiously. 'How you had the sheer *nerve* to say all those horrid things...' She waved her hands distractedly in the air. 'I don't care what you say about me, but I won't hear a word against poor Clive.'

'You asked for my opinion of your late husband,' Max pointed out quietly. 'However, I've no wish to speak ill of the dead, and I'm sincerely sorry if I've upset you in any way. After all, it's true to say that I hardly knew the guy, and so...'

'No, you didn't know him at all,' she flashed back indignantly. 'Because, when I was at my lowest ebb— not only having been deserted by you, but desperately worried about my mother, and almost suicidal with panic and fear at finding myself pregnant—it was *Clive Stanhope* who came to my rescue. So, don't you *ever* dare to make any more sneering remarks about a man who, out of the sheer kindness of his heart, provided a home for my family.

'And now,' she continued grimly, pleased to note that Max wasn't attempting to say anything, his face a blank mask as he stared silently at her across the kitchen. 'This seems to be the perfect time to show you over the house. I'm sure that you'll be interested to view my "rich inheritance" and in seeing just what an "easy, comfortable life" I have here,' she added sarcastically, not waiting to see whether he was following her as she stalked angrily from the room.

*   *   *

'Well—have you got the message at last?' she demanded some time later, throwing open the door of yet another room. Like so many of the others that she'd shown him, it was stripped of all carpets, curtains and furniture, consisting only of bare floorboards and blank walls.

Max's increasingly grim, stern expression as he'd followed her silently through the house from one empty room to another should have provided a sweet revenge for all the unkind, malicious remarks that he'd made earlier about her supposedly glamorous lifestyle. But Amber now found herself suddenly feeling weary of the whole exercise.

'There's lots more rooms like this, of course,' she told him with a heavy sigh. 'The truth is that we're more or less flat broke. Clive had gone through most of his inheritance long before he married me. But it didn't seem to matter when he was alive. I was just so happy to have a roof over my head and to be able to look after my mother and the baby. After Clive's death . . .' She paused for a moment. 'Well, for the past few years, I've been taking in paying guests to help pay some of the household bills. But now, without going into all the boring details, I'm having to sell this house simply because I can't borrow any more money to feed and clothe the family. In fact,' she gave a wry smile as she waved a tired hand around the empty room, 'your accusation that I married Clive just because he was a rich man now seems to be a bit of a grim joke, doesn't it?'

Max didn't immediately reply, giving her a sharp, penetrating glance from beneath his dark brows before walking slowly across the old oak floorboards covered in dust to gaze blindly out of a window.

'It looks as though I owe you a deep apology,' he said at last, his husky voice echoing eerily in the empty room as he continued to stare through the window at the parkland, now slowly becoming less visible in the softly gathering darkness of the late winter's afternoon. 'It's no excuse, of course, but I just assumed...' He paused, swearing softly under his breath as he brushed a hand roughly through his thick, curly dark hair. 'So, all those old portraits and antique furniture downstairs...?'

'Nothing but pure window dressing,' she told the man, who was still standing with his back to her. 'As you've seen, the entrance hall, sitting and dining rooms are still furnished more or less as they always were. Our own bedrooms are a bit Spartan, with just the basic necessities. However, I've managed to keep three guest-rooms in a fairly decent state, for when we have visitors. But that's it. Everything else went to the saleroom a long time ago.'

'*For God's sake*!' he exploded as he whirled around to face her. 'Why on earth didn't you tell me? I could have taken care of you all. There would have been no need for you to sell either the house or your possessions.' His lips tightened with anger as he gazed about the empty room.

She stared at him, completely dumbfounded for a moment, before leaning weakly against the wall, her slim frame shaking with hysterical laughter. 'Oh, Max, you're absolutely priceless!' She shook her head, lifting a shaking hand to wipe tears of helpless mirth from her eyes.

'I can't see what's so damn funny about your situation!' he grated angrily.

'Because, if I didn't laugh at such a ridiculously stupid statement, I'd probably scream with frustration and rage.' She gave a weary shake of her head. 'For Heaven's sake, I thought you were supposed to be such a clever, successful businessman. Haven't you yet worked out exactly *why* I accepted Clive's kind, generous offer of marriage?'

He shrugged. 'I'd always thought...I just assumed that you'd decided he was a better matrimonial prospect. After all, I hadn't anything to offer you at the time, and...'

'Oh, for goodness' sake, don't be such an idiot,' she retorted impatiently. 'The answer is, in fact, a very simple one. I couldn't tell you *anything* about myself and the baby because I had absolutely no way of contacting you.'

'That's simply not true!' he growled fiercely.

'What isn't true?' she demanded bleakly. 'The fact that you professed undying love and wanted to marry me? Or that after leaving me pregnant, you quickly skipped the country?'

'I promise you, I had absolutely *no* idea that you were expecting a baby,' he assured her earnestly, his face pale beneath its tan as he gazed at her with a tense, strained expression.

'You may not have been aware of my pregnancy— something that even *I* didn't know about until it was far too late. But you'd still disappeared off the face of the earth, making damn sure that I didn't have your new address in America. Right?'

'No! You're damn well *wrong*!' he ground out through clenched teeth, swearing violently under his breath as he began pacing up and down the room. 'How can you possibly believe that I set out to deliberately deceive you? For God's sake, Amber, you must know that I'd never do such a thing.'

'Oh, really?' she enquired with grim irony. 'Well, short of taking up clairvoyance, or placing a "Wanted" poster in every town in the United States, I'll be fascinated to hear just *how* I was supposed to get in touch with you. Even if I'd ever wanted to see you again—which I most certainly did not.'

'You don't understand,' he growled.

'You're quite right,' she snapped. 'I never did "understand" your rotten behaviour. And, quite frankly, it's now far too late for me to care one way or another,' she added with a heavy sigh, suddenly feeling tired to death of the whole wretched story.

So often, in the past, she had dreamed of being able to tell Max exactly what she thought of his vile, treacherous behaviour. But now that he was actually standing here in front of her, it all seemed so pointless somehow. In fact, by raking up the painful events that had taken place so many years ago, it looked as though she'd only succeeded in causing herself even more distress.

'You've got to let me explain . . .'

'Oh, no, I haven't! I'm simply not interested—and it's far too late for any "explanations". It's been eight years since you callously dumped me. Eight years in which I've made a new life for both myself and my daughter. And now, if you'll excuse me...' she added, glancing down at the watch on her wrist, 'I must go and dig up some vegetables before the light goes. Please feel free to continue your tour of this house, which, as we both know, you have no intention of buying,' she added grimly, before swiftly leaving the room.

THE clink of glasses and the noisy, cheerful sound of raised voices and laughter filled the large main area of the old Assembly Rooms.

Built in Regency times and carefully preserved by the efforts of the town council, the Assembly Rooms had originally been designed to cater for local meetings, dances and parties—providing a much-needed, central venue for a sparsely populated and rural area. However, as she gazed around the elegant room, filled with so many of her old friends and acquaintances, Amber realised that she and the other local inhabitants of the town were fortunate to still have the use of such a lovely old building.

'The party appears to be going well,' Philip said as he placed a fresh glass of wine in her hand. 'Everyone seems determined to press ahead with strong opposition to the new marina.'

'But it's going to be difficult to save the Tide Mill,' she sighed. 'Especially since the developers have already been given planning permission to pull it down.'

'Well, with snow forecast for the weekend, I don't reckon there will be much building work taking place—not until the new year, at least,' he pointed out. 'I just wish that I could say the same for my own profession. Unfortunately, this is by far my busiest time of the year.'

Amber looked at him with concern. 'I know you've been very busy this week. Are you on call again tonight?'

'I'm afraid so.' The young doctor gave her a tired grin. 'However, let's hope that all my patients stay well and healthy—for the duration of this party, at least! Incidentally, have I told you about the plans for my new surgery? I'm really very excited about the layout, and...'

But as Philip continued to expand on his architect's ideas for the new building, Amber suddenly stiffened, her green eyes widening in shock as the crowd of people parted for a moment, and she caught a glimpse of the tall, dark figure of a man standing across the room.

Max...? What on earth was he doing here? she asked herself, suddenly feeling panic-stricken as she watched his hard, determined features relaxing into a courteous smile as he turned to shake someone's hand.

How could she have been so stupid? She might have known that it was useless to try and avoid his baleful presence. But when she'd taken refuge in the kitchen garden—leaving Max to continue looking over a house which she was certain he had no intention of buying— she still hadn't been entirely convinced that he was seriously intending to stay at Elmbridge Hall. He had, after all, only returned to the town in order to see Lucy. And once he'd discovered that she wasn't due to return until tomorrow, surely Max would prefer the more convivial, lively atmosphere to be found in one of the small local hotels.

A bout of hard digging in the kitchen garden had, as always, helped to soothe her battered spirits. Although she'd eventually been driven back inside by a light snowfall and the gathering darkness, Amber had felt able to view the day's sequence of events in a slightly calmer frame of mind than when she'd first stormed out of the house.

It was, of course, no good trying to fudge the issue: she'd been a perfect idiot. Not only had she been guilty of underestimating Max's sheer ruthlessness, but also totally stupid to have allowed herself to be alone with him. Why hadn't she remembered that a leopard never changes his spots? That even as a teenager, he'd been like the awful nursery-rhyme character, Georgie-Porgie, 'who kissed the girls and made them cry'? Just about a *perfect* description of Max Warner—the root cause of so many tears and so much unhappiness in her life. But never, *never* again, Amber had grimly promised herself, returning to the house full of good intentions and firm resolve.

Pleased to discover that both Max and his car had disappeared, she knew that she hadn't seen the last of him—especially as he had yet to state his intentions regarding Lucy. However, when he still hadn't returned by the time she'd prepared an early supper for her mother, and Philip Jackson had arrived to give her a lift to the party, Amber had allowed herself to hope that he might even have decided to go back to London.

Fat chance! she told herself, staring glumly down at her glass. Goodness knows, she hadn't really wanted to come here tonight. But it had seemed important, if only for Lucy's sake, to try and appear to be behaving as normally as possible.

Attempting to pull herself together and concentrate on Philip's remarks about the plans for his new surgery, she heard the pager, which the doctor always carried in the top pocket of his jacket, give a sharp, high-pitched 'bleep'.

'I thought it was too good to last,' he told her ruefully, bending down to give her a quick peck on the cheek before hurrying off across the room in search of a telephone.

Sipping her wine and hoping that Philip wouldn't be long, Amber was startled when a hard, familiar voice spoke from behind her shoulder.

'Has the good doctor left you all alone? What a shame.'

Spinning around, she glared up at Max, who was grinning wolfishly down at her.

'He happens to be on call tonight,' she snapped before realising that Max must have been doing his homework. How else would he have known that Philip was a doctor? 'What are you doing here?' she demanded. 'I can't believe you're interested in what happens to the old Tide Mill?'

'Oh, I'm interested in all sorts of things,' he drawled. 'For instance, I'm looking forward to seeing how much the town has changed, meeting old friends and acquaintances, seeing Lucy...'

'I'm not prepared to talk about my daughter—certainly not *here*!' she retorted, glancing nervously around to see if anyone else had heard what he was saying.

'*Our* daughter,' he corrected smoothly.

'OK...OK!' she muttered, feeling almost sick with tension. Didn't Max know or care about the torture he was putting her through?

'You're quite right. This is neither the time nor the place for that sort of discussion,' he murmured, pausing for a moment as a waiter topped up their glasses. 'So...maybe we could discuss our own relationship instead?'

'What "relationship"?' she ground out through clenched teeth. 'As far as I'm concerned, we have absolutely nothing in common—except a very brief, unfortunate episode in the past. So, why don't you leave me alone? Go off and play your rotten games with someone else. And there's *just* the perfect companion for you,' she added grimly, nodding her head towards a noisy group of men, surrounding a beautifully dressed, glamorous ash-blonde woman. 'I hear that your old flame, Cynthia Henderson, can't wait to meet you again. And since everyone knows that Cynthia can never resist a man with a large bank balance, I'm sure she'll welcome *you* with open arms!' Amber taunted, not caring if she was sounding like a first-class bitch in her determination to hit back at him.

'Well, it certainly looks as if it's my lucky day, doesn't it?' he drawled sardonically. 'Because I thought that *your* arms seemed remarkably welcoming this afternoon.'

'Oh, shut up!' she snapped, her cheeks flushing with embarrassment and the realisation that she could never seem to get the better of this indomitable man.

Luckily, she was rescued from having to say anything more by the approach of Sally's husband, John Fraser.

'Hello, Amber, you're looking as lovely as ever,' the lawyer smiled at her. 'I'm sorry to be a nuisance, but I wonder if I could just have a quick word with Max? There are one or two people who would like to meet him, and...'

'Sure,' Max agreed quickly, promising to return in a moment, before following the lawyer back across the room.

Fervently hoping that she'd seen the last of Max, at least for this evening, Amber realised that she had a problem. However much she might want to leave this party as soon as possible, she had no way of getting home. With her old Land Rover in the local garage, and Philip busy with his sick patients, she was well and truly stuck. Desperately trying to find a solution to her dilemma, she was surprised to see Cynthia Henderson gliding purposefully across the floor towards her.

By far the most grown-up and attractive girl at school, Cynthia had managed to avoid the dire fate that—according to her teachers and the mothers of the other pupils in the class—lay in wait for such a boy-mad, sexually promiscuous teenager. Cynthia had, in fact, matured into a very glamorous and distractingly beautiful woman. Marrying and discarding at least two husbands along the way, she was now the owner of a very expensive boutique in the centre of town.

'Been abandoned, have you?' Cynthia drawled as she came nearer. 'Men really are the pits, aren't they?' she added, lighting a cigarette and casually blowing smoke in the other girl's face.

'You may have a point there,' Amber agreed grimly, raising a hand to fan the fumes from her eyes.

'Of course I do, sweetie,' Cynthia murmured, her eyes flicking contemptuously over Amber's plain black dress, which had clearly seen better days. 'I mean—just look at those stupid women.' She waved an elegant, crimson-nailed hand around the room. 'As soon as they set eyes on darling Max, they all immediately went on "red alert". A total waste of time, of course. You couldn't expect such an attractive man to even give them the time of day!' she added with a cruel laugh. 'By the way, I hear Max is staying at your boarding-house for a few days.'

'Yes,' Amber told her stonily, not finding it at all difficult to understand why Cynthia was so deeply unpopular with the other women in the town.

'Well, I don't suppose he'll be with you for long. As far as I can see, it looks as if Max hasn't changed one bit.' She gave another low, throaty chuckle of laughter. 'Because, if I remember rightly—and of course I do!—he always did get bored *very* easily.'

Amber shrugged, steeling herself against the poisonous darts of this equally poisonous woman, who was clearly intent on reclaiming her old boyfriend.

Well, the very best of luck to her! Amber thought sourly. If Max wanted to get heavily involved with this sexy, ash-blonde divorcee, that was entirely his own affair. She didn't give a toss *what* he did—just as long as he left her and Lucy alone. Right?

Unexpectedly overwhelmed by a sudden heavy weight of depression, her dismal thoughts were sharply interrupted as Cynthia gave a quick, breathless gasp of pleasure.

'Max, darling! How *wonderful* to see you again!' she cried as his tall, rangy figure crossed the room towards them. 'It was very naughty of you to abandon poor little Amber....' she added, winding her arms about his neck and giving him a long, lingering kiss on the lips.

Try as she might, Amber couldn't seem able to tear her eyes away from the glamorous blonde's voluptuous figure pressed so closely to that of Max, or to avoid noticing the way in which he was so enthusiastically responding to her kiss, his hands eagerly closing about her slim waist.

'Umm...we must *definitely* do that again—very soon!' Cynthia gave another husky, sensual laugh as she slowly removed her arms from around his neck. 'The whole town is buzzing with news of the prodigal's return. Is it *really* true that you're thinking of settling down here in Elmbridge?' she added, gazing hungrily up into his gleaming blue eyes.

Amber froze, her nails biting into the palms of her tightly clenched hands as she realised that the feelings tearing at her heart with such sharp, fierce claws were nothing more or less than an overwhelming surge of pure feminine jealousy. Feeling faint and almost sick, she stared down at the floor while she struggled to control her emotions. Like an animal in pain, she wanted only to escape, to seek the shelter of a deep, dark and private burrow in which to lick her wounds in secret. But of course, she couldn't. Sunk in misery, it was some time before she became fully aware of the conversation taking place beside her.

'... yes, I'll be in touch with you again, very soon. Unfortunately, I'm afraid that it's time Amber and I were on our way.'

'What...?'

'I've just bumped into your boyfriend,' he told Amber, who was staring at him in glassy-eyed horror. 'He was just rushing off to a bad car accident on the A45. Apparently it looks as if we're in for a heavy snowstorm tonight. So I said that I'd take you back home.'

'Surely there's no need to leave so soon?' Cynthia murmured, obviously not at all pleased by the turn of events. 'I'm dying to hear what you've been doing all these years you've been away. And is it really true that you're thinking of settling down here in Elmbridge? It would be such fun helping you to find just the *right* house. There are quite a few on the market at the moment, and...'

'Oh, that's no problem. I've already decided to buy Elmbridge Hall.'

'What a brilliant idea!' she exclaimed happily over Amber's muffled gasp of protest. 'And once you've renovated that poor, neglected house, there's only one more thing you'll need to make everything just *perfect*.'

'And that is?'

'Surely it's obvious darling. What you need is a wife!' Cynthia murmured huskily, throwing him a smouldering, sideways glance through her long, thick eyelashes.

'You're absolutely right,' Max agreed. 'In fact, I'm hoping to get married to an old girlfriend in the very near future.'

And we all know which 'old girlfriend' he has in mind, Amber thought miserably as Max led her from the room. If that smile of smug satisfaction and triumph on the glamorous divorcee's face was anything to go by, the only question in Cynthia's mind was precisely where she and Max would be spending their honeymoon.

The heavy, oppressive silence within Max's car seemed never-ending. As did the short journey back to Elmbridge Hall. Tense and nervous, Amber stared blindly through the windscreen, the rapidly falling snow glistening in the bright glare of the headlights. She could hardly believe that it was still only Friday night. Just how long was she going to have to put up with the ominous, baleful presence of this hard and indomitable man?

Desperately trying to combat a rising tide of fear and panic, Amber closed her eyes and leaned back against the headrest. It was nerve-racking to realise that they *still* hadn't discussed the all-important matter of Lucy. Or could it be that Max was just playing a game with her? Maybe he was deliberately keeping her in this ghastly state of overwhelming stress and anxiety, piling on the agony until almost the last moment before his departure.

And that wasn't all. On top of all her other problems, she now had to contend with his apparent decision to buy Elmbridge Hall. How *dare* he just casually announce the news to that nauseating woman, Cynthia Henderson? Surely he might have had the common decency to discuss the matter with her before telling anyone else. After all, it *was* still her home. It was up to *her* to decide whether or not she wished to sell it to Max.

Amber could almost tangibly feel the anger and fury raging through her veins at being treated as though she had no choice in the matter. For all he knew, there might be hundreds of people queuing up to purchase the Hall. The unfortunate fact that Max was the only person who'd expressed any interest in purchasing the old Tudor mansion merely served to increase her frustration at being treated in such a high-handed manner.

By the time Max brought the car to a halt outside Elmbridge Hall, she'd worked herself up into such a state that she could contain herself no longer. 'What are you intending to do about Lucy?' she burst out angrily as he came around to open her door. 'And if you think you can just calmly announce that you're going to buy my home, you've got another think coming!'

'I suggest we leave any discussion on those points until we get inside. It's freezing out here,' Max said, taking hold of her arm and leading her trembling figure up the icy steps to the front door. 'Why don't you go and check that your mother's all right?' he added as they entered the house.

'Why don't you mind your own damn business—and stop ordering me around?' she retorted furiously before stalking off across the hall towards Violet Grant's wing of the house.

After checking on her mother, who was fast asleep, Amber was still fuming by the time she made her way to the sitting room, where Max had set out a tray containing a bottle and two glasses. Casting a jaundiced eye over the large flagon of rare malt whiskey—it was years since she'd been able to afford anything so expensive—she was slightly mollified by the fact that Max had also put some more logs on the smouldering fire in the huge grate, whose flames cast a warm glow over the antique furniture and old velvet curtains.

'Here . . . this will warm you up,' he said, holding out a glass of pale tawny liquid towards her.

Backing away from him, she shook her head. 'No, I don't want anything more to drink. I've already had a lot of wine at dinner, and . . .'

'For God's sake, relax!' he retorted impatiently, firmly placing the glass in her hands. 'Believe me, this is purely medicinal. Far from intending to seduce you with the demon drink, I'm merely trying to prevent you from looking quite so cold and tired.'

'I really don't . . .'

'Drink it!' he growled, frowning fiercely down at her until she did as she was told before leading her towards a comfortable sofa by the fire.

'Whatever happened to the glamorous and charming "Mad Max" Warner? From what I can see, you appear to have all the charisma of a rattlesnake!' she grumbled, determined not to admit that the fiery liquor was indeed making her feel a good deal warmer and less weary.

'I've already told you to forget the past,' he told her firmly, sitting himself down on the other end of the sofa. 'I'm only interested in the present—and the future, of course. Which is why I want to discuss what we're going to do about Lucy.'

Overwhelmingly relieved to find that Max was, at last, prepared to broach the subject that had been tormenting her for so many weeks, Amber took a deep breath. Whatever the provocation, it was desperately important that she remain cool, calm and collected throughout their discussion.

'I know Elmbridge has changed and grown slightly larger since you've been away. But it is still a small market town, with everyone taking a close friendly interest in their neighbours. In other words,' she gave him a weak smile, 'it's very much the same hotbed of rumour and gossip that it's always been.'

He shrugged. 'You're not telling me anything that I haven't already seen and heard for myself.'

'Well, bully for you!' she exclaimed impatiently. 'However, I've lived in Elmbridge all my life, and Lucy was born and raised here. So, you can take it from me, that it's only going to need *one* person to see the both of you together, and just about everyone else will know—inside twenty-four hours—that Clive had to marry me because I was expecting your illegitimate baby. But that's only one small part of the problem,' she added quickly as he stirred restlessly on the sofa. 'You obviously don't give a hoot about *my* good name—but what about Lucy? She's only a little girl and hardly knows you from Adam. Can't you imagine the shock and distress she's going to feel, suddenly confronted by the fact that Clive wasn't really her father? Not to mention the poor child having to put up with being teased and laughed at by all her schoolfriends. I won't have her being subjected to...to that sort of ordeal!' Amber glared at him, her fists clenched tightly in her lap. 'There's *no way* that I'll let you ruin her life!'

'For goodness' sake, calm down!' he told her sternly. 'I'm well aware of the problems we have to face.'

'There won't be any "problems"—not if you drop your daft idea of buying this house,' she retorted quickly. 'All you have to do is to go straight back to London, or whatever, and I'll make sure that Lucy visits you as often as you like. We can take our time in explaining that you're her real father, and that way there won't be any need for...'

'No.' He gave a firm shake of his dark head. 'No, I'm afraid that idea of yours won't work.'

'But why not? So, OK, you've inherited your grandmother's estate. But that doesn't necessarily mean you *have* to live in Elmbridge,' she pointed out, striving to sound calm and reasonable. 'Even if you're fed up with London, there's bound to be some marvellous houses for sale not too far away. What about Cambridge, for instance? It's a lovely university town,

full of interesting people and only an hour away by
car from Elmbridge. On top of which, there's the Arts
Theatre, regular concerts in the Guildhall, and——'
She broke off as she saw his lips twitching with sup-
pressed laughter. 'I don't see what's so damn funny,'
she ground out through clenched teeth, desperately
striving to control an overwhelming urge to slap that
supercilious grin off his face.

'I was merely amused by your sales pitch for the
City of Cambridge,' he drawled. 'However, while I
agree that it's a lovely town, I can assure you that I
am definitely returning to live in Elmbridge, and that
I have every intention of buying this house.'

'But . . . but I don't see *why* . . .' Amber wailed, suddenly forced to realise that she had no hope of getting
this arrogant man to listen to any sound, logical arguments. 'Haven't you *any* idea of what you'll be
doing to my family? Surely you ought to be able to
understand . . .' She waved a hand helplessly in the air.

'I've heard a great deal regarding how *you* feel
about the situation,' he retorted grimly. 'How about
trying to understand *my* feelings for a change?'

'What . . . what are you talking about?'

'Have you actually bothered to think about anyone
other than yourself? To wonder how *I* must have felt
on suddenly discovering that I had a daughter?' he
demanded scathingly before rising impatiently to his
feet and striding about the room. 'Well, since it obviously hasn't, I can tell you that I was completely
and utterly shattered! One moment I was merely
calling to view a house, which I'd been told was for
sale, and then . . .' He brushed a distracted hand

through his thick, curly dark hair. 'For God's sake, Amber, that child is the spitting image of me. How in the hell did you think you could get away with claiming that Clive Stanhope was Lucy's father?'

'Clive had dark hair, although his was straight, of course. But children often have curly hair when they're young...' she muttered, her cheeks reddening as he gave a caustic snort of derision. 'Besides, you'd left the area years ago. There was no reason for anyone to make the connection between you and Lucy.'

'Did you ever intend to tell her the truth?'

'No, why should I?' Amber retorted defiantly. 'You'd had your fun before callously deserting me and my unborn child. I didn't—and I still don't, for that matter—see any reason for upsetting Lucy or causing her any distress by telling her that Clive wasn't her father. In fact, there was absolutely no problem. Not until you suddenly appeared out of nowhere— like the demon king in a pantomime,' she added bitterly.

'Thanks!'

'Well, what do you expect? I'm hardly likely to hang out the flags and cry "whoopee!" Not like your old girlfriend, Cynthia.' She gave a shrill, high-pitched laugh. '*You* may have only been back in the town for a day, but it looks as though *she's* already chosen her wedding dress, and all set for a quick canter up the aisle!'

'Can we please keep to the point at issue,' Max told her brusquely. Although he did not, she noted grimly, disagree with her assessment: that Cynthia was hell-bent on marrying him as soon as possible. 'My only concern at the moment is how both you and I can come to a sensible decision regarding Lucy's future. That's what you want, isn't it?' he demanded, sitting down on the sofa beside her.

'What I want . . . what I want is for you to go away and leave us alone!'

'Well, I'm afraid that isn't going to happen. Come on, Amber, you must try and pull yourself together,' he said in a softer tone of voice, taking her trembling hands in his. 'You may wish me a million miles away. But unfortunately, there are several good and valid reasons—inheriting my grandmother's estate, for instance—why I need to live in this area. I could possibly remain based in London, of course. But since I'm going to be visiting Elmbridge on a regular basis, you must see that it wouldn't be long before people started talking about the startling resemblance between Lucy and myself.

'I realise that my business trip to America came at a very bad time,' he continued as she remained silent, her cheeks flushed as she stared down at her fingers clasped within his large hands. 'However, once I'd recovered from the initial shock of discovering that I had a daughter, it did give me three weeks in which to think matters out. To decide on the best course of action—as far as Lucy is concerned. You and I may have messed up our lives,' he added sternly, 'but I'm sure you'll agree that we must try and do better for our child.'

She nodded, unable to speak because of a sudden heavy lump in her throat.

'First and foremost, I want to see as much of Lucy as I can,' he said firmly. 'It may not have been anyone's fault. But the fact remains that I've been denied any knowledge of her existence for the past seven years. I have no intention of being shut out of her life any longer.'

'But... but it will be such a shock. I... I haven't told her anything about the situation,' Amber protested tearfully.

'Relax! There's absolutely no need for you to get into such a state,' he said, placing a large white handkerchief in her trembling fingers. 'I'm perfectly capable of realising that we'll need time to get to know one another. Just as you must realise that I have no intention of trying to interfere with her place in your life. Or her memories of Clive.'

'Lucy was only a baby when he died,' Amber muttered, dabbing her eyes. 'But I have tried to tell her as much as I can about him, so she didn't feel too different from her friends.'

'You've obviously done a splendid job rearing our daughter. From what little I've seen, she appears to be a delightful child,' he told her warmly.

'Yes... yes, she really is,' Amber assured him, nervously twisting the handkerchief in her fingers. 'But, even if you do want to get to know Lucy, I can't see how to manage it. I mean... I know it's totally pathetic to care what people might say or do when the news leaks out. But how can I possibly explain what happened all those years ago? Absolutely *everyone* thinks that Clive is Lucy's father. I know you didn't like him,' she added, weak tears of tiredness filling her eyes and spilling out down over her cheeks. 'But I owe him more than I can say. Without his help and support I'd have been completely destitute, with no choice but to have the baby adopted. Do please try to understand,' she begged. 'I really can't *bear* the thought of Clive being made to look foolish in any way.'

'There's no need to cry,' Max murmured softly, taking the handkerchief from her shaking hands and carefully wiping the tears from her eyes. 'I now realise that I was completely wrong about Clive, and I'm really very grateful that he was able to come to your aid. You have my word that I'll never do anything that is likely to harm his memory.'

Amber leaned back against the cushions with a heavy sigh. 'I still can't see any answer to the problem.'

'Well, I've given the matter a considerable amount of thought, and as far as I can see, there appears to be only one sensible course of action. First of all, I intend to phone Mr Glover tomorrow morning, confirming that I have definitely decided to buy this house. As you've already pointed out, Elmbridge hasn't changed much while I've been away.' He gave her a sardonic grin. 'So, I imagine it will only take twenty-four hours for everyone to know about the sale...?'

Amber gave a weary nod. 'That's probably a conservative estimate,' she agreed listlessly.

'Right. So the scenario for public consumption is going to be a very simple one. Returning home after spending some years abroad—and anxious to settle down at last—I approached Mr Glover, who brought me here to view the house. Whereupon I promptly fell in love with this huge old Tudor mansion . . . *and* with its owner. So, the poor young widow—bravely struggling to support her aged mother and small daughter—agrees to marry the wealthy prince and they both live happily ever after. It is, as I'm sure you'll agree, a deeply romantic story,' he pointed out, his broad shoulders shaking with amusement. 'And one guaranteed to bring a tear to the eye of even the most hardened cynic.'

It was some moments before Amber, bone-weary and exhausted, was fully able to comprehend what he was saying.

'You must be crazy!' she gasped, sitting bolt upright and staring with horror up into his handsome face.

'On the contrary—it all makes perfect sense,' he drawled with a sardonic grin, completely ignoring her strangled protests of rage and fury as he continued to outline his proposed scenario.

'Since I've spent so many years in the United States—where life is, of course, lived at a much faster pace—everyone will quite understand my reluctance to hang around, once I'd made up my mind to a course of action. And what could be nicer than a Christmas wedding? Nothing flashy, of course, just a small, simple affair. And then, while this house is being put in order, we'll fly off to Switzerland for a combined honeymoon and skiing holiday. Which will give me a perfect opportunity to get to know Lucy.'

'I . . . I've   never   heard   such   stuff and nonsense!'

'It's the only possible solution to the problem,' he retorted firmly. 'My daughter needs a father. And I'm *quite* determined that she's going to have one.'

'So, OK, I may well get married to someone in the future. But not to you, of all people!' Amber cried, almost beside herself with rage. Who in the hell did this awful man think he was? God's gift to women?

Max gave a bark of caustic laughter. 'I hope you're not thinking of involving that young doctor in your plans. He's quite the wrong man for you.'

'What...what right have you to interfere in my friendship with Philip?' she gasped.

'As Lucy's father, I've obviously got strong views on the subject,' he drawled smoothly. 'Believe me, there's no way I'd approve of Philip Jackson.'

'What damned cheek!' Amber ground out, almost choking with fury. 'Well, I don't give *that* for your so-called "approval".' She snapped her fingers in his face. 'It's about time you realised that you have absolutely no rights as far as Lucy is concerned. And, in any case, you obviously know nothing about Philip,' she added defiantly. 'Because he's a very sweet, caring man, who's going to make someone a wonderful husband.'

'You may be right. But that's pure speculation because you're certainly not marrying him. As for my "rights" regarding Lucy...' His eyes hardened into frosty chips of blue ice. 'It would be *very* foolish of you to even think of denying me access.'

'I'm not listening to any more...I won't be threatened like this!' Amber lashed back angrily. She jumped to her feet, but her attempt to escape was foiled as he quickly reached up to clasp hold of her hands, pulling her back down on the sofa towards him. 'Let me go!' she panted, struggling helplessly against the iron grip of the fingers tightening cruelly about her wrists.

'It's not a threat—it's a *fact*,' he grated harshly. 'A quick blood test will instantly prove that I'm Lucy's father. And since I'm now a very rich man, I can easily afford to keep you tied up in the courts—until Doomsday, if necessary. Do you *really* want to spend the next few years harassed by a never-ending series of legal writs and injunctions? To have all the gory details of Lucy's conception and birth widely reported in the newspapers? It certainly won't do much for your mother's quality of life, will it?' he continued relentlessly, not bothering to hide the cruel, implacable menace in his voice. 'And what about our daughter? How do you think Lucy will feel as she grows older and realises that she's been deliberately prevented from seeing her real father? I'm told that young teenagers can be very difficult to handle. Quite frankly, Amber, I don't think that she'll ever forgive you.'

'You . . . you *devil*!' Amber gasped in horror, the blood draining from her face.

He shook his head. 'I'm merely trying to get you to see sense. To realise that I'm in deadly earnest.'

'This idea of a marriage is totally . . . utterly impossible! It would never work. That stupid story of yours . . . it's full of holes a mile wide,' she gabbled hysterically. 'No one... absolutely *no one* could possibly believe such a load of old rubbish. Not for one moment!'

'Oh, yes they will,' he retorted confidently. 'Everyone loves a romantic story, especially one that ends with the two lovers going off into the sunset together, hand in hand. In fact, now I think about it,' he mused reflectively, 'we might embellish the tale by letting it become known that I was crazy about you before I went to America. Only you, of course, were far too young. So, I've had to wait all these years before being able to claim my own true love. What do you think?'

'What do I think...?' Amber shrieked, her body shaking with baffled rage and fury as she tried to wriggle free of his grip. 'I think you must be completely *insane*. "A romantic story"? "My own true love"? Who do you think you're kidding?' she grated savagely. 'We both know that you were *never* in love with me. All you were interested in was sex!'

'And you...?' He raised a dark, sardonic eyebrow. 'Were you ever really in love with me?'

'Yes, of course I was,' she snapped, bitterly aware of a deep, hot flush rapidly spreading over her cheeks as she found herself being pulled closer to his broad torso. 'But only because I was far too young and stupid to know any better. Eight years on—it's now a *very* different story. I feel nothing for you. Absolutely nothing at all.'

He gave a low, husky laugh. 'Maybe we ought to test that last statement of yours,' he mocked softly, letting go of her hands, his strong arms closing firmly about her trembling body. 'Because I think you're still crazy about me.'

'You ... you arrogant swine! Haven't you heard a word I've been saying?' she demanded breathlessly, desperately trying to free herself from the embrace of the man whose face was now only inches away from her own.

'I don't think you're telling me the truth,' he murmured, studying her intently as his arms tightened about her like bands of steel.

'Oh, yes—yes, I *am*!' she protested, frantically trying to tear her gaze away from the gleam in his glittering blue eyes and the cruel, sensual line of his lips, the message they conveyed suddenly causing her stomach to churn wildly with shock and sexual tension. Staring up mesmerised as the black head came slowly down towards her, she couldn't seem to stop herself from shaking and quivering in response to the sudden fierce, deep hunger flooding through her body as he lowered her back against the cushions, almost holding her breath until his mouth firmly possessed her tremulous lips.

A second later she found herself swept up in a whirlwind of confused sensations. She was intensely aware of the fragrant aroma of his cologne and the warm, firm texture of his skin. Frantically striving to hang on to reality, she seemed unable to prevent her own senses from betraying her. Once again, the barriers which she'd so carefully erected against this man were being destroyed by the sweet seduction of his lips. With a faint, helpless moan she surrendered to the fierce wild excitement of his deepening kiss, the overwhelming need and desire for the caressing touch of his hands on her soft, trembling body.

It seemed a long time before Max raised his dark head to stare intently down at the figure in his arms. 'You may be a very desirable woman, Amber,' he whispered huskily, slowly running a finger down over her flushed cheek. 'But you always were a rotten liar!'

She gazed up at him in bewilderment and confusion, still dazed by the sudden assault on her newly awakened senses. As the heat and desire of a few moments before began slowly ebbing away from her trembling body, her vision was filled by the hard, ruthless gleam in his eyes, the sardonic curve of his lips betraying both mockery and satisfaction. A deep tide of crimson swept over her face and she almost groaned out loud, appalled at the pathetically spineless, feeble way in which—once again—she'd so weakly succumbed to his dark attraction.

Swiftly wriggling free of his relaxed grip, Amber quickly jumped up from the sofa.

'Just a minute,' Max drawled coolly, putting out a hand to catch hold of her wrist as she turned to flee from the room. 'I'm still waiting to hear your decision about our marriage.'

'What marriage?' she bit out savagely through nervous, chattering teeth as she jerked herself free. 'I wouldn't marry *you*—not even if you were the last man on earth!'

'Oh, yes, I'm very sure you will,' Max drawled flatly as she bolted across the room towards the door, his bark of harsh, sardonic laughter echoing in her ears as she stumbled up the stairs to the refuge of her bedroom.

CHAPTER SIX

A SHRILL ringing from the clock beside her bed broke through Amber's restless sleep. Yawning, she put out a hand to silence the alarm before raising her weary head to check the time. Eight o'clock—and time to get up.

Amber groaned, turning over to bury her face in the pillows. Tossing and turning throughout the night, she'd hardly had a wink of sleep. And it was all Max Warner's fault. Lying wide awake through the long hours of darkness, she'd been finally forced to accept that he was quite right. She really *was* still crazy about him! Even thinking about that torrid embrace last night was enough to set her stomach churning wildly, like a cement-mixer out of control. How on earth was she going to stagger through what promised to be a hideously long day?

If *only* she had some experience to fall back on. Some knowledge of both men and the world outside the provincial backwater in which she'd lived for most of her twenty-six years. Unfortunately, having fallen madly in love with Max at the age of eighteen, her subsequent pregnancy and marriage to Clive Stanhope had prevented her from taking part in the normal life of most teenagers. While her contemporaries had been going through the natural process of growing up— gaining some experience of the world and their own sexuality—she'd been looking after a small baby and, before the year was out, mourning the death of her young husband.

It was cringingly embarrassing to realise that her friends would undoubtedly react with screams of laughter, ridicule and sheer disbelief if they ever learned the truth. How could she possibly confess, even to Rose Thomas, that Max had been her first and only lover? That she now felt badly frightened, and completely out of her depth in trying to deal with such a hard, tough and sophisticated man?

With a heavy sigh of deep depression, Amber threw back the covers and swung her feet off the bed. Sitting on the edge of the mattress and staring blindly down at the floor, she realised that she had to pull herself together. Having to face the disastrous truth that she was still in love with Max was only a minor problem compared to the all-important fact that Lucy would be coming home later on this morning. She *must* try to work out exactly how she was going to handle the situation. Max was obviously a whiz at business affairs, but he clearly wasn't used to dealing with a seven-year-old little girl. And while she didn't really believe he would demand that Lucy should immediately be told he was her real father, he was plainly determined to push ahead with his mad idea concerning their marriage. He'd also made it clear that if she didn't agree to his plans for a Christmas wedding, he wouldn't hesitate to carry out his vile, cruel threats to keep her tied up in the courts for ever and a day, destroying both the life of herself and her daughter. So far, none of her protests or arguments had appeared to make the slightest bit of difference. What could she say, or do, that would make him change his mind?

Drawing back the curtains of her bedroom, she saw that there had been a heavy fall of snow during the night. The garden was now covered by a thick white blanket. Glancing up at the heavy grey sky overhead, Amber had no doubt that although it may have stopped snowing for the moment, it wouldn't be long before it started again.

By the time she was downstairs in the kitchen, preparing the breakfast trays for her mother and their guest, she was still feeling deeply depressed at having made no progress in finding an answer to her many problems. In what was clearly an either-or situation, Max seemed to hold all the cards. And it wasn't just the fact that he was insisting that she marry him. What about Lucy? What sort of father would he make for her little girl? Goodness knows it wasn't easy to be a parent these days. It was so important to try and set your children a good example, to bring them up in a steady, responsible manner, which you hoped would give them a sound foundation for their future life. But words like 'steady' and 'responsible' certainly weren't those she associated with Max's past behaviour. Was he likely to change his ways? Was he— hell! she thought grimly, recalling the disgusting way he'd so enthusiastically kissed Cynthia. And the glamorous divorcee had also made it blatantly obvious that, given half a chance, she'd happily jump into his bed.

How could she bear to marry a man who'd not only cruelly deserted her, but who had obviously spent most of his adult life having affairs with one beautiful woman after another? Let's hope he hadn't left any of *them* holding a baby, she told herself bitterly as she placed fresh, warm croissants and toast on his breakfast tray.

Not for the first time, Amber dearly wished that she'd never had the idea of taking in paying guests, which had enabled Max to gain a foothold in the house—something he'd never have been able to do in a private house. Praying that her visitor had passed a thoroughly uncomfortable night, she stomped aggressively up the stairs, not bothering to knock as she threw open the guest-room door, quite happy to chuck his tray at the awful man if he so much as dared to say a word out of place.

Unfortunately, far from still being fast asleep, Max had obviously been up for some time, having already shaved and had a shower. Amber gave him a quick, apprehensive glance, her cheeks flaming with embarrassment as she realised that the tall figure standing across the room was clearly naked, save for a short white towel about his slim hips.

'You must be a mind-reader,' he smiled. 'I was wondering about the arrangements for breakfast.'

'Yes...um...our guests normally prefer to eat breakfast in their rooms,' she muttered breathlessly, trying to tear her eyes away from the sight of his fit, lithe body. The faint drops of moisture still glistened on the bronze skin of his broad shoulders and the hard, muscular chest liberally covered with thick black hair.

Her heart seemed to be pounding like a sledgehammer, her pulse racing out of control as she desperately wished that she'd stayed down in the kitchen, well away from the sight of his strong, powerful frame and the long, tanned brown legs beneath that ridiculously small towel.

His eyes gleamed with unconcealed mockery as he walked slowly towards her. 'Poor Amber, you look tired. Didn't you sleep very well?' he drawled, his mouth curving with amusement.

'No, I didn't!' she snapped, backing nervously towards the door.

'Relax—there's no need to act like a frightened virgin,' he grinned. 'It's not as though we haven't seen each other's naked bodies in the past.'

'It's not an experience I'm in any hurry to repeat!' she retorted grimly, quickly placing the tray down on a nearby table, the infuriating sound of his laughter echoing behind her as she made a speedy exit from the room.

For the next hour or so, it seemed as though she was in a complete daze. She realised that she must have collected her mother's tray (wild horses wouldn't have dragged her back upstairs to Max's room again), done the washing up and run a vacuum over the carpets in the downstairs rooms. But she had no recollection of having done so. She couldn't seem to think of anything but Lucy's imminent return, and the catastrophic result of Max's strong, sensual appeal on her fragile emotions.

Goodness knows, she had tried to guard and protect herself, rightly fearing the impact of his overpowering attraction on her heart. But it was now far too late for any such dire warnings. In the past, she'd always regarded her love for Max as some sort of sickness or virus, from which she had slowly recovered over the years. How could she have guessed that it was a terminal illness—an acute infection that had no cure? How, when he'd treated her so badly, could she *still* be so deeply in love with him?

Her distressing, gloomy thoughts were interrupted by a phone call from the local garage, informing her that her old Land Rover was ready for collection. Gratefully thanking the mechanic for having fixed it so quickly, she was surprised by the man's chuckle of amusement.

'I wish all my jobs were that easy,' he told her. 'All the same, mind you tell young Lucy not to pull out them electrical wires from the back of the dashboard. Else you and she won't be going anywhere fast!'

'Lucy wasn't with me at the time,' she protested, but he only gave another rumble of laughter before putting down the phone.

Frowning in puzzlement, she didn't have time to think any more about the matter as she heard the toot of a horn. A moment later, her daughter raced into the house as fast as her young legs could carry her.

'Mummy...Mummy! I've had a really *fan-tab-ulous* time!' Lucy cried, throwing her arms about her mother's waist. 'Emily and I saw Father Christmas, and he gave me a lovely present,' she added breathlessly. 'It was terrific—really *wicked*!'

'I gather that's the very latest "in" word, at the moment,' Rose said, smiling at the bemused expression on her friend's face as she handed over Lucy's small suitcase. 'We loved having her and she was as good as gold,' she added, quickly brushing aside Amber's grateful thanks for giving her daughter such a treat. 'I'd love to be able to stop and tell you all about it, but I must get back home. There's a mountain of ironing to be done—and I haven't a clue what I'm going to cook for lunch!'

After waving goodbye to Rose, Amber hurried back into the house, but Lucy was nowhere to be seen. Only the tall figure of Max standing in the kitchen.

'Ah, there you are. Hurry up. It's time we were off.'

'Off where?' she demanded curtly, deeply resenting the sick feeling in the pit of her stomach as she viewed his firmly muscled legs in the tight-fitting, dark blue denim jeans topped by a thick, navy-blue sweater that emphasised his tan. He looked tough, formidable and—alas—so outrageously attractive that she had to swallow hard, fighting to control a mad impulse to leap into his arms. 'Where's Lucy?' she asked anxiously. 'I hope you haven't...'

'Relax! I haven't done anything,' he retorted impatiently. 'I merely suggested that both you and she might like to see my grandmother's old house—or more accurately, what's left of it—followed by lunch in the local pub. Lucy seemed to think that it was a splendid idea. Especially when I promised to help her build a snowman!'

Amber hesitated, longing to tell him to get lost. On the other hand, she knew that he'd already spiked her guns by telling Lucy, and to refuse to go along with his plans would only result in the little girl being disappointed and upset. Besides, like the rest of her neighbours, she'd never been invited to his grandmother's home, since old Lady Parker had been a recluse for the twenty-five years up to her death. The large house was now apparently a pile of rubble. However, she had to admit—privately, to herself— that it might be interesting to see the ruins.

'Well?'

She shrugged. 'Yes...all right. But I'm not sure about lunch. A lot of pubs aren't too keen on letting in young children.'

'That's no problem. I've already phoned up the Red Lion and checked that it's OK. However, don't forget that it's freezing outside, so make sure that you're both well wrapped up,' he added, glancing at her slim figure, clothed in a cream-coloured Aran sweater and tan cords. 'And it might be a good idea to take a thermos of coffee along with us, as well.'

The damned man thinks of everything! she thought gloomily as she finally tracked Lucy down in her mother's side of the house, excitedly telling her grandmother all about her wonderful time in London.

Anxious to assure her mother that they wouldn't be away from the house for too long, Amber was amazed to find the older woman up, dressed and in surprisingly good spirits.

'I'm feeling *much* better, so there's no need to worry about me, dear,' Violet told her with a beaming smile. 'You just run along and enjoy yourselves.'

Puzzled, but at the same time extremely grateful for her mother's sudden return to apparent good health, Amber hurried down to the kitchen, quickly filling a thermos before bundling herself and Lucy into some warm clothes.

Never having seen the old Victorian mansion, Amber had difficulty in imagining how it must have looked in its heyday. After the fire in which Max's grandmother had died, there now remained only a burnt-out shell, many of whose walls had been reduced to rubble, with broken statues and cracked urns lying discarded on the weed-covered terrace overlooking the wooded valley far below. However, most of the out-buildings, garages and stables were in reasonably good shape. As was the orangery.

'Did your grandmother ever grow oranges in here?' Amber asked as she gazed around at what appeared to be a large, elegant and surprisingly warm room.

'No, I shouldn't think so. But since I never met the old dragon, I really haven't a clue.' Max shrugged his broad shoulders. 'I'm far more interested, at the moment, in a hot cup of coffee. Quite frankly,' he added with a grin, 'I never realised that building a snowman would be such hard work!'

'It's harder than it looks,' Amber agreed with a laugh as she looked out of the window at Lucy, who was now busy decorating a decidedly lopsided, squat-looking structure with Max's long woollen scarf.

Despite having been so anxious about the situation, and deeply apprehensive about Max's desire to get to know his daughter, it was a relief to realise that her fears had been completely unfounded. He had treated the little girl very much as he might any other seven-year-old—not only laughing at her terrible jokes, but also laying down very firm, strict instructions to avoid going anywhere near the potentially dangerous ruins of the old house.

'It seems so extraordinary that you never met your grandmother,' Amber said a few moments later, filling their cups with hot liquid from the thermos as he brushed the cobwebs and dirt from two dusty old packing cases. 'Especially since you and your father were living only a few miles away.'

Max sighed and shrugged his shoulders. 'It's a long story, but basically it seems that my grandmother was a lonely, embittered old woman. Her husband had been killed in World War II, and when her only son was killed on the hunting field, she clung like grim death to her sole remaining child—a daughter called Imogen.

'It must have been a stifling, desperately boring life for my poor mother,' he continued, explaining how Lady Parker would never allow her daughter to go anywhere on her own, being deliberately rude and scaring off all her boyfriends, until the poor girl had become virtually a prisoner, clearly destined to spend the rest of her days as an unpaid companion to her elderly mother.'

'But why didn't she just take to her heels and run away?'

'Because she was, by all accounts, a very sweet and gentle person. She simply couldn't bring herself to be unkind to anyone—let alone her own mother. And in any case, by the time Imogen was approaching middle age, she'd become quite convinced that no one would ever want to marry her. However, it seems she did find her religion a great source of help and strength. Luckily, Lady Parker had no objections to her daughter visiting the local church in Elmbridge as often as she liked—which is how she came to meet my father.'

However, as the story unfolded, Amber was touched to hear how the Reverend Augustus Warner, a kind if somewhat absent-minded bachelor in his late forties, had fallen deeply in love with the unhappy, thirty-eight-year-old Imogen Parker. 'He wasn't the slightest bit interested in her mother's wealth, of course,' Max said, relating how his father had tried to gain his future mother-in-law's approval for his marriage to Imogen. But when she had resolutely refused to give the couple her blessing—even going so far as to forbid her daughter to ever see the vicar again—Imogen had, at last, found the courage to defy her mother. 'There was nothing she could do to stop the wedding, of course. But the old dragon never forgave her daughter for "running away" with my father.'

'It seems impossible to believe that *anyone* could be so cruel and heartless!' Amber exclaimed, shocked to hear how, when poor Imogen had died after giving birth to Max some eighteen months later, Lady Parker had continued to refuse to have anything to do with either the vicar or her grandson.

As he related the sad story, Amber suddenly gained a fresh insight into how lonely Max must have been as a small child, with no mother to care for him, and an elderly father who'd had no idea how to rear his son. No wonder the boy, brought up by a series of temporary housekeepers, had turned into a wild teenager. She could only think that it was a miracle he hadn't become involved in any really serious trouble.

However, gazing at the man who was sitting across the room from her, Amber was surprised to discover that they'd actually managed to spend some time together in perfect harmony. Was that because today he'd been in a quiet and reflective mood very different from the harsh and aggressive stance he'd displayed last night? It looked as though he was making a conscious effort to control the hard, forceful personality that she knew lay beneath that handsome exterior. Something for which she could only be thankful, she reminded herself quickly, profoundly grateful that Max had made no allusion to the events that had taken place last night.

But it seemed that he had been merely biding his time.

'This appears to be a good opportunity for us to have a quiet talk,' Max said, rising to his feet and strolling over to the window.

'I really don't think so . . .' she muttered nervously as he waved through the glass at Lucy, who was energetically assembling a large pile of snowballs. 'Besides, it will soon be time for lunch.' She glanced quickly down at her watch. 'So, maybe we ought to . . .'

'Relax! I don't imagine either of us is in the mood for any more rows or arguments,' he said firmly. 'But since you obviously consider me a double-dealing villain, it seems only fair that you should hear *my* side of the story.'

'There's no need...' she murmured, the rest of what she was going to say being lost as he gave an unhappy bark of laughter.

'There's *every* need.' He brushed a hand roughly through his thick dark hair. 'You have, after all, accused me of behaving with almost criminal irresponsibility by my abandoning a young teenage girl and leaving her to face a traumatic pregnancy without any help or support. Although—God help me!—that last charge *is* unfortunately true,' he added with a heavy sigh.

Amber gave a helpless shrug of her slim shoulders. 'Look, we've been through all this ad nauseam. I realise that I've given you a hard time, and said some horrid things to you, about what happened all those years ago. But that was in the past. We've both now made new lives for ourselves. What's the point in raking it up all over again?'

'The *point*, my dear Amber, is that your version of events does not tie up with mine,' he retorted bluntly, turning to give her a hard, searching look from beneath his dark brows. 'When, before leaving for America to join my uncle, I asked you to be my wife and to wait until I'd made arrangements for you to join me in the States, I meant *every word* of what I said.

'However, until the other day, I had no idea that in the flurry of my departure, I'd omitted to give you my uncle's phone number. All I knew was that we'd arranged for me to contact you on your arrival in London, when you'd have finished packing up your old home in Elmbridge and would know more about your mother's state of health and mind. Are we in agreement so far?'

She shrugged. 'Yes, I suppose so.'

'Right. Now, what you *don't* know is that shortly after I'd landed in the States, my uncle and I were in his car, due to attend a meeting in one of the factories he owned, when we were hit head-on by a large truck. I don't remember anything about the accident. All I know is that I eventually woke up to find myself in hospital with a broken arm, two broken legs and a bad case of concussion. I also learned that I was lucky to be alive—unlike my uncle, who'd been at the wheel of the car and had, unfortunately, been killed outright.

'However,' he continued as she gave an involuntary gasp of horror, 'while I was lucky not to have anything tricky, like amnesia, I did suffer from very intense, sick headaches for a long time after my limbs had healed and I was back on my feet. But that was nothing compared to the headache of trying to run my uncle's business. Although I was his only living relative, I was amazed to learn that he'd recently drawn up a will leaving me everything he owned.'

Max turned his dark head to give her a wry grin. 'As you can imagine, neither the other directors of the firm, nor the workforce, were too thrilled about *that*. And you can't blame them. Weeks seemed to go

by when I felt just so damn tired and ill that I didn't
know how I was going to be able to cope. So, by the
time I got my act together, I was not only having to
work my guts out to prove that I was capable of
running the company—if only to justify the faith
which my uncle must have had in me—but I also
realised that it was over two months since I'd been in
touch with you.'

She gave a helpless sigh. 'If only I'd known about
your accident. But I'd no idea . . .'

'Of course you hadn't,' he agreed swiftly. 'Just as
I had no idea of *your* problems. Believe me, if there
was ever a story of two star-crossed lovers, this is
definitely it!' He began pacing up and down over the
grey flagstones. 'Unfortunately, when I did get around
to phoning you in London, I got your aunt on the
line, thrilled to bits about the news of your forthcoming marriage to Clive Stanhope.'

'Oh, no!'

'Oh, *yes*!' he ground out. 'I was in such a state of
shock that it was some time before I understood what
the old trout was saying. I can still hear her now:
"They're so happy! It's *such* a suitable marriage—
just what her dear father would have wanted,"' he
savagely mimicked her aunt's plummy voice. '"Clive
is *so* wealthy. Have you ever seen Elmbridge Hall? A
wonderful old house—just perfect for two young
people to start their married life!" And a whole lot
more drivel on the subject of both Clive's wealthy
lifestyle and your past, *very* close friendship.'

'No, that's not true!' she was stung into retorting.
'I hardly knew Clive before he offered to marry me.'

'Not a word about the baby, of course,' Max continued grimly, ignoring her protest. 'For God's sake, Amber! Am I supposed to believe that your aunt was completely blind? Surely she *must* have known that you were pregnant?'

Amber hung her head. 'Yes... well, I suppose she probably did guess the truth,' she mumbled. 'But we never talked about it. She was very old-fashioned and... um...'

'... mightily relieved that her niece was getting married in the nick of time?' Max queried sardonically, pausing in his restless pacing for a moment to throw a searching, steely glance at the clearly unhappy, huddled figure of the girl sitting across the room. 'Well, there's not much more to tell,' he continued bleakly. 'As you can imagine, I went completely off the rails. However, when I eventually sobered up and realised there wasn't much point in drowning my sorrows in wine, women and song, I did the only thing I could—which was to throw myself into work. I developed and expanded my uncle's business, gobbling up many other companies on the way until going public and floating Warner International on Wall Street. Now, all these years later, I've also taken over a large business here in the UK. So, I guess it could be said that my story has a happy ending. Right?'

She nodded silently, not trusting her voice as she tried to come to terms with all that he'd said. It was absolutely shattering to realise that all her preconceived notions, all the unhappy and traumatic events of the past, should turn out to be the result of nothing more than a few unfortunate twists of fate. It seemed almost impossible to believe that a car accident and a missing phone number could be responsible for all the unhappiness of the past eight years.

Amber yawned, leaning back against the padded leather headrest. Goodness knows where Max had got hold of this huge, luxurious vehicle. But she had to admit that with the snow beginning to fall once again, a Range Rover was the perfect vehicle to cope with dangerous icy roads. Which made it all the more peculiar that Max, despite the obviously bad driving conditions, had insisted on taking her out to dinner. Like any other sensible person, she would have preferred to stay indoors by the fire. But Max, as usual, had managed to get his own way.

Turning her head to glare at the man sitting beside her, Amber's frustration at being ordered around was slightly mollified by the sight of a large bruise on his cheek. Good for Lucy! Although the little girl had never intended to hurt him, of course, she reminded herself quickly, recalling how when she and Max had left the orangery, they'd found themselves being pelted by snowballs. It had been an energetic fight, with Lucy—who'd already assembled her ammunition— screaming with laughter as Max had enthusiastically joined in the fun. Unfortunately, when the child had at last managed to score a direct hit on his face, it seemed that a large stone had become accidentally embedded in the snowball.

Although she was reluctant to give him any credit, Amber had to admit that Max had coped very well with the situation. Quickly drying Lucy's tears, he'd explained that it was a well-known hazard of the game, which he, as a veteran of many such fights had fully expected to happen, before suggesting that it was time for lunch. After providing her favourite meal of beef burgers and chips smothered in tomato sauce and, after returning home, playing innumerable childish card games in front of a roaring fire, it was no wonder that Lucy had taken such a shine to 'Mummy's old schoolfriend'. In fact, Amber thought sourly, by the time he'd been persuaded to read her a long bedtime story, it was not surprising that her daughter was beginning to think that Max was the best thing since sliced bread!

Confused by the conflict of emotions in her head, Amber gave a heavy sigh. She knew she ought to be pleased and happy that Lucy and Max were obviously getting on so well together. But she couldn't seem to help resenting their instinctive understanding of one another—or the way in which he seemed to have charmed the socks off her mother. With Violet, who appeared to have taken on a new lease of life, enthusiastically seconding Max's proposal to take her out to dinner, Amber hadn't been able to think of any viable reason for refusing the invitation.

'You're very silent,' Max said, breaking the heavy silence within the car.

'I...er...I'm still not happy about leaving my mother in charge of Lucy,' she muttered nervously, suddenly feeling threatened by the dominant presence of the man sitting so close to her. 'She hasn't been well, and...'

'Nonsense! There's nothing wrong with your mother,' he said crisply. 'In fact, Violet appeared to be in excellent spirits this morning when I told her I was buying your house.'

'You did *what*?'

'As a guest in your home, it would have been extremely bad manners if I *hadn't* seen your mother and also informed her of my plans,' he pointed out blandly. 'Which is why I also felt obliged to ask her for your hand in marriage.'

'Who are you k-kidding?' Amber spluttered furiously. 'I don't believe you've ever felt "obliged" to do anything in the whole of your damn life!' she grated, longing to slap that sanctimonious, holier-than-thou expression from his handsome face. 'You rat! If you've upset her in any way, I'll...'

'Oh, come on!' he gave a sardonic laugh. 'Violet is absolutely thrilled to bits at both being able to remain in the house and the idea of a Christmas wedding. However, I did extract a promise from your mother not to tell anyone. Certainly not until we'd both had an opportunity to discuss the matter with Lucy.'

He's done it again! The wretched man had found yet *another* weapon to coerce her into his insane idea regarding their marriage. Desperately wishing that she could lock herself away in a dark room and scream blue murder, Amber realised that Max now had her well and truly over a barrel. How could she possibly combat both her mother's delight at not having to leave Elmbridge Hall, *and* the fact that Lucy was bound to be thrilled to have a real father at last? On the other hand, how could she bear to marry a man who clearly wasn't in love with her? A man obsessively determined to pursue his mad plans for a Christmas wedding simply to gain parental control over Lucy?

Certain that she was going to disgrace herself by bursting into tears at any minute, she turned her head to stare blindly out of the passenger window. It was only then, as Amber caught a glimpse of an illuminated road sign, that she realised they were travelling along the main road leading to London—something she ought to have recognised long before now, if it hadn't been for the dark winter night and her own heavily depressed state of mind.

'What's going on?' she demanded. 'I thought you were supposed to be taking me out for dinner?'

'You're quite right—I am,' he agreed blandly. 'I merely thought you might like to dine at my apartment in London.'

'You must be out of your mind! Why on earth would I want to go all that way just for a meal?'

'I can give you any number of reasons,' he drawled smoothly. 'Because I thought you might appreciate eating something different from that served in the local restaurants; because my housekeeper is a first-class cook and has promised to leave us a delicious meal in the oven; because I thought it would do you good to get away from Elmbridge for a bit, and because...'

'OK, OK,' she snapped. 'But what about Lucy? My mother is normally a perfectly reliable baby-sitter, but....'

'Calm down,' he retorted firmly. 'Before we left, I told your mother exactly where we were going, and also gave her my phone number in case any problems should arise.'

Totally outraged and incensed at Max's continued interference in her life, Amber's fury intensified as she caught a glimpse, in the headlights of a passing car, of Max's eyes gleaming with unconcealed mockery, and became aware that his broad shoulders were shaking with amusement. But the infuriating man continued to ignore her protests that she wanted to return home, and unfortunately, it wasn't long before she found herself being driven into an underground car park beneath a large, modern building overlooking Hyde Park.

'*Good Heavens*!' she exclaimed some minutes later, finding it difficult to maintain her anger as she gazed around the sumptuously furnished sitting room of the penthouse apartment. Her eyes widened at the sight of so many marble columns and the huge floor-to-ceiling window providing a spectacular, panoramic view of the London skyline.

It was an amazing place, she thought, her shoes almost disappearing in the thick pile of a white carpet covering the floor of the large main room, which was decorated with ultra-modern chairs, sofas and glass tables of every shape and size. Staring at the huge, plate-glass windows draped with thick, cream linen curtains, she found herself wondering just how many women had spent time with Max in this opulent, luxurious apartment. Goodness knows, she'd never actually *seen* a male 'love nest', but it didn't take an overheated imagination to realise that this place with its long, black deep leather sofas and enormously large modern paintings of nude women must be the real thing!

'I thought this place might give you a bit of a laugh!' Max said cheerfully as she found herself staring incredulously at an *extremely* rude picture on the wall. 'Unfortunately, I inherited the apartment from a previous managing director of the company—who seems to have had more girlfriends than I've had hot dinners! So, please don't accuse me of having such ghastly, terrible taste, because, quite frankly, I can't wait to move out of here.'

To her surprise, Amber found herself smiling at his lugubrious expression as he gazed around the large room, and almost weak with laughter as later, during dinner, he entertained her with stories about the amorous exploits of his predecessor. 'You wouldn't believe some of the phone calls I've had here,' he grinned. 'I can't make up my mind whether the man was a regular Don Juan—or the Marquis de Sade!'

'I really ought to say I'm sorry for having been such a grouch earlier this evening. Because you were quite right,' she admitted when they were sipping their coffee and brandy in the drawing room. 'That was a really delicious meal—and it's a great treat for me to have the pleasure of eating someone else's cooking.'

'That's a more handsome apology than I deserve,' he told her quietly, falling silent for a moment and buried deep in thought as he stared down at the brandy glass in his hand. 'It wasn't just the shock of seeing Lucy, although, God knows, that left me completely traumatised for a long time,' he said at last, the raw bitterness in his voice causing her to look at him anxiously. 'It was discovering the many years of financial struggle and the sheer, grinding poverty that lay behind the seemingly wealthy façade of your house, which completely threw me for a loop. Even now, hearing you talk about the "treat" of enjoying someone *else's* cooking is enough to make me see red. I really don't think I'll *ever* be able to forgive myself for allowing you and Lucy to endure such an experience.'

Wincing as the harsh, savage tones echoed loudly in the small room, Amber instinctively turned to the man sitting beside her on the sofa to place a comforting hand on his arm. 'Please, Max, there's no need to torture yourself like this—or exaggerate my difficulties. Don't you realise that I'm so much luckier than thousands of other people? At least I've got a roof over my head,' she pointed out firmly. 'Nothing to do with my present situation could possibly be regarded as your fault.'

'It may not have been directly my fault,' he said with a heavy sigh. 'But I do have to take full responsibility for much that has happened to you. Which is one of the reasons why I'm so determined to make sure that Lucy has a father, and that both you and she are financially secure from now on.'

'I appreciate what you're saying—I really do,' she assured him earnestly. 'But you can be a perfectly good father *and* provide financially for Lucy without feeling that you have to marry me. I'll have plenty enough to live on, once the house is sold. Enough to buy a small cottage well away from Elmbridge, if need be, so that there won't be any gossip about Lucy's parentage. And of course you can see her—just as often as you like,' she added quickly as he gave a determined shake of his dark head.

'Once you're married to a rich, successful man—who's likely to attract business to the town—you'll find that there will be virtually no unkind gossip.'

'I don't know anything about such matters,' she said, brushing a distracted hand through her golden brown hair. 'But I'm quite sure that money isn't everything in life. It certainly can't buy you happiness, for instance.'

'No. But it can make damn sure that you're unhappy in comfort,' he retorted with a wry, twisted smile.

'My God, how can you be so cynical?' she accused him bleakly, angrily banging her coffee cup down on the low glass table in front of them. 'Is that the sort of marriage you're planning for us? Two people trapped in a thoroughly miserable existence? Surrounded by luxury, and yet not even talking to one another?' she demanded, jumping angrily to her feet. 'Well, I don't want *any* part of it! And I definitely don't want——' She broke off, eyeing him warily as she saw him rise slowly from the sofa and begin moving determinedly towards her.

'I know *exactly* what you want!' he drawled, his mouth twitching in silent humour.

'No, you don't'!' she retorted defiantly as she backed nervously away from his tall figure, her progress abruptly halted as she felt her back jar up against one of the cold, marble pillars decorating the room. 'I'm no longer that stupid little teenager that you once knew, Max,' she continued breathlessly, almost hating the diabolically attractive man gazing down at her, the hard, sensual gleam in his glittering blue eyes causing her stomach to clench with sexual tension. 'I'm twenty-six years old and perfectly capable of realising what you have in mind. Believe me, it's *not* the right answer.'

'Believe me, it most certainly *is*!' he mocked softly, taking another step forward.

'No... no, you're quite... quite wrong,' she protested. He was now standing so close to her that she could see the long, black eyelashes over his gleaming blue eyes, and the faint flush of arousal beneath the tanned skin stretched tightly over his high cheekbones and formidable jawline.

'Isn't it about time you stopped trying to fool yourself, Amber?' he drawled, raising his hand to run a finger lightly down the side of her face. 'What's the point of continuing to deny your own needs and desires?'

She could feel her heart beginning to pound at the feel of his soft touch on her skin. 'No, you're quite wrong about me,' she retorted breathlessly, desperately trying to pull herself together. But it was proving almost impossible to bring her weak mind under control, to stop herself trembling in response to the warmth of the long, muscular thighs pressed against her own, or to ignore the hand now trailing down over her neck, gently caressing the hollow at the base of her throat. 'You're making a great mistake...'

'God knows, I've made plenty of mistakes in my life. But *this* definitely isn't one of them,' he told her with a husky laugh, quickly sweeping her up in his arms and carrying her protesting, wriggling figure along a wide corridor to his bedroom.

'No, Max!' she gasped as he tossed her down on to the huge bed before swiftly trapping her beneath the weight of his strong, hard body. 'Let me go!'

'Stop fighting me,' he growled, the sound of his hoarse voice echoing in her ears as his blue eyes blazed down at the girl lying beneath him. 'It's no good trying to fool yourself, Amber. I *know* you want me as much as I want you. Every kiss...every movement of your body betrays that fact. My God, you nearly drove me wild last night! I could almost tangibly *feel* the heat of your desire as you trembled in my arms. Why continue to deny what we feel for one another?' he whispered thickly as his dark head came down towards her.

Once again, from the moment his mouth hungrily claimed her trembling lips, all the past years seemed to vanish as if they'd never been. The stark impact of their mutual desire, the force of his kiss and the hands swiftly pulling off her dress before possessively clasping her full breasts, were a potent reminder of the strong physical bond between them. Even now, as she moaned in protest, there seemed nothing she could do to stop herself from being swept along on a fast, rushing tide of heated desire and passion, helpless against the shivering excitement of his warm fingers moving enticingly over the flimsy barrier of thin silk covering her swollen nipples. And then, as the hard and angrily demanding pressure of his mouth softened, his lips and tongue now gently bewitching and beguiling her senses, she realised that he was right.

It was pointless to deceive herself any longer. Almost fainting with a tremulous, aching need for his possession, she knew that this was what she'd wanted—and had been fighting against with increasing desperation—ever since his return to Elmbridge. She wanted ... she *needed* to feel his mouth moving sensually over her lips, the excitement of the hard muscular body pressed tightly against her own and the erotic, scorching touch of the hands now setting fire to her flesh.

Raising his head, his breathing as ragged and unsteady as her own, Max stared down at her with eyes that blazed fiercely in the grey light of the unlit bedroom. 'Tell me, Amber,' he rasped, the hoarsely demanding, imperative note in his voice causing a fierce knot of desire to burst into flames in her stomach. 'Tell me that you want me.'

A deep, helpless shudder rippled through her body, her arms closing about him, her fingers curling into his thick dark hair. 'Yes—yes, I want you,' she whispered, oblivious of everything except her long years of emotional starvation and the driving, desperate compulsion to surrender to his possession, her desire and need of him so intense that it was like a deep physical pain.

Gripped by a primitive force that was completely beyond her control, she barely heard his low, husky laugh of triumph as he swiftly removed both his clothes and hers before tossing her back against the pillows. They both seemed possessed by a raw, animal hunger that had been repressed for far too long. Her emotions spinning wildly out of control, Amber felt no shame or regret as her hands moved over the strong contours of his body, feverishly savouring the breadth of his shoulders, his deep chest and flat stomach, the taut hard muscles of his thighs, the tanned flesh beneath her fingers so achingly familiar, despite the long years since she'd last held him in her arms.

If seemed as if Max, too, was possessed by a need to devour every inch of her bare flesh, the increasingly erotic, sexually explicit touch of his mouth and hands causing her to feel as though she were on fire, burning and melting with rampant desire. Overcome by the dynamic, potent force of her love and need for him, she cried out loud, the breath rasping in her throat as she panted for release from the tension that seemed to fill her whole existence. Absorbed by her own emotional needs, she barely heard his low, deep groan at the hard, driving thrust of his body as he finally entered her, responding to the pulsating rhythm of his powerful body with a wanton, erotic intensity that devoured them both, the white-hot heat of their passion exploding in a shimmering starburst before they fell shuddering into a deep, dark abyss of mutual joy and satisfaction.

Later, as they lay warmly and drowsily entwined together, Amber felt his fingers gently turning her face towards him. 'It's just as well we're going to be married in ten days' time,' he murmured with a wry smile. 'There's no way I'd be able to keep my hands off you for much longer than that!'

'Umm...?' she blinked sleepily up at him. Still dazed by her own frenzied response to his fierce, hungry possession and the overwhelming passion that had flared between them, it was a moment or two before she managed to comprehend exactly what he was saying. 'No...no, we can't possibly...' she muttered wildly as she broke free from his embrace. 'I must go back home...I shouldn't have left Lucy...and there's my mother, too...'

'Relax, darling,' he said huskily, firmly pulling her back into his arms. 'Surely you must realise why I deliberately brought you down here to my apartment in London.'

Not having any idea of what he was talking about, she stared blankly up at him, surprised to see a faint flush of embarrassment spreading over his tanned cheeks.

'Oh, Amber...how can you be so dim?' he groaned. 'Can't you see...there was no way I could make love to you in your own home without the risk of upsetting or disturbing Lucy, who doesn't yet know that we're to be married. On the other hand, I knew that I'd go stark, staring mad if we didn't make love tonight. Which is precisely why we're here in my bed! And don't worry,' he added quickly. 'I borrowed the Range Rover, so even if the roads are covered in snow, I could guarantee to get you home before breakfast. OK?'

'Of course it's not OK,' she retorted tearfully. 'I...well, I'm grateful for your thoughtfulness. But as far as I'm concerned, this has been a really...really terrible mistake!'

'Making love to you was never a mistake,' he said thickly. 'My one great error was not to have married you before I left for America all those years ago. Which is why I intend to rectify that mistake as soon as possible,' he vowed, his hands sweeping possessively over her trembling, quivering body. 'Because it's you I want—and it's you I'm going to have!'

Amber shivered at the flat, hard, determined note in his voice. All the barriers she'd erected over the years had fallen too fast, too violently, and she was frightened at how clearly she had given herself away. She might love this tough, difficult man, but she had no real clue to his innermost feelings, no certainty that he felt anything for her other than a strong, sexual attraction.

'But...but it won't work. I need more time....' she muttered helplessly, her flesh quivering beneath his dominant touch on her naked body.

'Time for you to think of some puerile, weak excuse? Sorry, Amber, but I'm not feeling that generous,' he drawled with silky menace, his fingers gently brushing the hard, swollen points of her breasts with such a slow, enticing sensuality that it was all she could do not to groan out loud as fierce, wild tremors of pleasure flashed through her body like forked lightning. 'So, you're going to promise—here and now—to marry me in ten days' time. Right?'

Quivering with ecstasy, her senses spinning out of control in a frenzy of delight and excitement beneath the overwhelming mastery of his touch, Amber could only give a deep, helpless sigh as she abandoned herself to her fate. 'Yes...' she gasped helplessly before sinking beneath great waves of overwhelming desire and passion. 'Yes, Max, I... I'll marry you.'

CHAPTER SEVEN

ALTHOUGH she'd spent some anxious moments wondering how to break the news of her impending marriage, Amber realised that she needn't have worried. Now, four days after agreeing to marry Max, and with only a week to go until the wedding, everyone in the town seemed to be fully aware of what was going on and delighted to hear that the Hall wasn't going to be sold after all.

Everyone, she reminded herself, except 'Gloomy Glover'—clearly regretting the loss of his commission on the sale of her home—and Cynthia Henderson, who'd suddenly decided to leave an assistant in charge of her shop before swiftly departing on a month's cruise around the Caribbean. Unfortunately, today's post had also included a letter from Philip Jackson, who clearly wasn't at all happy about her decision, either.

Sighing as she gazed down at the letter lying on her desk, Amber made yet another attempt to decipher the squiggly writing, which looked more like an inky trail left by a demented spider than heartbroken outpourings full of doom and gloom from the young doctor.

She'd been amazed at the speed with which the news had raced through the small town. When she'd told Max how much she dreaded having to tell everyone, he'd merely grinned. 'Just leave everything to your mother and some of her old cronies. I guarantee that the story will be around Elmbridge and back to you inside twenty-four hours!' He'd been quite right, she acknowledged ruefully, thankful that she'd taken the precaution of telling her own friends first of all. Sally Fraser, for instance, would have been mortally wounded if she hadn't heard the glad tidings from Amber's own lips.

While she could only marvel at how everyone seemed to have swallowed Max's romantic fairy tale lock, stock and barrel, she'd been determined to tell her old friend, Rose Thomas, the truth about her secret love affair in the past and the reasons behind the announcement of her wedding.

'Oh, Amber, I'm *so* happy for you!' Rose had cried joyfully, jumping up from her kitchen table and rushing over to throw her arms about her friend. 'None of us ever guessed that you'd had a romance with Max all those years ago. Or that you were carrying on one during these last few weeks, for that matter! Although, now I come to think about it, I wonder why it never occurred to me that you two would be *perfect* for each other?' She beamed at her friend. 'And what's going to happen about the sale of your house? Are you going to take it off the market?'

'Well, it's no longer for sale, of course, but I expect we'll probably own it jointly,' she explained. 'Actually, I'm feeling a bit overwhelmed at the moment because Max is insisting on paying the full asking price into some sort of investment account for me. He says that he wants to make sure that I always have some private money of my own.'

'How kind and generous. He must be crazy about you!' Rose exclaimed, grinning as the other girl's cheeks flooded with colour.

'I'm not sure...' Amber muttered with a helpless shrug. 'I know that he wants to make sure Lucy has a proper father, but I'm really not certain about anything else. We've got all that past history between us, of course, but it's different now....' Her voice trailed unhappily away.

'Look, whatever took place in the past happened to two young people who've now grown up,' Rose told her firmly. 'You're not the same person you were then, and neither is Max. You've both made mistakes—haven't we all!—but now you've got a chance to start a new life together. And if you think he's marrying you just because he feels a deep sense of responsibility towards Lucy—I reckon you must be out of your mind! Quite frankly, Amber,' she added with a wry laugh, 'Max didn't strike me as someone who'd allow himself to be pushed into doing *anything* he didn't want to. So, my advice is to forget all the unhappiness of the past. It's the here and now that's important, for both you and Lucy.'

'Yes, I know you're right. It's just that it's such a big step, and I can't help being nervous. However, I really don't want anyone else to know the full story,' Amber cautioned her friend. 'Quite apart from anything else, I wouldn't like there to be any gossip about Clive, who was so very good and kind to me.'

'You've no need to worry. I won't breathe a word,' Rose promised quickly.

'Over the years, there were so many times when I longed to be able to tell you everything,' Amber sighed. 'But somehow I just lost my nerve at the last minute. However, for everything to come out now...well, it could be very awkward,' she added quietly. 'Especially as far as Lucy and my mother are concerned.'

'Well, for Heaven's sake, whatever you do, don't tell Sally!' Rose grinned. 'All the same, I do wish that you *had* taken me into your confidence. If only because it can sometimes be helpful to talk over one's problems with a friend. And I know that your life as a single parent can't have been easy.'

'It was really tough at times,' Amber agreed. 'You want to do the very best for your child, but it's basically a no-win situation.'

'Well, I think you've done brilliantly. Especially since you also had to cope with your mother's problems, as well. However, I must say that I've never seen Violet looking so fit and sprightly, while Lucy appears to be over the moon with excitement. I take it that she fully approves of both Max and your wedding plans?'

'That's an understatement! She's totally *thrilled* at the idea of having a real father like all her other friends. On top of which, she and Max don't just look so much alike, they also seem to instinctively understand each other, as well. Quite honestly, I can't think why I got myself into such a state.' Amber smiled and shook her head, remembering how she'd almost worried herself sick, desperately anxious that her daughter should be happy with the idea of her mother's remarriage. But, once again, Max had taken charge of the situation after Amber, almost trembling with nerves, had spent a considerable amount of time alone with the little girl, carefully explaining the plans regarding their future.

'The fact is, Lucy,' he'd said with a warm smile as he joined them in the sitting room, 'I've always been madly in love with your mother. However, she—very sensibly, I may say—chose to marry your father. Clive Stanhope was a good, kind, very caring man, and there's no way I can hope to take his place. So, I'm not going to even try, OK? On the other hand,' he added with a grin as the small girl had given him a cautious nod, 'I think we could have a lot of fun. There are so many things we can all do together as a family, which maybe your mother didn't have time for in the past. Such as the three of us going off, straight after the wedding, for a Christmas skiing holiday in Switzerland. Only don't tell anyone, because it's supposed to be a big secret. OK?'

'OK,' Lucy had grinned, obviously pleased to be trusted to keep such an important item of news to herself.

'However,' Max had continued more seriously, 'I reckon that the *most* important thing I have to tell you is that I promise to do my best to make your mother very happy.'

Lucy had regarded him silently for a moment. 'Mummy told me that you're a very clever businessman. Are you *very* rich?'

Max had shrugged his shoulders. 'Yes, I guess I am. But as your mother will tell you, money doesn't necessarily buy happiness. Loving and caring for people is far more important.'

'Well, Mummy needs a new car 'cos the Land Rover is always breaking down. And she ought to have some nice new clothes,' the little girl pointed out firmly. 'Can you afford to buy her lots and lots of *really* glamorous dresses?'

'As many as she wants—and all of them absolutely *dripping* with glamour!' he'd agreed with a grin, ignoring Amber's strangled protest at the down-to-earth, almost mercenary attitude that her daughter seemed to be taking over her mother's proposed marriage.

'And...um...can I be a bridesmaid?' Lucy asked hopefully.

'Of course!' Max laughed. 'Anything else on your shopping list?'

'Well...did Mummy tell you that I've been wanting a pony of my own for simply *ages*?' Lucy gazed up at him with wide, guileless blue eyes. 'If Mummy is having a new car, will you buy me a pony?'

Almost cringing with shame, Amber had held her breath as Max regarded his daughter blandly for some moments before giving a deep chuckle of amusement.

'No, you crafty, hard-bargaining, artful little girl! I'm not giving you a pony. Not straight away. You'll have to wait until the morning of your eighth birthday,' he'd said firmly, smiling as Lucy had dissolved into a fit of giggles before throwing herself joyfully into his arms.

'It wasn't at all funny at the time. I nearly *died* with embarrassment!' Amber said as her friend laughed at the story of Lucy's bargaining session with her new stepfather.

'Except, well . . . he isn't her stepfather, is he?' Rose pointed out gently. 'I mean . . .' she hesitated, 'isn't it going to be a bit of a problem deciding when and how to tell her that Max really *is* her father?'

'I've been worried about that,' Amber agreed with a sigh. 'Especially as she looks so much like him. However, Max feels that we shouldn't rush into telling Lucy too much, too soon. He seems to think that a warm, loving family life will make the fact that he's her real father more or less irrelevant. I can only hope he's right.'

'I'm sure he is,' Rose had said firmly. 'Just as I'm quite sure that he's the man for you. I was never too happy with the idea of your marrying Philip Jackson. To tell the truth, I always thought he was the sort of person who takes himself far too seriously.'

Her friend was right, Amber realised, grimacing down at the long letter from Philip, still lying reproachfully on the desk in front of her. Having her own doubts and worries about the wisdom of marrying Max, she really didn't need to have them reiterated by anyone else, and she was grateful to be distracted by a telephone call from Rose's husband, David Thomas.

'I just thought I'd give you a ring, Amber,' he barked down the phone, the noise of his busy office clearly audible in the background. 'You remember those house deeds you lent to me . . .?'

'Oh, Heavens! I'd forgotten all about them,' she exclaimed.

'I think you'll be pleased to hear that I've made an interesting discovery. *Very* interesting indeed!'

'Really? What have you found out?'

'Well, maybe I ought to call in and explain it all to you. It's a bit involved—quite complicated, really. But it looks as though there's a chance of saving the Tide Mill.'

'That's terrific!' She smiled down the phone with delight. 'Come on, David, don't keep me in suspense. I want to hear all about it—right now!'

However, by the time she put down the receiver, leaning back in her chair to gaze blindly out of the window, Amber's mind was in a complete whirl.

According to David—whose idea of perfect bliss was delving into dusty historical records—when Clive had sold the old Tide Mill, the sale had only included the building and the land on which it stood. He had *not* sold either the tide pool adjacent to the mill, or the ancient rights and ownership of the spit of land surrounding the tide pool where it jutted out into the river.

'I don't know why Clive didn't include the tide pool in the sale. Although, maybe the builder, who originally bought the old mill, wasn't interested in paying extra for what was nothing more than a huge pond,' David suggested. But, as he'd gone on to explain, the old deeds included an ancient Crown Grant of 1667, made under the great seal of Charles II, which gave the owner of Elmbridge Hall a 'good and perfect title' to the whole of the land enclosing the pool *and* most importantly, the river bed itself.

'I'm sorry to be so dim, David, but I really don't understand what you're talking about. I never knew that anyone could own the land *under* a river. Why would they want to do that?'

'Well, the river is tidal, isn't it? So, maybe in times gone by, there were oyster beds laid in the river beside the pool. That could have been a ''nice little earner'' for whoever owned Elmbridge Hall at the time.'

'There speaks the accountant!' she laughed. 'But I still don't really understand why that old deed is so important.'

'OK, I know it's complicated. But if you looked at a map of the area, you'd see the old mill on the riverbank, and the land that surrounds the tide pool jutting out into the river like a large U. Now, what this ancient deed proves is that all the land forming the outline of the U is still owned by you—and you also own the river bed, which lies between the pool and the other side of the river. I've checked up with a friend in the County Record Office,' he added, his voice crackling with excitement. 'He tells me that if you own the land around the pool *and* the land under the river as far as the river-bank opposite, you are entitled to demand a licence fee of anyone wanting to tie up their boat on to your land.'

'You mean . . .' Amber frowned as she tried to concentrate on what he was saying. 'You mean, anyone can sail up and down the river, but if they want to come ashore anywhere on my land, they have to have my permission to do so?'

'Got it in one!' David agreed crisply. 'Moreover, since you own the river bed itself, no one can build moorings or drive piles into the earth beneath the river. Which is going to be one big headache for Suffolk Construction, right? Because they may own the Tide Mill, but unless you sell them the pool, the land surrounding it *and* your rights to the river bed, they haven't a hope in hell of building their marina!'

'Wow! I can't wait to tell Rose the good news,' she laughed before realising that she would soon no longer be the sole owner of Elmbridge Hall. 'I'll have to tell Max what you've discovered, although I'm sure he'll be as pleased as I am to hear the news. He's working in London this week, but as I'm going down to do some shopping and then join him for lunch on Friday, I'll be able to tell him all about it. However, don't you think that we ought to let the people at Suffolk Construction know about the old deed?' she added tentatively. 'It does seem a bit unfair to leave them completely in the dark.'

'Yes, you're right,' he agreed. 'I haven't a clue who actually owns the firm. But maybe John Fraser can help? As a solicitor, he's bound to know how to go about finding out that sort of thing. Sorry...I'll have to go,' David had added hurriedly as the background noise in his office suddenly increased in volume. 'I'll give you a ring as soon as I have any more information. Bye.'

'I wish you'd both stop yakking away about the boring old Tide Mill!' grumbled Sally as she helped herself to another cup of tea.

'But that's the whole point of this meeting,' Rose pointed out as she passed around a plate of chocolate biscuits. 'We have to decide whether we're going to close down the committee now that Suffolk Construction can't build their new marina. Or whether we should wait for a while and see what happens.'

'Yes, well...you're right,' Sally agreed with a shrug. 'But, quite frankly, I'm *far* more interested in hearing about the plans for Amber's wedding. You haven't told us what sort of dresses you and Lucy are going to wear.'

'That's because I haven't bought them yet,' Amber grinned, still feeling slightly light-headed after yesterday's phone call from Rose's husband, David.

It seemed almost impossible to believe that everything in her life was suddenly coming up roses. When she recalled just how terrified she'd been at the prospect of Max's return to Elmbridge only a few weeks ago, it was really quite extraordinary the way all her problems appeared to have melted away. It wasn't just her forthcoming marriage to Max in a few days' time—which meant being able to stay in her old home, and which had led to Lucy's joy and happiness at the prospect of gaining a stepfather—but now, thanks to Rose's husband examining those old deeds, it was almost certain that they would be able to save the Tide Mill, as well.

'David said that he's trying to discover who owns Suffolk Construction. But as so many companies have been gobbled up by huge conglomerates these days, it may take him some time,' Rose warned her friends.

'I hope you're not going to try and buy any wedding outfits in Cynthia Henderson's boutique,' Sally demanded, refusing to be sidetracked in her determined pursuit of the latest up-to-date news on Amber's marriage. 'That assistant she's left to run the shop is absolutely *hopeless*!'

'No,' Amber shook her head. 'The sort of clothes Cynthia sells in her shop were always far too flashy for me. I'm going down to London tomorrow, to meet Max for lunch and to do some shopping. I'd thought I might find a suit or...'

'A dress and matching coat would be a better choice, especially since it's freezing cold at this time of year,' Sally wisely pointed out. 'And don't forget that the heating system in the church is always breaking down. You don't want to spend the next two weeks trying to recover from a nasty dose of flu. By the way,' she added casually, 'exactly where *are* you planning to go on your honeymoon?'

Amber laughed. 'Give me a break, Sally! If I tell you, everyone else in Elmbridge will know all about it in five seconds flat!'

'How can you say that? I'd never tell *anyone*,' her friend assured her earnestly, pointedly ignoring Rose's loud snort of amusement and disbelief. 'Are you going somewhere nice and warm, like the Caribbean? You could get a wonderful tan, and...' she paused as David Thomas entered the kitchen.

'Hello, darling. You're home early.' Rose smiled over at her husband before frowning as she noted the slightly apprehensive, worried expression on his face. 'What's wrong? Is everything all right at the office?'

'The office is fine, no problem,' he assured her, coming over to help himself to a cup of tea. 'I didn't know...I didn't realise that you were both here.' He turned to give Sally and Amber a strained smile.

'We were just discussing what you'd discovered in my old deeds,' Amber said. 'However, I think it's probably time we left. Just lately, I seem to be spending more of my life in Rose's kitchen than I do in my own home!'

'There's no need to go,' he assured her quickly. 'I just popped in to see Rose for a moment.'

'Have you had a chance to find out who owns Suffolk Construction?' his wife asked. 'We realise that it may take some time, of course, but——' She broke off as he turned his head to give her a quick glance of warning. 'What is it? It's something to do with the old mill, isn't it?'

'Well...er...I don't suppose it's all that important. We can always talk about it later,' he muttered evasively.

'Come on, David. If what's worrying you concerns the Tide Mill, you can't leave us in the dark,' Rose told her husband impatiently. 'I think you'd better hurry up and let us know the worst.'

'Yes, I suppose so,' he sighed, pulling up a chair and sitting down at the table. 'Although it's not a *major* problem, of course. Just a bit awkward, if you see what I mean?'

Rose groaned. 'No, we don't know what you mean. So, for Heaven's sake, get to the point!'

'Well, there's definitely no problem with the deeds,' he told Amber. 'At the moment, you really do own all rights to the land and the river bed, as I told you on the phone yesterday.'

'What do you mean by "at the moment"?' Sally queried sharply. 'Surely she either does or she doesn't own the damn things. I've never heard of any deeds with a time limit on them—not ones dating back to 1667.'

'You're quite right,' he agreed. 'But don't forget the deeds go with the house. So, there's no problem while Amber has sole ownership of Elmbridge Hall. However, when she marries Max, I understand that he's either buying the house outright from her, or they are going to share the tenancy.' He turned to Amber. 'Is that right?'

'Yes, I suppose so. We haven't really had much time to sort it out.' She shrugged. 'Why should it matter one way or another?'

David hesitated for a moment. 'Well, I don't know...it just seems a bit odd. You see, I can't understand why Max hasn't told you that it's *he* who owns Suffolk Construction.'

'*What*?'

'I don't believe it!'

'You must be kidding.'

'Hang on!' David protested above the loud exclamations of shock and horror that had greeted his statement. 'It's only a small problem. We're not exactly talking about the end of the world!'

'He's right. There's bound to be a simple reason why Max hasn't told anyone,' Rose said firmly, putting an arm about Amber's dazed, trembling figure. 'But, first of all, David, I think you'd better tell us how you discovered that Max owns Suffolk Construction. Are you *quite* sure that you haven't made a mistake?'

He shook his head. 'It was Sally's husband, John Fraser, who told me when I asked him to do some digging and find out the owners of the construction firm. From what I gather, it seems that he's been looking after Max's business interests here in Elmbridge for some time. For instance, he arranged the appointment of the present manager, a Mr Cruickshank, and . . .'

'John never said a thing about it to *me*!' Sally protested. 'I'd have told you straight away, if I'd known that Max owned the company.'

'Hmm, yes, I'm quite sure you would have,' Rose agreed, having no doubts about exactly *why* her friend's husband, not wishing the news to be broadcast far and wide, had remained silent on the subject.

'Is it all to do with his grandmother's estate?' asked Sally. 'Was she the original owner of the firm?'

'No, I don't think so,' David said slowly. 'From what John said, it appears that Suffolk Construction was taken over some time ago by a European company that, in turn, was recently taken over and absorbed into Max's firm, Warner International.'

'I'm sure that there's a very simple answer,' Rose told them firmly, throwing a worried, sideways glance at Amber, who was still sitting frozen in her seat, her face ashen with shock as she stared blindly down at the kitchen table.

'Yes—but what?' asked Sally, frowning with bewilderment before bluntly putting into words the un-
spoken question in the forefront of everyone's mind.

'I mean...Max couldn't *possibly* be marrying
Amber to get hold of her house deeds, so that Suffolk
Construction can go ahead and build their
marina...could he?'

It was a cold, damp, dismal day; the streets of London
were even more crowded than usual with people intent
on last-minute Christmas shopping, the air thick with
exhaust fumes and noisy with the incessant honking
of cars, buses and taxis.

Amber had never particularly cared for life in the
big city. But she'd forced herself to get the train down
to London this morning, fully intent on telling Max
exactly what she thought of his despicable behaviour.
Luckily, she wouldn't have to beard him in his office,
since she knew that he was working at home this
morning before being due to meet her for lunch at an
expensive restaurant in Mayfair. Well, that was a lunch
that wouldn't now be taking place, she told herself
grimly, impatiently tapping her feet as her taxi was
reduced to crawling through the heavy traffic.

Following a sleepless night, mainly spent pacing up
and down over her bedroom floor, she had slowly
progressed from a state of complete and utter shock
to one of boiling rage and fury. How *dare* Max make
use of her for his own evil and nefarious plans? The
devious rat had obviously sweet-talked his way back
into her life—and her heart—with only one aim in
mind: to further his own lousy business interests!

Now the scales had fallen from her eyes—she could see it all! He'd clearly had *no* intention of marrying her—not when he'd first called with Mr Glover to look at her house. It was now obvious that Max had merely intended to buy the property in order to gain access to her deeds. And it didn't take a very high IQ to realise exactly *why*, after seeing Lucy, he'd suddenly come up with the idea of marriage. All that business about the little girl needing a father had been nothing but *hogwash*! Amber had told herself furiously. It was obviously her daughter's startling resemblance to Max that had immediately changed his plans. After all, since he had already made arrangements to return to Elmbridge—a fact that he'd freely admitted—he couldn't afford a scandal. And there most certainly *would* have been plenty of scandal and gossip once everyone realised—as they were bound to do sooner or later—that Lucy was his illegitimate daughter. Definitely *not* a good idea for someone who was intending to become a pillar of the local business and social community, Amber thought savagely, almost kicking the door open as her taxi came to a halt outside the large modern apartment block overlooking Hyde Park.

Waiting for the lift to take her up to the top floor, Amber couldn't seem to stop herself shaking with tension. In fact, ever since learning of Max's vile treachery yesterday afternoon, she hadn't been able to think straight—or prevent her limbs and body trembling as if in the grip of some raging fever. 'It's just shock. It will soon wear off,' Rose had told her, clearly worried about letting the stunned, dazed girl drive the few miles back to Elmbridge Hall. But although her friends had been very kind, their distress and sympathy with her plight had left her desperately anxious for the sanctuary and shelter of her own home.

It wasn't that she didn't care about the old Tide Mill because, of course, she did, Amber told herself as the lift swept her upwards at breakneck speed, towards the penthouse suite on the top floor of the large building. It was the overwhelming humiliation and embarrassment of being such a credulous fool that she found so hard to bear. Unfortunately, it was no good trying to blame anyone else for the catastrophic situation in which she now found herself. It was *she*, overcome by her own weak, starved emotions and Max's devastating attraction, who was responsible for raising the false hopes of both her mother and daughter. Poor Violet would now undoubtedly lapse back into her deeply depressed state of mind. And as for Lucy...? Amber almost whimpered aloud at the thought of having to deal such a dreadful, crushing blow to her young daughter's joy and happiness at the prospect of having, at long last, a father of her very own.

'Hello, darling, I wasn't expecting to see you until much later this morning,' Max said as he opened the front door of his apartment.

It was acutely dismaying to find herself almost weakening at the sight of Max's lean figure in the casual, slim-fitting dark trousers, his broad shoulders covered by a soft, black cashmere sweater over an open-necked shirt. Just a glance at his tall, lithe body was enough to make her legs wobbly, her stomach feeling as though it were full of butterflies. Someone should arrange to have him locked up and then throw away the key, she told herself grimly. Because this man was clearly nothing but a damn menace to the whole female population!

'What's brought you here so early?' He raised a quizzical dark eyebrow. 'Have you been on a spending spree and run out of money?'

'No, I haven't run out of money. And, if I had, I certainly wouldn't ask *you* for any,' Amber retorted grimly.

'So, what's the problem?' he murmured smoothly, leading her across the well-polished, shiny parquet flooring of the large hall. 'I'm sorry that I've been rather tied up lately. But we'll soon be able to spend plenty of time together. I'm really looking forward to Christmas.'

'Well, I'm glad at least one of us has something to look forward to! Unfortunately, it won't be either Lucy or myself.'

'Really?' he drawled, his dark brows drawing quickly together in a frown as he registered the sharp, acidic note in her voice. 'Well, maybe I can change your mind. Because, while this apartment is hopeless, I'm still going to need an occasional base in London. So, I was hoping that we'd have time this afternoon to look at some houses that are for sale. They all have large gardens, which I thought would be perfect for Lucy to play in whenever she's down here.'

'You can look at what you like. I couldn't care less one way or another.'

'OK, let's have it,' he shrugged. 'You're obviously
upset about something. Although I can't think what—
other than the fact that I do seem to have been heavily
immersed in business lately.'

'I don't give a damn about your business!' she
grated angrily, her fury and resentment returning with
a vengeance as she gazed at his tall figure, now
lounging casually against one of the marble pillars in
the room, his glinting blue eyes regarding her with
some amusement. 'Although that's the reason why
I'm here, of course,' she continued. 'I just wanted to
tell you, face to face, that you can forget any idea of
marrying me—because I wouldn't touch you with a
ten-foot bargepole!'

'Don't be such an idiot!' he laughed. 'You're just
suffering from pre-wedding nerves. I've now got hold
of the special licence for our marriage next week,
and . . .'

'Didn't you hear what I said? I told you to forget
it!' she snarled. 'And you can also forget any idea of
getting hold of my house, as well. Which—as we both
know—will rule out any chance of you making yet
more millions out of Suffolk Construction.'

'What in the hell are you talking about?'

'Oh, come on, do me a favour!' She gave a shrill,
high-pitched laugh. 'Unless they own the deeds of my
house, Suffolk Construction hasn't a cat in hell's
chance of being able to build the new marina in
Elmbridge, right? And *who* owns Suffolk
Construction? *Who* persuaded this stupid, gullible
fool that he wanted to marry her, so that he could
buy her house *and* lay his hands on the deeds? Well—

surprise, surprise!—it's clever Mr Warner. Only I'm afraid it turns out that he wasn't *quite* clever enough,' she added savagely as he straightened up, regarding her with a dangerous gleam in his suddenly hard, blue eyes.

'So, you can forget your precious marina *and* that rotten, bogus marriage you've so carefully arranged,' she continued venomously. 'You can also forget *any* idea of getting your hands on Lucy. Because I don't care if I have to spend my whole life in court! I'll never, *never* let you get your slimy hands on her.'

'That's quite enough!' he thundered angrily, striding over the thick carpet towards her. 'You must be having a brainstorm! I don't know what the hell you're talking about.'

'Can you deny that you own Suffolk Construction?' she yelled angrily.

'No, of course not. Why should I?' He came to a halt, placing his hands on her shoulders as he frowned down into her blazing green eyes. 'God knows, it's only a tinpot little company, going nowhere fast. Why should you be interested in it one way or another?'

'Why indeed?' She glared defiantly up at him, refusing to be intimidated by the superior height of the man looming over her. 'Except that I've *now* discovered the truth about that "tinpot little company" of yours.'

'Oh, really?' he drawled coldly.

'Yes, *really*!' she lashed back, desperately trying to control the tears that threatened to fall at any moment. 'I know all about your wicked plans. So you can forget any idea of a wedding, or of buying my house, *or* the effort of having to pretend to be the stepfather of the year! And . . . and what's more——'

But she didn't have a chance to finish what she was saying, as he propelled her swiftly towards a pair of deep leather armchairs.

'OK, that's it!' he said sternly, pushing her down into a chair before seating himself firmly in the other. 'Now, I want you to take a deep breath and tell me— as calmly as possible, please—exactly what has been going on since I left Elmbridge.'

'Why should I?' she glared at him tearfully. 'You know it all anyway.'

'I know *nothing*!' he ground out savagely through clenched teeth. 'Only that you seem to have flipped your lid, and are apparently accusing me of a quite ridiculous, crazy scheme, which sounds more like something dreamed up by Hollywood than real life. So, get on with it, Amber. And it had better be good!' he added with grim warning. 'Because I'm sick and tired of always being cast as the villain of the piece, as far as you're concerned.'

Haltingly at first, and then speeding up her narrative as he clicked his fingers with terse impatience, she told him about David Thomas's discovery of both the ancient deed and Max's connection with Suffolk Construction. 'I . . . I nearly died with humiliation when Sally pointed out the truth,' she gulped, raising a trembling hand to brush the weak tears from her eyes. 'I couldn't . . . I couldn't believe just what a stupid fool I'd been.'

'I certainly won't disagree with *that* diagnosis!' He gave a harsh bark of angry laughter before slowly rising to his feet and pacing up and down over the white carpet. 'OK, I'll agree that the story you've outlined would make a great movie,' he said at last. 'There's only one problem. How long have you known about this ancient Crown Deed?'

'I only heard about it when David phoned two days ago.'

'Right. And how long has *he* known about this mysterious document?'

'I...I'm not sure,' she muttered. 'He only said that he'd discovered it buried amongst my house deeds.'

'Well, that's very interesting,' Max drawled, walking slowly towards her. 'So, maybe you can tell me how in the blazes *I*—who only returned to this country a few months ago after spending the past eight years in the United States—was supposed to have discovered the deed?

'It would obviously take some time to lay my evil, wicked plans,' he pointed out grimly as she gazed open-mouthed up at him, her brain in a total whirl. 'So, tell me, where and how did I manage to discover such a vital piece of information? Especially when David Thomas, who apparently prides himself on his local knowledge, has only just discovered the damn thing?

'Don't worry, Amber, it's only a small, technical hitch,' he added with cruel sarcasm as she stared at him in dawning horror, the blood draining from her face as she slowly began to comprehend the truth behind his remorseless, logical questions. 'I'm quite sure that your totally overwrought, fertile imagination can come up with an answer. Maybe I hired

James Bond to secretly investigate your house deeds, just in case they might contain something interesting? Or, did I persuade the little green men from Mars to...'

'*Oh, God* ...!' she groaned, gazing at him for one long, grief-stricken moment before covering her face with trembling hands, her slim body shaken by a storm of tears, weeping her heart out both because of her own stupidity—and for the certain loss of the one and only man she'd ever loved.

CHAPTER EIGHT

'WHAT an idiot you are, my darling!'

'I...I know...' she cried, her tears increasing as she felt a warm hand gently stroking her hunched shoulders. 'I know that you'll *never* be able to forgive me for being so...so *incredibly* stupid....'

'Oh, yes, I think I probably will,' he murmured, his blue eyes gleaming with amusement as he bent down to tenderly gather her sobbing figure up into his arms before carrying her out of the room and down a long corridor.

'Where...where are you taking me?' she muttered, burying her tear-stained face in the warm curve of his shoulder.

'Where do you think?' he demanded with a husky laugh as he entered his bedroom, lowering her gently down on to the enormous bed.

'Oh, no! We can't possibly...'

'Don't give me any of that nonsense, Amber,' he growled. 'Trying to persuade you to marry me has been—without a shadow of doubt—one of the most difficult and exhausting tasks I've ever had to face. It's only because I love you so much that I've kept on banging my head against what has so often seemed like a brick wall.'

'You...you really *do* love me?' she whispered, gazing incredulously up through her wet, spiky eyelashes at the man towering over her. 'But I thought...'

'Of course, I do, you stupid woman!' he ground out with exasperation, impatiently brushing a hand through his thick, dark hair as he sat down on the bed beside her. 'And now, after putting me through the wringer this morning, I have every intention of stripping off that boring tweed suit you're wearing. Because it's definitely about time that you soothed my injured feelings!'

'But, Max, we can't!' she gasped, adding quickly as he glared ferociously at her, 'It's only eleven o'clock in the morning, for Heaven's sake!'

'Oh, God! Who cares whether it's midday—or midnight?' he breathed, roughly pulling her into his arms, fiercely moulding her trembling body to his strong, lean figure with an urgency that made the blood race in her veins.

The musky, masculine scent of his cologne filled her nostrils as his lips fastened urgently on hers, his kiss deepening with possessive force as her soft, helpless moans of pleasure and the warm, yielding response of her slim figure provoked his increasing ardour. There was a desperate hunger in his hands as he swiftly removed her clothes, quickly peeling away his own and clasping her naked form to his hard masculine body, his powerful frame shaking with the force of an urgent, passionate intensity barely under control.

'I love you. I've never stopped loving you—however hard I tried to do so,' he murmured thickly against her soft skin, his lips trailing down over her breasts, provoking helpless gasps and moans of pleasure as his mouth closed over first one swollen nipple and then the other. 'You belong to me—and I'm *never* going to let you go. Never, ever again!'

His hoarse voice was almost the last thing she heard as she sank beneath the fierce tidal waves of overwhelming passion and desire. Feverish tremors of delight shook her body, each lingering caress, each sensual and erotically intimate touch making her ache with the desperate intensity of her need for his possession. Trembling with ecstasy as he placed his hands beneath her, parting her quivering thighs and lifting her up towards him, she was unaware of crying out in a wild, almost inhuman voice as she arched to meet the hard, powerful thrusts of his body. Their driving hunger and need forging them together as they became one flesh and one soul; the universe seeming to explode about them in brilliant, searing fragments of fiery light and heat.

'But, darling, surely you *must* have known how I felt about you?' he murmured softly as she lay curled within the warmth and shelter of his arms. 'How could you have doubted my love? Why else would I want to marry you?'

'But, I . . . I thought it was mainly because of Lucy. That you wanted to look after and provide for her. It wasn't long before I finally realised that I was madly in love with you, of course. But I was so confused about what you felt towards me that I simply wasn't able to think straight. Otherwise, I'd never have leapt to all the silly, wrong conclusions about that awful deed.'

'Oh, my love,' he gave a low, soft laugh. 'You're such an idiot!'

'I know,' she agreed sadly. 'I can't believe that I've been *so* stupid. But when David Thomas mentioned the name of your manager in Elmbridge as being a Mr Cruickshank, and I remembered you talking to someone of that name on your mobile phone in the car—well, it all seemed to make some kind of terrible sense. That, and the fact that you and John Fraser were obviously involved in business together...' Her voice trailed unhappily away.

'It's all right, darling,' he murmured tenderly, gathering her closer to his hard, naked body. 'The misunderstanding wasn't all your fault. Because, while I can promise you that I *didn't* have anything to do with that deed, I haven't been entirely straight on the matter of my business affairs in Elmbridge.'

'What do you mean?'

'Well, when I took over the large firm in London, it was some time before I discovered that it included a lame-duck company, Suffolk Construction, that was planning to build a marina in Elmbridge. However, I soon realised that there was a considerable amount of local feeling about the plans, and so I decided to put everything on hold until I'd found out the true facts of the case. I reckoned people might talk to me more openly if they *didn't* know I was the owner.'

'Yes, well...I can see that makes sense,' she acknowledged. 'All the same, I do wish that you'd at least told *me* the truth. I'd never have got myself into such a stupid muddle, or made such a fool of myself, if I'd known what was going on.'

'I see now that I should have trusted you,' he agreed. 'But although finding that I'd become the owner of Suffolk Construction was a complete accident of fate, it did give me a good and valid reason to hang around the neighbourhood, quite apart from the fact that I'd suddenly inherited my grandmother's estate. And that's what I needed. Because I was quite determined—once I learned that Clive had been killed in a car accident some years ago—to return to the town and, somehow, renew my relationship with you.'

'But you can't have intended to marry me? Not before you discovered that Lucy was your daughter?'

He gave a heavy sigh. 'I honestly don't know *what* I intended to do. For years I'd burned with resentment at the way you'd thrown me over—and for a man whom I thought of as an idle, rich, landowning ne'er-do-well. Yes . . . yes, I know,' he added quickly as she stirred restlessly in his arms. 'I now realise the truth of what happened in the past. But when I returned to Elmbridge, I . . . well, I guess I must have had some sort of half-baked idea in the back of my head. Not of carrying out any kind of punishment or revenge, of course. But, somehow, hoping that you were now bitterly regretting not having married me.'

'Oh, Max!' she murmured, raising herself up on one elbow to gently brush the damp curls from his brow. 'That sounds almost as foolish as some of the silly things I thought, and did.'

He gave a rueful laugh, his cheeks flushing beneath her fond smile. 'Frankly, darling, I'm deeply ashamed at having to confess anything quite so pathetic and juvenile. However, when I discovered the truth—that far from living in rich, glamorous surroundings, you were existing virtually on the poverty line—I quickly realised that I had an opportunity to grab you for myself at last! Unfortunately, my courtship proved to be a very difficult and tricky undertaking.'

'*Courtship*...?' Amber exclaimed, gazing at him with incredulity for a moment before falling back against the pillows, her body shaking with laughter. '*What* courtship? I've had nothing but dire threats and menace from the first moment we met—and well you know it!'

'Yes, you have a point,' he grinned. 'But I don't think you realise just how difficult it was to try and get close to you. I wasn't even entirely sure how much you still cared for me—although I knew from your response to my kisses that we were still strongly attracted to one another. And while you may laugh about my so-called courtship, just trying to get myself through the door of Elmbridge Hall nearly stumped me,' he added with a sigh. 'In fact, I'm afraid to say that it was only when I resorted to underhand methods, by pulling out the electric wiring of your car, which you'd left unattended in the High Street, that I finally managed to inveigle my way into your house.'

'Do you mean to say...?' She glared at him indignantly.

'Yes, I'm afraid so!' he admitted with a grin. 'I was worried about that handsome doctor, Philip Jackson. I'd already heard from John Fraser that he was keen on you. But when I saw him kissing you in the middle of the High Street, I knew that I was going to have to move damn fast,' Max added grimly. 'I had to make sure that I'd got you well and truly committed to *me*, before that guy had a chance to propose marriage.'

'Actually, he'd already asked me to marry him—about six months ago,' she murmured, secretly thrilled to the core to learn that Max had been jealous of the young doctor.

'And . . .?'

'And—nothing,' she replied quickly as his arms tightened possessively about her. 'I always knew that he wasn't the right man for me.'

'What about Clive?'

She blinked at him in puzzlement. 'But I've already told you about him. You know all about our marriage.'

'Er . . . no, not quite,' he murmured. 'Don't forget that before I actually saw Lucy, I was well aware of the fact that you had a young daughter. I naturally assumed that Clive was her father. That you and he . . .'

'Oh, no,' she said quickly, her cheeks flushing beneath his steady gaze. 'Clive and I . . . we never . . . we didn't . . .' She took a deep breath. 'There's never been anyone else. I know it sounds feeble, but . . . but you're the only man who's ever made love to me.'

'Oh, *darling*!' he groaned. 'You wouldn't *believe* just how jealous I've been of that poor guy. I knew I had no right . . . and God knows I'll always be so grateful to him for looking after you, but . . .' His mouth claimed hers in a deeply possessive, passionate kiss that seemed to last for ever. When he at last let her go, she lay flushed and breathless in his arms. 'My sweet one,' he whispered. 'I love you with all my heart—which you captured for all time eight years ago. And while I can't say that I've lived like a monk since we parted, I can promise you that I've never become seriously involved with anyone else.'

'Oh, yes? What about Cynthia Henderson?' she teased.

'Well...' he paused, grinning down at her as he pretended to give the matter some considerable thought. 'I was pleased to note that you showed definite signs of being extremely jealous when she threw herself all over me at the party in the Assembly Rooms.'

'Now just a minute!' Amber protested. 'I wouldn't bother getting *too* swollen headed about that fact, if I were you. Because, given half a chance, Cynthia can be relied upon to leap into just about *anyone's* bed!'

'Hmm... that's interesting. I've always been very partial to voluptuous ash-blondes,' he drawled provocatively, laughing as she quickly rose to the bait, angrily thumping his chest with her clenched fists. 'But what I *really* can't resist is a girl with tawny hair and green eyes, who's going to be my wife in a few days' time. Right?' he demanded huskily, rolling over to trap her beneath his powerful body.

'Oh, *yes*!' she breathed ecstatically as he softly brushed his mouth over her trembling lips. 'You are absolutely, one hundred per cent *right*!'

'Doesn't Amber look simply *lovely*!' Sally murmured, staring across the room at the newly married couple, clearly oblivious of the photographer's flash-bulbs as they gazed deep into each other's eyes.

'Yes,' Rose sighed, wiping away a tear. 'I don't think I've ever seen her looking so beautiful—or so happy.'

'I thought that this was going to be a quiet wedding with only one or two guests,' Sally said as she gazed around the large, oak-panelled walls of Elmbridge Hall. 'But as far as I can see, they must have invited at least half the town to the wedding!'

Rose laughed. 'According to Max, his first mistake was to give Violet Grant a blank cheque as far as expenditure on the wedding was concerned. And his second major error was not checking the number of people on the guest list before Violet had issued all the invitations!'

'Well, it's no secret that Amber's mother is a bit dotty. Sometimes not quite "all there", if you know what I mean,' Sally murmured quietly as Violet, wearing a very smart lilac chiffon-and-lace dress, smiled vaguely at them from across the room. 'But you have to admit that she's always had wonderful taste. I don't think that I've ever seen this house looking so lovely. In fact,' she added confidentially, 'I'm told that the bill for those magnificent flower arrangements came to many *hundreds* of pounds. And goodness knows what Amber's gorgeous coat and dress must have cost—it doesn't bear thinking about!'

'Hmm...' Rose murmured, well aware of *exactly* how much had been spent on the bride's outfit from one of the top fashion houses in London.

'I know my darling bride-to-be,' Max had told her a few days before the wedding. 'She's so used to not spending anything on herself that she'll buy the first thing she thinks is even vaguely suitable. So, I want you—as her oldest and dearest friend—to make sure that both she and Lucy are dressed up to the nines. Money is no object,' he added firmly, scribbling a note on the back of one of his business cards. 'Just tell them to send the bill to me.'

It had taken a considerable amount of arm twisting and plain speaking, but Rose had eventually persuaded her friend that she owed it to Max—if not for any other reason—to look her very best at the wedding. And once they'd been shown the simple but beautifully cut, pale cream woollen dress with its matching cloak and hood, lined in cream-coloured fur, Amber had immediately agreed that it was the perfect choice.

'I wish it was *real* fur,' Sally was saying. 'Goodness knows, Max can afford it.'

'But Amber wouldn't wear it,' Rose retorted, knowing that her friend shared her own feelings of revulsion at the slaughter of innocent wild animals. However, before they could disagree any further on the merits, or otherwise, of the anti-fur lobby, Lucy danced up to them, almost beside herself with excitement.

'Look at me, Aunt Rose! Don't I look *stu-pen-dous*!'

'You certainly do!' she laughed as the little girl twirled around in front of her. Indeed, Lucy was almost heartbreakingly lovely in her cream silk dress, with its lace-trimmed petticoats edged in palest pink, matching the wide sash about her waist and the large bow in her hair. 'In fact, I thought you made a really beautiful bridesmaid.'

'As beautiful as Mummy?'

'Well...almost—but not quite,' she murmured, gazing misty-eyed at the radiant glow on Amber's lovely face.

'But my new daddy is *easily* the most beautiful man,' Lucy said firmly before dashing across the room.

'She's so right—it's no contest!' Sally grinned, watching as the child's handsome new stepfather laughingly swept the little girl up in his arms. 'Incidentally, I can't help thinking that it's lucky Lucy looks so much like Max,' she added, thoughtfully viewing the two dark, curly heads pressed closely together. 'It makes them seem more of a real family somehow.'

'Umm...but don't forget that Clive had blue eyes and dark hair exactly the same colour as Lucy's,' Rose pointed out as calmly. 'Not as curly, of course. But then, most children's hair tends to grow straighter as they become older, doesn't it?'

'Yes, of course, you're quite right,' Sally agreed, immediately dismissing the vague, very faint question mark that had just floated through her mind. 'I sometimes think children are like puppies, who often mature into dogs that closely resemble their owners. So, I expect that will happen with Lucy and Max. Because anyone with half an eye can see that she absolutely *adores* her new father.'

Sighing with relief at having successfully deflected Sally's inquisitive nose for gossip, Rose quickly changed the subject. 'I know that he was very unhappy about losing Amber to Max, but I'm so pleased that Philip Jackson accepted an invitation to the wedding.'

'He was never the right man for her,' Sally said firmly, conveniently forgetting that for the past year she'd been quite certain that her friend would eventually decide to marry the young doctor. 'In fact, now that Amber is no longer available, I can think of one or two other girls who'd be just about perfect for him.'

'Hold it!' Rose grinned. 'We'll both have to stop matchmaking, because it's obviously a pure waste of time! Just look at Amber and Max. *They* didn't need anyone's help to get together.'

'Oh, I don't know...' her friend murmured, nodding towards where Mr Glover, the house agent, was pursing his lips as he frowned suspiciously down at some of the oak panelling in the hall. 'I know it might seem a bit far-fetched...but old "Gloomy Glover" does seem to have acted the part of Cupid in this marriage, doesn't he?'

Grown-ups really did act *very* peculiarly sometimes, Lucy thought as she skipped back across the floor towards Aunt Rose and Mrs Fraser. Everyone was very happy today, of course, but she really didn't understand why these two ladies should have suddenly collapsed into gales of laughter.

'Mummy says to tell you that they've finished having their photographs taken,' the little girl said, tugging at Rose's skirt to gain her attention. 'And I heard my new daddy say that he was "damned well not going to make a speech'' she added with a giggle. 'But Mummy laughed and said, ''no speech—no honeymoon!'' So, he's decided to say something after all.'

'What a sensible man,' Rose grinned.

'And a clever new wife!' Sally agreed with a laugh before gazing down at Lucy. 'I hear that you're a lucky girl, and that your mummy and daddy are going to be taking you off with them on their honeymoon?'

Lucy nodded. 'I'm not supposed to tell anyone where we're going, 'cos it's a great secret! But I'll tell you, if you like.'

'Yes, I . . . er . . . I'd love to hear all about it,' Sally murmured, casting a guilty, nervous glance at the expression of strong disapproval on Rose's face.

'Really, Sally!' she muttered in an undertone. 'I *know* that you're an incorrigible gossip, but it's quite disgraceful to try and wheedle secrets out of a child, for Heaven's sake!'

'Ac-shally . . .' Lucy lisped, pressing her tongue against a loose tooth, which had been threatening to fall out all day. 'Ac-shally, we're going off in a balloon, and then a plane, and then it's a long, long journey by boat—all the way up the Amazon!'

'Really?' Sally gasped.

'Really and truly,' Lucy nodded, gazing up at her with wide, innocent blue eyes, grinning as the blonde woman made a swift, hurried excuse before hurrying off across the room.

'That was *very* naughty!' Rose told the little girl sternly, struggling to keep her face straight as she observed Sally grabbing a friend's arm, clearly intent on spreading the news. 'I know exactly where you're going, and I'm sure your mother would be very cross to hear you telling such a thumping lie!'

'But I had my fingers crossed behind my back,' Lucy protested with an engaging smile. 'And I know Mummy won't mind, 'cos I've heard her say that Mrs Fraser likes nothing better than listening to other people's stories!'

'You're so sharp you'll cut yourself one of these days!' Rose told her with a grim bark of laughter. 'In fact, I can see that your new daddy is going to have his work cut out, keeping an eye on you! However, I think it's about time we joined your parents. Although I'm not quite sure where they've got to,' she added with a slight frown, leading Lucy through the crowd and trying not to bump into the black-uniformed waiters, busy keeping the guests' glasses filled to the brim with vintage champagne.

'Well, Mrs Warner...?' Max murmured, having swiftly clasped his wife's hand and whisked her away from the crowd into a small book-lined study off the main hall. 'So, how does it feel to be a married woman once again?'

'Since I was never *really* married before, I'm afraid that I can't speak with any authority on the subject!' Amber told him with a loving smile, amazed that such a hard, tough businessman should have looked so pale and nervous during the few days leading up to their wedding. 'However, *Mr* Warner...' she added, stars in her eyes as she gazed mistily up at her handsome husband, 'I can definitely tell you that, so far, I'm feeling *ecstatically* happy!'

'Oh, my darling!' he groaned, his arms closing tightly about her slim figure. 'I know it was stupid of me to even think about it. But I was terrified that you might change your mind and decide not to marry me after all. In fact, I don't think I had a wink of sleep last night!' he added with a bark of wry laughter, raising his hands to gently cup her face, his long, tanned fingers trembling with emotion.

'When I saw you coming up the aisle towards me this morning, I...well, it was all I could do not to shout out loud for joy! I still can't believe my luck at having found you once again. To know that all the secret heartache and deep unhappiness from which we both suffered is now behind us for ever.'

'For ever and ever,' she whispered, feeling as though she was floating on a cloud of pure bliss and over-whelming happiness as he lowered his dark head, firmly possessing her lips in a long, passionate kiss of total commitment before Lucy's high-pitched, excited voice cut sharply through the mists of their mutual desire.

'Everyone's looking for you—but *I* guessed where you'd be!' the little girl said as her new daddy grinned down at her, his arms still clasped about his new wife's slender waist. '*Do hurry up!*' she added impatiently. 'Aunt Rose says that it's time for you to cut the cake, and for the speeches to begin.'

Max groaned. 'Do I really *have* to make a speech?' he begged in a last-ditch attempt to wriggle out of such an onerous duty. 'I don't mind talking to any number of businessmen, but I'm sure to look a fool...'

'You only have to say a few brief words,' Amber told him firmly.

'Don't worry, Daddy,' Lucy said quickly. '*I* don't think that you look a fool. I told Aunt Rose that I thought you looked really beautiful!'

'Well, after *that* vote of confidence, it doesn't seem as if I have any choice in the matter,' he grinned down at his daughter, ignoring his new wife's gurgle of laughter.

'Although, flattered as I am, Lucy,' he continued as he led his new family back to join their guests, 'I must tell you, that if you want to see *real* beauty— together with a loving, tender heart—then you only have to look at your mother!'

A family feud...
A dangerous deception...
A secret love...

by Sara Wood

**An exciting new trilogy from a
well-loved author...featuring romance,
revenge and secrets from the past.**

Join Tanya, Mariann and Suzanne—three very special
women—as they search for their destiny. But their
journeys to love have very different results, as each
encounters the irresistible man of her dreams....

Coming next month:

Book 1—*Tangled Destinies*
Harlequin Presents #1790

Tanya had always idolized Istvan...well, he *was* her brother,
wasn't he? But at a family wedding, Tanya discovered a
dangerous secret...Istvan wasn't related to her at all!

Harlequin Presents: you'll want to know what happens next!

Available in January wherever Harlequin books are sold.

HARLEQUIN PRESENTS®

Don't be late for the wedding!

Be sure to make a date in your diary for the happy event—
The seventh in our tantalizing new selection of stories...

Wedlocked!

Bonded in matrimony, torn by desire...

To Have and To Hold by Sally Wentworth
Harlequin Presents #1787

"Gripping and enticing..."—Romantic Times

Marriage to Rhys might seem the answer to all Alix's
dreams...after all, she'd fallen in love with him at first sight.

But Rhys only proposed to Alix because she'd make him
the *perfect* wife.

Then Alix decided to take control of her own destiny, and Rhys
found that he couldn't live without her!

Available in January wherever Harlequin books are sold.

HARLEQUIN PRESENTS®

Ever felt the excitement of a dangerous desire...?

The thrill of a feverish flirtation...?

Passion is guaranteed with the seventh in our new selection
of sensual stories.

Indulge in...

Dangerous Liaisons

Falling in love is a risky affair!

The Sister Swap by Susan Napier
Harlequin Presents #1788

Acclaimed author of *The Cruellest Lie*

It began as a daring deception....
But Anne hadn't bargained on living next door to
Hunter Lewis—a man who wanted to know *everything*
about her!

Still, Anne managed to keep up her act for a while. Until she
realized that hiding the truth from Hunter meant that she
was also hiding from love!

Available in January wherever Harlequin books are sold.

HARLEQUIN PRESENTS®

Harlequin brings you the best books, by the best authors!

Coming next month:

Harlequin Presents #1785
Last Stop Marriage by Emma Darcy

Award-winning author
"Pulls no punches..."—*Romantic Times*

Dan's wanderlust had spelled the end of his marriage to
Jayne...or *had* it?

But if he despised stability, how could he suddenly be a
daddy, and to *such* a cute baby?

Jayne found herself hoping that the last stop on Dan's
journey would be a passionate reunion...with her!

Harlequin Presents #1786
Dark Apollo by Sara Craven

"Ms. Craven does a magnificent job."—*Romantic Times*

Nik Xandreou *dared* to accuse Camilla's sister of being
a gold digger. So a furious Camilla set out to prove
Nik wrong! But in the clash of personalities that followed,
Camilla found herself hoping that Nik would win their
contest *and* her heart.

Harlequin Presents—the best has just gotten better!
Available in January wherever Harlequin books are sold.

Their Inseparable Bond

Jill Weatherholt

LOVE INSPIRED

INSPIRATIONAL ROMANCE

LOVE INSPIRED®
INSPIRATIONAL ROMANCE

Recycling programs for this product may not exist in your area.

ISBN-13: 978-1-335-59716-8

Their Inseparable Bond

Copyright © 2024 by Jill Weatherholt

For questions and comments about the quality of this book, please contact us at CustomerService@Harlequin.com.

Love Inspired
22 Adelaide St. West, 41st Floor
Toronto, Ontario M5H 4E3, Canada
www.LoveInspired.com

Printed in U.S.A.

But Jesus beheld them, and said unto them,
With men this is impossible;
but with God all things are possible.
—*Matthew* 19:26

For Derek.
Thank you for your enduring patience
during my perpetual meltdowns.

Chapter One

Canine trainer Jake Beckett peered at his twins in the rearview mirror. Being a single father at the age of fifty had never been part of the plan. Then again, neither had losing his wife and their unborn child.

"Do you think Miss Myrna will bake her yummy snickerdoodle cookies for the class picnic?" Six-year-old Kyle called out from the back seat of Jake's cherry-red extended-cab pickup truck.

Myrna Hart's cookies were famous in the small town of Bluebell Canyon, Colorado. Without Myrna, the most beloved resident in town, Jake would have never survived that first year after his wife passed away.

"I don't see why not, but you can ask her yourself when we get to her house."

Jake stole a glance at his son. With his dark brown eyes and sun-kissed brown hair, Kyle was the spitting image of his late mother. His twin sister, Kayla, had many of his wife's features, like her thick, wavy brown hair and rust-colored freckles that dotted the bridge of her nose, but Kyle favored their mother more.

Jake brought the vehicle to a stop at the intersection.

Cumulus clouds drifted over the Rocky Mountains. He glanced over his shoulder and noticed Kayla gazing out the window, lost in thought. "Are you okay, Kayla? You haven't said a word since we left the school."

"She's upset about the mother-daughter fashion show." Kyle nudged his sister's arm.

"Stop it." Kayla pushed back and stuck out her tongue.

The family dog, Tank, a three-year-old Border collie nestled between the children, raised his head and released a snort.

"Settle down, kids. What's this about a fashion show, Kayla?"

The sudden silence was ominous. As time passed, Jake was coming to realize that as Kayla got older, not having a mother would bring challenges he might not be prepared to handle.

"Nothing… It's stupid." She choked back tears.

"Yeah, who cares about seeing a bunch of girls walking around wearing different clothes?" Kyle said. "It's silly, Kay. Forget about it. We can go fishing or something instead."

Jake was proud of his son. Kyle always tried to protect his sister. It was best to drop the subject for now. The event obviously upset her.

Moments later, Jake pulled into the circular driveway in front of Myrna's house. Rocking chairs lined the large wraparound porch, tempting a person to settle down with a glass of icy lemonade. For the past two years, Myrna's door was always open. After Laura died while giving birth to what would have been their third child, Myrna's home had become a refuge for Jake and his children.

Jake raked a hand through his cropped salt-and-pepper

hair, unbuckled his seat belt and opened the cab door. Tank sprang from the truck.

"I'll race you!" Kyle called out to his sister before sprinting toward the front porch.

Kayla zipped off with Tank on her heels.

The children thundered up the steps, ran across the wide-plank flooring and jerked open the squeaky screen door. Myrna had told them long ago they didn't need to call ahead or knock—they were family.

Jake's long, muscular legs circled to the rear of the truck to retrieve the replacement stairway railing. Myrna's diagnosis of macular degeneration had propelled him on a mission to make her house more accommodating and safer. Jake and others in the community looked after Myrna following the death of her husband, Jeb, five years ago.

He walked across the driveway carrying the railing and ascended the stairs. Tank circled the porch twice, exploring the wood with his wet nose. Then he headed to the oversize dog bed Myrna had bought specially for him.

"Lie down, Tank."

The dog spun around three times before flopping on the pillow and releasing a sigh.

"Good boy." Jake opened the door and stepped into the foyer. The toe of his leather work boot caught on the runner that covered the hardwood floor. Jake made a mental note to inspect the entire house for throw rugs. They were a tripping hazard. To ensure Myrna's safety, they would have to go.

Voices echoed from the kitchen. Jake moved past the baby grand piano to the back of the house. He inhaled the aroma of sweet cinnamon. He stepped inside the kitchen and Myrna's face brightened. Measuring in at barely five feet tall, Myrna kept fit by her constant motion. Her seventy-year-old skin showed no sign of the hours she spent outdoors in her garden.

"Jake, I just told the children your timing is perfect. Not only are there fresh snickerdoodles, but you finally get to meet my beautiful granddaughter and brilliant doctor, Olivia." Myrna winked and ran a finger through her short silver hair. "She flew into town last night for an overdue visit. It was a delightful surprise."

Jake's pulse ticked up when he spotted a striking young woman sitting on one of the stools surrounding the granite-topped island in the kitchen. Kyle was chatting up a storm with her like she was an old friend. Olivia's auburn, wavy hair cascaded over the tops of her shoulders.

Jake placed the railing against the laundry room door. He approached Olivia and extended his hand. He swallowed hard against the knot in his throat. "I've heard a lot about you. It's nice to meet you in person. I'm Jake Beckett."

Olivia smiled. She stood, revealing her long limbs and slender stature, and accepted Jake's hand. "Hello. Olivia Hart. It's a pleasure to meet you."

According to Myrna, Olivia worked long hours as an ER doctor in Miami, Florida. She was married, but he didn't remember Myrna ever mentioning children. Jake released her hand. At six foot one, it wasn't often he met a lady almost equal in height. "I didn't mean to interrupt your reunion. I thought I'd stop by and install the railing. I picked it up at the hardware store this morning since I'll be taking the kids to the car show tomorrow."

Myrna set the pitcher of sweet tea on the counter, then removed glasses from the cabinet. She glanced in her granddaughter's direction. "He has a mile-long list of improvements he'd like to make on the house. Jake is the most thoughtful young man you'll ever meet. He's always doing for others."

Jake's face warmed. "I'm not exactly young, but that's kind of you to say. I've added something to the list. We need to get rid of that runner in the foyer, along with the other throw rugs. They're a hazard."

"See, Gammy? Jake agrees with me. It's not safe for you to be living alone." Olivia addressed Myrna with a pointed look.

Jake shook his head. "I wouldn't say that. With some improvements and the help of a service dog, I think your grandmother will be fine."

"You're getting a dog?" Olivia glanced at her grandmother.

"Yes, and she's just the sweetest thing. Her name is Callie. Jake is training her." Myrna smiled and took a seat at the island.

Jake removed his wallet from his back pocket. He pulled out a business card and passed it to Olivia. "My brothers and I run a business together. They're out of town on a hunting trip, otherwise they'd be here devouring your grandmother's cookies."

Olivia examined the card. "Beckett's Canine Training. So you train service dogs?"

He nodded and straightened his shoulders. "Yes, ma'am, along with herding dogs. We train and place service dogs across the state. I also host a camp four times a year for Puppy Raisers."

"Why don't you bring Callie with you for Sunday dinner so Olivia can get to know her?" Myrna suggested to Jake.

He'd thought about bringing Callie along today, but she wasn't behaving well this morning. Jake left her at his brother's house. Callie had proved to be a slow learner. She would never make it as an official service dog, but Jake was confident she could meet Myrna's needs if her vision deteriorated. "I'll do that." He grabbed two glasses Myrna had left next to the pitcher. "Do you want some tea, kids?"

"Yes, yes!" Kyle bounced on his toes.

Kayla remained silent while sneaking looks at Olivia.

"Kayla, what about you?"

"I'm not thirsty," she whispered.

"Don't forget the cookies." Myrna pointed to the large porcelain Cheshire cat. "I had forgotten all about the car show tomorrow."

"We haven't," Kyle chirped. "Daddy said we could even stay until dark to watch the fireworks. It'll be so cool!"

Myrna looked at Jake. "Maybe you can take Olivia. I want her to experience everything that small-town life offers."

Olivia released a sigh and addressed Jake. "She's trying to convince me to give up my job and uproot my life in Miami." Olivia rolled her eyes. "Small-town life isn't for me."

"So, quaint and hospitable isn't your thing?" He laughed.

"I don't mean to be disrespectful. It's fine for some people." She drew her shoulders back.

"If you stick around long enough, you might change your mind." Jake couldn't imagine living anywhere else. He'd enjoyed growing up in Virginia, but after he and his brothers inherited the land in Bluebell nearly twenty years ago from their aunt who passed, the entire family had moved out West.

Olivia trailed her finger along the top of her glass of

sweet tea. "I don't see that happening. But I will stay long enough to convince my grandmother to move back to Miami with me. So, the safety improvements and the dog training probably aren't necessary."

Jake's mouth dropped open. Wait. What? Was she serious? There was no way Jake could allow that to happen. Sure, he wasn't blood, but Myrna was family to him and his children.

Kyle moved closer to his father. Anguish filled his eyes. "Is Miss Myrna moving?"

Myrna sprang from her stool with the agility of a teenager. She opened the oak cabinet, removed a serving platter and scooped the cookies from the jar. Carefully, she placed them in a semicircle on the dish. "I'm not going anywhere. My home is here. It's where I plan to stay until I go home to be with the Lord." Myrna hurried to the island with the baked goods. "Let's change the subject and enjoy these cookies."

Kayla gave Olivia a callous once-over. After losing her mother, Kayla clung to Myrna. Two years had passed and their bond was stronger than ever. Kyle loved the older woman too, but Kayla and Myrna had a special connection that the little girl wasn't about to allow this interloper to destroy.

"Now, about the car show. You should go with Jake and the kids, Olivia." Myrna sat, broke off a piece of cookie and popped it into her mouth. "I think you'd have a good time. I won't be able to take you since I'll be baking cupcakes tomorrow morning and preparing for Bible study."

Jake considered Myrna's suggestion. It might be a good idea for Olivia to go to the show. She'd hear firsthand how much the people in the community loved her grandmother. There wasn't a person in Bluebell who wouldn't help Myrna in a time of need. Maybe then Olivia would drop this outlandish idea to move her. "If you're interested, you're welcome to join the kids and me," Jake offered.

"Yes!" Kyle jumped off his stool and circled to Olivia. "Please come with us, Dr. Olivia. It'll be so much fun. We're going to have a picnic. Daddy's going to make us his special triple-decker club sandwiches. We even get to have soda, too!"

Olivia looked at Jake. Her brow arched. "What about your wife? Shouldn't you check with her?"

Silence covered the room like mist drifting across a pond.

Jake's stomach twisted. His eyes darted between the twins. Kayla's face turned to stone. Kyle's lower lip quivered.

"Our mommy is dead." Kayla's abrupt response shattered the silence.

Kyle ran to Jake and buried his face in his father's hip.

Embarrassed, Jake addressed his daughter. "Kayla, I think you should apologize to Dr. Olivia."

Kayla eyed her father. "It's true. I don't have a mommy anymore."

"That may be, but I didn't like your tone."

The adults exchanged glances. Kayla remained silent, crossed her arms and rolled her lower lip.

Olivia cleared her throat. "I'm so sorry." Olivia turned to her grandmother. "I guess I didn't remember."

The refrigerator's motor hummed. Outside, a car door slammed, and Tank barked twice.

"It sounds like I have more company." Myrna clapped her hands and rose from her seat. "So it's settled. Jake, you and the kids can swing by tomorrow morning and pick up Olivia on your way to the car show. I'll have a batch of cupcakes ready for the picnic."

Jake nodded. There was no point in arguing with Myrna.

Myrna headed to the door. Kayla remained quiet, and Olivia kept her eyes glued to the floor. Kyle inched toward Olivia's stool. "So, you'll go with us to the car show?"

"That's sweet of you, Kyle, but your father might want to keep this a family outing." Olivia looked up at Jake as though asking for permission.

"We would be happy for you to join us," Jake said.

"Please, will you come?" Kyle asked.

Olivia turned her attention back to Kyle and smiled. "I've always loved triple-decker sandwiches. Of course I'll go."

Kyle pumped his fist and whispered a *yes*, perhaps not wanting to upset his sister, but it was too late. Kayla frowned at Jake before racing out the kitchen door and into the backyard to take refuge in the tree house. After his wife died, Jake had built the house for the kids on Myrna's property since the family spent so much of their time with Myrna.

"Please come and have some tea and cookies, Larry." Myrna returned to the kitchen with her guest.

For as long as Jake could remember, Larry Walker had been the branch manager of the only bank in town. He sometimes overlooked late payments when someone in the community experienced tough times. Larry was a good man. Jake extended his hand. "It's nice to see you. What brings you out this way?"

Larry placed his briefcase on the island and reached inside. "I need a couple of signatures from Myrna."

"For the home improvements. Don't you remember?" Myrna directed her question at Jake. "I took out a home equity line of credit to cover the cost. I know I mentioned it to you."

"You did. But I told you a loan wasn't necessary. I can do all the work for you."

Myrna smiled. "That's generous of you, but I can't let you work for free. Besides, I have to pay for the materials."

Jake wouldn't be working for free. He couldn't count the number of meals and counseling sessions Myrna had provided him since his wife died. He'd never be able to repay her in his lifetime. "You can pay for the material, but I won't accept a dime from you for the labor."

Myrna rolled her eyes and looked down at the papers Larry had placed in front of her. "Where do I sign?"

Larry flipped the pages and pointed to the signature block at the bottom of page three. "Right here."

Myrna blinked her eyes before rubbing her fingers over her eyelids.

"Where? Let me put on my reading glasses." Myrna removed the eyewear from the top of her head and slid them on her face.

The three adults watched as Myrna squinted to see the signature line. Her glasses didn't appear to help.

"Gammy, when was the last time you saw the eye doctor?" Olivia moved closer.

"I had a follow-up appointment a month ago, but I had to cancel."

"Why?" Olivia asked.

"Elizabeth from my prayer group needed a ride to Denver for her cataract surgery."

Myrna always put others ahead of herself.

Olivia shook her head. "This is exactly why you should come to Miami. It's not safe for you to drive a car if you can't see to sign your name. I can't allow you to put yourself in danger. You have macular degeneration. If you don't stay on top of this disease, you could lose your eyesight."

Jake agreed about the seriousness of Myrna's condition. Since her diagnosis, he'd researched the disease. He was aware of what could happen if Myrna didn't receive proper treatment. Jake had found a well-regarded specialist in Denver and put Myrna's name on the waiting list for an appointment. But if Olivia had her way, Myrna would never have that appointment. Jake couldn't allow that to happen. Completing the safety improvements on Myrna's home and training Callie would be his top priorities. Jake had every intention of proving to Olivia that Myrna belonged in Bluebell, surrounded by the people who loved her.

"Good morning, sleepyhead." Myrna stood at the six-burner gas stove. A white-and-yellow apron hugged her waist.

A heavy sensation filled Olivia's chest. Her father used to call her "sleepyhead." Olivia often reflected on how different her life would have been if her father hadn't died when she was young. Her bare feet padded across the pinewood floor leading to her grandmother's kitchen. "Good morning." She hugged the woman and held on a little longer than usual. The tension she hadn't known she'd been carrying eased. "It's nice to be here with you, Gammy. I've missed you."

Myrna smiled. "I've missed you, too."

"I'm sorry I let so much time pass."

"There's no need to apologize. I still carry fond memories of the cruise you took me on several years ago. And remember, you visited a couple times when you attended medical conferences in Denver."

"Those were brief evening visits before I had to get back to Miami." Olivia lowered her gaze. "I should have spent more time with you."

"You're a busy doctor. And with the divorce, I'm sure it's been difficult. I only wish you would have told me about your marital issues before you arrived in Bluebell. Maybe I could have helped you."

Olivia hadn't shared the details of the breakup with Gammy or anyone. She'd been in shock when her ex-husband told her he no longer wanted to have children. Her world went into a tailspin when Mark filed for divorce. Olivia wanted to work on their differences, but Mark believed it was best to end the marriage since he no longer shared her dream of having a family. "I'm not sure anyone could have helped, but there's no excuse for me not to have called you more frequently."

"You're here now. That's what's important. Breakfast is almost ready. I'm sure you're starving."

The aroma of bacon with a hint of sweetness caused her stomach to rumble. "I am. Why didn't you wake me up last night?" Olivia headed to the coffeepot. She removed a cup from the mug tree and poured. A baking sheet lined with a dozen cupcakes cooled on the countertop.

"After Liz dropped me off from my caring cards meeting, you were sleeping so sound, I didn't have the heart."

Myrna speared a strip of bacon with a fork and turned it over. She reduced the flame. Hot grease hissed inside the skillet.

Olivia couldn't remember when she'd slept so soundly. During the separation and following the divorce, with no one waiting for her at home, Olivia often covered for her colleagues who had families. "I don't think I've slept that long since I was in high school." She laughed and took a sip of the hot brew.

Myrna slid four slices of whole wheat bread into the toaster. "Between the time difference and the stress of traveling, you needed your rest. Since you slept through dinner, I've cooked you a big breakfast."

"That's so thoughtful. Thank you." Olivia took notice of the farmhouse table with five place settings. "Are you expecting company?"

"Since Jake was so sweet with his offer to take you to the car show today, I thought inviting him and the children over for breakfast was the least I could do." Myrna removed the second batch of cupcakes from the oven.

"Here, let me help you." Olivia grabbed a pot holder from the counter and took the baked goods from her grandmother. "It's only nine o'clock. I can't believe how much cooking and baking you've done. Do you ever slow down?"

"I could ask you the same. I worry about you working such long hours at the hospital." Myrna opened the refrigerator and removed a plate of cupcakes.

Olivia wanted to cut back her hours now, but when her marriage was crumbling, she'd used her job to escape the truth. The man she'd vowed to spend the rest of her life with had decided he no longer wanted to have children. "If you move to Miami, we can look after each other. I can reduce my hours. Or maybe I can leave the hospital and start a small family practice of my own that could offer more flexibility." Olivia bit her lower lip. "What if something happened to you? You're all alone in this big house."

Myrna placed the dessert on the counter and rested her hand on Olivia's arm. "You're thinking about your father, aren't you?"

Since Olivia had learned about her grandmother's diagnosis, reliving the day her father died had become an everyday occurrence. If only she'd come straight home from school instead of disobeying her mother and going to the playground with her friends. The thought of her grandmother dying alone in her home, like her father, had consumed her mind. "I don't want to leave you here by yourself."

"I appreciate that, but my life is here. The people in this town have been my family for almost twenty years. I couldn't imagine ever leaving Bluebell." Myrna pulled her hand away and pushed herself from the table. "Jake will be here soon. I better get the icing on these so you can take them with you."

The mention of Jake reminded her of the struggle she had earlier deciding what to wear. She looked down at her black jeans and pink blouse. "Is this outfit okay? I didn't know what to wear. I've never been to a car show." Since Olivia first woke up, she'd had reservations about spending the day with Jake and his children. "Are you sure you can't come with us to the car show? Jake is your friend. I feel uncomfortable going with him and his kids."

"Your outfit is perfect." Myrna glanced at the clock on the wall. She carried the plate of cupcakes and the bowl of icing to the table. "Come and sit with me, dear."

Olivia followed her grandmother and pulled out a

chair from the table for each of them. She sat down and took a sip of her coffee.

"Why are you so apprehensive about going to the show with Jake and his children?" Myrna asked as she ran the knife with a glob of vanilla icing over the chocolate cupcake.

"I should have never asked about his wife. I feel terrible. To be honest with you, I didn't remember you mentioning that Jake had lost his wife. I guess I wasn't paying attention. I'm sorry." The coffee soured in Olivia's stomach.

"Don't be so hard on yourself. I never shared the details of what that family has endured with you." Myrna pulled in a slow breath and released it. "It should have been a happy time for Jake's family. His wife, Laura, was seven months pregnant when she went into labor. She had issues with her blood pressure and had a heart attack." Myrna wiped a tear.

"And the baby?"

Her grandmother shook her head. "It devastated Jake. He lost his wife and baby boy in a matter of minutes. If it weren't for his strong faith, I don't think he would have survived."

"That's so sad." Olivia placed her hand over her mouth and shook her head.

"Laura was a wonderful wife and mother. She kept the Beckett house running. Poor Kyle and Kayla, they didn't understand what had happened to their mother. Kyle had terrible nightmares, and Kayla wouldn't talk."

"How did Jake handle it by himself?"

"Oh, he wasn't alone. His brothers were here to support him. Plus, the entire town rallied around him."

Myrna brushed a tear from her cheek.

"After Laura was gone, it paralyzed Jake. The poor guy couldn't operate the washing machine. He didn't know that Kyle liked sliced bananas on his peanut butter sandwich. Or that Kayla won't drink orange juice that has pulp. That was Laura's department. Jake's brothers were there to support him, but the kids needed a mother figure, so I stayed at their house for the first month."

"Why?"

"That's what family does. We support one another. We give our time and effort to someone other than ourselves."

"But you're not family." Olivia couldn't deny feeling a twinge of jealousy. Since the day she'd come home from school and discovered her father nonresponsive on the kitchen floor, all she'd wanted was to be part of a family again.

Myrna reached for Olivia's hand. "It's not blood that makes you family, dear. Love and loyalty bind people together. It's what makes Bluebell Canyon so special. Give it time. You'll see."

Olivia considered her grandmother's words. Olivia's mother had been blood, yet after losing her husband, the only thing her mother seemed to care about was getting her next drink. Had her mother ever considered the effect that finding her father had had on Olivia?

"For weeks, Kyle couldn't fall asleep unless I was in bed with him. Jake and Kyle have come a long way, but Kayla is still in a lot of pain. I think it might be a good thing for her to spend time with you."

"Why would you think that?"

"Let's just say I have a good feeling about the positive effect you could have on her."

Olivia didn't plan to stay in Bluebell Canyon long

enough to affect anyone, much less a child who had lost her mother. She still had unresolved issues after losing her father and later being abandoned by her mother. How could she help Kayla? It was clear to her that Jake's circumstances were going to make it more challenging to convince Gammy to come back to Miami.

Outside, car doors slammed. Children's laughter filled the air. Olivia's stomach tightened. It was too late to back out. She'd have to go to the car show with Jake and his kids. It was what Gammy wanted. But after today, Olivia would have to keep her distance from the Beckett family. Getting involved with a grieving widower and his two children wasn't part of her plan. And she certainly didn't want to develop ties to the other townspeople, either. She needed to focus on getting Myrna out of Bluebell Canyon.

Chapter Two

"Every time your grandmother feeds us breakfast, I feel like I've gained ten pounds," Jake joked, to lighten the mood inside his truck. Kyle had been a chatterbox since they'd left Myrna's house. Kayla had barely said a word at breakfast and remained quiet. Olivia sat in the passenger seat with her back ramrod straight, twisting the ends of her hair around her index finger. She stared out the window. The sunlight showcased her creamy complexion. Jake quickly shifted his eyes back to the road as he approached the four-way stop.

"Have you ever attended an antique car show?" Jake raised an eyebrow in Olivia's direction.

"No, I can't say that I have. What exactly happens? Do we drive the cars or go for a ride?"

Kyle's giggles carried from the back seat to the front of the truck's cab. Jake peered in the rearview mirror and saw Kayla rolling her brown eyes.

"Kayla, would you like to explain some car-show etiquette to Dr. Olivia?"

"No."

"I will! I will!" Kyle called out. "Ouch! Stop it, Kay."

"Kids, settle down."

"But, Daddy, Kayla is pinching me."

"Kayla, leave your brother alone. We'll let him explain the protocol to Dr. Olivia."

"There's a certain way to behave?" Olivia questioned.

"Yeah, but it's still fun. You can't touch the cars or lean against them. Stuff like that," Kyle explained. "You need to be respectful of the cars and the owners. They spend a lot of money—" his eyes grew wide "—like a humongous amount to make their cars nice again."

Jake listened to his son with pride. Kyle's mother had grown up going to car shows. Her father had been an enthusiast. Jake and his wife started taking the twins to shows when they were only a year old. Laura made sure as the children got older that they learned the proper etiquette. It was important to her to carry on the tradition she'd shared with her father. Jake couldn't blame Kayla for getting upset that Olivia had joined them. It was difficult for him to have another woman in his wife's seat on a family outing. If Myrna hadn't insisted Olivia join them, he would have never extended the invitation on his own. It didn't feel right.

Olivia looked over her shoulder. "Thank you for educating me." She turned to Kayla. "Is there anything else?"

Kayla stayed quiet while Kyle nodded his head. "Ask a lot of questions. The owners like that."

Olivia smiled. "Okay, I'll remember that. You seem to know a lot about car shows. Where did you learn all of this?"

"Our mommy taught us," Kayla responded curtly. "My family went to shows." She crossed her arms. "You're not in our family."

"Kay!"

"What?" Kayla shot a look at her brother. "She's not."

"You don't have to be so mean," Kyle said.

"Your brother is right. I don't like your attitude, young lady." Jake looked at Olivia. "I'm sorry."

Olivia simply nodded.

Jake turned on the radio to extinguish the silence inside the vehicle. The plan to have a nice outing with his children wasn't going as expected. Kayla made it clear she didn't want Olivia to spend the day with them, yet Kyle seemed thrilled. It would be a long day if he didn't turn things around soon.

Thirty minutes later, they arrived at the fairgrounds. A cloud of dust swirled behind the truck as Jake searched for a parking space in the field. "We've got some time before the show starts. Do you want to go on a couple of rides?"

"Yay!" Kyle cheered and pumped his fist. "Kayla and I are tall enough to go on some by ourselves."

The group exited the vehicle. Food trailers lined the trampled path that led to the rides. The smell of popcorn and sugary-sweet funnel cake filled the air. The children took off running and headed toward the merry-go-round.

"Are they okay going by themselves?" Olivia's eyebrow arched.

Jake stuck his hands into the back pockets of his jeans and laughed. "This isn't Miami. We know practically everyone here. That's what makes living in a small town so great."

The twins took their place in line behind two girls who looked to be in their early teens.

"Do you want to have a seat over there?" Jake pointed to a wooden bench underneath an oak tree where he could see the kids and get to know Olivia. He had to try.

It might be the only way to convince her how much everyone in Bluebell loved her grandmother.

They sat, and Olivia fingered her necklace and looked toward the children. "I feel like I'm spoiling Kayla's day. I don't think she wants me around."

"Give her time. She's not as comfortable around strangers as Kyle is." Jake wasn't so sure Kayla would soften up to Olivia. He knew his little girl. She was strong-willed when she set her mind to—or against—something. He planned to talk with Kayla tonight at bedtime about being more respectful toward Olivia.

"We didn't exactly get off on the right foot. I shouldn't have made that comment about asking your wife for permission. I'm sorry."

Jake adjusted his cowboy hat to shield the sun from his eyes. "Like I mentioned yesterday, there's no need to apologize. You didn't know."

Olivia resumed twisting her hair around her finger. "I know now. This morning, Gammy told me about Laura and the baby." She dropped her hands and folded them in her lap. "I'm sorry for your loss."

Jake noticed Olivia brushing a tear from her cheek. "Thanks. It's been a rough couple of years." When his wife had gone into distress, they had rushed him out of the delivery room. The staff raced in and out of the room. Jake stood by the door, feeling as if he were floating outside of his body. He'd been unable to escape the beeping machines. He knew something wasn't right, yet no one offered to tell him what was happening. When the doctor finally stepped into the hallway, his worst fear became a reality. Laura and the baby hadn't survived. His knees had buckled. He had dropped to the tiled floor. Thoughts of his children coloring in the waiting room with Myrna swirled in his mind. They weren't aware their mother was gone. He thought that taking the children home that night without their mother would be the hardest thing he'd ever do, but telling them what had happened nearly broke him. Jake's eyes scanned over to the children. "Kyle has handled it a little better than Kayla. I think he's trying to be the tough guy."

"Growing up without a mother isn't easy for a young girl," Olivia said.

"Are you speaking from experience?"

"Kind of. I had a wonderful and caring mother, until I lost my father when I was eight." Olivia looked up at the sky.

"I'm sorry." Jake knew Myrna's only son had passed years ago. He didn't recall anything about her son's wife.

Olivia nodded. "After he died, my mother kind of checked out."

"What do you mean?"

Olivia rubbed her palms down her thighs. "She started drinking…a lot. I was too young to realize she abused alcohol to mask the pain of losing her husband. About a year after he died, my mother left. That's when Gammy and Pops rented out their home down the road from ours in Denver and moved in with me. They stayed until I went off to college. Gammy didn't want me to lose the only home I'd known. For years, no one knew where my mother had gone. There was a part of me that was happy she had left. She wasn't the same person after she started to drink. Once I finished college and moved to Miami, Gammy and Pops sold my childhood home and moved to Bluebell."

"Do you ever hear from your mother?"

Olivia shook her head. "While I was in medical school, my mother died in a car accident."

"Even though she'd been absent from your life, that had to have been tough for you," Jake said.

Olivia paused and turned to Jake. "Really, the day my father died, I lost both parents. If it weren't for Gammy, I don't know what would have happened to me."

"She's a special lady. When my wife passed, your grandmother put her life on hold to help the children and me. She stepped in to help my brothers and took over, starting with the funeral arrangements. I couldn't think straight. I tried to stay strong for Kyle and Kayla, but my heart had shattered." Myrna never pretended to have all the answers. She was simply there during the darkest and most isolating time of his life. Jake had kept sinking further into a depressed state. "Myrna helped put the pieces of our lives back together again. She reminded me to lean on my faith, to look for the light through the darkness." Jake rubbed his eye. "She's an important part of our family."

"I'm glad she was there to help you and the children, but she's my only family and she's an important part of my life, too. That's why I want to help her. I can hire a full-time nurse until I work things out with my job." Olivia turned to Jake. "You saw her yesterday. She couldn't even see the signature line on the papers Larry brought her to sign."

Jake nodded. "I think we can both agree that Myrna's eyes are deteriorating. Over time, she'll need more help."

"So we agree? She shouldn't be living on her own." Olivia straightened her shoulders.

"Hold on a minute. I never said that." Jake didn't like the direction of this conversation.

"Daddy!" Kyle called out. The twins smiled and waved as the merry-go-round powered up. Jake was relieved to see Kayla smiling. His heart squeezed for his little girl, who smiled exactly like her mother.

Jake focused his attention back on the discussion at hand. "I hope you'll hear me out before you decide about moving your grandmother."

"I'll listen, but I can't make any promises."

"Since Myrna's diagnosis, I've been making modifications around the house to make it safer if her eyes worsen."

"I understand and appreciate that, but from what I saw yesterday, it's not a matter of if her eyes get worse. They already are. I don't think she should live alone." Olivia's eyes filled with sadness.

"That's the reason I wanted Myrna to get a service dog." Jake had known it wouldn't take much to convince Myrna. She'd always loved dogs and often had Tank over for sleepovers. Myrna even periodically volunteered with his business when things got too busy with him and his brothers. "At first, she didn't want to admit that she might need help, but she came around. She agreed having a service dog was the best solution to maintain her independence. Remaining independent is very important to her."

Olivia nodded. "I've seen many people come into the ER with service dogs, but I think a nurse would provide better companionship."

"Service animals are excellent companions and much more." The animals provided their handler with the confidence to get out and continue to live their lives to the fullest. Seeing these dogs change people's lives for the better made his work rewarding.

"Training dogs to assist people with disabilities is an admirable business."

Jake couldn't imagine doing any other type of work.

"Thank you. It's wonderful to see the hard work pay off when the dog graduates and meets their new handler."

"Yesterday, you mentioned a camp for Puppy Raisers. What's that?"

"Puppy Raisers are individuals who commit to fostering a potential guide or service dog puppy in their home for the first year of the dog's life before formal training can begin."

"Interesting. I'd like to hear more."

Olivia was showing interest. This was good.

"My goal with Camp Bow Wow is to socialize and educate the puppy about everyday life and outdoor experiences while training the animals to work and perform tasks for people with disabilities. I expose the puppy to things they'd encounter working as a service dog, so they become comfortable and confident in any situation. For example, they visit grocery stores and restaurants, and learn how to behave and help their owners in all potential real-life scenarios. We meet Monday through Friday from three thirty to five thirty for three weeks. These hours allow the twins to help. I want them to see how blessed they are and to have compassion toward the disabled. After camp is over, I do follow-ups by video and make myself available to answer questions."

"Do all the puppies enrolled in your camp advance to train as service animals?"

"Usually, but now and then, we have a dog owner interested in training their own dog. The current group is all volunteer Puppy Raisers who will give up their dog after a year. Our business usually works with breeders who have ancestry lines that have proved to be successful in the past with specific disabilities. It's important to keep in mind that not every puppy is cut out to work as a service animal. That doesn't mean they'll make a bad pet. They just don't have what it takes to provide the critical support required of a service dog."

"Is Callie enrolled in your camp?"

Jake smiled. "Yes, but Callie is what you might call a work in progress. She's been a slow learner, but your grandmother fell in love with her the first time they met. I'll admit, I haven't had a lot of time to work with Callie, but I think she'll be a great help to Myrna."

"Did you get her through one of your breeders?"

"No, a local veteran named George Waters rescued Callie from a shelter in Denver when Callie was two months old. He planned to be her Puppy Raiser, but then he got sick and passed away. When he was diagnosed with cancer, he asked that I go forward with training Callie. I mentioned Myrna might need help in the future because of her recent diagnosis of macular degeneration. Since he and Myrna were good friends, he insisted I train Callie to help Myrna. I promised George I would carry out his request."

"So, you're training Callie to be Gammy's eyes?"

Jake nodded. "Myrna could live independently for years to come." Maintaining Myrna's independence—and keeping her and her friendship close—was Jake's goal.

"What if I take over as Callie's Puppy Raiser? Then she could get used to living with Gammy. I could help you train Callie. You said yourself that you've been busy."

Jake hadn't expected this from Olivia. With a hectic schedule at the hospital, he figured she'd be more likely to own a cat since they could be less maintenance. "Do you like dogs? I don't require my Raisers to have experience training, but they must have a love for dogs."

"Who doesn't love puppies?" Olivia smiled.

"Callie won't stay a puppy forever. A fully grown golden retriever can be quite large."

"I'm familiar with the breed. I think Callie and I will get along fine."

"It takes an enormous commitment. It would be your responsibility to oversee the care of Callie, like feeding, grooming, socialization and exercising. Do you think you'd have the time?"

"I've taken a sabbatical from my job with no set return date, so I can stay as long as it takes to get Callie trained. By then, I'll be able to better assess whether it's in my grandmother's best interest to stay in Bluebell or move to Miami and live with me."

Didn't Myrna get a say in the matter? Of course, that was between Olivia and her grandmother, so he held his peace on the subject. "Okay then." He extended his hand and gave a single nod. "It's a deal. We'll work together to get Callie trained if you agree to hold off on any decision about moving Myrna."

Olivia accepted Jake's hand. "All right, but Callie must prove to me that Gammy will be safe living independently."

Jake glanced up at the sun and released a slow and steady breath. Maybe having Olivia along today hadn't been such a bad idea. "I'll bring Callie over after church tomorrow so you can meet her." Once Olivia got firsthand experience with the service a trained dog could provide, she'd feel much more at ease with Myrna staying in Bluebell. At least, that was what he was hoping for. But not just for himself—for Kyle and Kayla. It would devastate them if Myrna moved away.

"Daddy, Daddy! Come quick!"

Jake's eyes shot toward the sound of Kyle's frantic cry. He sprang from the bench and bolted toward Kayla. Arms and legs flailed in all directions as Kayla rolled on the ground with a girl he'd seen in the line earlier.

"Ouch! My hair!" Kayla yelled.

"Kayla! Stop!" Jake reached down to pull his daughter off the other girl, who appeared older and bigger than Kayla.

"Let me go!" Kayla squirmed in Jake's arms.

Another girl who'd been in the line ran to the scene. "Come on, Lisa. Just say you're sorry. We have to go meet Aunt Jane at the concession stand."

"Would either of you care to explain what this is about?" Jake asked as Olivia joined the group.

Neither child said a word.

"I was talking to Jeremy, so I don't know what happened. I came back, and they were rolling around on the ground, pulling hair and stuff." Kyle spoke up.

Jake glanced at his son before addressing the girls. "Lisa, I think I know everyone in town, but I can't say I recall ever seeing you before."

"We're visiting our aunt Jane." Lisa's voice shook.

"Jane McWilliams?"

Lisa nodded and brushed her hair from her face.

"Okay, so do you want to tell me your side of the story?" Jake asked.

Lisa nodded. "We were waiting in line to go on the merry-go-round again. I said her mother was pretty. When I turned around, she jumped on me and punched me."

"Stop saying that!" Kayla lunged toward Lisa. "She's not my mother! She's not my mother!" Kayla wailed and pointed.

"Whoa, hold on." Jake reached for Kayla's arm before she could tackle Lisa once again. Kayla's body was stiff. Jake had never seen her this way. "Kayla, you need to calm down."

Jake turned in the direction Kayla was pointing. Olivia. He should have known. Lisa thought Olivia was Kayla's mother. A lump formed in his throat. He scooped up Kayla. Her torso went limp as she surrendered her tears.

"It's okay, sweetie." Jake stroked the back of Kayla's head.

"It's never going to be okay without my mommy."

"I'm sorry." Lisa looked up at Jake. "I didn't mean to make her cry."

Jake gave an understanding nod. "I know you didn't. Kayla shouldn't have lashed out at you. I'm sorry. I hope you and your sister can forgive her."

Lisa nodded.

"Let's go." Lisa's sister took her sibling's hand, and they walked away.

"I miss my mommy." Kayla's lip quivered as she buried her face into Jake's shoulder. His knees nearly buckled.

Olivia kept her distance to give Kayla space.

Jake hated to disappoint Kyle, but he had to take Kayla home. "I think we better forget the car show."

"But, Daddy!" Kyle whimpered. "You promised."

"I'm sorry, buddy, but your sister is upset. I think it's best if we go home."

"I want to see Miss Myrna." Kayla whimpered.

Kyle kicked his boot into the ground, stirring up a puff of dirt. "It's not fair."

Tension grew in Jake's neck, but he knew what he had to do. Myrna was the only one capable of calming Kayla down.

"Maybe I can stay here and take Kyle to the show," Olivia offered.

Kyle's eyes brightened. "Yes! Please, Daddy!"

Jake considered Olivia's offer.

"Let her stay. I don't want to ride in the car with her," Kayla whispered. Jake looked at Olivia, hoping she hadn't heard Kayla's request. It wasn't Olivia's fault, just like it wasn't Lisa's fault, either. Both were innocent victims of Kayla's grief.

"Are you sure you want to do that? You didn't seem too thrilled about the car show from the start." Jake tried to give Olivia an easy out.

Olivia looked at Kyle and smiled. "Actually, after listening to Kyle, I think we'll have a great time."

Kyle flew toward Olivia and wrapped his arms around her waist. "We'll have fun, Dr. Olivia! I promise!" Kyle turned back to his father. "Can me and Dr. Olivia still have a picnic and see the fireworks?"

How could he disappoint Kyle? Jake glanced at his watch. "It's not quite lunchtime."

"Maybe Kyle and I can walk back to the truck with you. I saw some picnic tables close to where you parked. We can take our sandwiches and hang out for a little while," Olivia suggested.

Kyle grinned. "Don't forget Miss Myrna's cupcakes."

Jake laughed. "I won't, but you might need to skip the fireworks this year, buddy." Having lunch and taking Kyle to the car show for a couple of hours were one thing, but staying for the fireworks would make a long day for Olivia.

"But we always stay and watch. Why do we always have to do what Kayla wants?" Kyle rolled his lower lip and crossed his arms across his chest.

"We can stay for the fireworks. I'd love to see them."

Olivia placed her hand on Kyle's shoulder. "Kyle and I will have a great time."

Kayla buried her head deeper into Jake's shoulder.

"Can we, Daddy?" Kyle pleaded.

The thought of having both of his children upset was more than he could handle. "Okay, I'll come back to pick you up later. Maybe by then Kayla will change her mind and want to watch the fireworks."

"No! I want to stay with Miss Myrna." Kayla stiffened.

"If it's all right with Myrna, I'll come back to catch the fireworks with you two." Watching the incredible light show had always been his wife's favorite way to close a perfect day. Of course, today had been anything but perfect. Given Kayla's feelings toward Olivia, Jake wondered if working with the doctor to train Callie was asking for more trouble.

"Are you sure the pressure cooker is okay, Gammy? Look at it shake. I think it's going to blow its top." Olivia covered her eyes and retreated from the pot. When she was a little girl, her mother had tried to cook in one of these. After her father arrived home from work, the pot blew its lid. Black beans exploded all over the room. A few even stuck to the ceiling. Olivia never saw her father laugh that hard again. A few weeks later, he passed away. She brushed off the reminder that the only two men she'd ever loved had left her with a broken heart.

"The green beans are fine, dear. That's what it's supposed to do." Myrna wiped her hands down the front of her apron. "Did you and Kyle have fun yesterday?"

Spending the day with Kyle had filled her heart with joy. "I don't remember when I've had a better day."

Gammy's eyes shifted to Olivia.

"That makes me happy. You work too much. Life's short. You need to slow down and enjoy the moment. Trust me. It goes fast. I don't want you to have any regrets when you're my age."

Olivia considered her grandmother's words. When she and Mark were first married, Olivia thought they'd have at least two children. In the early years, she couldn't put all the blame on her husband. Olivia was beginning her career. She thought there'd be time for children. But at thirty-six and single again, it felt like time was running out. The one thing she wanted more than anything was to have a family. But how could she trust another man after Mark had revealed he didn't want children after all? "I'll be fine."

"I know Mark changed his mind about having children, but that doesn't mean you don't have other options. Have you considered adoption?"

Olivia had plenty of friends who had adopted children, but they were married. Olivia wanted a family like she'd had before her father died and her mother turned to alcohol. "Unless I changed my schedule, raising a child on my own would be difficult."

"Keep your options open, dear. You could always marry a man who already has children."

Olivia couldn't ignore the twinkle in Gammy's eyes.

"Speaking of, did you enjoy the fireworks? I'm happy Jake joined you and Kyle for the show."

Her grandmother's motives were becoming questionable. "Yes, we had a wonderful time." Olivia had only wished Kayla had been with them.

The timer on the oven beeped. Olivia was thankful for the interruption.

"Can you get the biscuits?"

Olivia grabbed the pot holders and opened the door. She removed the cookie sheet and placed the tray on the trivet. "Since you were asleep when I got home from the car show, I wasn't able to tell you what Jake and I discussed."

"Jake phoned this morning and filled me in on your plans to work together to train Callie. I'm excited to have the dog here full-time. You're going to love her. Over the years, I've met many of the Puppy Raisers. I think this might be what you need."

"What do you mean?"

Myrna removed the lid from the slow cooker. The savory aroma of succulent beef and vegetables mixed in a spicy broth filled the air. "Between working long hours and the stress you were under during the divorce, maybe it's time to reevaluate your life."

"And you think training a puppy is the answer?" Olivia laughed.

"I'll let you come to your own conclusion over the coming weeks." Myrna replaced the lid. "The pot roast is nearly ready." She glanced at her watch. "Jake and the kids should be here any minute."

Olivia's suspicions mounted. "Did you invite Jake and the kids to dinner because of me? If you're trying to play matchmaker with the car show and dinners, it won't work." Olivia needed to put a stop to this. Sure, Jake was gorgeous, and he seemed nice enough, but putting her trust in another man wasn't in her plans right now, or perhaps ever. Her heart couldn't handle more pain. Besides, one of his two children probably wouldn't mind if she dropped off the face of the earth.

"I'm doing no such thing. I've had Jake and the children over for Sunday supper since Laura died."

Olivia's cheeks warmed. "I'm sorry. I didn't mean to be disrespectful. I just need time to myself."

"Don't take too much time alone, dear. Like I said earlier, you have options. You don't want to put it off too long. Raising children takes a lot of energy."

"I can't jump and marry a man because I want children."

"No, but you could keep your heart open to the possibility. My grandmother always said there's a lid for every kettle. You'll find your lid."

"We're here!" Kyle's voice carried through the house.

Olivia turned to the sound of the front door opening. Dogs barked, and toenails skittered on the hardwood floor, rapidly approaching the kitchen.

A loud crash sounded.

"Oops! Sorry, Miss Myrna," Kyle called out. "Callie knocked over your plant stand."

Gammy didn't seem fazed by all the commotion. Olivia questioned if she could handle the dog. She raised her eyebrow at her grandmother. "This is okay with you?"

Myrna turned the setting on the slow cooker to warm and wiped her hands with the dishcloth. "I wouldn't have it any other way. Go grab the dustpan and broom from the pantry. Let's get it cleaned up so we can eat dinner."

Myrna pivoted on her heels and exited the kitchen.

Olivia sprinted from the pantry at the sound of more breaking glass.

Once in the living room, Olivia noticed the toppled plant stand had sent shards of broken porcelain and dirt all over the floor. The Oriental rug was a mess.

"Kids, grab the dogs and take them outside until we get this cleaned up. And put Callie on a leash so she doesn't run off," Jake instructed. "I'll get the other broom from the garage."

Olivia directed her attention to Jake. "Is she always like this?"

"Tank gets her riled up. Like I mentioned yesterday, Callie has a lot to learn."

"Obviously," Olivia mumbled.

"If Callie is going to live here full-time, we'll need to doggy proof the house. That will involve removing easily accessible items from dressers, tables and countertops. You don't want to leave things like shoes, socks, clothing, medications, chemicals, electrical cords or food lying around. If there are rooms where you'd rather Callie didn't enter, then I'd recommend you close the door or put up a baby gate. It's better to be safe than sorry." Jake spun around and headed toward the garage.

Olivia scanned the area. There was potting soil strewn over the floor and a second plant knocked over. "How did that one fall? It's on top of the end table."

Myrna laughed. "When puppies get excited, they like to jump. Like Jake said, if Callie can reach it, then move it."

"Look at this mess." Olivia went to work with the broom.

"You need to loosen up a bit, dear. Real life is messy. Everything doesn't have to be neat and organized," Myrna stated.

Olivia bit her lower lip. Gammy was right. She'd lost her joy when she discovered her father unconscious on the kitchen floor. In the years that followed, she'd buried her grief and replaced it with a determination to carry out her father's legacy to become a prominent doctor. Did her ex-husband believe she'd never make time for children? Was she the reason he'd changed his mind about having kids?

Chapter Three

❧

"Okay, I think we're all done here. Everything seems to be back in its place." Jake swept the last pile of dirt and broken glass onto the dustpan.

Olivia placed her hands on her hips. "What about Gammy's plants? The dogs destroyed them."

"I'll replace them. It's not like this hasn't happened before." Jake chuckled and looked at Myrna. "Right?"

Myrna nodded. "Remember the first time you brought Tank over to the house? He snatched the rib-eye steak from the countertop and ran all over the house. It took us twenty minutes to get our hands on him."

"I remember. He'd hidden under the guest room bed, and by the time we found him, all that was left was bone," Jake recalled. It was the first time since losing his wife that he'd laughed.

"Well, nothing like that will happen to Callie. I'll have her house-trained in no time," Olivia said.

"Yeah, right," Kayla mumbled from the corner of the living room.

Jake focused his attention on his daughter. Her tears from yesterday had faded, but her attitude toward Olivia

remained. "Didn't I tell you last night if you don't have something nice to say, hold your peace?"

"But, Daddy, you said Callie was difficult and training dogs is your job." Kayla frowned at Olivia. "She's probably never been around one. You always say to be a Puppy Raiser, you have to love dogs."

Jake watched Olivia's face flush. When he'd told the kids Olivia would help train Callie, Kyle had been ecstatic. Kayla had run out of the room in tears.

Myrna moved toward Kayla and placed her hand on her shoulder. "You've helped your father with other Puppy Raisers. Maybe you can help Dr. Olivia, Kayla. She doesn't have a dog of her own, but I know she's always loved animals."

"I can help, too!" Kyle raced toward the two women and bounced up and down. "I'm pretty responsible. I put Callie and Tank in the fenced area before we came inside."

Jake smiled. "Good thinking, son."

Kyle straightened his shoulders.

"She doesn't want my help. I don't think she likes kids, either." Kayla shrugged Myrna's hand away.

"Stop being so mean." Kyle frowned at his sister.

Jake approached his daughter. "That's enough, young lady."

"But she's old, and she doesn't even have any kids." Kayla's words rolled quickly off her tongue.

"I don't know where you left your manners today, but I believe you owe Dr. Olivia an apology."

"Sorry." Kayla kept her eyes focused on the floor and crossed her arms.

Olivia nodded.

An awkward silence hung in the air. Outside, the only train that crossed through the town sounded its whistle.

"Let's all take a deep breath and go have our dinner. I've made your favorite, Kayla, pot roast with baby carrots." Myrna motioned her arms toward the kitchen.

"Can we go outside after we eat?" Kyle asked. "I can show Dr. Olivia some stuff that might help her with Callie. Kayla can help, too."

Jake glanced in Olivia's direction. Sadness filled her eyes. Yesterday, Jake could excuse Kayla's actions toward Olivia, since the car show was her mother's favorite family activity. The day had stirred memories for Kayla, but today was a new day and her behavior was inexcusable. He'd discuss her punishment once they got home. Jake was proud of his son for trying to be the peacemaker. "I think that's a great idea."

Myrna stooped in front of Kayla. "You're good with Tank. Maybe you can show Dr. Olivia a few things."

A tiny smile parted Kayla's lips. "Okay."

Jake's shoulders relaxed. He would never have been able to convince Kayla to help Olivia. Myrna had a special touch with his daughter.

"I'll race you to the kitchen, Kay!" Kyle yelled. Kayla accepted his challenge and took off running. Myrna followed the children.

Olivia kept her feet firmly planted.

"Are you ready to eat?" Jake stepped closer and noticed the scent of lavender surrounding Olivia.

"I do like children. I guess I'm just not comfortable around them." Olivia twirled a strand of her hair. "I don't have experience with kids, except in the ER."

"Kayla's behavior toward you is unacceptable. I'll be sure and speak with her when we get home later."

"Don't be too hard on her."

Jake ran his hand across his chin. "Sometimes I feel like I can't do anything right as far as Kayla is concerned. Your grandmother is so good with her. Myrna always knows exactly what to say to make her feel better."

"Is that your subtle way of saying Gammy should remain in Bluebell Canyon?"

"I'd like that, but it wasn't what I meant. Besides, you agreed to postpone any decision until we get Callie trained and I finish more of the home modifications. I have some great ideas that I'd like to run by you."

"I'm sorry. You're right." Olivia nodded. "Thank you for offering to share the improvements you'd like to do on Gammy's home. I appreciate it. Maybe I could help you with them."

"I can always use an extra hand." Jake smiled. "I'm starving. What do you say we head back to the kitchen and get something to eat before the kids devour everything?"

"I'll be there in a minute." Olivia slid her hands into the back pockets of her jeans.

Jake walked away, leaving Olivia alone in the living room. He sent up a silent prayer that going forward everyone would work together for the shared goal of helping Myrna.

Later, with their stomachs full, Jake and Olivia headed outside with the children. Olivia offered to help Myrna, but she insisted cleaning the kitchen was relaxing and something she preferred to do alone.

The late-afternoon sun peeked through the large oak trees lining Myrna's property.

"Come over here." Kyle reached for Olivia's hand and

led her toward the fenced area where Tank relaxed in the shade. Callie circled the property, looking for a way to escape.

Kyle looked up at Olivia and squinted. "The most important thing you need to remember is that puppies are hyper."

Olivia laughed. "Is that so?"

"Tell her, Daddy."

"Kyle's right, but she'll grow out of that stage. Eventually you won't have to worry about her running through the house destroying things like you saw earlier. But for now, we need to keep things out of her reach."

"Has she been potty trained?" Olivia asked.

"She is now. When George rescued Callie, he learned that was the reason she'd ended up in the shelter." Jake never understood people who purchased puppies but didn't have the patience to put in the time required to train them properly. "It's one of the main reasons dogs end up in shelters. People don't want to come home from a long day at work to find their flooring or rugs destroyed, but they won't train their pet."

Olivia glanced between Jake and Kyle. "Isn't having accidents a given for a new puppy?"

"It doesn't have to be if the owner puts in the effort. But it doesn't end after the animal is potty trained. Dogs need exercise, especially service dogs," Jake explained.

"That's not a problem." Olivia shrugged her shoulders. "If Gammy and Callie end up coming home with me, there are several dog parks near my condo in Miami."

Jake laughed.

Olivia directed her gaze at Jake. "What's so funny?"

"Taking Callie out once a day for a walk in the dog park won't cut it. Puppies can go all day long. By night-

fall, they'll still have the same energy they had from the start of the day. In addition, pups must have exposure to a variety of indoor and outdoor sounds, especially if they are to become a service animal."

"Why is that necessary?"

"This is something we cover in camp, but have you ever tried running a vacuum cleaner near a puppy?"

Olivia shook her head.

"Whether a vacuum, a lawn mower or a leaf blower, motorized tools can terrify a puppy and result in a fight-or-flight reaction. It's important they have repeated exposure in order to become accustomed to the noises. In time, the puppy will learn it is safe as long as it has a history of being safe around it."

"I never realized there was so much involved with training a dog."

Jake nodded. "Most people don't." He looked across the yard. "Come here, boy!"

Immediately, Tank was up and running toward Jake. Once at his feet, Jake reached down and scratched the dog behind his ear. "Tank might not be a puppy, but he benefits from outdoor activities like most dogs." Jake pushed his hands into his back pockets.

"I'm fairly active, so I'm sure I won't have any trouble keeping up with Callie," Olivia explained.

Kyle looked up at his father. "I don't think she understands."

Jake shrugged his shoulders. He couldn't say he hadn't warned Olivia. He hoped in time, she'd realize the effort and patience that were necessary to train a puppy. "I'm going to run inside and get their food. It's time for the dogs to have their dinner. Keep your eyes on her, kids."

"Dr. Olivia or Callie?" Kayla questioned.

"Both." Jake winked and jogged inside the house.

"How's it going out there?" Myrna called out over her shoulder as she rinsed the dinner plates.

"I'm afraid Olivia doesn't realize training Callie won't be easy. I know she's a doctor, but I'm not sure she understands the time and energy required to be a Puppy Raiser."

Myrna turned off the faucet and dried her hands on the dish towel. "I think she got a little taste of it earlier," she said with a smile.

"Believe it or not, Callie has settled down a bit since I've gotten her into a routine. She's rowdy when she's first let out of the car, but at least she hasn't gotten her teeth into my wallet again." After Callie had chewed up a one-hundred-dollar bill, Jake learned quickly to keep his wallet in his nightstand drawer.

"I'm happy Olivia wants to be a Puppy Raiser and help with Callie's training at Camp Bow Wow." Myrna smiled.

Jake hoped that after Callie completed her training, Olivia would see firsthand how much Callie could help her grandmother. "So am I, but best of all, she said she will put off deciding on moving you until I have time to finish the modifications to your home and see how things progress with Callie."

"That sounds promising, but don't worry about me leaving Bluebell." Myrna swatted her hand in the air. "That will never happen."

"Daddy!" Kyle raced through the kitchen door.

"What is it? Is Kayla hurt?" Jake's pulse quickened.

Kyle blinked rapidly. "No! It's Callie. Dr. Olivia accidentally put her outside the fence without her leash. Callie took off like a rocket ship."

"Oh, dear." Myrna placed her hand against the side of her face.

"Hurry, Daddy!" Kyle cried out.

"You and your sister stay here and feed Tank. I'll go after Callie. Don't worry. I'll find her." Jake sprinted out the door and right past Olivia.

"Jake, I'm sorry!" Olivia yelled. "Let me help!"

Jake ignored the apology and her offer to help. He had to find Callie. He increased his pace as he neared the steep hill. On the other side were deep woods, and with the cloud cover that had moved in, it would be dark soon. Jake pumped his arms as he neared the top of the hill. If Callie continued into the wooded area, finding her would be impossible.

"Dear, please sit down and have some tea. Jake will find Callie. He knows those woods inside and out."

Olivia continued to pace the wraparound porch. The moment Callie had taken off, guilt had consumed her mind. Jake had warned her about removing Callie's leash. Her eyes scanned the property. The wildflowers covering the fields were quickly fading into the shadows. Olivia shuddered to think what could happen if it got too dark to keep searching for the puppy. "What if he doesn't? I'll never forgive myself if something happens to her."

"Relax. You worry too much. Jake will find her."

Myrna stood up from the rocking chair and picked up the teakettle from the side table. She filled a cup and placed it on a saucer. "Here, drink this. It's chamomile. It will calm your nerves."

Olivia accepted the beverage and sat on the edge of the rocker. A brisk breeze whooshed up the porch steps and caused a shiver to move down her spine. *Callie is too small to be off on her own. What if there are coyotes in the area? Why in the world did I remove the leash knowing Callie isn't trained?*

"Miss Myrna!" Kyle called out as he and Kayla raced through the yard and scaled the steps. Tank trailed behind, secured on a leash. "It's almost dark. Do you think we should take Daddy's truck and look for Callie? He keeps the key under the floor mat." Kyle sank into the empty rocking chair. Tank plopped on the floor beside him.

Olivia didn't have to look in Kayla's direction. She could feel the child's eyes burning into the side of her face. This was all her fault. "That sounds like a good idea. I could drive."

Kayla crossed her arms. "You'll make it worse."

"Kayla! Didn't your father tell you to hold your peace if you don't have something nice to say?" Myrna asked.

"Yeah, Kay. Dr. Olivia can't help it if she doesn't know anything about puppies. She's not a dog doctor. Besides, maybe Daddy should have used the crate from his truck to keep Callie from running loose."

"Isn't that cruel to lock a dog up in a cage?" Olivia asked.

Kayla rolled her eyes.

Myrna motioned for the child. "Come over here and sit with me. I think we all need to relax and take a deep breath. There's no point in us rushing off to help with the search. Your father will be back with Callie any minute. We just have to be patient."

Kayla's shoulders slumped and her lower lip rolled as she crossed the porch. "What if Callie is gone forever?" Kayla climbed on Myrna's lap and nuzzled her face against the woman's shoulder.

Myrna's phone rang. Olivia hoped it was good news.

Following a brief exchange, her grandmother ended the call and slid the phone into the pocket of her apron. "That was Jake."

"Did he find Callie?" the twins asked in unison.

"Yes, and she's fine. So you can stop worrying. Why don't you two run inside and start working on that jigsaw puzzle you dumped on the dining room table? I'll be along to help you in a minute."

All smiles, the children hurried into the house. The screen door closed with a bang.

Olivia released a slow and steady breath. "I'm glad Jake found Callie safe." Despite the good news, her grandmother looked concerned. "What is it? Did you say Callie was okay for the children's sake?"

"No, it's Jake I'm worried about."

"What's wrong?"

Myrna stepped toward the screen door. "I don't want the children to hear. After losing their mother, they're so afraid something will happen to their father—especially Kayla."

Olivia understood. After her father died, she raced home from school each day to ensure her mother was okay, especially after her mother started abusing alcohol. Olivia's heart would pound in her chest as she got closer to the kitchen. Flashes of her father on the floor would replay in her mind. For months leading up to her mother leaving, Olivia refused to go out and play with her friends, afraid that something would happen to her mother.

Myrna pulled the door closed, silencing the laughter echoing through the foyer. "I need you to drive to the Pearsons' ranch and pick up Jake and Callie."

"Of course. I can do that." With the sun setting soon, Olivia assumed it might be too far to walk.

"Jake twisted his ankle. He says it's no big deal, but I think you should check for broken bones. Ronnie can't drive him and Callie back here because the truck he uses to putter around the ranch has a dead battery and his wife took their SUV to visit her ill sister."

"Don't worry. I'll pick them up." Olivia ran inside to grab her car keys.

Ten minutes after Olivia left her grandmother's house, the sun had set as she navigated the vehicle down the winding road. With assistance from the high beam headlights, she spotted a two-story farmhouse with a large wraparound porch up ahead. She often dreamed of a home like this. With children chasing each other around the property while a dog nipped at their heels. Her shoulders slumped at her current reality. Her home in Miami was empty.

Olivia arrived at the end of the driveway and two porch lights turned on. She placed the vehicle into Park. A door slammed while she fumbled with her seat belt. Olivia looked up and spotted Jake.

She exited the car and released a sigh of relief when Jake approached with the puppy nestled in his muscular arms. Her heart pumped a little faster. What was it about a man with a puppy?

"Your grandmother sure is stubborn. I told her I could walk back. I'm sorry to trouble you." Jake lifted his foot and gave it a shake. "It feels fine now."

"You know Gammy. She never takes no for an answer." Olivia looked down. "Are you sure your ankle is okay?"

"Not even a limp." Jake gave a reassuring nod.

"That's good to hear, but you still might want to ice it once you're home."

"Okay, Doc." Jake saluted.

"How's Callie?" Olivia moved toward the animal and scratched her head.

"She's fine, but she'll sleep well tonight. For being so young, she covered a lot of ground." Jake secured the leash around Callie's collar before placing her back on the ground.

"I'm sorry I took Callie off the leash." Olivia gazed at the animal. "If anything had happened to her, I would have never forgiven myself. Please, I hope you'll accept my apology."

Jake nodded. "There's no need to apologize. I should have crated her, so let's forget about it. The important thing is that we work together to get Callie trained, so that she can assist Myrna." Jake looked down at Callie. "Are you ready to go home?"

Callie jumped to her feet and barked.

Jake turned to Olivia. "I think she's hungry. Let's head home."

Olivia took quick, shallow breaths as they headed toward the SUV. Why did the thought of being alone in the car with Jake suddenly make her nervous?

Once inside, they both secured their seat belts. A spicy, masculine scent filled the air. Whatever their disagreements were about moving her grandmother, she couldn't deny the man was easy on the eyes. Way too easy.

Chapter Four

Tuesday afternoon, Olivia squinted against the sun's light as her SUV crested the top of the hill. With the window cracked, she inhaled the crisp air while taking in the picturesque scenery of the Rocky Mountain range, the complete opposite of the views in Miami. The sight of the palm trees that lined the Florida streets had always calmed her nerves, but there was no disputing that the Sunshine State was almost shockingly flat compared to Colorado.

From the back of the car, Callie whined three times and then started to bark nonstop. She obviously wasn't happy to be inside the crate.

"Settle down, Callie," Olivia called out over her shoulder. She pushed away a strand of hair that had escaped her ponytail. The dog wasn't the only one who was nervous. Thinking about spending the afternoon with Jake at Camp Bow Wow had Olivia's nerves rattled all morning. At least there would be other Puppy Raisers in attendance to keep her from being distracted by Jake's rugged good looks. She needed to focus on Callie.

Cruising down the winding dirt road, Olivia slowed

the vehicle to steal a glance at the handwritten map lying on the passenger seat. She chuckled at the map Gammy had drawn for her. It triggered childhood memories of the maps she and her friends drew when they played treasure hunt.

About a mile and a half back, Olivia had made a turn off the main road, but she hadn't yet spotted any houses. According to Gammy, Jake's two younger brothers and business partners, Cody and Logan, lived on the massive plot of land they'd inherited years ago. It was divided into several parcels with five homes. A third brother, Luke, a retired professional bull rider, lived in Virginia with his family, but he maintained a residence on the farm. Jake's father also had a house on the land, but he resided in Denver to be close to his wife, who was in late-stage Alzheimer's. The family had cared for Mrs. Beckett at home, even providing her with a trained companion service dog. But in the end, she needed the professional care of doctors and nurses not available in Bluebell. Their father believed moving her to a nursing home was best for his wife. Jake had a close-knit family, something Olivia always dreamed of for her future. But was Gammy right? Had she allowed her job to consume her to where it may become the only future she could have?

Callie barked twice and released a whimper.

"I know. You're ready to get some exercise." On Sunday, Jake had given Olivia a flight kennel to transport Callie in the car. It was a plastic cage, but smaller than the crate he planned to give her today at Callie's first day at Camp Bow Wow. "We should be at Jake's any minute."

Callie's nails scraped incessantly against the plastic.

Olivia bit her lower lip. "I forgot to let you go to the bathroom before we left the house. Is that it?"

Callie barked.

"Was that a yes?" Olivia laughed.

Another bark echoed inside the vehicle. Olivia eased her foot off the accelerator and hit the brake. "All right, we'll make a quick pit stop, but you'll have to hurry. We don't want to be late for your first day of camp. I have a feeling the instructor doesn't appreciate tardiness."

Olivia stepped from the car and quickly rounded to the back passenger door. The tantalizing aroma of wildflowers decorating the open field along the road scented the air. She reached inside the car and gripped the plastic latch of the kennel. "What in the world?" Callie's wet tongue covered her hands, making it difficult for Olivia to unlock it. "Hang on. I'll have you out in a second."

Finally, the lock released. Olivia opened the sliding door and lifted Callie from the kennel. She squirmed and kicked her hind legs.

"Wait just a second. I need to get your leash," Olivia pleaded as Callie's head butted against her chin.

Callie continued to wiggle. Her sharp toenails pierced Olivia's arms. "Ouch! Settle down, Callie." With one powerful jolt, the animal escaped from Olivia's grasp. She hit the ground and took off running.

"Wait!" Olivia's heart hammered against her chest.

The thought of running after Callie crossed her mind, but the dog had already nearly covered an entire football field. Seizing her on foot would be impossible. Olivia pivoted on her heel and hurried back to the driver's side of the car. Once inside, she pushed the ignition button, fastened her seat belt and peered through the windshield. Between the glaring sunlight and the film on the glass, she struggled to see. Since the dirt road wasn't parallel to the field, the chances of finding Callie by car seemed as hopeless as traveling on foot. How could she face Jake? What would she tell him? In nearly forty-eight hours, she'd lost Callie for the second time. Perspiration peppered her forehead. Olivia jammed her foot on the accelerator, kicking up a cloud of dust. There was no way she could show up at the camp without Callie. What kind of Puppy Raiser lost her dog on the first training day?

"Look, Daddy!" Kyle ran from the inside of the barn and pointed. "It's Callie."

Jake pulled his attention from his iPad and shielded his eyes from the sun. He spotted Callie across the north pasture, racing toward the barn.

"Oh, man. Dr. Olivia let her off the leash again." Kayla rolled her eyes.

Jake wasn't sure what had happened. Olivia had agreed to bring Callie to the camp, but he'd expected they would arrive together.

As Callie approached, the four other puppies enrolled in the camp rose to their hind legs and barked. The Puppy Raisers held tight to their leashes.

Callie ran to Jake and jumped up and down before flopping on the ground at his feet. "How did you get here?" Jake bent over and scooped up the dog. He ran his fingers through Callie's coat. "Run and grab a leash, Kyle."

Kyle sprinted to the barn and returned with the leather strap.

Jake secured Callie's collar and glanced at his watch. "Kayla, why don't you handle Callie so we don't hold up the class?"

"Okay, Daddy." Kayla took the leash and joined the group.

Jake moved inside the center of the orange cones that formed a large circle. He scanned the group and sent up a silent prayer, giving thanks for these dedicated volunteers. "Since we have already been chatting online in the Puppy Raiser group, I won't waste your time with introductions. Thanks for being here. As a Puppy Raiser, your role is critical and the first step your puppy will need if he or she will advance to formal service dog training." Jake turned to the youngest in the group. "Rebecca, this is your third puppy, isn't it?"

Rebecca stepped forward with her golden retriever. "Yes, this is Honey. My other two puppies were Labradors. This is my first golden. Being a Puppy Raiser has been a rewarding experience. It's hard to say goodbye to your puppy once they are ready to train to become a service dog, but knowing I've helped to make a difference in someone's life makes it all worth it."

The group broke into applause. Jake smiled. He was proud of Rebecca. She took her role as a Puppy Raiser seriously, as did most of the volunteers.

"Thank you for sharing with us, Rebecca. That's exactly the reason my brothers and I started this academy. The goal of Camp Bow Wow is to teach each puppy about trust, bravery, basic obedience, socialization and love. These skills will give them the foundation to eventually, with further training, become service dogs if that's your goal. Many enroll in the camp to train their family pet."

Off in the distance, tires crunched along the gravel road. Before Jake saw the vehicle, he knew it was Olivia.

"There's Dr. Olivia's car!" Kyle pointed to the SUV cresting the hill.

"She's driving way too fast!" Kayla yelled.

Jake shot his daughter a look. "Remember what I told you about holding your tongue?"

"But she is!"

The SUV came to a screeching halt, stirring up a cloud of dust. Olivia haphazardly parked her vehicle in the lot next to the barn. She sprang from the car and raced toward the group. "Callie got away from me again." Olivia stopped long enough to catch her breath. "We have to find her!"

Jake moved closer and caught the faint scent of Olivia's perfume. The citrus aroma smelled like freshly cut oranges. He placed his hand gently on her shoulder. "Relax."

"I can't! I got out of the car to let her use the bathroom and she got away from me again. She sprang from my arms before I could put the leash on her." Olivia pushed her hair away from her face. "I've lost her again. Maybe I'm not cut out for this."

"Don't be so hard on yourself. Callie is safe." Jake knew he was wasting his breath. In Olivia's eyes, losing Callie for a second time was unacceptable.

Kyle stepped closer to the adults. "It's okay, Dr. Olivia. Look over there." Kyle grinned and pointed toward Callie, stretched out on the grass, enjoying the warmth of the sun. Kayla had a firm grip on the leash. "Callie is okay."

Olivia ran to the dog and dropped to the ground. She scooped up the animal and snuggled her close against her chest. "I was so worried about you." She kissed the top of Callie's head. "I'm glad you're safe."

Callie returned the affection, licking the side of Olivia's face. It was the first time Jake saw Olivia connect with Callie. This was a good sign. Progress was being made.

Olivia giggled as the dog continued to give her wet kisses. "This won't happen again. I promise." Olivia placed

Callie on the ground and stood to address the class. "I'm sorry if I held everyone up today."

"No harm done." Jake looked out at the group. "Everyone, this is Olivia Hart. She hasn't been a part of our online group, but she'll be joining us. She's my good friend Myrna's granddaughter."

"Hello," the class responded in unison.

Jake clapped his hands. "Is everyone ready to get started?"

"Yes." The group cheered. The outburst caused the dogs to jump to their feet and bark.

"Okay. First, we'll touch a little on your puppy's socialization skills. We want to ensure they become a friendly and confident adult. At home, it's important to introduce your dog to different sounds and to teach them to be okay being alone."

Harry Dearwester, the oldest in the group, raised his hand.

"Yes, Harry. Did you have a question?" Jake asked as the class turned their attention to the portly, gray-haired man.

"Why would we want to teach them how to be alone if they're going to work with people who might have a disability? Shouldn't they learn how to be with other people?" He bent over and patted his eight-week-old retriever, Tex.

"Being comfortable around strangers is a brilliant point, and one I'll touch on in a moment." Jake strolled around the group and eyed each animal. "First, teaching your dog how to remain calm while home alone can help prevent the animal from developing separation anxiety. I can't tell you the number of stories I've heard of dogs becoming destructive when left home alone. Callie is a prime example. Two weeks ago, while the twins were at school, I ran out to the store. Callie appeared to be having a good day, so I let her have the run of the house, rather than crate her."

"Uh-oh," Harry remarked.

"Yes, it was a big mistake. I should have known better. I'll post a couple pictures of the aftermath of tornado Callie on the website."

The group laughed.

"It wasn't a pretty sight, but a prime example of the importance of using a crate early on. That's why purchasing one is at the top of the list of essentials I provided in your welcome packet. I know a couple of you probably already have one. The crate will create a safe place that the dog will want to keep clean. In addition, keeping them in the crate and allowing them out to use the bathroom will teach them that going outside is good."

Jake took notice of Olivia's furrowed brow.

"Is everything okay, Olivia?"

"This just seems so involved. Won't most of this come natural to the dog?"

Being an ER doctor, Olivia knew a lot about human behaviors. Dogs? Not so much. "Has that been your experience so far with Callie?"

Olivia's face reddened. "Not exactly, but I haven't had a lot of time with her."

"These foundational skills need to be taught early on. A good example is the leash."

"I know, I know. Keep it on. I have that rule memorized." Olivia rolled her eyes. "Trust me, I've learned my lesson."

"Do you know why it's so important to keep the animal leashed early in their training?" Jake waited for a response from Olivia, but only received a shrug of her shoulders. "Anyone?" He scanned the group.

A black crow called out overhead.

Jake continued. "It's imperative for your dog to know their limits. Trust me, they will constantly test you. The leash is one way to teach the animal to keep their focus on you, not on their surroundings."

"Like the squirrels running around in the yard," Rebecca called out.

"Exactly. When my dog Tank was a puppy, he tried to go after every squirrel and rabbit that crossed his path. I spent a lot of time chasing him around the ranch. That was a great point, Rebecca," Jake said. "We'll use the leash, along with a dog bed or mat, to teach your puppy the Place command."

George Thielhorn, a middle-aged man who'd recently inherited a nearby ranch from his father, cleared his throat. "What's that?"

By the blank expressions on the faces of the group, except for Rebecca, Jake realized no one was aware of the most essential command to teach your dog. "Some people say it's a magical cue." Jake laughed. "Seriously, though, most new owners think Sit, Stay and Down are the basic training commands to teach. They make the mistake of believing that's all the animal needs to know. But they couldn't be more wrong."

"Yeah, when I first became a Puppy Raiser, my friend told me I was wasting my money on this camp. She said dogs weren't able to learn a bunch of stuff," Rebecca told the group.

"Your friend must not have any experience with service dogs. I'd venture to guess that if she's a dog owner, her dog barks when you ring her doorbell." Jake had a lot of experience with dog owners who believed their animal needed little training.

"She has a Jack Russell. Every time I go to her house, the dog barks nonstop." Rebecca shook her head.

"That's exactly why the Place command is so important. It will teach your dog, in any situation, to settle down onto a dog bed, a blanket or even the dog's favorite place in the house. It will give them a job to do instead of allowing them to choose one for themselves. They might choose jobs like barking at the doorbell, jumping up on people, begging for food at the dinner table, running wild through the house and destroying everything in their path, or jumping out of a car without permission." Jake glanced in Olivia's direction. "These are just a few of the undesirable behaviors of an untrained dog."

George cleared his throat. "If I can teach Maggie this command, I'll be confident with my investment. She's been shredding everything she can get her mouth on. My wife is close to shipping her off to her sister's ranch."

"I don't think that will be necessary, George. Once Maggie learns that Place simply means for her to go to the spot you tell her and stay there until you release her, your wife will be happy. I guarantee it. Maggie will have no choice but to stay. And she'll do it like it's her job, because it is."

"That's a relief," George stated while the rest of the group chatted among themselves.

Olivia remained quiet and attentive. After the way Callie had acted out at Myrna's during Sunday dinner, Jake was reminded that the dog might need extra attention beyond the camp. At the end of the three-week program, he'd have to evaluate Callie's progress. Either way, he'd made a promise to his friend George. He'd train Callie to assist Myrna, and he planned to keep his word.

"Okay, I'd like for you to pair up and switch dogs with a partner so the animals can get used to being handled by a stranger. We'll circle the ring a few times before you take control of your dog, and then we'll practice a few commands. After that, we'll work a little on your dog's attentiveness by using dog treats to give them a lesson on eye contact. You'll find detailed instructions in the packet I provided. You can practice at home."

Two hours later, the animals and their owners were ready to wrap things up for the evening. While the group said their goodbyes and headed toward their cars, Olivia and Callie lingered behind.

Jake moved toward Olivia, where she sat in the grass, scratching behind Callie's ear. "Did you have a question?" Jake knelt and patted the dog.

Olivia lifted her head and fixed her eyes in his direction. Jake's pulse increased when their fingers brushed.

"I wanted to apologize if I sounded like a know-it-all in class. It's pretty obvious I don't know what I'm doing with Callie."

Olivia stood, and Jake followed her lead.

"There's no need to apologize. You're no different from any other first-time Puppy Raiser I've had in previous camps." Jake doubted his words. Olivia was different. He'd never had to teach someone as beautiful as Olivia, which he had to admit made it difficult to keep his attention on the class. "As I mentioned before, training a dog properly takes a great deal of patience, and trial and error. Keep in mind, Callie is adjusting to her new environment now that she's living at Myrna's house. It's also important to remember that every dog is different. Each will have their own strengths and weaknesses, just like humans."

Olivia nodded. "I see that now. I can't believe how naive I've been to think I could train Callie on my own."

"Well, to quote Myrna, you are a brilliant doctor. It's only natural for you to believe training a dog would come easy to you."

Olivia's face flushed, and she playfully swatted Jake's arm. "Oh, please. I'm far from brilliant." She paused and gazed out over the field. "In fact, lately I've wondered if I'm truly cut out to work in the ER."

"From what I've heard from your grandmother, I'd say you're probably just exhausted. She's mentioned your long hours."

"I didn't realize how tired I was until I boarded the plane from Miami. The flight attendant had to wake me when we landed." Olivia laughed.

"It sounds like this trip is exactly what you need. I'm sure your husband is missing you, though." Myrna had told Jake about Olivia's husband and his successful career. Maybe that was why he hadn't traveled with her.

"I don't think so. We're divorced." Olivia's face reddened and she avoided eye contact.

"I'm sorry." Jake reached his hand toward her shoulder, but quickly dropped it to his side. "I didn't realize. Myrna never mentioned it." Jake only remembered her talking highly about Olivia's husband. He couldn't deny he was curious as to the reason for their breakup, but it wasn't his place to ask.

"She only learned about it a couple of days ago. I wanted to tell her in person. It's not something I'm proud of."

"I'm sure it's been difficult for you." Jake had a friend

who'd gone through a divorce last year. It was tough, especially for his children.

"He didn't want kids." Olivia volunteered the information. She shook her head and looked up at the sky.

Unsure how to respond, Jake remained silent.

"I know what you're thinking. That's something we should have discussed before we got married."

"Didn't you?"

"Many times. In fact, we talked about it early in our relationship. He came from a large family. He told me he wanted a lot of children."

"What changed his mind?" After losing his wife, Jake's children were his world.

Olivia released a sigh and shrugged her shoulders. "He decided he didn't want the responsibility or expense."

Olivia wiped away a stray tear.

"After he told me, he filed for divorce. It all happened so fast, but in retrospect, I wonder if there were signs I had missed. I guess it doesn't matter now. Having kids has been a lifelong dream for me. Maybe he thought he was doing me a favor?"

"You should have children if it's what you want. I couldn't imagine my world without Kyle and Kayla."

A comfortable silence passed before Kyle approached. "Can we take Tank and Callie for a walk?"

Jake glanced at his watch. "I don't think so. You've got math homework to finish before dinner."

"Oh, man." Kyle kicked his tennis shoe into the ground. A cloud of dust erupted.

Jake looked at Olivia. "Math isn't his strongest subject."

"I'm pretty good with it. Maybe I can help," Olivia offered, twisting a strand of her hair.

"That would be awesome!" Kyle bounced on his toes.

"That's kind of you to offer, but I'm sure you have more important things to do."

Olivia shook her head. "Actually, Gammy is having dinner with a friend from church this evening, so I'm on my own."

"Maybe Dr. Olivia can stay and eat with us! Can she, Daddy?"

Jake couldn't help but notice the smile that parted Olivia's lips. Was she open to an invitation to have dinner with his family? Perhaps if she got to know the children better, Olivia might have a more difficult time uprooting her grandmother and taking her away from people who loved her, too. It was worth a try. "We'd love for you to join us. We planned to make homemade pizza, so there will be plenty."

Kayla remained silent. She obviously wasn't as enthused as her brother.

Olivia tilted her head and tucked a strand of hair behind her ear. "I'd love to."

Jake fought to temper the thrill of spending an evening with Olivia and his children. Knowing now she was single, he had to take a deep breath to wrangle his emotions under control. It wouldn't be wise to go down that road with Olivia. She was only here temporarily. Besides, he was all too familiar with the pain of losing someone you loved. He couldn't take that risk a second time.

Chapter Five

"Do you want me to show you how to roll out the dough, Dr. Olivia?" Kyle offered with a smile. "I had to practice, but I'm pretty good at it now."

An hour after agreeing to come to dinner at Jake's house, Olivia wiped her flour-covered brow with the back of her hand. She always loved to bake, but her ex-husband did most of the cooking, including making pizza from scratch. He considered himself a master chef. Olivia had loved the conversations they shared while he cooked at the beginning of their marriage. She'd sit on the island stool and watch Mark slice and dice. He had the remarkable skill of turning simple ingredients into a mouthwatering meal. But when her schedule at the hospital consumed more of her time, he spent less time in the kitchen and more time at his office.

Olivia took in the spacious kitchen. Apart from the ingredients and bowls strewn across the quartz counter-top, the room was immaculate. Except for the kids' drawings on display, the stainless steel appliances sparkled. Olivia would give anything to one day be able to cover her own refrigerator with drawings her children created.

She returned her attention to the task at hand. "This is the most stubborn stuff I've ever seen. I push it forward and it pulls right back." She placed the rolling pin on the counter and kneaded her fingers into the cool dough while appreciating her local pizza shop back home.

Jake laughed and moved toward the roll of paper towels next to the sink. He turned on the faucet and ran the towel twice under the water. While Olivia continued to struggle, he reached across the island. "Here, let me get that." He brushed the dampened paper towel across her forehead. "You had a little flour up there." He pointed to her brow.

His gentle touch ignited warmth in Olivia's cheeks. A moment of awkward silence filled the room.

"Thank you. I guess my secret is out."

"What's that?" Jake asked.

"That I have the local pizza place back home on speed dial."

Jake grinned. "I didn't want to say anything, but that dough has had you tangled up for quite a while. Don't be so hard on yourself. I probably should have kept the dough at room temperature for a while longer. Would you like a hand?"

Olivia pulled away and rotated her palms face up. "Yours are probably cleaner than mine." Sticky clumps of dough clung to her fingertips.

Kyle clattered around in a nearby drawer and pulled out another sparkling rolling pin. "My mommy taught me and Daddy all the secrets to make a pizza. It's pretty easy once you get the hang of it."

Callie and Tank both barked in the backyard.

"I thought Kayla was going to feed the dogs?" Jake looked down at Kyle.

"She said she was." Kyle shrugged his shoulder.

The barking continued, but this time, it was only Callie. Olivia walked to the sink, rinsed her hands and peered out the window above the faucet. Tank was curled up underneath the weeping willow while Callie ran circles around the yard. Kayla was nowhere in sight. "Do you mind if I go check on Callie?" She reached for the hand towel and then turned to Jake.

"Do you want me to go with you?" Kyle volunteered. His eyelashes fluttered.

Olivia smiled. Kyle was such a thoughtful little boy. Thoughts swirled in her mind. He was exactly the type of child she dreamed of having one day. "Maybe you should stay here and help your daddy with the pizza. The two of you are much better at handling the dough than I am."

"Okay, but what toppings do you want? I hope not those fishy things." Kyle crinkled his nose.

Olivia knelt in front of Kyle. "No way. I love cheese. In fact, I've never met a cheese I didn't like."

The corners of Kyle's mouth tilted up into a smile. "Me too!" He jumped up and down.

"What about the pepperoni lovers over here?" Jake waved his arms.

Kyle rolled his eyes. "My daddy and Kayla love pepperoni."

Olivia stood and gazed down at Kyle. "Let me go outside and get Callie settled. I'll ask Kayla if she wants to help. The two pepperoni fans can make their pizza and we'll make ours. How does that sound?"

"Awesome! After dinner, can we do the jigsaw puzzle in the dining room? It's got tons of cool farm animals." Kyle's smile lit up his face.

Jake placed his hand on his son's shoulder. "That will have to wait. Remember, you have math homework to do."

Kyle's smile faded, but quickly returned when he looked up at Olivia. "But you're going to help me, right?"

"Of course. Earlier, I said I would help you. I always keep my word." Olivia understood the importance of keeping her word, especially to a child. After her father died and her mother began to abuse alcohol, broken promises were ubiquitous.

"Some grown-ups don't, so I was just checking." Kyle returned his focus back to the dough. "I won't touch it until you come back. Daddy told me that Mommy always said don't work the dough too much because it will fight back."

"I think she was right. I'll be back." Olivia headed to the back door.

Outside, Olivia's steps slowed. She admired the bright yellows and reds of the snapdragons lining the backside of the privacy fence. Their sweet fragrance drifted through the late-spring air. Unable to recall the last time she'd slowed long enough to notice flowers, she wondered when the season had changed. Living in Miami was a never-ending race from the moment her feet hit the floor each morning. As she studied the flower bed, she wondered if Jake's wife had created the garden or if the family had planted the flowers together. The latter was a beautiful image. Something she'd often dreamed of doing one day with her family.

Callie raced toward Olivia, pulling her mind back to the moment. She reached down and pulled the dog into her arms. "Hey, girl. What's got you so riled up?" Callie licked the side of her face. "You want some attention? Is that it?"

Olivia scanned the yard, but there was no sign of Kayla. A hint of a breeze cooled her face. On the opposite side of the grounds, she spied a small house with light pink shutters and a lime-green roof. It looked like the playhouse her best friend had when they were in grade school. Kayla had to be inside.

With Callie still in her arms, Olivia advanced across the grass, careful not to frighten the child if she was inside. The door to the house was ajar. Olivia peeked through the crack. White twinkle lights lined the ceiling. Her heart squeezed at the sight of Kayla sitting on the floor with a picture frame in her hands and tears racing down her cheeks.

Olivia's first instinct was to retreat. Go back into the house and pretend she hadn't seen Kayla. But how could she? Kayla was obviously upset. If Olivia entered the house uninvited, she could make matters worse. Kayla had made her feelings toward her apparent.

Olivia contemplated her next move. During her career, she'd treated plenty of children in the ER. What if she couldn't help Kayla? But what if she could? She straightened her shoulders, raised her hand and gently knocked on the pink wooden door. "Kayla, may I come inside?"

A bumblebee buzzed past while Olivia waited for an answer that never came. She took a deep breath, reached out and tightened her grip on the doorknob. She opened the door and stepped inside. To her surprise, despite the small outer appearance of the house, once inside Olivia didn't have to hunch or lower her head. It was spacious enough for two people. "Are you okay, sweetie?" Olivia froze. With closer proximity, she could see the picture of a strikingly beautiful pregnant woman contained inside the frame. The woman had brown hair that cascaded well past her shoulders.

Tears streamed down Kayla's face.

Olivia took a deep breath, trying to compose herself. Her first instinct was to drop to the ground and wrap her arms around Kayla. She'd tell her that the pain wouldn't last forever, but Olivia knew that wouldn't be the truth. The ache of losing her father still clung to her like a weighted vest. Losing a parent was something a child should never have to experience, but the stark reality was she and Kayla shared the same heartache. Olivia remained quiet, allowing Kayla time to respond to her uninvited guest.

Callie wiggled and whimpered in Olivia's arms. She placed her down and Callie's toenails scratched the wooden floor as she ran to Kayla. The dog pounced on her lap and licked her hands that were still clutching the frame.

Next, Callie slid her tongue along the child's face. A slight giggle erupted from Kayla's lips.

"Okay, Callie." Olivia patted her hand against her leg to get the dog's attention. "That's enough."

"She hasn't learned her place yet," Kayla whispered.

Olivia stared at Kayla for a moment before realizing what she was referring to. "You're right. Once she learns her place, when I put her on the ground, she'll stay, right?"

Kayla nodded and wiped her cheek. "Yeah."

Olivia knelt to face Kayla. "Is it okay if I sit with you?"

Kayla gave a slight shoulder shrug. Olivia took it as a yes.

Positioned on the floor, Olivia pulled her knees against her chest, looked around the room and sighed. "When I was your age, my friend had a clubhouse just like this, except it didn't have electricity. I always wanted one of my own."

Callie finally settled down on the floor and rested her head against Kayla's leg.

"My daddy built it for me." Kayla scratched the top of Callie's head.

"That was nice of him." Olivia took in the space. She admired the pink lace curtains covering the two windows. A table with two chairs sat on top of a thick pink throw rug. Kayla was certainly daddy's little girl. "It feels so cozy."

Kayla looked down at the photograph and ran her fingers across the glass. "He made it after my mommy died."

At a loss for words, Olivia remained silent.

"He thought I might want it to get away from the boys in the house." Kayla kept her eyes fixed on the photo. "But I think he didn't want to think about Mommy."

A lump formed in Olivia's throat. It was a wise observation for a six-year-old. Olivia could remember her mother responding the same way after losing her husband. The day after the funeral, Olivia's mother decided she wanted to repaint the interior walls of the entire house. Day after day, her mother went nonstop, never sleeping or taking time to eat, which meant she didn't prepare any meals. Olivia ate cereal for breakfast, lunch and dinner until the milk ran out. Then she ate the cereal dry. It wasn't until Gammy and Pops moved in that she finally had some normalcy.

"Do you mind?" Olivia reached for the photograph.

Kayla clung to the frame for a moment and then finally let go. She handed it to Olivia. Her eyes never left the photograph.

"Your mother was beautiful." Olivia studied the woman who looked so much like her children. Her brown eyes sparkled with glints of gold. Her skin was like that of a porcelain doll. "What's the best thing you remember about her?"

Kayla's eyes widened. She bit her lower lip and shook her head.

Olivia passed the picture back to Kayla. "You know, it's okay to talk about your mommy."

Her brow crinkled. "It is?"

"Yes, that's how we can hold tight to the memories. I know that's what your mommy would want."

"Every time I try to tell a story about her, my daddy and Kyle talk about something else. Kyle says it hurts Daddy too much. He says we shouldn't mention Mommy. But I'm afraid if I don't, I'm going to forget her."

Olivia gazed around the space before meeting Kayla's eyes. "Well, right now it's just me and you. I'd love to hear a story about your mommy."

"Really?"

Olivia nodded.

Kayla inched closer to Olivia and smiled. "My mommy loved snow. We used to make giant snowmen in front of the house and dress them in Daddy's clothes." She giggled.

Olivia pictured the scene in her mind and her heart warmed. "That sounds like fun."

"Yeah. She made everything fun. After, we'd come inside and have cocoa and warm brownies with strawberry Jell-O."

"Tell me more," Olivia encouraged Kayla.

"Before school, on days when it was cold, my mommy would put my coat, hat and gloves over the heat vent on the kitchen floor. Everything was warm and toasty when I got ready to catch the bus."

"I'm sure it felt nice." It sounded like something Olivia's father would have done for her. He was always doting on her.

Kayla looked up with tears in her eyes. "I really miss her."

For a second, Olivia hesitated, but when Kayla leaned into her arms, Olivia provided an embrace. She stroked the back of Kayla's head and held her tight. Her hair smelled like sweet honeysuckle. "I know you do, sweetie."

"It's not fair. All my friends have mommies. They get to do fun stuff together like me and my mommy used to do."

"I'm sure that's hard." Olivia kissed the top of her head.

Kayla pulled back and looked up. "I'm sorry I was mean to you when you lost Callie." Kayla blinked several times.

Olivia laughed. "You were just being protective."

"My daddy was right."

"About what?"

"He says sometimes my mouth speaks before my head has time to think."

"I used to do the same when I was your age." Olivia recalled many times that her mouth got her into trouble. "You know, you and I have a lot in common."

"Like what? I'm not as pretty as you. I'd like to be a doctor one day, but I'm not smart like you."

Kayla's lack of confidence was unsettling. "You're a beautiful young lady. Don't compare yourself to anyone else. God made you exactly how He wanted you to be. Did you know there is no other person in the world with the same fingerprints as you?"

Kayla looked down and examined her fingers. "Really? That's cool."

"I hope you'll always remember that you can do anything you put your mind to. If you want to be a doctor, then work hard in school and you'll reach your goal." Olivia placed her hand underneath Kayla's chin, tipping it upward. "Sweetie, don't let anyone steal your dreams."

Kayla nodded. "Okay. I promise." She bit her lower lip. "So, what do we have in common?"

Outside, a woodpecker drilled the side of the clubhouse as daylight faded.

"When I was a little older than you are right now, my daddy died."

"He did?" Her brow crinkled. "I'm really sorry."

"Thank you." The years had passed, but the pain was like a wound that kept getting bumped and never healed. If Olivia closed her eyes, she could picture her father lying on the kitchen floor. She had opened her mouth to scream, but there was no sound. Dropping to the floor, she'd rested her head against her father's chest and cried. "The kids at school never seemed to understand. Sure, they were nice and apologetic at first, but as time passed, they seemed to forget about it, but I never could."

Kayla's head quickly bobbed up and down. "That's exactly how I feel."

"It's important to remember that your friends aren't doing it on purpose. They've just never been in your shoes. It's like being in a private club. Only the members truly know what's going on."

Olivia wasn't sure if this made sense to Kayla. Even as an adult, it was difficult for her to understand why God would allow a child to lose a parent. She thought of Jake and his loss. How did anyone move past such a heartbreaking event?

Kayla pushed her hair away from her face. "I sure wish I wasn't a member of this club. I don't like to feel this way."

"Even though it doesn't seem like it, you can always talk to your daddy or Kyle." After Olivia's father passed, without siblings, it wasn't until Gammy came to live with them that Olivia had someone to reminisce with about her mother.

"But I don't want to make my daddy sad. I can see the look on his face when I mention Mommy. And Kyle seems like he's already forgotten about her."

"People grieve a loss in different ways, sweetie. It might be too painful for your father and brother to talk about her."

"But I'm afraid we're going to all forget. I always feel better after I talk about her. Sometimes I even tell my stuffed animals stories about her."

"I did the same thing." Olivia paused. "I have an idea. Maybe while I'm here, you can talk to me about your mommy and I'll talk to you about my father. Does that sound like a good idea?"

Kayla lunged forward and wrapped her arms around Olivia's neck. Warmth surged through Olivia's body. She'd never held a child in this way. It felt good—too good. Getting attached wasn't part of her plan. She was here to help her gammy and convince her she'd be better off in Florida. Olivia would never be happy living in a small town. Yet the feeling she had with Kayla in her arms seemed to bring her more happiness than she'd felt in years.

Jake rubbed his eyes and did a double take. Were his eyes playing tricks on him? He blinked three times and once again looked through the kitchen window. He wasn't mistaken. Olivia and Kayla were walking through the backyard holding hands. After Olivia's arrival, Kayla avoided interaction with her, but now they looked like best friends. Kayla and Olivia becoming buddies wasn't good. Kayla's heart could break if this new friendship continued to blossom. Olivia's time in Bluebell was temporary.

"Wash your hands, sweetie," Olivia instructed Kayla as they stepped into the kitchen.

"Okay." Without hesitation, Kayla skipped to the sink, humming a tune.

"Do you want to help me make our pizza?" Jake asked Kayla as he drizzled olive oil on the dough.

Kyle glanced up from the counter. "Yeah, Kay. You help Daddy. Me and Dr. Olivia are making this pizza." He motioned with his hand across the ingredients. "See all the extra cheese? This is ours."

"I want to work with Dr. Olivia," Kayla said. "After dinner, she's going to help me with my book report."

It wasn't his imagination. Something had occurred outside between Olivia and Kayla. But what?

"I thought Dr. Olivia was going to help me with my math after?" Kyle kicked his shoe against the wood floor.

Jake and Olivia looked at each other. Her brow arched while she appeared to wait for him to resolve the dispute.

"Dr. Olivia offered to help your brother with his math first. You know he's been struggling."

Olivia cleared her throat. "Maybe, if it's okay with you, I can help both of them."

"That's kind of you to offer to help Kayla too, but I'm sure you'll want to get home after we have our pizza." Jake assumed Olivia was being nice, so he offered a way out.

"I'd love to help. I'd just be going home to an empty house. Gammy said not to expect her until at least ten o'clock." Olivia pinched a mound of cheese and sprinkled it over the pizza. "I offered to drive her, but she said she'd be fine. With her poor vision, I worry about her being on the road after dark, so it might be best for me to stay and keep myself busy. I'll just sit up worrying otherwise."

Jake nodded. "She can be as stubborn as a rusty bolt."

Olivia chuckled. "I think you're right. She probably shouldn't be driving day or night. I need to find out when she last had her license renewed."

Jake agreed. He also worried about Myrna being out on the road, particularly at night. But taking away someone's driving privileges was a sensitive topic. It would be best for a medical professional or someone at the DMV to handle it. "I believe Myrna renewed last summer, but it appears her eyes have deteriorated since then."

"Quit touching the dough, Kyle. You're going to ruin it." Kayla interrupted the adults, bringing them back to the task at hand.

"All right, I think it's time to get these pizzas into the oven. Kyle, do you want to help me with the pepperoni? We don't want to keep Dr. Olivia out too late."

Kyle jumped off the step stool and sped to his father's side. He snatched a piece of pepperoni and popped it into his mouth.

"I said help, not eat." Jake ruffled the top of his son's hair.

Kyle giggled, and the oven beeped.

"Ours is ready to go in," Olivia announced.

"Great. The pot holders are in the top drawer to the right of the oven." Jake placed the last sprinkle of garlic powder over the pizza.

Olivia's eyes popped as she peered inside the oversize oven. "The oven is huge. We can put the pizzas side by side."

"Daddy bought the oven for Mommy. She loved to cook. He said one Thanksgiving she baked three turkeys at once for the homeless shelter in Denver." Kayla spoke with pride.

Kyle nudged his sister in the arm.

"What?" Kayla flinched.

"It makes Daddy sad when we talk about Mommy."

"But Dr. Olivia told me it's okay. She said it's good to remember. It's what Mommy would want." Kayla shot a look in Olivia's direction.

Olivia's eyes shifted to Jake.

Jake cleared his throat. He couldn't miss the redness in Olivia's face. "Dr. Olivia is right. We should never forget your mommy."

"Then how come you don't like us to talk about her?" Kayla wrapped her arms around her stomach.

It was true. When his children or someone from town mentioned Laura, he did his best to change the subject. Despite the advice from Pastor Kidd, Jake struggled to keep her memory alive. It was too painful. It wasn't fair to Kayla and Kyle. He prayed about it every morning. "I believed not talking about your mommy protected you, but really, I wasn't giving you the opportunity to grieve the loss of your mother in your own way. It was easier for me not to talk about what had happened. I've been wrong. I'm sorry."

Kayla moved toward Jake and wrapped her arms around his waist. "It's okay, Daddy. I don't want you to be sad. When I was outside, I told Dr. Olivia stories about Mommy, and it made me feel good. Maybe you should try it, too."

Jake's heart warmed. "I think that's the best idea I've heard in a long time."

Kayla's smile lit up her face. "You do?"

"Yes. In fact, I think I have the perfect way to share your stories about your mother."

Kyle and Kayla moved closer to Jake. Their eyes grew wide. "How?" they both asked.

"Maybe each night before we say our bedtime prayers, you can take turns sharing something you remember about your mommy."

"We can talk about Mommy?" Kayla questioned as though she were asking for the impossible.

Jake nodded. "If you'd like, we can start tonight."

"Yes!" Kyle did a fist pump. "I can't wait to go to bed!"

The adults laughed.

"But what about you, Daddy?"

Jake looked down at Kayla.

"You knew Mommy a lot longer than we did. You must have tons of stories. Can you share, too?"

Jake's heart squeezed. *God, give me the strength.* "There's nothing I'd rather do more." He'd known Laura since college, so there'd be an endless amount of stories to share with Kyle and Kayla. He'd do his best to remember every detail about his wife. In his desire to protect his children, he'd actually done more harm than good. But thanks to Olivia, that was all about to change. He glanced in her direction and she smiled. A twinge of excitement coursed through him, but he quickly pushed it away. He had to remain loyal to Laura's memory.

Chapter Six

Late Friday afternoon the sun dipped behind the Rockies, prompting Olivia to check her watch for the third time in twenty minutes.

"Come, Callie." She clapped her hands three times, and the puppy obeyed the command. "Good girl. Let's head inside and get your dinner." Since returning from Camp Bow Wow, Olivia had worked on the homework Jake had assigned at the end of their session. Callie was making good progress, but according to Jake, she still had a lot to learn. Olivia couldn't deny the idea of spending more time with Jake was appealing. He was easy on the eyes, but she needed to remind herself this trip was for Gammy, not to fall for a handsome service dog trainer and his adorable children.

Noting the time, Olivia shivered. It would be dark soon, but Gammy was still out. When Olivia had arrived home from camp, a scribbled note was on the kitchen table. Gammy had taken Ruth Westerly for a medical procedure after her ride had fallen through. Olivia admired her grandmother's generous heart, but the idea of her driving home in the dark didn't sit well. She didn't have a phone number to call Ruth to check if Gammy had dropped her off. She'd have to try her grandmother's cell for the second time.

Olivia stepped inside the laundry room. Callie jumped up and pawed at Olivia's feet. "I know you're hungry. Just give me a minute." Callie released a bark, followed by a whimper.

Olivia removed the sealed canister of dry food from the shelf and poured it into Callie's dish. The ravenous pup pushed her face into the bowl and gulped the meal. "I guess Jake was right when he said puppies have enormous appetites. All that exercise at camp made you hungry. Didn't it, girl?" Olivia scratched the top of the animal's head. "Eat your dinner. I'm going to fix something for me and Gammy. I'm starving, too."

Outside, thunder rumbled in the distance. Olivia scanned the contents of the refrigerator as she rubbed the back of her neck. A flash of lightning filled the kitchen at the same time as her phone sounded an alarm. Olivia dropped the head of lettuce she'd pulled from the shelf.

A tornado watch has been issued in your area.

What? Living in Florida, Olivia was used to the occasional tornado warning, but even living in Colorado as a child, she'd never realized the state experienced these weather patterns, too. Or maybe she didn't pay much attention to the weather as a child. Her heart hammered against her chest. She snatched the phone off the countertop to check the radar. Two quick taps on the screen caused her hands to shake. A huge red blob covered the map. Severe weather was heading toward Denver and it appeared to be moving toward Bluebell Canyon.

Olivia quickly pulled up her contact list and smashed her finger on Gammy's name. Again, the call went straight to voice mail, but this time Olivia left a message. "Gammy, please call me as soon as you hear this. There's a severe storm coming. Wherever you are, wait for me. I can come pick you up. Please call me." She pressed End and slipped the device into her back pocket. An engine rumbled outside. Was Gammy finally home? She raced to the front window and peeked through the slats of the plantation shutters. A delivery truck was in the driveway. A man stepped from the vehicle and climbed the front steps carrying a large box. Before he rang the bell, Olivia flung open the door to greet him.

"I have a package for Mrs. Hart." He peeked around Olivia's shoulder. "Is she home?"

Olivia accepted the delivery. "Thank you." She turned and placed the box on the chair inside the foyer. "No, she's not here right now, but I'll be sure she gets the package."

"I wanted to thank her for the cookies she baked for me last week. They were the best I've ever had. She's okay, isn't she?"

The young man's genuine concern touched Olivia. This would only happen in a small town like Bluebell. "She's fine, thank you. She drove a friend to a medical appointment."

"It must be Mrs. Westerly. She had her colonoscopy scheduled for today. I would have driven her, but I couldn't get the time off from work." His brow knit. "I hope Mrs. Hart gets home before the storm hits. The radio says it could be a big one."

The pulse in Olivia's neck fluttered. "I hope so, too. I'll let her know you enjoyed the cookies." Olivia glanced at the name tag pinned to his company shirt.

"You be safe too, Jeff."

Olivia closed the door and considered her next move. Jake. He would have a phone number for Ruth. Actually, she should have asked Jeff. He probably had the entire town on his phone.

Olivia slipped her phone from her pocket and intently scrolled her contact list. When Jake's number appeared, she tapped to call. Her fingers tightened against the phone. He answered on the first ring.

"Hey, Olivia. What's up?"

"I'm sorry to bother you. It's Gammy." Her voice shook. "She's not home and there's a storm coming. I'm worried."

"I'll be right over."

The last thing Olivia wanted to do was disrupt his evening with the children, especially if it was a false alarm and her grandmother walked through the door any minute. "I don't want to trouble you. I wanted to know if you had a telephone number for Ruth Westerly?" Olivia explained the situation.

"I'll call Ruth and call you back." Jake quickly ended the call.

Olivia paced the floor and prayed her grandmother was safe. Maybe it was only a poor cell signal. But something gnawed at her, telling her otherwise.

Olivia's phone gave a half ring before she answered Jake's call. "Did you reach Ruth?"

"There was no answer. But I'm not surprised. Ruth lives alone. Her husband passed away a few years ago."

Olivia sensed the concerned tone in Jake's voice. "What should I do? I don't have a good feeling about this. Gammy should be home by now. The weather report mentioned tornadoes."

"Stay put. I'll be right over." Jake hung up.

Despite the situation, knowing Jake was coming over instilled a sense of comfort in Olivia. Something she hadn't felt since before the dissolution of her marriage.

Less than fifteen minutes later, she heard the crunching of tires on gravel out front.

Callie jumped to attention and raced to the door. Olivia followed.

Before Jake knocked, Olivia flung it open.

"It's raining," he announced as he wiped his feet on the welcome mat and stepped inside.

"Where are the children?" Olivia asked.

"I dropped them off at my brother's house. I didn't want them to worry when it turns out to be nothing."

Olivia admired Jake. He always put his children first and would do whatever he could to protect them. "Good thinking."

"You mentioned a medical appointment. Do you know what time?"

Olivia nodded. "Her note said it was three o'clock."

Jake rubbed his hand across his chin. "Anything else?"

"No."

Jake walked across the floor, then pivoted. "I can try to call Dr. Dickerson. He's the town doctor. Most likely, he referred Ruth to a doctor in Denver, or perhaps he set up the medical procedure."

"That's a great idea."

"Don't get too excited. I'm not sure how much Dr. Dickerson can share, given the confidentiality laws." Jake pulled his phone from his back pocket and tapped the screen.

Olivia's shoulders sank. Jake was right. She should have asked Jeff the delivery boy since he knew about Ruth's appointment.

Jake looked up from his device. "I'm not getting a good signal in here—could be the storm. Do you mind if I go out on the porch to make the call?"

Heavy rain pelted the roof. Water overflowed from the gutter.

"Of course not." Olivia appreciated Jake asking permission. She wondered if Jake realized how much she loved her grandmother. Her thoughts quickly returned to Gammy being out on the road in these treacherous conditions. Why didn't she push the issue more? Olivia should have tried harder to convince her grandmother that with her vision deteriorating, it was too dangerous to drive—particularly after dark.

Jake stepped back inside the house. His face was wet from the driving rain.

"Did you find out anything about the doctor? We need to find her!"

Jake approached and gently placed his hands on her upper arms. His stormy eyes connected with hers, creating another wave of nausea, along with a swarm of butterflies. "Please, try to calm down. Dr. Dickerson said he referred Ruth to a gastrointestinal doctor in Denver. Ruth had told him her appointment was at one. He's calling the doctor's office now to find out what time they left his office. He said he'd call right back."

Olivia inhaled a deep breath and released it.

"If Ruth's procedure was on time, they should have been on the road long before four o'clock." Jake glanced at his watch. "It's after six now. They should be home any minute."

Outside, a gust of wind rattled the shutters before tapping sounded against the windows.

Jake turned at the noise. "That sounds like hail." He

walked toward the window and opened the plantation shutter. "I think small pellets are falling. It looks like the winds are picking up, too. Make sure you have a full charge on your phone in case we lose power."

Olivia hurried into the kitchen and retrieved her charger from her purse. She plugged the phone into the outlet, keeping the phone turned on so she wouldn't miss a call. A chill raced up her spine thinking about Gammy in the storm.

Jake stepped into the kitchen and his cell phone rang. He answered on the first ring. Olivia heard a voice on the other end. Thankfully the connection was better. She busied her hands by dumping the cold pot of coffee from earlier in the day into the sink and sent up a silent prayer for her grandmother.

Jake pocketed his cell and approached Olivia.

"What did Dr. Dickerson say?"

"It looks like we'll be making a road trip. Dr. Dickerson spoke with the physician who performed the colonoscopy. He'd had an earlier cancellation, so he actually finished up with Ruth around three fifteen."

The sudden turn of events was unsettling. She had hoped her grandmother's absence was because of the doctor running behind schedule, but Jake just confirmed that the opposite was true. Olivia ran her fingers through her hair. "Then why hasn't Gammy dropped off Ruth? Something isn't right." A sudden beeping from her phone made her jump.

A severe thunderstorm warning has been issued in your area.

Olivia read the message and shuddered.

"I'm going to put a call in to my friend. He's a state

trooper in Denver. Maybe he can tell us of any accident reported." Jake drew his phone from his pocket.

Olivia could barely breathe. If anything happened to Gammy, she would be all alone in the world. "We have to go find her," Olivia pleaded with Jake while he searched his device for his friend's number.

She paced the kitchen floor. Callie nipped at her heels while Jake spoke on the phone.

Minutes later, he ended the call and approached Olivia.

"Has he heard of any accidents?" Olivia wrapped her arms tight around her waist.

Jake's expression was solemn. "My buddy Nick isn't on duty, but I spoke with Dispatch. They don't have any accident reported along the route Myrna would have been traveling."

Olivia dropped her arms to her sides and grabbed her purse off the counter. She unplugged her phone from the charger and tossed it inside her bag. "I need to go find her."

Callie barked twice.

"I can't sit here waiting." She bit her lower lip. The tears she'd fought to hold back broke free and streamed down her cheeks. "My grandmother is all I have."

Jake moved closer and pulled her into his arms. "Please don't cry. She'll be okay. We'll find her. I promise."

For a moment, Olivia found comfort in Jake's warm embrace, but that was a dangerous place to be. She quickly pulled away, turned toward the window and the pounding rain, and shivered. "Let's go find my gammy."

Minutes later, they were on the road. Jake gripped the steering wheel and willed the windshield wipers to move faster. The heavy rain was blinding. The car's high beams did little to assist Jake with the poor visibility.

Despite his cautious speed, he suddenly lost control of the car.

With the treacherous weather, Jake would have preferred to make this trip alone, but he couldn't blame Olivia for wanting to help with the search. She loved her grandmother and was concerned for her safety.

Olivia leaned forward with a paper towel in hand, frantically wiping the fog that the defroster failed to eliminate. "Can you see?" Her voice shook as she leaned closer to him.

Their shoulders brushed, providing a moment of comfort despite the weather conditions. Jake shook off the feeling. He needed to keep his focus off Olivia and on the road. This was another reason he'd wanted to search for Myrna on his own. Lately, Olivia's presence made him feel like a nervous schoolboy.

"Do you think it would be better if we use the main interstate to get to Denver? These country roads have huge potholes. I don't think Gammy would go this way." Olivia continued her attempt to clear the windshield, which seemed to be a losing battle.

"You're right about the highway being a safer route, but Myrna won't travel on the interstate. She always avoids the highway and takes the back roads because she doesn't like to drive over forty miles per hour."

Olivia tore another towel from the roll. "I guess her eyes are worse than she wants any of us to know."

"Long before Myrna's diagnosis, she wouldn't get on the interstate. She said merging into fast-moving traffic caused her blood pressure to skyrocket." Jake laughed.

Olivia leaned back against the leather seat. "It sounds

like you know my grandmother better than I do. It's kind of sad, don't you think?"

"Don't be so hard on yourself. It happens. Things aren't like they used to be."

"How so?"

Jake eased his foot from the accelerator as the car rounded a sharp curve. A flash of lightning lit up the sky. "Families used to live closer to one another. They were there to help each other during times of need."

"From what I hear, you still honor that tradition. Gammy told me you and your family all live on the same plot of land. She also shared how you and your brothers worked together to help your father care for your mother before she went into the nursing home." Olivia paused and released a sigh. "It must be a comfort to know there's always someone around who has your back."

"Yeah, it's nice to have family nearby, but it doesn't take blood to make a family. Your grandmother is proof of that. Of course, my brothers always come through for me, but your grandmother was my rock after my wife died. She helped me and the kids so much in those first few months. I'm not sure I would have survived without her."

Olivia squirmed in her seat. She wrapped her arms around her stomach. "I'm glad she was there to help you. She did the same for me after my father died. Once my mother turned to drinking as a coping mechanism, I had no one to help me deal with the loss. I honestly can't fathom what would have become of my life if Gammy hadn't come to take care of me. I hope you can understand why it's important for me to bring her back to Miami. I want to help her like she helped me. With her eyes getting worse, she can't continue to live alone, with or without a guide dog. Tonight is a perfect example. Callie wouldn't have stopped Gammy from driving her friend to Denver, but I could have."

"I don't want to argue with you about moving Myrna. We both want what's best for her. I agree she shouldn't have made this long drive, but I think her heart over-powered her logic." Now wasn't the time to debate the moving issue. Jake knew plenty of disabled people who lived independently with the help of a service dog and upgrades to their home.

They rode in silence for the next few miles. Olivia continued with her attempts to reach Myrna, but the calls went straight to voice mail.

"Look! Do you see those lights flashing ahead?" Olivia pointed.

Jake slowed as the wipers continued at a rapid pace, trying desperately to keep up with the deluge. "That's the driveway to the Potters' farm. It's been empty since Sam died over a year ago. They have everything tied up in probate court."

"There was a car. I saw it. Pull over!"

Jake hit the turn signal and navigated his extended-cab truck off the road. The headlights hit the familiar white sedan and his pulse slowed. "That's Myrna's car."

"Thank You, God!" Olivia cried out. "I hope they're okay."

Jake placed the car into Park and turned off the en-gine. "You wait here. I'll go check on them." He unfas-tened his seat belt, pulled the hood of his jacket over his head and opened the door.

"Not on your life." Olivia repeated Jake's actions. "I'm going, too." She jumped from the car.

Jake jogged to Myrna's vehicle with Olivia close behind and tapped on the driver's-side window. He didn't want to frighten the women. With the rain coming down so hard, it was likely they couldn't see him and Olivia.

A second later, the window rolled down about half an inch. "I've been praying that you would come," Myrna said.

"Why didn't you call? Are you two okay?" Jake scanned Myrna's face. His shoulders relaxed when he saw no sign of distress.

"When the weather got bad, I pulled over at the first safe spot. I tried to call, but my cell phone battery went dead."

Olivia peered into the back seat. "Is Ruth okay?"

Jake looked through the glass. He spotted Ruth stretched out across the back seat with a yellow afghan covering her.

"She fell asleep ten minutes outside of Denver. I guess the anesthesia is still working on her." Myrna glanced over her shoulder at her friend. "Poor thing. On our way out of the doctor's office, she said she was starving after fasting. She wanted a double cheeseburger. Then, within seconds of getting into the car, she was out."

"I wish you would have used Ruth's phone to call. I've been worried sick." Olivia sighed.

Myrna unbuckled her seat belt. "Ruth doesn't have a cell phone. I gave her one last year for Christmas, but she donated it to Penny, who runs the women's shelter in Smithville. She said Penny could use it more than her."

Olivia frowned. "With your eyes, you shouldn't drive without a fully charged phone. In fact, you shouldn't drive, period. What if we hadn't found you?"

Myrna pulled her hood over her head. "Maybe we should wait and discuss my driving privileges when we're all safely home."

"Okay, ladies, we'll talk about this later. Olivia, you can follow me. We'll swing by Ruth's house and drop her off first."

Olivia nodded.

Jake helped Myrna from the car and circled her around to the passenger side while Olivia took the driver's seat.

With the women safely inside the car, Jake trudged across the muddy driveway to his truck. Based on their earlier conversation, it was clear Olivia still believed Myrna would be better off in Florida. However, the more he learned about Olivia's past, he was gaining a better understanding of Olivia's position. She loved Myrna as much as he and his children did. Of course, protecting Kyle and Kayla from any additional pain and suffering was his number one priority. He'd have to continue with the upgrades on Myrna's home and pray Olivia would reconsider her plan. Bluebell would not be the same without Myrna Hart…or without the woman who was slowly stealing his heart.

Chapter Seven

Olivia used the back of her palm to wipe the moisture from her cheek. She tugged the cool satin sheet under her chin and squeezed her eyes closed. A soft whimper filled the guest room, followed by another round of wetness across her eyebrows. She slowly opened one eye and found herself face-to-face with a shiny brown nose.

"What are you doing up so early, Callie?"

The puppy dug her paws furiously into the fluffy down comforter and barked.

Olivia eyed the digital clock on the dresser and jerked her head off her pillow.

Eleven fifteen.

Kicking the covers tangled around her ankles, she sprang from the bed. When her bare feet hit the floor, she nearly tripped.

Callie barked and raced to the door.

Jake had stressed the importance of keeping Callie on a schedule. Last night, before going to bed, she'd double-checked the alarm on her phone. Had she been so tired that she slept through it?

Olivia sprinted to the closet and quickly dressed. The

shower could wait until after she took Callie for a walk and fed her breakfast.

"Come on, girl." Olivia opened the bedroom door and raced for the staircase. Halfway down, her socked feet skidded to a stop.

"Whoa!"

Olivia stopped just short of running full force into Jake, who was hunched over on the landing.

"Where's the fire?" Clutching a piece of carpet in his right hand, Jake pushed himself up. His biceps bulged through his Beckett's Canine Training T-shirt.

Olivia's messy hair and flannel lounge pants were proof that the last person she had expected to see this morning was Jake. Had she known he was in the house, she would have at least run a comb through the tangled mane.

"I overslept." Olivia glanced down at Callie. Warmth filled her cheeks. "I never oversleep. The day is half-gone! I should have taken Callie out hours ago. I marked my calendar for a two-hour hike this morning."

"Relax. Not everything in life needs to be planned. You must have needed the sleep, and it's hard to resist the positive effects of the mountain air." Jake winked. "Don't worry. Myrna took Callie out before she left."

Guilt took hold. First, Callie ran off on her watch, not once, but twice. Now Olivia got caught slacking off on her puppy-raising duties.

She twisted a strand of hair. "I'm sorry. We'll get out of your way." Olivia called to Callie. "Come on, girl. Let's get your breakfast before it's lunchtime."

"Myrna fed her already. I think she got up with the chickens." Jake laughed.

If Olivia wanted to keep up with her grandmother,

she'd have to get a louder alarm clock. "Where did Gammy go?" Getting her grandmother to sit still long enough to talk to her about relinquishing her driver's license and relying more on neighbors for transportation would be a challenge. Following yesterday's scare, Olivia was more convinced that driving was no longer safe for Gammy.

"She's working her volunteer shift at the library from eight until noon. Then she was meeting Hilde for lunch in Denver. They also planned to do some shopping for the twins' birthday party."

"Boy, I hope I have that kind of energy when I'm her age. Gammy has a way of making me look like a lazy bum."

Jake laughed. "She doesn't allow a blade of grass to grow under her feet. She loves to do for others."

Since arriving in Bluebell, Olivia kept witnessing the positive impact her grandmother had on her community. "When is the twins' party?"

"It's a week from today. I still can't believe they're going to be seven years old." Jake shook his head. "You're invited, of course."

"That's nice of you. It sounds like fun." Olivia admired Jake. Raising his children without their mother couldn't be easy, yet he seemed to handle things effortlessly.

"I'll add you to the guest list. The kids will be happy."

Olivia wasn't sure about Kayla. She had hoped they'd connected after she told Kayla about losing her father, but she still sensed the child didn't fully trust her. Olivia couldn't blame her. She understood how Kayla felt. "I'm sure you and Gammy have everything under control, but I'd love to help."

Jake smiled. "With ten kids currently on the guest list, we could use an extra set of hands."

As an adult, Olivia had never been to a child's birthday party. When her desire to have children started growing, she used to imagine throwing big birthday celebrations with pony rides, face painting and inflatable bouncy houses. "I'd be happy to help. Do you have anything special planned outside of the typical birthday festivities?"

"I do. I plan to take the children to the county fair. It just so happens that opening day is on their birthday."

"That sounds like perfect timing."

"I thought Kyle would burst with excitement when I told him. He's been marking the days off on our calendar hanging in the kitchen."

Olivia laughed. "What can I do to help get ready for the party?"

"Are you sure you'll have the time? Your plate seems pretty full with Myrna and Callie."

"I like to stay busy. Besides, I need to repay you for all that you've done for Gammy. Remember, I told you I'd like to help with the repairs you're doing around her house." Olivia paused and pointed to the floor. "Like this. If I had known you were coming over, I would have made a point of getting up in time to help you."

Jake slid the tape measure into the back pocket of his jeans. "No worries. You're up now. Are you ready for some coffee?"

"I work in the ER. I'm always ready for coffee." Olivia smiled.

"That's right." He palmed his forehead. "You probably live on the stuff."

"In moderation. I've seen the effects too much caffeine can have on the body."

"But a cup or two is good, right?"

Olivia nodded. "Absolutely."

"I made a fresh pot about ten minutes ago. Get yourself caffeinated and then we can go over my plans for the steps."

"Sounds like a plan." Olivia turned to head to the kitchen.

"You can let Callie out back. The kids are out there with Tank." Jake picked up his coffee from the foyer table and took a sip.

"Great. I'll be right back." Olivia continued down the hall.

The aroma of bacon lingered in the kitchen. Her stomach rumbled. Of course, Gammy had cooked breakfast for Jake and his kids. If only she'd woken up earlier, she might have enjoyed a hot meal. For now, coffee would have to do.

Radiant sunshine filled the room. It was a glorious day to be outdoors, but she'd already committed to helping Jake.

Outside, the children's laughter reminded Olivia of recess on the first warm day following a long, cold winter spent indoors. She moved to the open kitchen window. Callie followed and whimpered, longing to join in the fun. "I know, girl. I feel the same."

Olivia peered through the screen. Her heart squeezed. A backyard filled with children was her dream. Had she missed the warning signs during their marriage that her ex-husband had changed his mind about having children? Were those years with Mark wasted? Olivia shook off the thought and reminded herself of what Gammy believed. *Choices don't determine your future. God does.* Olivia released a steadying breath. Mark was only part of her story. She couldn't allow him to put an end to her dream.

Unable to pull herself away from the window, Olivia laughed as Kayla yanked Kyle's baseball cap from his head and raced through the yard, determined to win the game of keep-away. Kyle chased his sister while Tank barked and nipped at the boy's tennis shoes.

Callie barked and scratched at the door.

"Okay, just a minute."

Olivia opened the cupboard next to the window and grabbed a large mug. She filled the cup three-quarters full and contemplated letting Callie outside without going out to greet the children herself. The last thing she wanted to do was spoil Kayla's fun.

Callie continued to scratch at the door. Olivia's stomach fluttered. She placed her sweaty palm on the door handle, but quickly dropped it to her side. She wiped her hand down her leg, knowing the fear behind her hesitation. Olivia saw herself in Kayla—a little girl who had put up walls to protect her broken heart.

Kayla's giggles filled the kitchen. Olivia opened the door to let Callie outside to join the fun. She closed it slowly. It was probably best to keep her distance. The last thing she wanted to do was steal Kayla's joy.

A slow and steady breath parted her lips. Olivia couldn't deny the truth. She was thirty-six and alone. With each passing year, her desire to have a child grew stronger. Olivia brushed away a tear racing down her cheek and turned away from a glimpse at a future that she feared would never be.

Jake pulled up the piece of carpet runner covering the last step of the staircase. Maybe the busy pattern was in style years ago, but with Myrna's eyes deteriorating, it was an accident waiting to happen. The solid carpeting he planned to place down the hardwood steps along with a colorful strip of tape on the edge of each step would provide additional contrast to ensure Myrna's safety.

The sound of dishes clattering in the kitchen surprised Jake. He assumed Olivia would have taken Callie outside to join the children and Tank. Of course, Kayla still wasn't exactly rolling out the welcome mat for Olivia.

"The coffee tastes fantastic."

Jake lifted his head from the task at hand. His pulse quickened at the sight of Olivia standing in the foyer. The sunlight streaming through the large window over the front door highlighted her delicate bone structure.

"I'm glad you like it. I brought it over this morning. It's one of my favorite blends. Myrna enjoys it, too. Are you ready to get to work?"

Olivia approached and tucked a strand of hair behind her ear. "I'm all yours. You're doing so much for Gammy. It's not fair for you to do it all alone."

"I can't think of anything I'd rather do more after all Myrna does for me and the twins."

Jake tossed the piece of rug into the pile.

"I appreciate everything you've done for Gammy. You're a good man, Jake."

He stood and dusted his hands off on his jeans. "There's nothing I wouldn't do for your grandmother. She means the world to me, like she does to you, too."

"I'm pretty sure Gammy feels the same about you."

The back screen door closed with a bang. Feet padded against the hardwood.

"Hi, Dr. Olivia!" the twins called out.

"Hello." Olivia tossed up a hand.

"Daddy, we're hungry," Kayla announced.

Jake turned with a smile. "After the big breakfast Miss Myrna cooked for you? Your tummies must be bottomless pits. Between the two of you, I think you polished off at least a dozen silver-dollar pancakes."

"That was hours ago." Kayla rolled her eyes.

"Yeah, besides, those pancakes are little. Can we go to Charlie's?" Kyle tugged on Jake's tool belt.

Jake glanced at his watch. "Well, I had planned to go into town to pick up some new light bulbs for Miss Myrna."

"Yay!" The children cheered.

Kyle stepped closer to Olivia. "Do you want to come with us?"

"Who's Charlie?" Olivia looked down at Kyle. "Is he a friend of yours?"

Kyle giggled. "No. It's a place to eat."

"Charlie's Chuck Wagon is a local diner in town. It's owned by Mary Simpson. Charlie was Mary's great-great-grandfather," Jake explained.

"They have the best cheeseburgers in the world!" Kyle looked at his father. "Not as good as yours, Daddy."

Jake ruffled the top of Kyle's head. "Thanks, son, but my burgers can't compete." He turned to Olivia. "You're welcome to come along. We can show you around town a little. If you're going to stay for a while, it might be a good idea to familiarize yourself with some of the local establishments."

Olivia chewed her lower lip. "Actually, I wanted to check out some of the local markets and also the bank."

Jake laughed. "It won't take long to check out the markets since we only have one here in Bluebell."

"I guess people shop at the big-box store instead?"

Jake had never been to Miami, but he'd read enough about it to know that it was a different world from Bluebell. It would take time for Olivia to become acclimated in a small town. "Most make do with what we have here locally. For the bigger stores, you need to travel to Denver."

"Well, since I won't be here permanently, I'm sure I'll be fine."

Jake hoped when Olivia returned home, she'd leave Myrna and Callie here in Bluebell, where they belonged. "Okay, let's feed the dogs and secure them before we hit the road."

Thirty minutes later, the foursome sat inside Charlie's Chuck Wagon. Dark wood paneling surrounded their corner booth. Peanut shells covered the hardwood flooring.

Olivia peeked over her menu. "I feel like I've stepped onto the set of a Western movie. I'm surprised there isn't one of those mechanical bulls."

"Oh, they got rid of that in the early '90s after Seth Davis nearly broke his neck. He had one too many root beers minus the root and tried to ride the bull standing up." Jake laughed.

"Cool!" Kyle exclaimed. "Maybe I can try that on the merry-go-round at the park?"

Jake tossed his son a look and shook his head. "You'll ride sitting down, young man."

"Hi, Jake. It's nice to see you and the kids."

Evelyn Simpson, Mary Simpson's older sister, had worked at Charlie's for as long as Jake could remember. She greeted the customers with a warm smile, along with a side order of the latest gossip. If you wanted to know what was going on around town, you asked Evelyn.

"Well now, who is this pretty young thing?" She cast

her eyes on Olivia. "Wait a minute. You must be Myrna's granddaughter."

"She's a doctor!" Kyle announced.

Evelyn nodded. "ER, from what I hear. That's quite impressive. Bluebell isn't as exciting as Miami, but I hope you enjoy your stay. Of course, I have a sneaking suspicion you'll fall in love with our town and never want to leave."

"It's nice to meet you. I'm Olivia Hart." She extended her hand to Evelyn. "I don't have plans to stay since my home is in Florida, but I'm enjoying my visit."

"You might have a change of heart." Evelyn winked. "Now, what can I get everyone?"

"Cheeseburgers?" Jake scanned the table.

"Don't forget the fries and chocolate shakes, Daddy." Kyle bounced up and down. "You'll love the fries, Dr. Olivia. They're curly!"

"Did you get that, Evelyn?" Jake winked at the server.

Evelyn scribbled on the pad and slid the pencil behind her ear. "I'll get your orders back to Henry, pronto." She pocketed the pad and scurried toward the kitchen.

"Daddy, can I have a quarter for the jukebox?" Kyle reached his hand across the walnut tabletop.

Jake reached into the pocket of his jeans and fished out a handful of change. He eyed Kayla. She hadn't spoken a word since they'd left the house. "Kayla, do you want to play your favorite song for Miss Olivia?"

The child shrugged her shoulders.

"Come on, Kay. You always love to hear that song about Jeremiah the bullfrog." Kyle tugged on his sister's arm and took off.

Without saying a word, Kayla jumped off the seat and ran across the restaurant, chasing her brother.

Olivia kept her eyes on the children. "Kyle is protective of his sister. That's so sweet."

Jake was thankful Kyle kept a watchful eye on Kayla. "After their mother died, he thought it was his responsibility to look after her. Sometimes I think he does a better job with her than I do."

"You shouldn't be so hard on yourself. You're doing an amazing job. It can't be easy. Kayla told me you built her the clubhouse after you lost your wife."

After Laura passed away, life went on for his brothers and they went back to living their normal lives. Jake no longer knew what normal was. How could he go on without his wife? She gave him the two greatest blessings he'd ever received—his children. Laura brought joy and inspiration to his life every day. "Kayla wouldn't talk for weeks. I took her to the doctor, but he said to give her time. The more time that passed, the more helpless I became, so I built the clubhouse. When I couldn't sleep at night, I'd work on it. Constructing that little house kept my hands busy and my mind occupied. Your grandmother was staying with us and she kept the coffee coming. On those really dark days, she'd share stories about Laura. She stressed how important it was to talk about her, just like you taught Kayla, but that was so hard for me. I thought if I didn't bring her up, my pain would go away."

"And did it?"

"No, it stayed fresh. I caused a lot more pain for Kayla." Jake glanced over at the kids dancing near the jukebox. His heart warmed. "Thank you for opening my eyes to what I was doing wrong."

Olivia leaned back in the booth. "So, last night's story time must have ended well?"

Jake couldn't have asked for a more perfect night. With

the children fresh out of a bubble bath, they'd cuddled up in their pajamas. The three snuggled into Jake's bed while he reminisced about their mother. "I slept better than I had in the last two years. I told the kids about the night I proposed to their mother." Jake remembered the evening as though it were yesterday.

"I'm sure they enjoyed hearing that story." Olivia's chin tilted and she tucked a stray piece of hair behind her ear. "I'd love to hear it, too."

"Really?"

Olivia nodded. "I would."

Jake smiled. "I picked up Laura at her house. I still remember the feeling I had in the pit of my stomach as I drove to her house."

"Butterflies?"

Jake shook his head. "More like bats. Not just one or two, but a swarm. I had spoken with her father the day before, so he and Laura's mother had given us their blessing, but I wasn't sure if Laura would say yes."

"How long had you been dating?"

It was difficult to remember his life without Laura. "Since the seventh grade. That's when her family moved to Virginia, where I'm from. Two weeks before the first dance of that year, a friend told me Billy Parker was going to ask Laura to be his date. I couldn't let that happen, so that day in the cafeteria, I asked her if she wanted to be my girlfriend. Of course, at that age, neither one of us really knew what that meant."

Olivia laughed. "I remember."

"We were together until we graduated from high school. That's when I realized I wanted to marry her."

"That's sweet. You married your high school sweetheart."

Jake explained to Olivia that he had sat at his desk in his bedroom the night before, mapping out his plan to propose. He even checked the time the sun would set the next day. "I had everything planned out. First, we'd go to an afternoon movie. After, a sunset picnic at Sawyer's Canyon. That's where I wanted to propose to her. At the movie theater, I remember her asking me what was wrong. I was so nervous I spilled our jumbo bucket of popcorn. When she passed me the box of sour balls, I dropped it, and the candies flew all over the floor."

Olivia covered her mouth before a giggle escaped.

"Yeah, there I was, the star quarterback, and I was so nervous I couldn't even hold on to a little box of candy." Jake paused and looked up at Olivia. Her smile lit up her entire face. "Trust me, it gets worse."

"I have a feeling it has a happy ending, though." Olivia picked at the folded napkin on the table.

"After the movie, we went outside. The film had run a little longer than the guide had stated. I still needed to make the twenty-minute drive to the canyon, but the sun was setting fast."

Olivia moved toward the edge of her seat. "You made it, didn't you?"

"Well, I had to hurry. I opened the door for Laura and then I raced around to the other side of the car. I stumbled on a rock in the street and dropped the car keys." Jake paused, picked up his glass of water and took a sip.

"And?"

"The keys bounced down inside of the sewer."

Olivia's brown eyes doubled in size. "Oh, no!"

"It gets worse." Jake shook his head. "Within seconds, the rain came. That was something my teenage brain didn't consider when making my plan. I forgot to check the weather."

Olivia stifled a laugh.

"Laura unlocked the driver's-side door so at least I could get inside. For the next half hour, it poured. Water gushed down the street and into the sewer."

"And the keys?" Olivia's brow arched.

"Never found them."

"But you still proposed, right?"

"Well, that's where the story takes another twist. Our geometry teacher, Mr. Preston, pulled up. After I told him what happened, he drove me and Laura home."

"I'm sorry your plan didn't work out that night. Did you surprise her another time?"

"Actually, her mother did." Jake laughed.

"What happened?"

"By the time we arrived at her parents' house, the rain had stopped. When we pulled into the driveway, Laura's mother came running from the house. You would have thought there was a fire. We got out of the car and her mother grabbed Laura in her arms and cried. She told her how happy she was that we were going to get married."

"No! Oh, Jake!" Olivia couldn't hold back her laughter. "I'm so sorry."

Jake burst out laughing. "It was like being in a sitcom. Her mother was grabbing her hand and looking for the ring. Of course, at first, Laura was clueless. Then her father came out and welcomed me into the family. In the end, we all had a good laugh about it. Her parents were ecstatic because they got to see the proposal live."

"So you asked her that night?"

"Yep, right there in the driveway."

Olivia sat back. "That's the best proposal story I've ever heard."

For a moment, Jake remained silent. In less than twenty-four hours, for the second time, talking about Laura had come easy for him.

Olivia reached across the table and rested her hand on top of Jake's. "Are you okay?"

He released a long breath and looked at their hands. "Life doesn't always go as we plan, does it?"

Olivia shook her head. "I know mine hasn't."

Jake watched the smile Olivia had worn while he'd shared the proposal story slip away.

"Thank you for listening."

"I appreciate you sharing the story with me."

Silence hung in the air as the server approached with their orders.

"Okay, I've got two burgers with double cheese."

Olivia flinched and quickly pulled away her hand.

For a split second, Jake longed to feel her touch again, but out of respect for Laura, he forced the thought away.

Chapter Eight

"I've made a list of the things we need to pick up for Kayla and Kyle's birthday party." Myrna flipped through the pages of a brown leather journal.

Olivia approached the light signal and eased her foot off the accelerator. "I wish I had one-half of your organizational skills, Gammy."

"I just write everything down in here." She lifted the journal. "I have boxes of these at home filled with every store list, appointment, Bible study, recipe and thoughts from the day. You name it and it's recorded."

Olivia worried what Gammy would do when she could no longer see to write about her daily events. It was obviously an important ritual. Maybe she could use the recording feature on her cell phone. "So, what's first on the list?"

"Hank Garrison will drop off the tents tomorrow afternoon. There's only a slight chance of rain in the forecast for Saturday, but Jake thought it was best to play it safe. Hank and his crew will set up the tents in front of the house."

"I thought the party was going to be at the fairgrounds?" One year, Olivia and her father attended the Colorado State Fair and made some of her fondest memories. Her mother had planned to attend, but she'd come down with the flu. Olivia remembered her father had let her eat as much cotton candy as her stomach could hold. "I remember seeing the dog stunt show. It was hilarious. Daddy and I laughed so hard our stomachs hurt."

Gammy smiled. "It makes me happy when you recall the good times."

Olivia only wished she'd had more time to create memories with him.

"Make a left here, dear." Myrna pointed to Garrison's Mercantile Company.

Olivia hit the turn signal.

"I guess Jake didn't mention that the twins' party is an all-day event. Garrison's will have most of what we need." She closed her journal and slipped it inside her purse. "We celebrate big here in Bluebell. Once you get a taste of it, you won't want to leave." Myrna laughed. "We'll spend the morning and afternoon at the fair. After, we'll come back to Jake's place for a cookout, fireworks and other activities."

"Sounds like fun, but a lot of work for Jake."

Myrna swatted her hand. "He'd do anything for those kids. Besides, practically the entire town has volunteered to help. In fact, I put you in charge of baking the cakes. We'll pick up the ingredients today."

Olivia loved to bake, but once she went to work in the ER, she began purchasing her baked goods. She navigated the SUV into an open parking spot in front of the store. "Of course I will. What's their favorite?"

"They both love my recipe for German chocolate cake. It's been in the family for generations."

Olivia smiled. "I remember. You baked it when you and Pops came to stay with me and Mom."

"One Minute" Survey
You get up to **FOUR books** <u>and</u> a Mystery Gift...

> **ABSOLUTELY FREE!**

Romance

Suspense

> YOU pick your books – WE pay for everything!

See inside for details.

YOU pick your books –
WE pay for everything.

You get up to FOUR new books and a Mystery Gift…
absolutely FREE!
Total retail value: Over $20!

Dear Reader,

Your opinions are important to us. So if you'll participate in our fast and free "One Minute" Survey, YOU can pick up to four wonderful books that WE pay for when you try the Harlequin Reader Service!

As a leading publisher of women's fiction, we'd love to hear from you. That's why we promise to reward you for completing our survey.

IMPORTANT: Please complete the survey and return it. We'll send your Free Books and a Free Mystery Gift right away. And we pay for shipping and handling too! *We pay for EVERYTHING!*

Try **Love Inspired® Romance Larger-Print** and get 2 books and fall in love with inspirational romances that take you on an uplifting journey of faith, forgiveness and hope.

Try **Love Inspired® Suspense Larger-Print** and get 2 books where courage and optimism unite in stories of faith and love in the face of danger.

Or TRY BOTH!

Thank you again for participating in our "One Minute" Survey. It really takes just a minute (or less) to complete the survey… and your free books and gift will be well worth it!

If you continue with your subscription, you can look forward to curated monthly shipments of brand-new books from your selected series, always at a discount off the cover price! Plus you can cancel any time. So don't miss out, return your One Minute Survey today to get your Free books.

Pam Powers

"One Minute" Survey

GET YOUR FREE BOOKS AND A FREE GIFT!

✓ Complete this Survey   ✓ Return this survey

1 Do you try to find time to read every day?

☐ YES   ☐ NO

2 Do you prefer books which reflect Christian values?

☐ YES   ☐ NO

3 Do you enjoy having books delivered to your home?

☐ YES   ☐ NO

4 Do you share your favorite books with friends?

☐ YES   ☐ NO

YES! I have completed the above "One Minute" Survey. Please send me n Free Books and a Free Mystery Gift (worth over $20 retail). I understand that I a under no obligation to buy anything, as explained on the back of this card.

☐ **Love Inspired® Romance Larger-Print** 122/322 CTI G2AK

☐ **Love Inspired® Suspense Larger-Print** 107/307 CTI G2AK

☐ **BOTH** 122/322 & 107/307 CTI G2AL

FIRST NAME

LAST NAME

ADDRESS

APT.#

CITY

STATE/PROV.

ZIP/POSTAL CODE

EMAIL ☐ Please check this box if you would like to receive newsletters and promotional emails from Harlequin Enterprises ULC and its affiliates. You can unsubscribe anytime.

LI/LIS-1123-OM

▼ DETACH AND MAIL CARD TODAY! ▼

© 2023 HARLEQUIN ENTERPRISES ULC
™ and ® are trademarks owned by Harlequin Enterprises ULC. Printed in the U.S.A.

"It was your father's favorite." Myrna unfastened her seat belt and patted Olivia's hand. "Let's only think good thoughts today."

"That sounds like a plan."

Olivia stepped inside the store and took in the rustic surroundings. The uneven floorboards and rough wood walls gave the mercantile a warm and welcoming feel. It was the complete opposite of the high-end boutiques with modern designs that lined the streets of Miami. The aroma of cedar sent a flood of memories through her. She pictured the chest that sat at the foot of her childhood bed. After her father died, she'd packed away pictures and special gifts he'd given her. Over the years, the chest had traveled with Olivia as she moved from one home to another.

"Look who's here."

Olivia spotted a petite, gray-haired woman coming from the back room and walking around the checkout counter at a swift pace. An oversize box in her arms didn't hinder her speed. Every strand of her short silver hair was in place, as though she'd just returned from the hairdresser.

"This is Nellie Garrison, Hank's wife and co-owner of the mercantile." Gammy made the introduction. "Nellie, this is my granddaughter, Olivia."

The woman set the box on the counter and approached her customers. "I'd recognize that beautiful face anywhere." Nellie placed her hands on Olivia's cheeks. "Your grandmother is so proud of you. She's shared many photographs of you. I knew who you were the moment you walked in. I'm glad you finally got away from that ER and made it to Bluebell. You'll never want to leave."

What was it about this place? It was like everyone who lived in town worked for the chamber of commerce. Was there something about Bluebell Olivia couldn't see?

"My work is back in Miami, so I'll only be here long enough to convince Gammy it's time for someone to take care of her."

"Is she still on that silly idea?" Nellie tugged on Myrna's arm and laughed. "There's no one in this town who would think twice about helping your grandmother, so there's no need to worry about her. Of course, if you moved to Bluebell, you could keep a close eye on her yourself," Nellie said with a wink.

Olivia bit her tongue to keep the peace. Her stomach twisted as she realized it wasn't only Gammy she'd have to convince that moving would be in her best interest. The entire community might be an obstacle for her. But if she didn't feel confident in Callie's abilities, Olivia would have no option but to carry out her original plan.

The front door swooshed behind them.

"Look who's here." Nellie nodded her head toward the customer.

Olivia spun on her heel in time to see Jake strolling into the store. His boots scraped across the hardwood. His normally straight posture was gone and instead he appeared hunched. Underneath his dark brown cowboy hat, Olivia saw lines crinkling along his forehead.

"Jake, is everything okay?" Myrna asked.

She hadn't imagined it. Even Gammy noticed the weight Jake carried.

"Jake," Olivia asked, "is everything okay?"

"I don't want to interrupt…"

Nellie took advantage of his brief pause. "I'm just getting to know Myrna's gorgeous granddaughter. You should show her around Bluebell!"

Olivia's face warmed. She quickly changed the subject to the twins' birthday. "Gammy and I just stopped in to pick up some things for the party."

Jake's expression darkened further. "That's what I wanted to talk with Myrna about."

Nellie took Olivia's hand. "We'll leave you two alone to talk."

"No, I'd like to get all of your opinions." Jake removed his hat and raked his hand through his hair.

"What is it, Jake? I'm worried," Myrna said.

"Kayla came home from school today and announced she wasn't going to her birthday party." Jake slipped his hands into the back pockets of his mud-splattered jeans.

"Oh, my stars, that's the silliest thing I've ever heard." Nellie pulled out a stool. "Here, dear, take a seat." She patted her hand against the larch wood stool next to the counter. "It sounds like you need a good cup of strong coffee." Nellie scurried to the back room, but Jake didn't sit. Instead, he paced the floor.

Myrna cleared her throat. "Does Kyle have any idea why his sister had this sudden change of heart? Just last week, Kayla was so excited about the party. She'd chattered endlessly about all the different animals she wanted to see at the fair."

Jake shook his head. "Kyle said during recess he saw a couple of Kayla's friends whispering and pointing at her while she was getting a drink from the water fountain. A couple of minutes later, Kayla ran to the far side of the playground and hid behind a tree. He went to check on her, but she wouldn't talk to him."

"Poor Kayla. Sometimes children can be cruel when they decide to gang up on one of their friends," Myrna said.

Olivia saw the pain in Jake's eyes.

"I suspect the teasing may have been about the mother-daughter fashion show. Kyle mentioned it recently, but I kind of brushed it off because I didn't hear more about it." Jake sighed.

Nellie crossed the room with a tray of cups, along with a carafe of coffee. "I got an email the other day from my women's club about volunteering for the fashion show. I signed up. It sounded like fun."

Jake dipped his chin. "Maybe not for a little girl who lost her mother. I'm afraid this event is triggering a lot of sad memories for Kayla."

Olivia's heart ached for Kayla. A few months after her father passed away, her elementary school hosted a father-daughter dance for all grades. Weeks before the event, her girlfriends talked nonstop about what they'd wear and how their dads were all taking them out to a fancy, grown-up dinner.

"You okay?" Gammy whispered to Olivia.

Olivia nodded and smiled. She found comfort in knowing that her grandmother remembered the dance as well. If it hadn't been for Gammy, that evening would have been the worst night of her life. Instead of the dance, they got dressed up and went to the movies. After, Gammy took her to the most expensive restaurant in town. It was the first time Olivia had eaten at a table draped with a linen tablecloth and with a candle as the centerpiece. For one night, thanks to her grandmother, the pain of losing her father waned.

"The kids raced out of the house so fast when the bus honked its horn for school this morning, I wasn't able to talk with Kayla. But after they left, I went up to their rooms to strip the sheets from their beds and I found this under Kayla's mattress. It's the flyer announcing the fashion show." Jake slipped a folded piece of paper from his back pocket and passed it to Myrna.

Olivia watched as Gammy opened the paper and nodded. "There's no doubt about it. It's the fashion show that has Kayla upset. We'll have to put our heads together to come up with an idea to help her."

"I can take her." The words spilled out of Olivia's mouth before her brain could process the offer. She was usually an overthinker, always weighing the pros and cons of her ideas before speaking or acting.

"That's a wonderful idea." Gammy wasted no time with her response. She rested her hand on Olivia's arm.

The touch brought her back into the moment. Was this the right thing to do? What made her think Kayla would even want to go with her? Although they had a moment of connection in Kayla's clubhouse, their relationship appeared to have regressed to its original state when they first met. It was obvious Kayla felt threatened by her presence. In her mind, Olivia was trying to replace her mother.

"I appreciate the offer, but I'm not sure if that's a good idea." Jake kept a close eye on Olivia.

Now was her opportunity to back out. But as much as Olivia wanted to run out of the store and take the offer with her, her heart had a different idea. Olivia had been in Kayla's situation. She knew the agony of losing a parent. How could she walk away?

"You've come a long way." Olivia scratched Callie underneath her collar and, with the other hand, fed her a treat.

After skipping lunch with Gammy on Friday, Olivia packed up Callie and headed to Jake's place. She wanted to work with the pup before camp started.

"Not quite."

Olivia looked up and squinted into the late-afternoon sun. Jake towered over her, twisting a piece of straw between his teeth. She wasn't sure if there were any magazines that featured cowboys, but if so, Jake could be on the cover.

"Why would you say that?"

Jake squatted and rubbed Callie's head. "I think we've got our hands full with this little one."

"Are you saying Callie can't help Gammy? I remember you said some dogs don't have what it takes to work as service animals."

"That's true, but I still have hope." He picked up Callie and rubbed his nose into her coat. "It's okay, girl. I believe in you."

Callie covered Jake's face with sloppy kisses.

"You certainly have a way with her." Olivia laughed. "I wish I could say the same about Kayla."

Olivia hoped Kayla would change her mind about attending her birthday party, but according to Gammy, she hadn't mentioned it.

"It's obvious you mean the world to her. Losing a parent is a lot for a child to handle, but it's a blessing Kayla and Kyle have each other. After my dad died, I'd pretend my stuffed animals were my siblings, so I could have someone to talk to." Olivia stood.

Jake reached out and placed his hand on Olivia's arm. "Thanks for sharing that with me. I appreciate it."

A warm sensation traveled up her arm. She moved her eyes toward his hand. "You're welcome."

"Daddy! We're home!" Kyle called out from across the pasture.

Jake's hand pulled away and Olivia looked up. His eyes

remained fixated on her as though neither wanted to be the first to look away. Warmth spread across her face. What exactly was happening? She'd missed lunch. Maybe it was her blood sugar dropping. That had to be the reason.

"I aced my spelling test!" Kyle smiled, revealing a missing front tooth.

"That's wonderful, son. Congratulations."

"Hey, when did that happen?" Olivia pointed at Kyle's mouth. She looked over and noticed Kayla walking slowly toward them with her head down.

"This morning! Isn't it cool? Daddy said if I put it under my pillow tonight, I might get a surprise."

Kayla joined them but remained silent.

"Did you have a good day, sweetie?" Jake asked.

Kayla shrugged her shoulders.

Olivia noticed the redness around her eyes.

"Run inside and change. I need your help to set up the cones for camp."

"I'll be right back," Kyle called out over his shoulder as he sped toward the house.

"Daddy, do I have to help with camp today?"

"What's wrong? You're not sick, are you?" Jake brushed Kayla's hair away and placed his hand on her forehead. "Cool as a cucumber."

"I feel okay."

Jake's brow arched. "Did you do poorly on your spelling test?"

Kayla shook her head. "I didn't miss any words."

"That's great, sweetie. Then why so glum?"

Kayla glanced at Olivia before turning her attention back to the ground.

Olivia could see Kayla was upset, but her gut told her it had nothing to do with a spelling test. It was more.

When Kayla's eyes met hers for a second time, Olivia sensed maybe Kayla wanted to talk, but not necessarily to her father.

"Sweetie?" Jake kept a close eye on his daughter. "Do you want to talk about what's bothering you?"

Olivia took a step back. "I'm going to take Callie and get her some water. You two talk."

"No!" Kayla snapped. Her face turned red.

Jake turned to Olivia, then back to Kayla. "I can't help you if you don't talk to me."

Kayla kicked her tennis shoe into the ground and bit her lip. "It's just— Forget it. You wouldn't understand." Kayla pivoted and ran across the yard to her clubhouse.

Jake slid his hands into his back pockets. "What am I missing here?"

"You're just being a guy."

Jake sighed. "That's the only thing I know how to be." He scratched his head and looked toward the clubhouse.

"Sometimes a girl needs—"

"Her mother. Is that what you think this is about? Girl talk?"

A look of understanding washed over Jake's face. He was a good father and sensitive to his daughter's needs. "Exactly. May I?" She pointed at the clubhouse.

"Would you?"

"Of course I will." Olivia handed Callie's leash to Jake.

Jake took the leather strap. "Thank you."

"Don't thank me yet." Olivia smiled and headed across the yard.

The closer she got to the little pink house, the more her stomach knotted. Olivia's steps slowed. What if it had all been a mistake and Kayla didn't want to talk with her? It was a chance she would have to take. Olivia had seen the pain in Kayla's eyes. She couldn't allow her to keep everything bottled up. It wasn't healthy.

Outside the door of the clubhouse, Olivia leaned close to the little building, but no sound came from the other side. She gently tapped her knuckles against the door. "Kayla. May I come in?"

Olivia waited in silence. She fought the urge to push the door open, take Kayla into her arms and tell her everything would be okay. She had to remain patient. The last thing Olivia wanted to do was push Kayla even further away.

The second she raised her hand to knock again, the door slowly opened.

"I was hoping you'd come." Kayla peered around the door.

Olivia's breath hitched. Kayla wanted her there? The child's eyes looked redder than earlier. Clutched in her left hand was the photograph of her mother.

Olivia's heart broke as memories of her father and how she'd felt after he died flooded her mind. "Do you want some company?"

Kayla pulled the door open wider. Olivia stepped inside.

A music box played. Kayla moved toward the table with two chairs. Olivia followed behind, recognizing the song. "Bridge Over Troubled Water."

Frozen, Olivia stared at the music box in the middle of the table. She closed her eyes and saw her mother and father dancing in the kitchen. It was the only time Olivia had ever seen her parents holding each other. Olivia could still picture the joyful smiles on their faces. Her mother had giggled softly when her father whispered something in her ear. After her father died, Olivia never heard her mother giggle again.

"Dr. Olivia, are you okay?"

Kayla's voice startled her back into the moment. "Yes. I'm sorry."

"It's okay." Kayla looked at the music box. "Do you know that song?"

Olivia nodded. "Yes. I remember my parents dancing to it."

Kayla turned her attention to the picture frame. "It was my mommy's favorite song. She gave me this music box the day after she told me I was going to have another brother."

"That's a very special gift."

Kayla put the picture frame on the table and picked up the music box. "She shouldn't have given it to me."

"Why would you say that? I'm sure your mommy bought it special just for you."

She ran her tiny fingers around the gold-plated casing. "I was mean to her."

"Why, sweetie?"

Kayla bit her lower lip. "I didn't want another brother, or another sibling." She tipped her head down. "Kyle was born first. If Mommy had another kid, I wouldn't be her baby anymore."

"And you were afraid she might not love you as much anymore?"

Kayla nodded. "But I did something bad."

Olivia couldn't imagine Kayla doing anything bad outside of the ordinary things that children did. "Maybe it's not as bad as you think." Olivia pulled out a chair for Kayla and then took the other seat. Outside the clubhouse, dogs barked. Olivia glanced at her watch. They had twenty minutes before camp began. "Do you want to tell me what happened?" She reached across the table and took Kayla's hand.

"I prayed." Kayla spoke barely above a whisper.

"Well, that doesn't sound too bad."

"I asked God to make me Mommy's baby forever."

Olivia's stomach twisted. Kayla blamed herself for the death of her mother and baby brother.

"It was my fault they died."

"Sweetie, you can't blame yourself for that. Your mommy had a medical emergency. What happened to her and your brother had nothing to do with your prayers."

Kayla's brow crinkled. "Really?"

"I promise." She gave Kayla's hand a squeeze.

"Last week, I told Cindy, my best friend, about my prayer, and she told Missy, the mean girl in my class. Yesterday, on the playground, Missy told me it was my fault."

That was why Kayla didn't want to go to her party. It wasn't only because of the fashion show.

"I never told my daddy. I thought he'd get mad at me."

Olivia offered a small smile and leaned in. "You can always tell your daddy anything. He might get upset or disappointed, but he'll never stop loving you."

Kayla wiped at the tear racing down her cheek. She looked up. "Kind of like God?" Her eyebrows drew together. "I learned in Bible school that God will love me no matter how much I mess up. Is that true?"

Olivia nodded. "Yes, thankfully it is the truth. And your daddy will always love you too, no matter what you do."

A tiny smile parted Kayla's mouth. She sprang from the chair and wrapped her arms tight around Olivia's waist. "Thank you for making me feel better. I think I'll tell my daddy about my mean prayer tonight when we say our prayers together."

Olivia embraced Kayla and closed her eyes, savoring the connection. "I think that would be the perfect time."

Kayla pulled back. "You know what else I'm going to tell him?"

"What's that?" Olivia gently brushed a strand of hair away from Kayla's face.

"I'm going to tell Daddy that I'm going to my party tomorrow." She grinned.

"That will make him very happy." Olivia checked her watch. "Maybe you should go help your daddy get ready for camp?"

"Okay." Kayla gave Olivia another quick hug.

"I'll be there in a minute," Olivia added.

Kayla skipped out the door, taking a piece of Olivia's heart with her. Olivia wrapped her arms around her body. If only she could forget the past so easily. A painful lump formed in her throat. She picked up the music box, turned it over and wound the key. Thoughts flooded her mind as the familiar song played. She recalled her father's death, her failed marriage, and thought about a possible future without children. Alone in the clubhouse, she rested her head on the table and wept.

"Wow! This is so cool!" Kyle squeezed Jake's right hand and bounced on his toes.

Jake couldn't have asked for better weather. The prediction of rain earlier in the week had failed to materialize. The tents Hank Garrison set up at the house weren't necessary unless people wanted to escape the bright sunshine.

"Where are we going to meet everyone, Daddy?" Kayla held tight on to Jake's left hand.

Jake still didn't know what Olivia had said yesterday

in the clubhouse, but he was thankful she had somehow convinced Kayla to attend her seventh birthday party.

"We have some tables set up near the concession area." He and Myrna had concluded being close to the food would be the best place for the party guests to gather. The kids and their parents could come and go while having a home base to rest or grab something to eat.

"That's good because I'm hungry," said Kyle.

"You're always hungry." Kayla rolled her eyes at her brother.

Jake smiled at his children's banter. Although today was a day to celebrate, he couldn't help but think about Laura and the baby. Early this morning, before the kids were out of bed, Jake had gone for a long walk on his property. He thanked God for all his blessings and prayed for the strength to remain present for this special day for his children. Over breakfast, the children shared memories of their mother.

"Look over there at the big sign, Kayla. That's for us!"

"Wow! Cool!" Kayla ran toward the sign. Kyle pulled his hand free from Jake's grip and followed his sister.

Jake had ordered a personalized "Happy Birthday" banner designed by a Denver company he'd found on the internet. It showcased his children's names in large block-style lettering. It thrilled Jake to see the children so happy.

A group of people swarmed below the banner. Judging by the size of the crowd, it looked like everyone had already arrived. His shoulders slouched when he didn't see any sign of Olivia.

"Daddy!" Kyle raced to his father's side. "Uncle Logan said he and Uncle Cody want to take us to the rodeo. Can we go?"

"Of course you can, but what about the stunt dogs?

That's going to start at the same time." Jake had carefully studied the schedule of events. He wanted to make sure Kyle and Kayla didn't miss a thing.

"I'd rather see the bull riders. I see dogs all the time." He giggled.

Jake recalled growing up in Whispering Slopes in the Shenandoah Valley of Virginia. His parents took him and his brothers to the state fair, where seeing everything was impossible. Kyle was smart to choose something new. "Today is your day, so you get to decide, but first it's important for us to greet your guests. They're here to celebrate with you and your sister."

Kyle pulled his father toward the group. The aroma of sugary funnel cake teased his sweet tooth. Jake spotted Olivia. He narrowed his eyes and watched her talking with his younger brother Logan. He was taken aback by how beautiful she looked with her hair pulled back in a ponytail and a cowboy hat on her head. It appeared the city doctor was fitting right in with the locals.

Logan noticed Jake's arrival first. "Hey, bud, I thought you were going to miss your own kids' party," Logan joked.

Jake smiled. "Welcome back. How was the trip?"

"Alaska was amazing. Cody is already talking about going back. Our flight was late getting in last night, so we're both a little worn out."

"I'm sure you are. I appreciate you both coming to celebrate today," Jake said.

"We wouldn't have missed it." Logan palmed Jake's shoulder. "I was just getting to know Myrna's granddaughter. We could use a doctor like her in town. I've heard some chatter that Dr. Dickerson might be retiring."

Jake shook his head. "Those beauty shop women gossip too much. Doc Dickerson will keep practicing medicine as long as he's upright."

"You're probably right." Logan tipped his hat to Olivia. "It was a pleasure talking to you. I better start rounding up the kids who want to go to the rodeo. Are you interested in going?"

Olivia glanced in Jake's direction. "Is everyone going as a group?"

"No. While we're here, everyone is kind of doing their own thing. There's too much to see to please everyone. Later at the ranch, we'll have more organized events." Jake placed his hand on his brother's shoulder. "I had a little surprise planned for Olivia, which is scheduled to begin in fifteen minutes. So, if she's game, we'll pass. Thanks for taking the twins, buddy."

"Sounds good. A couple of parents are going along, so don't worry about me losing any of the kids." Logan laughed, turned on his heel and moved to the group of parents congregated around one of the picnic tables.

Olivia cleared her throat. "You probably don't know this, but I'm not big on surprises. I'm more of a routine person."

"I never would have guessed." Jake nudged her arm. "Sometimes it's good to be spontaneous and not follow a schedule."

Olivia placed her hands on her hips. "You sound like Gammy. Just the other day, she said that exact thing to me."

"Well, you are on vacation, aren't you? Maybe now is a good time to start some new habits. Make some changes that might make you happier."

"What makes you think I'm not happy? Did Gammy say something to you?"

The last thing he wanted to do today was upset her.

"I'm sorry. Maybe my advice was out of line. I know how precious life is, that's all. I have a habit of trying to make sure people I care about don't take life for granted. Putting things off until they fit into your schedule isn't the way to live. There's no guarantee for a tomorrow."

A look of understanding crossed Olivia's face. "You're right. I am on vacation, after all. What better time is there to do things a little spur of the moment?"

"There you go." Jake smiled. "By the way, nice hat." He winked.

She fingered the brim and her cheeks flushed. "Gammy bought it for me." She looked down at her feet. "She purchased the boots, too. Do I look silly?"

That was not how Jake would describe her. Between the hat, the faded jeans and the pair of cowboy boots, she was the prettiest cowgirl he'd seen in a long time. "You look great. No one would ever know you're a city girl."

Olivia's eyes widened. Her hand cupped her cheek. "I just realized this all plays into Gammy's grand plan to keep me here in Bluebell."

Jake laughed. "I wouldn't worry. It will take more than some Western clothing for you to uproot your life and move."

"You're right. Miami is my home. That will never change."

Olivia's words ignited a sinking feeling in his stomach. While they headed toward the arena to watch the dog stunt show, Jake struggled to brush off the disappointment Olivia's comment had sparked. Today was a day to celebrate the twins' birthday. This wasn't the time to lose his heart to a woman who lived a couple thousand miles away and wanted children of her own. Having more children wasn't part of his plan.

Chapter Nine

From the moment Olivia had arrived on the grounds with Gammy, a sense of nostalgia consumed her. She loved everything about the fair. And the best part was the day had just begun. The cheerful sounds of children enjoying themselves, the food trucks lining the trampled grass, the air filled with the sweet smells of treats, all brought back wonderful memories of the trip to the fair with her father. Jake's advice from earlier entered her mind. For most of her adult life, she'd allowed work to dominate both her schedule and her ability to enjoy the gift of life. She could never imagine the pain Jake had endured. If anyone understood the reason to live each day as if it were your last, it was Jake Beckett.

"I can't believe you're not asking where I'm taking you. I thought you'd want to pull out your cell phone and put it on your schedule."

Jake playfully nudged his arm against Olivia, making her keenly aware of his broad shoulders. "Stop it." She pushed back against him, giggling like a child. "I've decided my phone is off-limits today."

"Good for you. But I know from experience, sometimes old habits are hard to break."

"I'll keep that in mind." Olivia knew all too well about breaking habits. Lately, she'd been more guarded of her time off from the hospital. At first it was difficult to say no to colleagues who once relied on her to cover when she wasn't on the schedule. But now she looked forward to those days where she was able to do something for herself. Going to a coffee shop and reading for hours was her latest obsession. "So, are you going to tell me where we're headed?"

"You're worse than the twins." Jake laughed. "Are we there yet?" His voice mimicked the twins' higher voices.

Olivia rolled her eyes and laughed. A group of senior women approached from the other direction.

"Hello, Jake."

"Hi, Mrs. Hinton. I hope you ladies are enjoying yourselves."

"Yes, we are. It looks like you are, too." The elderly woman winked as she and the others moved toward the line at the cotton candy vendor.

Since their ten-minute walk to wherever they were going began, Olivia noted that everyone who passed seemed to stop and say something to Jake. "Is there anyone you don't know?"

"That's the best part about living in a small town. I couldn't imagine raising my children anywhere but Bluebell." Jake stopped at the metal gate that surrounded an enclosed building. "We're here."

Olivia's heart raced. She didn't know what was behind the gate, but the anticipation was exhilarating. "Can you tell me now?"

Jake turned, wearing a smile. "We're going to watch the stunt dogs perform."

For a second, Olivia had to remind herself to breathe. Her mouth was dry. She struggled to find the right words.

Jake gently placed his hand on her shoulder. "Are you okay?"

Olivia bit her lower lip. Tears peppered her eyelashes.

"What is it? I thought you'd enjoy this."

Olivia shook her head. "I haven't seen the stunt dogs since I was a kid. They were my dad's favorite."

"Your grandmother mentioned it. That's why I thought you'd like to come to the show."

Jake's thoughtfulness was endearing. She'd forgotten she'd mentioned to Gammy about going to the dog show with her dad. She inhaled a deep breath. "I'd love to go with you."

"I'm happy to hear that. Shall we?" Jake gently clasped her hand, creating a reaction she couldn't quite identify. Whatever it was, she liked it.

Ten minutes later, Olivia sat alone in the stands while Jake was off getting popcorn. He said one of the best parts about seeing the show was the butter-laden popcorn. She couldn't argue with that. She even ordered a diet soda. After all, she was on vacation.

Her shoulders relaxed as she took in the crowd of mostly children with their parents. A longing tried to take hold, but she forced it aside. Today was a day to enjoy life. She refused to dwell on the past.

Olivia spotted Jake working his way through the crowd, carrying a cardboard tray with their snacks. Her pulse ticked up a few beats. Western-style clothing was never her thing, but Jake sure looked good in his long-sleeved denim shirt with silver buttons down the front, paired with khakis. As he moved toward their seats, she couldn't ignore the way the shirt brought out the blue in his eyes.

"Okay, I got buttered popcorn and your diet soda. I think we have a couple of minutes before the show starts." He settled in the seat next to her and passed the drink.

Olivia put the straw between her lips. She drank as though she'd been in the desert for days, while sneaking peeks at his freshly shaven face.

"You are hooked on that stuff. I think you'll need a refill before the show starts." He laughed.

She wasn't sure if it was the syrupy sweet taste or the carbonation of the soda, but whatever it was, the cool drink settled her nerves. Olivia didn't recall ever feeling nervous during their classes at camp. Today, something seemed different. She was relieved when the announcer came over the loudspeaker to say the show would start in a few minutes.

Jake settled the tub of popcorn on his right knee and helped himself. "The stuff is great." He crammed a handful into his mouth.

Olivia reached inside the bucket and grabbed an equally large handful. "I better eat up because it looks like it will be gone before the show even gets started," she teased.

"Don't worry. They have free refills." Jake laughed.

"You better pace yourself." Olivia smiled, feeling more at ease with her one-on-one time with Jake as their conversation continued.

"Are you kidding? When I was little, I could eat this stuff all day." He raised the tub and took another handful.

Olivia scanned the program she'd picked up on the

way inside. "This looks like a great lineup of stunts. I guess dogs have gotten smarter since I was a kid. I remember the juggling. It was hilarious, but also impressive. I never understood how they trained the dogs to do that."

"What about the dancing? Last year two Border collies did the tango. I tried to get Tank to do it, but he didn't want any part of it."

Jake's comment triggered a fond memory of her father. She closed her eyes for a moment. "Once, when I was little, my dad took me to a minor-league baseball game. Like my mother, I thought baseball was boring, but if I was with my dad, I was happy to go. Before they threw out the first pitch, a group of Jack Russell stunt dogs performed. I'll never forget it. I didn't know dogs could jump so high. They were even jumping rope. When we got home after the game, I remember my dad had convinced himself he could teach our dog, Tootie, to do the same."

"And did he?"

Olivia shook her head. "Tootie was a one-hundred-plus-pound Saint Bernard. What do you think?"

Jake laughed. "Excuse me for a second. My phone is vibrating." He reached into his back pocket and pulled out the device.

Olivia watched while Jake tapped the screen to open a text message.

He jumped to his feet. "I have to go. Logan said Kayla is upset."

Olivia stood.

"No, you stay and watch the show. I know how much it means to you."

That was true. Watching the stunt dogs was a trip

down memory lane for Olivia, but Kayla's well-being meant more. "If you don't mind, I'd rather go with you."

"I don't mind at all. Lately, it seems like you're able to handle Kayla's issues better than I am. Let's go."

Outside of the building, Olivia heard the announcer introducing the first stunt dog. The laughter grew distant as they moved at a brisk pace toward the rodeo venue.

Moments later, Olivia spotted Logan. He jogged in their direction. Kyle trailed behind.

"Where's Kayla?" Jake scanned the area.

"She's inside the women's bathroom." Logan pointed to a nearby toilet rental as Kyle caught up with the group.

"Is she sick?"

"No, Daddy. It was that mean ole Missy. She was teasing Kayla again about the fashion show," Kyle explained.

"Before the show started, the kids went outside to get a snow cone. Missy and some other girls were in line. Kyle came back inside to tell me Kayla had locked herself in the bathroom and that's when I texted you. I'm sorry, man. I should have gone with them to get the snack." Logan rubbed the side of his temple.

"It's not your fault. This fashion show has had Kayla upset for over a week. Maybe I need to speak with Missy's mother. I know kids tease each other, but this is a sensitive issue for Kayla."

Logan nodded his agreement.

Olivia's chest tightened. She glanced toward the bathroom. "Would you like for me to talk to her?"

"Yeah, if anyone can get her to come out, it's Dr. Olivia," Kyle added.

Jake agreed with his son. He turned to Olivia. "Like I said earlier, lately Kayla seems to respond better to you," Jake said.

Olivia rested her hand on Jake's arm. "Don't take offense. I'm sure you've tried your best. It may be easier for her to talk to another female. After my father died, the mean girls chased me into hiding many times."

Kyle moved closer to Olivia. "I'm sorry you got teased, Dr. Olivia."

Olivia's heart squeezed. "Thank you, Kyle." She patted his shoulder. "Let me get Kayla and maybe we can all watch the rodeo together."

"That sounds like a great idea. We'll just hang out here for a while," Jake said.

"But, Daddy, I never got my snow cone. Can we get one now? We can get one for Kayla when she comes out of the bathroom." Kyle tugged on Jake's hand.

"Sure." Jake looked at Olivia. "We'll meet back here?"

"Hopefully we won't be too long." Olivia turned and headed toward the restrooms. She sent up a silent prayer to be able to comfort Kayla and convince her to come out of the restroom and enjoy the fair.

Outside the door to the restroom, Olivia raised her hand and knocked. "Kayla, can you open the door, sweetie? It's Dr. Olivia." She scanned the area surrounding the two bathrooms for signs of Missy or any other children. "There's no one here except for me. I'd like to talk to you, but I'd rather see your face than talk to a door."

A soft giggle came through the vent at the top of the bathroom. This was promising. "Your daddy told me how word spreads in a small town. Can you imagine what people would think if they heard the lady from Florida talks to toilets?"

Another giggle sounded, but this time the door slowly opened. Kayla cautiously stepped outside. Her eyes were red and swollen. She hesitated for a moment before lunging into Olivia's arms.

The lump in Olivia's throat prevented any words from escaping her lips. Instead, she clung to the child like her life depended on it. At that moment, it did. Nothing else mattered but to protect Kayla and lessen the pain of losing her mother. Olivia had carried the same pain throughout her childhood and into her adult years. Yet the time spent with Kayla seemed to ease the heartache.

"Missy is so mean." Kayla sniffled and choked on her words. "She ruined my birthday."

"Let's go sit over there." Olivia pointed to a bench perched under an old weeping willow tree.

Kayla loosened her arms from around Olivia's waist but kept hold of her hand. They walked to the tree and took a seat.

"Do you want to tell me what happened earlier?"

Kayla inched closer to Olivia. "Missy said I wear boy clothes because I don't have a mommy to teach me."

Olivia's stomach clenched at the cruelty Kayla had experienced. "That wasn't nice of her to say that to you, sweetie. Sometimes words have more power than we realize. I'm not excusing Missy, but I don't think she's learned that lesson. We have to be careful when we choose our words. When I was a little girl, Gammy always told me sometimes it's best to say nothing." Olivia wasn't sure if Kayla understood. After Olivia's father died, a couple of kids at her school spoke horrible words to her. They said she should have done something when she'd come home from school and found her father on the floor. They told her his death was her fault.

"Like when Daddy says to hold my tongue?" Kayla nuzzled her head against Olivia's side.

Olivia smiled. "Exactly."

"Yeah, sometimes I probably say things I shouldn't, especially to Kyle." Kayla wiped her eyes and looked up. "I'm sorry, Dr. Olivia."

"For what, sweetie?"

"I said some mean things to you when you first got here."

Olivia ran her fingers through the back of Kayla's hair. "It's all forgotten." She kissed the top of her head, inhaling the sweet scent of her shampoo.

"I'm glad you came to get me. You made me feel better."

"Well, today is your special day. You shouldn't spend it hiding."

Kayla nodded. "It wasn't the best place to hide. It didn't smell too good in there."

Olivia laughed. "I'm sure it didn't. Are you ready to join the others and watch the rodeo?"

Kayla jumped off the bench. "Can I ask you something first?"

"What is it, sweetie?"

Kayla pushed the toe of her red tennis shoe into the grass. "Will you take me to the fashion show?"

"I didn't think you had any interest in watching the show."

"I don't want to watch. I want to be in it with you." Kayla twisted a strand of her hair.

Excitement coursed through Olivia's veins. Yesterday at Garrison's Mercantile, she'd eagerly volunteered to accompany Kayla to the fashion show. But then her heart sank when she recalled Jake's words. He didn't think it would be a good idea. How could she say no to Kayla? It would break her heart.

Kayla's eyes filled with hope as she waited for an answer. Olivia couldn't disappoint her. She wanted to put an end to Missy's teasing once and for all. But was that the real reason? Or was it because it would give Olivia an opportunity to be a mother? Even if it was only for one night. "There's nothing more that I'd rather do."

"I'm going to run a few errands. Do you need anything?" Myrna tapped on the counter.

Jake peered from underneath Myrna's kitchen cabinet beside the sink. "I think I'm good, thanks. Are you sure it's nothing I can run out and get for you?"

Myrna snatched her purse off the island and flung it over her shoulder. "Not unless you're interested in getting your hair permed." Myrna scurried toward the door and turned around. "Olivia and I took Callie out earlier this morning to work with her, but she's still not back. Can you check on her? I know she didn't have breakfast. That girl doesn't eat enough. I don't know how she survives living alone in Miami."

"Sure, I'd be happy to check on them." Jake had hoped to see Olivia while he was working at Myrna's house. Lately, he couldn't stop thinking about her.

Myrna fumbled in her purse. Her keys dropped to the ground.

Jake approached as Myrna got on her knees and felt around on the floor.

"Here they are." Jake picked up the leather strap right in front of her. Myrna should have been able to see it. But maybe not. While researching online, he remembered reading about blind spots in the center of the vision of patients with macular degeneration. "Maybe I should take you to the hairdresser and whatever other errands you have to run? We can go out for lunch, too. I can finish installing these lights underneath the cabinets later."

Myrna stood and brushed her hands on her pants. "You sound like Olivia."

"What do you mean?" Jake asked.

Myrna released a heavy sigh. "Just because I didn't see my keys on the floor, you're ready to take away my driver's license and lock me up in the house."

Jake put his hands in the air. "Hey, wait a minute. Remember, I'm on your side to continue to live independently. That's why I'm trying to get Callie trained and doing all the upgrades around your house. I want you to maintain your freedom for as long as you can."

"I'm sorry. I didn't mean to sound so defensive. I appreciate everything you and Olivia are doing for me. Olivia cares about me and her motives come from her heart. Perhaps my actions don't reflect it, but I know my limitations and I don't plan on doing anything foolish. As difficult as it is for me to admit, I need help. I've reached out to my friends and I'll continue to do so."

Jake was coming to his own realization that Olivia's motives were coming from a place of love. Saturday night, after the twins' party, while Jake tucked Kayla into bed, he learned Kayla had asked Olivia to take her to the mother-daughter fashion show. Olivia had agreed, even though he had told her he didn't think it was a good idea. Initially, Jake had jumped to conclusions. Since Kayla had been so upset about the show, he believed she didn't really want to go. Perhaps Olivia had pressured his daughter. But after talking with Kayla, he learned his conclusions were way off base. Olivia knew how much the fashion show meant to Kayla. She understood what it felt like for a child to be left out because they'd lost a parent. "So what's got you upset?"

"Olivia's been struggling with Callie acting out. The pup basically goes bonkers when someone comes to the door or when a phone rings. I told her it takes time to train the animal, but being the perfectionist she is, she thinks if it hasn't happened yet, it won't."

Jake ran his hand through his hair. This wasn't good.

Myrna sighed. "Bless her heart. Even as a little girl, Olivia lacked patience. I remember one Christmas I took her to see Santa Claus at the local department store. When she saw the line snaking through the store, she told me she'd rather just write him a letter than wait. I can't help but think Olivia's patience is wearing thin with Callie because she's eager to return to Miami. And of course, when she leaves, she wants to take me with her." Myrna placed her hands over her stomach. "I know she believes she's doing what's best for me, but just the thought of moving makes my stomach sour."

Jake couldn't stand to see Myrna upset. He was upset, too. It would crush the twins if Myrna left. The town wouldn't be the same.

Myrna glanced at her watch. "I need to get going. I don't want to miss my hair appointment. Maybe when you go outside you can remind Olivia that training a dog doesn't happen overnight. Otherwise, I'm afraid she's going to pack my bags." Myrna turned on her heel and scurried out the door.

Jake cleared his tools from the kitchen counter. He'd have plenty of time to finish the lighting installation before camp started this afternoon. He grabbed his insulated cup and unscrewed the lid to top off his coffee before going out in search of Olivia.

Outside, the midmorning sky was overcast. With a 70 percent chance of rain in the forecast for later today, he'd have to set up a few things inside the barn in case he needed to move the camp inside.

Jake scanned the open field, but Olivia was nowhere in sight. Off in the distance, he could hear Callie barking. Olivia must have taken her to the pond. He crested the hill and followed the grassy path that led to the benches Myrna's husband had built before he passed away. Jeb was handy with a hammer. He'd built the home where his wife still lived.

Jake squinted into the sunlight peeking through the clouds. He spotted Olivia sitting on the bench. She was leaning forward with her elbows resting on her thighs. Both hands covered her eyes.

Callie barked twice and came running toward him. Olivia didn't seem to notice the puppy was off her leash.

Jake scooped up the dog and moved closer to the bench. Olivia's shoulders quivered. She was crying.

He wasn't sure if she wanted to be alone to deal with whatever had her so upset. He didn't want to pry into her personal business, but he couldn't just leave her there.

Cautiously, Jake continued in Olivia's direction. He didn't want to startle her.

A gentle breeze blew and swept a tissue from Olivia's hand. She reached to pick it up, but Jake beat her to it. "Are you okay?"

She startled and quickly wiped her eyes on the back of her hand before pushing herself off the bench. "I didn't know you were here." Her brows rose as she looked at Callie. "Oh, I'm sorry. I was working with her and I got a phone call. I should have put her back on the leash before I took the call." Her arms dropped to her sides. "You're right. I'm not cut out to be a Puppy Raiser. I don't know what I'm doing."

"Hold on." Jake reached up with the tissue and blotted away the tears running down Olivia's cheeks. "I never said that. This is all new to you. It takes time. You're doing a great job with her."

"But I don't have time. I'll be thirty-six next month." Olivia flopped back down on the wooden seat.

Jake considered Olivia's words along with her actions. Something told him this wasn't only about training Callie. He took a seat next to her and put the puppy at his feet. "What does your birthday have to do with training Callie?"

Olivia shook her head. "It doesn't. I'm not talking about Callie."

Jake didn't want to pressure her, but it seemed like she was open to talking about what was bothering her. "I know you don't know me very well, but people tell me I'm a good listener. Maybe if you feel like talking about what's got you upset, I can help you."

"That's sweet of you, but I don't think anyone can help me."

"You'll never know unless you talk about it. Come on. I can't stand to see you like this," Jake said.

Olivia sat up straighter and pushed her shoulders back. She slowly turned to Jake. "My college roommate Beth called me. Mark, my ex-husband, got remarried last week."

"I'm sorry. I would imagine that's hard news to hear." Since Jake hadn't experienced a divorce, he couldn't imagine how this kind of turn of events would affect him. He always believed marriage was for life, but from what Olivia had shared, Mark had wanted out. *How do you stay with someone who no longer wants you?*

"It's not the marriage that surprises me. It's the rest of the story that—"

Olivia burst into tears again.

Callie perked up and jumped to her feet, releasing a cheerful bark.

Jake reached down and picked up the dog. He gently scratched her under the collar. "It's okay, girl."

Olivia sniffled and then shook her head, as if she wanted to shake out the last of her tears. "They are expecting a child."

Jake's stomach twisted. Unsure how to respond, he waited.

"I'm such a fool. Why did I ever marry him?"

This was unfamiliar territory, but he knew it was wrong for Olivia to blame herself. "You loved him. That's why you married him. Look, I don't know what happened, but I can tell you that Mark is the fool, not you."

Olivia rubbed her eyes. "Since we split, I kept telling myself it was all for the best. I wanted to have children, and he didn't. But that was all a lie. He wanted kids."

Jake's heart broke for Olivia. He couldn't imagine experiencing that kind of betrayal.

"He just didn't want to have them with me," she sobbed.

Jake squeezed his fists together. He'd never been the violent type, but if Mark was here, it would take every ounce of restraint not to punch the guy's lights out. Look what he'd done to Olivia, a beautiful and vibrant woman. But his actions had filled her with self-doubt. He placed Callie back on the ground and reached his arm around Olivia, not sure how she would respond.

Olivia slowly rested her head on Jake's shoulder. "Why did he stop loving me?"

Jake didn't know what to say. Olivia was only trying to process this devastating news. A part of him was glad he was there for her, yet a bigger part felt this was way too personal. The last thing he wanted to do was become invested in Olivia's personal life. Eventually, she'd be leaving with or without Myrna.

"It's my fault. He didn't believe I could ever slow down long enough in my career to raise a family."

From what Myrna had told Jake, she didn't believe Olivia could, either. Although Myrna said she had prayed about it constantly, she thought Olivia believed giving up her career would disappoint her father. "Could you slow down? You invested a lot of time to become a doctor."

"If slowing down meant having a family, then yes, that's more important to me. After the divorce, I stopped taking extra shifts on my days off."

"That's a positive step in the right direction," Jake said. Maybe Mark and Myrna were too quick to judge Olivia.

"Having a family is something I've dreamed of since I was a little girl. It might sound silly to you."

Jake shook his head. "Dreams are never silly if they're what God has put into your heart. You should never give up on a dream."

A gust of wind blew, swirling the smell of honeysuckle in the air.

Jake glanced up at the sky. The clouds were thickening. "It looks like we might get some rain this afternoon."

"That's not good. I don't think Callie can afford to miss a class. I've been having a hard time with her."

"Myrna mentioned your recent challenges with Callie.

I'll help you. She'll be fine. As for camp, it goes on—rain or shine."

Olivia flinched and pulled away. She'd been so upset maybe she hadn't realized how close they were sitting on the bench. "I'm sorry I dumped all this Mark stuff on you. That wasn't really fair."

"There's no need to apologize. I'm glad I was here to listen. I guess I'm returning the favor. You've been listening to Kayla a lot lately. I really appreciate it."

"Yeah, I've wanted to talk to you about that. I'm sorry if I was out of line when I accepted Kayla's invitation to the mother-daughter fashion show. I should have spoken with you first, but it broke my heart to see her so upset about Missy teasing her that when she asked, I couldn't say no." Olivia tucked her chin against her neck. "If you'd rather I didn't take her, I understand."

"Are you kidding? Ever since you agreed, she's been talking about it nonstop. If I told her she couldn't go, she'd never speak to me again." Jake smiled.

Olivia laughed. "I doubt that. She worships the ground you walk on."

"Well, my sources say you're high on her list of favorite people yourself," Jake stated.

Olivia smiled, and her face radiated. "I'd be dishonest if I said I didn't feel the same way about her—about both of your children. Getting to know them has been the greatest joy of my trip. I'm honored Kayla invited me to the show. I honestly can't think of anything I'd rather do—so thank you for allowing me to accompany your daughter."

Jake leaned in closer. "You know what?" He took both of her hands in his. "I think one day you're going to make a terrific mother."

Olivia took a deep breath. "Thank you, Jake."

Across the field, a black crow landed at the top of a pine tree and cawed.

"There is one thing I'm a little concerned about." Olivia squirmed on the seat. "Gammy has told me how people like to talk in Bluebell. I wouldn't want anyone in town to think—"

"What? That there's something going on between us?"

Olivia's cheeks blossomed into pink blotches. "Well, yes."

"It might shake things up a little around here." Jake wiggled his eyebrows. "Maybe a few people need to learn to keep their noses out of their neighbors' business."

Olivia poked her elbow into his arm. "Be nice. I think they all do it out of concern."

"Oh, look who's defending the small-town people now. I was joking, but you're right. We all take care of one another. That's the way it's always been."

Olivia gazed out into the open field and took a deep breath. "You know, the longer I'm here, I'm realizing that might not be such a bad thing."

Jake agreed. It was a great thing. Bluebell was the perfect place to settle down and raise a family. Once upon a time, his life had been proof of that. But he'd been there and done that. If Olivia changed her mind and stayed in Bluebell, could he take a chance on love for a second time? Or would his fears prevent any possibility of a future with Olivia?

Chapter Ten

"Good girl. You're doing great." Olivia dropped to her knees and kissed the top of Callie's head. She couldn't be prouder. The puppy's tail wagged back and forth as she devoured the attention.

All the credit went to Jake. He knew training Callie would require extra work and the skills Olivia didn't possess, but he went the extra mile. Despite his objection about her desire to move Gammy to Miami, he'd been generous with his time. Camp would end soon, but Jake planned to continue to work with Callie.

"It looks like she's finally got the Place command figured out," Jake said.

Olivia got to her feet and spun around in the open field. She spotted Jake approaching, dressed in faded jeans and a crisp white buttoned-up shirt. Despite the warm air temperature, goose bumps peppered her skin. His good looks were something she couldn't deny. Lately, they'd become more of a distraction. "I think you're right. Did you see her in camp today? Not only did she take her place on the mat without being told, but she stayed down, too. I felt like a proud mama."

Jake laughed. "You should be proud. You've worked hard with Callie."

"The extra time you've spent with us has helped. You're good at what you do."

"It helps when you love your work, but you probably know that."

Olivia believed practicing medicine was what she loved. She also believed it was what her father would have wanted. Had she been wrong? Honestly, she hadn't missed Miami and the stress of working long hours. She could never admit it to Gammy or to Jake, but Bluebell was part of the reason she had mixed feelings about returning home. "I don't think I love my work as much as you do. I used to, but sometimes seeing so much pain and death takes its toll."

Jake shook his head. "I don't know how you do it. I remember after Laura died, I wondered how the doctors dealt with death day in and day out."

"In our defense, sometimes we save lives or bring new life into the world." Olivia tried to convince herself that the good outweighed the bad, but she had the battle scars to prove that wasn't always the case.

"Daddy!" Kayla yelled as she and Kyle skipped across the field. "We finished putting away all the cones. Are you ready to go over to Miss Myrna's?"

"What's going on over there?" Jake asked.

"The church bake sale is this Sunday. We're going to help Miss Myrna bake snickerdoodles. I told you the other day." Kayla rolled her eyes.

Olivia's ears perked up. "That's right. I'm supposed to pick up some ground cinnamon on my way home today. I totally forgot."

Olivia had her face buried in her hands.

Jake sat down and waited for her to speak. He'd wait all night if need be. Shoot, he'd wait forever. He loved her.

Olivia lifted her head and cleared her throat. "The text was from my supervisor. There's a major staff shortage at the hospital because of the flu. She's booked me on the next flight back to Miami."

His stomach dropped. "When?"

Tears streamed down her face. "Tomorrow evening."

"What about Kayla? The fashion show is on Friday. You promised her." He squeezed his fists tight. Every muscle in his body tensed. He'd known this would happen, yet he'd done nothing to prevent the relationship between Olivia and Kayla from growing. Now his baby would have her heart broken, exactly like he'd predicted.

"Don't you think I know that? I've been looking forward to it as much as Kayla."

Jake shook his head. "That doesn't matter. She's a child. She won't understand why you have to go, only that you're leaving her."

"It's my job, Jake. I don't know what I can do."

"Can't you ask for your return to be delayed a couple more days?"

"I've ignored her emails, texts and phone calls for the past week. She's not cutting me any slack. It's tomorrow or I won't have a job."

Jake raked his fingers through his hair. How would he tell Kayla?

Olivia inched off the bench. "I'll talk to Kayla. Maybe Gammy can take her in my place."

"No!" Jake grabbed her hand. "I don't think you understand how much this means to Kayla."

"How can you say that? I've walked in her shoes. Growing up without a father, I missed out on countless special events. I know exactly what she's going through." Olivia wiped the tears from her face. "Please don't say I don't understand. That's not fair."

Jake forced his shoulders to relax. He was being too hard on Olivia. It wasn't all her fault. "I'm sorry. I know you understand. My protective instincts are getting the best of me, I suppose. I just hate to see her disappointed. She's been looking forward to the show since you agreed to go with her." Jake couldn't forget the look on her face when she'd come home from their shopping trip last weekend. Kayla had talked nonstop about their matching outfits. Olivia leaving before the fashion show would crush her.

"If there was any way I could stay until Friday, I would, but I can't risk losing my job."

Jake nodded. "Let's go back inside and have our dessert. But don't mention this to Kayla."

"Don't you think I should be the one to tell her?"

"No. I'll talk to her when we get home. It will be better if it comes from me."

Olivia rubbed her arms. "Can't I even say goodbye to her and Kyle?"

"No, I think it's best if you just leave. Let me handle everything." Jake pushed himself off the bench. "We better go back inside."

A couple of minutes later, Jake and Olivia rejoined Myrna at the table. Thankfully, the children were at the indoor play area.

"What's going on?" Myrna asked. She looked at Olivia. "Have you been crying?"

Jake leaned back in his chair while Olivia explained the situation to her grandmother.

Jake opened the back door of his truck and unfastened the car seat. "I'll just slip this into your back seat and we'll hit the road."

Kayla and Kyle raced to the cars.

"I'm going with Daddy!" Kyle announced.

"It's just us girls in your car, right?" Kayla looked at Olivia.

"That's right. Girls only." She winked.

"Okay then, we'll all meet up at Miss Myrna's house," Jake suggested.

Jake fastened Kayla into her seat. Then he and Kyle got into the truck and drove away.

"Come on, Dr. Olivia. Let's go," Kayla called out.

Olivia crated Callie and then climbed behind the wheel of the SUV. She settled against the leather seat and peered in the rearview mirror at Kayla. Her body shivered. This was what it felt like to have a family.

For the first five minutes of their trip to Gammy's house, Kayla chattered nonstop about the fashion s

"When do you think we'll go shopping, Dr.

"Maybe next weekend, if your father says

"Why do we have to wait so long? I wis today." Kayla giggled.

"You have school. That always con said.

"School ruins everything."

"Also, Callie's camp graduation is this Saturday. I'll need your help to get her ready." Olivia was looking forward to spending the day with the twins.

"But you and Daddy are still going to train her since she's a slow learner."

"That's true. Callie needs more work if she's going to help Gammy, but she's coming along." Olivia admired

"I guess it slipped my mind, too." Jake looked at Olivia and shrugged his shoulders.

Olivia picked up Callie. "I better get to the store."

"I need to pick up a couple of things from the store, too. Why don't I grab the cinnamon and you go ahead to Myrna's house?" Jake suggested.

"Can I ride with Dr. Olivia to Miss Myrna's house?" Kayla tugged on her father's arm.

Olivia nodded to Jake.

"We'll have to get the car seat loaded into Olivia's car first."

"We should buy Dr. Olivia a car seat since we'll be together a lot," Kayla suggested.

Olivia's heart warmed at the thought of a car filled with child seats. She forced the thought away. This was only temporary. Once she got back home to Florida, there would be no need for a child restraint system.

"It's only a trip to the grocery store, sweetie," Jake ___ered.

___ve'll be doing a lot of shopping for the mother-___hion show, right, Dr. Olivia?"

___d herself to stop thinking about the future ___oment. "You're right. We have a lot of ___n fact, we might need to take a trip to ___ with your father."

___ddy? Please! Please!" Kayla pleaded.

"Are you sure about this?" Jake asked.

"Of course. We can make a day out of it. We'll have lunch out, maybe get our nails done." Olivia rested her hand on Kayla's shoulder. "How does that sound?"

"Great! Maybe we'll run into mean ole Missy!"

Olivia and Jake shared a laugh as they headed to their vehicles.

guished. "Why don't we follow my daddy's advice and enjoy each moment of every day?"

"Okay, but I'm still going to pray that you change your mind and stay."

Ten minutes later, Olivia navigated the SUV down the long driveway leading to Gammy's house. She filled the silence with music from an oldies station. Olivia always enjoyed listening to music from the 1950s. It surprised her to learn Kayla enjoyed the same. She said it was the station her mommy liked. "Okay, let's get inside and see what Gammy is up to. Your daddy and Kyle will be here soon and we can get started baking for the sale."

Olivia turned off the ignition and exited the vehicle. She opened the back door and reached in to unfasten Kayla's car seat.

Kayla wiggled out of the chair and jumped to the ground. "What's your favorite kind of cookie?" she asked as she took hold of Olivia's hand.

"Of course, Gammy always bakes the best snickerdoodles, but I've never told her that my favorite is oatmeal chocolate chip."

"Mine too! Do you think we can make those today?"

"I don't see why not. Gammy's pantry is well stocked, so I'm sure we can find some oats."

"Let's go inside and check," Kayla said.

They scaled the front steps. Olivia opened the screen door, and they moved inside.

"Miss Myrna! We're here," Kayla called out from the foyer.

The house was eerily silent. Olivia had seen Callie sniffing around in the side yard when they pulled into the driveway. "Gammy? Are you up there?" Olivia yelled from the bottom of the stairs.

"I'm in my bedroom," Gammy finally answered.

"Come on down so we can get started with the cookies. Jake and Kyle are on their way with the cinnamon."

"I need to wait a few minutes."

Something wasn't right. Her tone sounded weak. Olivia looked at Kayla. "Let's go check on her."

At the top of the steps, Olivia paused and sent up a silent prayer that Gammy was okay. They headed toward her bedroom at the end of the hall.

Olivia stepped inside. Gammy sat in her reading chair. She had her left foot propped up with a pillow on top of her footstool. In her right hand, she held an ice pack. "What's wrong?" Olivia raced to her side and dropped to her knees.

"It's nothing, dear." She fanned her hand in the air. "Go on and get started on the cookies. I'll be down in a minute."

"You never sit during the day except at mealtime. And even then, you're jumping up to do one thing or another."

Her grandmother laughed. "I just tripped, that's all."

"Where? Do I need to take you to the emergency room?" Olivia asked.

"Should I call my daddy?" Kayla cried out.

"You both sure have a lot of questions." Myrna rested her hand on Kayla's arm. "I'm fine."

"How can you sit there and say that? Tell me exactly what happened," Olivia demanded.

"My cell phone rang, so I was rushing from the family room into the kitchen. I tripped on the step. I shouldn't have been walking around in my socks."

Olivia released a heavy breath. That step was nothing but trouble. Her grandmother had no business living in a house with a sunken family room. "So you didn't see the step? Your eyes are getting worse."

"I just missed the step. I've done it thousands of times over the years, even when I was a lot younger."

Olivia wet her lips. "How did you get up here?"

"I just took it slow and exhibited a little determination." Myrna gave a dismissive glance. "Exactly the way your grandfather used to handle difficulties in life."

Olivia's fists tightened. Sometimes, her grandmother was as stubborn as a coffee stain on a white shirt. She would never admit to being in pain, her failing eyesight, or that this house couldn't accommodate her needs. It didn't matter how many changes Jake made—her gammy couldn't stay in this house. She took the melted ice bag from Gammy. "Kayla, stay here with Gammy while I go downstairs and get some fresh ice. Make sure she doesn't get up."

"I'm not a child, Olivia. I don't need someone watching me." Myrna attempted to stand, but winced in pain and dropped back into the chair.

Olivia stood and shook her head. "I'll be right back." She stormed from the room and rushed down the stairs, not sure who she was angrier with, Jake or herself. She shouldn't have made this agreement to train Callie. Obviously, the dog did not help prevent the fall. Olivia shuddered at the thought of how much worse it could have been.

Outside, car doors slammed. Jake and Kyle were home.

Olivia moved to the refrigerator and opened up the freezer. The icy blast of air did little to cool her temper. She needed to talk to Jake, but not in front of Kyle. The sooner she got her gammy moved to Miami, the safer she would be.

* * *

"Can you take this bag for me, son?"

Kyle reached for the grocery bag. Jake unloaded the other three bags from his truck.

Callie raced to the fence to greet them.

"Let's go inside and see what the girls are up to," Jake suggested.

Jake entered the kitchen and spotted Olivia wrestling with the ice maker. Her back was to the door. She murmured under her breath, but Jake couldn't quite make out what she was saying.

"I thought the place would smell of baked cookies by now," Jake announced.

Olivia jumped. "I didn't hear you come inside."

"Maybe it was because of the racket you were making with the ice maker. Is something wrong with it?" Jake moved a little closer and placed the grocery bags on the counter.

"Not the machine, but Gammy." Olivia slammed the freezer door closed.

Jake couldn't miss the anger washed across Olivia's face. He turned to Kyle. "Why don't you go find your sister?"

"She's upstairs in Gammy's bedroom," Olivia answered.

Kyle zipped out of the room.

Jake spotted the ice bag sitting on the counter. "What's going on?"

"Gammy fell and hurt her foot."

Jake's pulse ticked up. "You should have called me. Do we need to take her to the emergency room?"

Olivia picked up the ice pack and screwed the lid tighter. "She said she's fine, but I think she's only saying that because she knows I'm upset. She tripped on that stupid step from the family room into the kitchen."

Jake knew of the step. He had it on his list of things to address. "I know that's an issue in this house."

Olivia placed her hands on her hips. "I don't see how it can be fixed without remodeling the entire family room area."

"Relax. We can install a ramp. It's not that big of a deal," Jake explained.

"Well, it sounds like another costly expense. You know my grandmother is on a fixed income."

"Myrna has been open with me about her finances. A couple of guys plan to do the job for free. This is a small town, remember? Your grandmother has done so much for this community, it's the least we could do for her. I know it's hard for you to understand, but we take care of each other in Bluebell."

"So you've said." Olivia shook her head. "I'm afraid that step is just one of many issues in this house. What about the fact that her bedroom is upstairs? Are you going to install an elevator or something?"

"Look, I don't have all the answers now. I'm doing the best I can to help your grandmother stay at her home. It's what she wants."

"I'm not sure Callie is the answer. She obviously wasn't there for Gammy today."

Jake raked his hand through his hair. "Of course she wasn't. She's a puppy who's not fully trained. It takes time. It's what we agreed."

"Daddy, why are you fighting with Dr. Olivia?"

Jake spun around at the sound of Kayla's voice. "We're not fighting, sweetie." He glanced at Olivia, who simply shook her head.

Kayla shrugged her shoulders. "It sounded like it." She walked over to Olivia. "Miss Myrna wanted me to get the ice." Kayla took the bag.

"Thank you, Kayla. Tell Gammy I'll be up in a minute."

"Okay." Kayla raced out of the kitchen.

"I'm sorry. I didn't mean to pounce on you. I was upset about Gammy."

Jake understood Olivia's concern. She loved her grandmother. "You don't have to apologize. I know you're worried. Let's drop this for now. We agreed to help with the bake sale, so let's get the kids and have some fun."

"You're right. I'm going to run up and check on Gammy. I'll be right back with the kids." Olivia scurried out of the kitchen.

Jake slipped his cell phone from his back pocket and scrolled through his directory. He connected the call, but it went straight to voice mail. "George, hey, it's Jake. Remember that project I mentioned at Miss Myrna's house? Can you order the material this week? I'd like to get going on the ramp sooner rather than later. Call me when you have a chance."

Footsteps echoed down the front staircase. Jake moved to the cabinet that stocked all of Myrna's cookbooks.

"I don't know why you won't stay upstairs and keep the ice on your foot." Olivia guided her grandmother into the kitchen.

"I did ice it."

Olivia rolled her eyes. "For like two minutes."

"Ice, smice, I'm perfectly fine. I told you I just tripped. It was nothing. You worry too much, dear." Myrna walked toward Jake. "Hand me that cookbook. It's the one that has the biggest collection of cookie recipes."

Kayla moved close to Myrna. "Dr. Olivia said you probably have some oats in your pantry. She likes oatmeal chocolate chip cookies, too."

Just like Laura. Jake pulled the canister of oats from the bag and passed them to Olivia. "I bought these today."

"Thank you." She took the container and their fingers brushed. When their eyes connected, Jake noticed the pink hue that covered Olivia's cheeks before he pulled his eyes away.

Myrna slid a stool closer to the island and took a seat. "Okay, we've got a lot of baking to do. Olivia, did you pick up the cinnamon?"

"I got it," Jake answered and removed two bottles from the grocery sack.

"Perfect. We'll need at least eight dozen snickerdoodles to start. After we finish with those, you can bake the oatmeal chocolate chip. I also had a request for a few dozen peanut butter kiss cookies."

"We might be here all night." Jake rolled his eyes.

"That would be so cool!" Kyle cheered.

"Not when you have school in the morning, buddy. We better get cracking."

"Your father is right. Since I only have one oven, I think it's best that we each grab a mixing bowl and start making the batter." Myrna pointed to a stack of stainless steel bowls on the counter next to the sink. "Once the dough is ready, you can use these scoopers to make the balls." She passed a utensil to everyone. "I have more than enough cookie sheets, so we should be able to take one batch out and pop another into the oven. I've got the cooling racks lined up over there." She pointed to the counter on the other side of the kitchen.

"I feel like we just stepped inside Betty Crocker's kitchen," Jake joked.

"Who?" the twins asked in unison.

"Don't pay any attention to your father. He's just being silly." Myrna got up and scurried to the pantry. "Let me get everyone an apron so you don't mess up your clothes."

"Gammy, I wish you'd sit down and rest your foot."

"I've forgotten all about that. I wish you would too, Olivia. Really, I'm fine." Myrna passed a yellow apron to Olivia. "Here, put this on and get to work."

Olivia did as she was told. Jake locked eyes with her and smiled. Olivia moved to the empty counter space next to him. He leaned closer. "You better do as you're told or she might make you stay after class," he said with a laugh.

Three hours later, Myrna's kitchen smelled of sweet cinnamon and chocolate. Racks of cookies lined the countertop. A dusting of flour covered the floor.

"My hand is getting tired from stirring." Kayla dropped the wooden spoon into the cookie batter.

"Here, Kay. We can switch. I'm getting bored scooping the cookies off the baking sheet." Kyle extended his hand, offering the spatula.

Kayla snatched the kitchen tool and ran toward the cookies fresh out of the oven. She reached for the first tray. "Ouch! My hand!"

Jake jumped off his stool and ran to Kayla. "Did you touch the hot cookie sheet?"

"Yes. It burns!" Kayla cried out.

Olivia sprang into action. "I'll get my medical bag." She ran from the kitchen.

Jake heard Olivia's feet hit the wooden steps. A door slammed overhead. She was back in the kitchen in less than thirty seconds.

"Let me see." Olivia reached for Kayla's hand.

"Ow, it hurts."

"Right here?" Olivia pointed to the red mark.

"Yeah, it burns."

"I know it does, sweetie. I've got some gel in my bag. It will make it feel better."

"Will it stop the burning?"

"Yes, but first let's put your arm under some tepid water."

"Okay."

Olivia guided Kayla to the sink, turned on the faucet and gently placed her arm under the running water.

"Ouch!" Kayla cried out.

"I'm sorry, but I've got to get the area clean before I can put on the cooling gel. Are you okay?"

Kayla nodded and her lower lip quivered.

"You're being very brave. This is going to feel much better once I get the medicine on it."

"Okay." Kayla chewed on her lower lip.

Olivia squirted a dollop of the gel onto the burn. "Does that hurt?"

Kayla shook her head. "No. It feels kind of cold."

"That's how it's supposed to feel. That means the medicine is helping." Olivia continued to rub the ointment into Kayla's skin.

Jake stood close as Kayla's tears subsided.

Olivia placed the tube of medicine back inside her bag. She pulled out a bandage and unwrapped the packaging. "I'm going to cover the burn loosely with this bandage, okay?"

Kayla nodded and kept her eye on the wound.

"Now, you let me know if it hurts."

"Okay."

Olivia wrapped and taped the burn. "I'll send the medicine and bandages home with your daddy, so he can do the same before you go to bed tonight."

"Can't you do it later?" Kayla pleaded with Olivia.

"You'll be at your house and I'll be here looking after Gammy. I'll show your daddy how to doctor the burn just the way I did, okay?"

Kayla lunged from her stool and wrapped her arms around Olivia's neck. "Can't you come to our house? I only want you to do it."

Jake watched as Kayla squeezed Olivia tight, with no sign of letting go. His daughter's affection toward Olivia was both endearing and worrisome. The last thing he wanted was for Kayla to get too attached to Olivia. Her heading back to Florida soon would only leave a void in Kayla's life.

"Sweetie, come on now." Jake attempted to pry Kayla's arms from around Olivia, but she refused to let go.

Olivia looked up at Jake and shook her head, telling him it was okay. But was it?

"Thank you for taking care of me, Dr. Olivia. I wish you were my mommy." Kayla nuzzled her head into Olivia's shoulder.

Kyle sprang off his seat. "That would be so cool!"

Jake noticed Myrna's smile before she covered her mouth.

Kyle danced around the kitchen and glided toward

Jake. "Why don't you marry Dr. Olivia? Then you won't be lonely anymore."

This was getting out of hand. Jake didn't doubt that Olivia was as uncomfortable with the direction of this conversation as he was.

Myrna clapped her hands. "Okay, now. Who's hungry?"

"We are!" the twins cried out.

"Who would like pizza?" Myrna called out to the group.

"We do, we do!" Kyle and Kayla cheered.

Myrna grabbed her purse off the counter. She removed her wallet and glanced at Jake. "Why don't you and Olivia run out to Mr. Pepperoni and pick up a couple pizzas for our dinner?" She passed her credit card across the island. "I'll call in the order."

"Pizza party!" Kyle jumped up and down doing a fist pump.

"You don't have to feed us dinner. I've got some leftovers from last night in the refrigerator."

"We don't want meat loaf again, Daddy. Pizza is much better," Kayla chimed in.

"Quit arguing with me. After all the help you all have given me, we're having pizza. Take my card. Olivia, you go along with Jake. The kids and I can finish the cookies."

Olivia grabbed her purse and looked at Jake. "You're wasting your breath."

"I know, I know. Shall we?" Jake motioned with his arm for Olivia to head out. He turned to Myrna. "Give them my cell number," he said.

Several minutes later, behind the wheel of his truck, Jake fiddled with the radio. "What kind of music do you like to listen to?"

Olivia pulled down the sun visor. "I like oldies music."

Jake's heart squeezed. "That's what my wife used to listen to. She loved it."

"Kayla told me that was why she liked it, too. We were also talking more about our girls' trip to Denver. I'm sorry I didn't check with you first before I mentioned it in front of Kayla." Olivia tucked a piece of hair behind her ear. "I guess I got excited about the idea. It's been a long time since I had a day out with the girls."

"You don't need to apologize. I just hope Kayla didn't talk you into it. The fashion show might not be your thing."

Olivia ran her hands across the top of her jeans. "Actually, I'm excited about the show and spending time with Kayla."

"I know she's crazy about you." Jake hit the brake as the railroad crossing lights flashed.

"She certainly wasn't when I first got to town." Olivia laughed.

"True, but that's obviously changed. I hope she's not getting too used to having you around. I don't want her to get hurt when it's time for you to go home to Miami."

"I would never intentionally hurt Kayla. She's been through so much already."

"I'm sorry. I guess I worry too much."

"Kayla isn't the only one getting attached. Believe me, I've thought about how hard it will be for me to say goodbye."

"You could always stay in Bluebell." He hadn't meant to say that out loud. Or had he? He looked over at Olivia.

She examined her fingernails and turned her head.

They held each other's gaze.

Did she want to stay? If she did, it wouldn't be because of him. He was too old for her. There was too much baggage from his past. Yet the sparkle in her eyes told him *maybe*.

Excitement coursed through him and he leaned in.

Olivia followed his lead until their lips almost brushed, but then she glanced away.

"I can't. I'm sorry," Olivia said, turning away.

Heat filled his face. "No, I'm sorry. I don't know what I was thinking." Jake leaned back against the seat.

"I'm not sure what either of us was thinking." She pushed the hair away from her face.

Olivia broke the silence with a sigh. "Gammy is dropping hints for me to stay every chance she gets. During dinner last night, she even mentioned me becoming the town doctor. Luckily, she got a phone call and dropped that topic."

"There's been chatter about Dr. Dickerson retiring." Jake wasn't sure what would happen. Most doctors probably weren't interested in working in a small town where they might get paid with homemade apple pies. "We're hoping Doc hangs around a little longer. It's a long trip to Denver."

"There's no doctor's office closer?"

Jake shook his head. The train passed, and the gate lifted. He eased his foot on the accelerator. "Unfortunately, no. Doc tried to retire over a year ago, but he couldn't find anyone to take his place. His son, David, is also a doctor. We had hoped that he'd fill his dad's shoes upon retirement, but David went for the big bucks at a research hospital in California."

"I guess for some, it's all about the money."

After Jake lost his wife, he realized having money

helped, but family and friends mattered the most. "Not you?"

"I'll admit, the money was nice as far as paying off all my student loans was concerned, but a few years into my career, I went to work in the ER. That position was what I'd worked so hard for. It was a lifelong dream finally realized. I make a real difference every day in the ER, and I think my father would be proud of me."

"So now you have your dream job?" Jake asked.

Olivia remained quiet and gazed out the window. "Have you ever wanted something so bad, or looked forward to an event, but when it finally happens, you're left feeling…?"

When Olivia couldn't find the right word, he took the lead. "Empty?"

"Yes. That's exactly how I feel." Olivia sighed.

Jake hit the turn signal and pulled in front of the local pizza parlor, Mr. Pepperoni. He turned off the engine and unfastened his seat belt. "I don't want to sound like I'm getting into your business, but maybe you're one of those people who prefers the race over the finish. I think that's common in goal-driven people."

"You might be right. After I finished my residency, I became obsessed with reaching my next goal. People who took time off were slackers. I volunteered to speak at seminars and covered coworkers' shifts. I did anything to keep my mind occupied. I worked nonstop."

"What were you avoiding? Or what *are* you avoiding?" Jake asked.

Olivia turned to Jake and unbuckled her seat belt. "What makes you think there's something I'm avoiding?"

"It's been my experience that people who fill every

minute of their day with work are usually trying to avoid something or someone."

Olivia squirmed in the leather seat. "You're a wise man, Mr. Beckett. Are you speaking from experience?"

Jake laughed. "I think we all go through times where we bury ourselves in our work in order to cope with something we want to but can't control."

For a moment, silence filled the cab of the truck.

"Any advice on what to do when the person you're trying to avoid is yourself?" Olivia laughed half-heartedly.

"Maybe not advice, but like I said, I'm a good listener if you want to talk about anything on your mind."

Olivia looked at her watch. "What about the pizzas? I don't want to keep everyone waiting."

"Don't worry about that. Mario is always running behind on his orders. Besides, he'll send me a text when the order is ready for pickup. Tell me what's going on. Is this about your ex-husband and his expanding family?"

"I can't put all the blame on him. He spent years listening to my excuses about why I couldn't make it home for dinner. Or why I couldn't attend a function at his work. He put up with me for a lot longer than I would have."

"Why did you make excuses?" He hoped Olivia could trust him enough to share the burden she'd been carrying.

"After my father died, I blamed myself for his death."

Jake shook his head. "But why? You were only a little girl."

"I should have been there for him, but I wasn't. I know I can't change that, but I've lived my entire life trying to make up for my shortcomings. Trying to make sure that I lived a life he would be proud of. I've done everything for him, and in doing so, I've lost the opportunity to have the one thing I've always wanted—a family of my own."

Silence hung in the air. There was nothing more Olivia wanted to share.

Jake's phone signaled an incoming text message. He checked the device resting on his console. "The pizza's ready."

"Great. I'm starving." Olivia opened the truck door and stepped from the vehicle.

Jake considered Olivia's words, and something struck him in his heart. The feelings for her that were growing in him needed to be pushed away. He wouldn't be responsible for denying her of her only dream. Olivia wanted kids, and on the day he lost his wife and child, he vowed never to have more children. The risk was too great. That chapter of his life had come to a heartbreaking close.

Chapter Eleven

"Thank you all for coming out today." Jake scanned the crowd and smiled. "The last day of camp is always bittersweet for me, but it's time for you and your puppies to spread your wings."

The crowd broke into cheers and applause.

Olivia reached down and picked up Callie. "Today's your day," she whispered in the puppy's ear before turning her attention back to Jake. It was becoming more difficult to not notice him, especially after their almost kiss in the car the other day. As much as Olivia didn't want to admit it, she wished the pizza had taken a little longer to bake.

"Today is a special day. It represents not only the culmination of all your hard work, dedication and love over these past several weeks, but also the beginning of your puppy's journey toward the opportunity to change someone's life. There will be a lot of blood, sweat and tears ahead for each of you because raising a puppy isn't easy. It's downright hard sometimes, but trust me when I say the day you see your puppy helping its assigned handler, you'll forget those challenging times.

"Since Rebecca has the most experience with being a Puppy Raiser, she has volunteered to help with any concerns now that camp has concluded. If you have questions or problems, Rebecca and I will be available to support you either by phone, email or video conference. You'll never be alone, so don't forget that. After we eat, I want to get a photo of each of you with your puppy. Now Kayla and Kyle will pass out your certificate of completion while I go fire up the grill."

The class clapped and cheered, and shouts of "thank you" could be heard.

Jake handed Kyle and Kayla the folder with each participant's certification.

"My tummy doesn't feel good, Daddy," Kyle moaned.

"I can pass them out by myself." Kayla glanced at Kyle.

Olivia's ears perked up. Even though she wasn't working at the hospital, she was always on call. She moved closer to Kyle. "Does your tummy hurt or do you feel sick?"

"I don't know. It just feels funny."

"Can you show me where?" Olivia asked.

"Right here." Kyle held his belly button.

"Maybe you should go lie on the sofa for a while," Olivia suggested.

Jake felt his head. "He doesn't seem to have a fever. Maybe he's hungry. A piece of barbecue chicken or maybe a hamburger might make you feel better. He ate little at breakfast this morning."

Kyle wrinkled up his nose and shrugged his shoulders.

"Would you rather your sister take care of the certificates?"

"No, I want to." Kyle and Kayla left and headed toward the class.

Maybe Jake was right about Kyle just being hungry. She'd check on him later.

Jake packed his tablet inside his backpack and zipped it closed. "I guess I better get the grill started. Do you want to help me?"

"Of course. Just tell me what I can do," Olivia said.

"Myrna is up at the house getting some of the side dishes together, so that's covered." Jake flung his bag over his shoulder.

Gammy had left the house this morning while Olivia was still having her coffee. She said she had a list of things a mile long she wanted to do before the cookout. "Do you think I should go give her a hand?"

"You know your grandmother likes to take total control of the kitchen. Besides, I thought if we worked together, we'd get the food out quicker. We have a hungry crew here." Jake laughed. A light breeze blew a few strands of hair from Olivia's ponytail as they strolled toward the patio area.

"Watch your step." Jake reached for her hand as they climbed up the steep hill that led to an oversize brick patio. Once at the top, Jake let go of her hand. Olivia looked down and missed the feel of his large, calloused hand.

"Wow! This is quite a barbecue. It almost looks like you have a full kitchen." Olivia strolled toward the large barbecue with a brick base. The impressive design had a six-burner grill, a stainless steel refrigerator, a side burner and an abundant amount of counter space.

"This is incredible. It almost makes me want to take up cooking." Olivia opened the steel doors below the countertop and noticed a supply of plates, serving dishes and skewers.

"I built this a few years ago. My brothers and I like to have family cookouts in the summer months, so I thought I'd make it big enough for all of us to enjoy. Hopefully, our hectic schedules will slow down so we can plan something."

"You did a fantastic job. It looks like something you'd see in a home-and-garden magazine. I can't even have a small grill at my condo."

"Thanks. Another perk to living in the country, I guess." Jake scanned the property. "I'd like to do a bit more landscaping."

Olivia put her hands on her hips and looked out across the land. "With that incredible view of the Rockies, I don't think you need to do anything." She spotted an oversize swing situated underneath a massive Douglas fir. "I'm sure that's a beautiful place to watch the sunset."

Jake nodded. "It's one of the best views on the property. Maybe you'd like to check it out sometime?" Jake held her gaze.

Once again, their almost kiss came to mind, igniting a warmth on her face.

"Are you okay?" Jake asked. "Your cheeks look a little flushed."

Olivia placed a hand on the side of her face. "It must be this warm sun."

"Jake, dear," Gammy called from the open back door. "Do you want me to wrap up the corn on the cob in some tinfoil to throw on the grill? I've got all the hamburger patties ready to go. I still have to put the sauce on the chicken."

This was the perfect opportunity to put some space

between her and Jake. The reaction Olivia had in his presence was becoming more confusing. "I'll come inside and help you." She turned to Jake. "If you want to get the grill started, I'll go bring out the food."

"That sounds good. Maybe I can throw some hamburgers and hot dogs on first, since they'll cook faster."

"I'll get them." Olivia turned on her heel and hurried into the house, unable to get the thought of watching the sunset with Jake out of her mind.

Two hours later, with everyone's stomach filled, Olivia stood alone in Jake's kitchen. Gammy and Kayla had gone to help Nellie with the inventory at the mercantile, so Olivia had volunteered to clean up while the guests played a game of horseshoes outside.

She walked toward the kitchen sink. The twins' drawings covering the refrigerator captured her attention. She'd seen them before, but a few more had been added. Her heart ached.

"Need some help?"

Olivia jumped, her fingers losing their grip on the top plate in the stack, and the porcelain dish crashed to the floor. "Oh, I'm sorry." She quickly set the other dishes on the counter so she could clean up the mess she'd created.

"No, it's totally my fault. I shouldn't have snuck up on you. It was obvious you were lost in thought." Jake moved toward the pantry, stepping over the broken dish. "Let me get the dustpan and broom. I'll have this cleaned up in no time."

Olivia picked up the remaining dishes from the counter and brought them to the sink. She turned on the water and began washing each by hand. Her thoughts stayed with the drawings on the refrigerator.

Jake swept up the remaining pieces, carried the dustpan out to the laundry room trash can and returned to the kitchen.

"What's on your mind?" Jake leaned in over her shoulder.

For the second time, Olivia flinched in surprise, but this time nothing shattered. She turned off the water and placed the plate into the drying rack. "What makes you ask?"

"When I walked in, you were a thousand miles away. Remember, I'm a good listener." Jake gently nudged his shoulder into hers.

Olivia took in a breath and moved to the refrigerator. "Can you tell me about some of these?" She pointed to the colorful drawings.

Jake followed her steps. He reached his hand toward the picture of a purple turkey. "I know the holiday is far off, but I found these when I was cleaning out my desk. They make me smile." Jake pointed to one of the drawings. "You're probably familiar with the traditional trace of your hand into a Thanksgiving turkey."

"I can take a wild guess who drew it—Kayla. She told me purple is her favorite color."

Jake nodded. "Even if it wasn't her favorite color, she would have picked something out of the ordinary. Kayla always likes to think outside the box, as noted by the red-and-yellow socks the turkey is wearing."

Olivia chuckled. "Unlike her brother." She pointed to the other turkey colored a rich brown.

"Kyle is exactly like his mother. She always followed the rules."

"What about this?" Olivia touched another drawing with a note written in the picture.

Jake rubbed his hand across his chin. "I remember that day like it was yesterday."

Olivia studied the attempt of a self-portrait created by Kyle. The boy in the drawing, dressed in a pair of denim overalls, stood with his hands behind his back and a tear streaming down his cheek. "What was he sorry for?"

"Kyle had gone fishing with his friend Zack and his father. They went to Mirror Lake, which is one of the largest in the area. Without my permission, Kyle took my pocket watch given to me by my father when I graduated from high school. It belonged to my grandfather. The watch didn't run, but my family had passed it down from many generations. My plan was to gift it to Kyle when he graduated. Unfortunately, it's somewhere at the bottom of the lake."

Olivia placed her hand to her mouth. "Poor Kyle. He must have felt so terrible."

"When Zack's father brought him home, Kyle was so upset he couldn't tell me what happened. He ran straight to his room and hid under the bed. I couldn't get him to come out. The bed didn't have enough clearance for me to go under after him, so I slept on top. Laura had passed a couple of months earlier. If she'd been alive, he would have gone straight to her. She always knew the right thing to say."

"So, when did he draw the picture for you?"

"I'm not exactly sure. When I got up the next morning, it was at my place on the kitchen table. He must have come out from underneath the bed in the middle of the night long enough to make the drawing, because when I woke up, he was still under the bed sleeping."

Olivia swallowed the lump in her throat. "That's the

sweetest story I've ever heard." She tried to hold back the tears.

"Hey, don't cry." Jake reached for a napkin, tore it in half and gently blotted her eyes.

"You're blessed to have such wonderful children."

"I thank God every day for them. If it weren't for Kayla and Kyle, I don't think I'd have a purpose in this world."

Jake spoke the truth and didn't mean any harm, but his words were like acid on her open wound. Had she wasted her life believing her purpose was to follow in her father's footsteps and be a successful ER doctor?

"Daddy, I don't feel good." Kyle entered the room. His face looked drawn and colorless.

Olivia cast her feelings away and raced to his side. She placed her hand on his forehead. "He's burning up."

"I've got to call Doc Dickerson." Jake slapped his hands against the back pockets of his jeans. "I must have left my phone outside by the barbecue."

"Here, you can search the internet for his number and use mine." Olivia grabbed the device off the counter.

"After Kayla's reoccurring bouts of strep throat last winter, I've got Doc Dickerson's number embedded in my brain." Jake stepped aside to make the call.

"Do you want to go lie down?" Olivia dropped to her knees, holding Kyle's hands.

"I feel like I'm going to—"

Before Kyle could finish his sentence, vomit projected onto Olivia's shirt.

"I'm sorry," Kyle whispered.

"It's okay, sweetie. Let's get you to the bathroom while your daddy calls the doctor."

Minutes later, Jake ran into the bathroom. "Doc is out of town on a family emergency."

"He doesn't have an on-call doctor who covers for him?" With Kyle in her arms, sitting on the bathroom floor, Olivia held the cool washcloth across his head.

Jake shook his head. "Only you." He knelt beside Kyle. "Are you feeling any better now that you threw up?"

Kyle nuzzled his face against Olivia's torso.

"I'd like to get him into his bed. I don't think he has much left in his stomach. Are you ready to go rest, sweetie?" Olivia asked.

Kyle flinched in her arms. "Ow!"

"What is it, son?"

"My tummy hurts."

"Can you show me where you feel the pain?" Olivia flung the cloth onto the vanity.

"Here." Kyle placed his hand against the lower right side of his abdomen.

"We need to get him to the hospital." Olivia rose to her feet with Kyle in her arms, careful not to alarm him.

"I don't want to go!" Kyle cried out.

"What do you think is wrong?" Jake's eyes widened.

"It could be his appendix. Has he ever had it removed?"

"No, but how can you tell?"

"The pain he experienced earlier was around his navel, but it's moved to his right side. Of course, I can't be sure without an ultrasound or CT scan."

"We'll have to take him to Denver. I'll go tell Logan what's going on. He can take over for me and wrap things up with the graduation festivities. I'll give Myrna a call, but I'd rather she not let Kayla know what's going on until we know anything for sure," Jake said.

"Good idea. Let me clean up my shirt a little and we'll get going." Olivia kissed the top of Kyle's forehead.

"I'll meet you outside in my truck." Jake sprinted out of the bathroom.

"I'm scared. I don't want to go," Kyle whimpered.

"There's nothing to be afraid of. You need to go to the hospital so the doctor can fix your tummy." Olivia brushed her hand across Kyle's cheek.

"But why can't you fix it?"

"Because the doctors at the hospital have everything they'll need to make you feel good again," Olivia reassured Kyle.

"But what if it hurts?"

"You'll be asleep, so you won't feel a thing. Then, when you wake up, your tummy will feel better."

"Will you be there when I wake up?" Kyle asked.

"I promise." Olivia took Kyle's hand and gave it a gentle squeeze.

"Okay, I'll go." Kyle rested his head on Olivia's shoulder.

With Kyle held tightly in her arms, Olivia raced outside to Jake's truck. The sound of birds chirping filled the air. She looked up and prayed silently to God that if Kyle was experiencing appendicitis, they'd make it to the hospital before the organ ruptured.

"I think I'm going to be sick again," Kyle moaned from the back seat.

Jake gripped the steering wheel and glanced in the rearview mirror, easing his foot off the accelerator as he navigated the two-lane mountain road.

"It's okay. I have this pan for you." Olivia held it underneath Kyle's chin.

Since Kyle first got sick, Olivia had been tending to

his every need. She'd climbed in the back seat and held him close.

Kyle heaved, but nothing came up. He slumped against Olivia, and she reapplied the cloth to his forehead.

When Jake had explained to Logan they were taking Kyle to the hospital, his brother jumped into action. He'd taken the sodas from the cooler and loaded the icy water into Jake's truck, along with some washcloths. He'd thrown the pan into the back seat, which had come in handy three times since they'd left Jake's house.

Olivia continued to monitor Kyle's temperature.

"We should be at the hospital in about five minutes, buddy."

"I'm scared to go there, Daddy," Kyle whimpered from the back seat.

Jake's heart hurt for his son. What he wouldn't give to be the one in pain. "There's nothing to be frightened of. I'll be with you."

"But you were with Mommy and she never came home," Kyle cried.

This would be the first trip to the ER since he'd taken Laura that fateful night. Jake was afraid it would spark some memories for Kyle. It certainly had for him. He'd driven this route with the same sense of urgency. *Lord, please don't let it be the same outcome.*

"You're going to be just fine," Olivia reassured Kyle. "I promised you, remember?"

After what felt like an eternity, Jake spotted the entrance to the hospital and hit his turn signal. "We're here."

Two hours later, Jake sat in the familiar chapel where he'd prayed for his wife and son. This time, he prayed for Kyle.

By the time they'd arrived at the hospital, Kyle was in serious condition. Following a scan, the doctor came into the waiting room and delivered the news. If they'd been a few minutes later, Kyle's appendix would likely have ruptured. But thanks to Olivia's expertise, Kyle would be okay.

He should have never brushed aside Kyle's initial complaints of not feeling well.

"Would you like some coffee?"

Jake looked up. Olivia's smile warmed his heart. He rose to his feet and took her into his arms, not caring if he spilled the beverage all over himself. "Thank you."

"It's only coffee." Olivia laughed. "If you're not careful, it's going to end up all over your nice shirt."

He pulled back and reached for the cup. "Thank you for what you did for Kyle. If it wasn't for you—"

"Stop. It's nothing any trained doctor wouldn't have done."

Jake shook his head. "I brushed him off. He came to me because he didn't feel well and I told him it was only because he was hungry."

"You had no way of knowing at that point it could be something serious."

With their mother gone, Jake was his children's sole protector. It was his job, and he had failed. "But you knew. I don't want to even think what could have happened if you hadn't taken charge of the situation and realized what was going on with Kyle's stomach."

"Remember, I get paid to know when people are sick." Olivia rested her hand on Jake's arm. "Try not to be so hard on yourself."

Jake captured her gaze. "You were wonderful with

Kyle. I know you're trained to treat people, but the way you were with him—the way he responded to you…"

"You're welcome." Olivia smiled, and they both took a seat.

Thoughts swirled in Jake's mind. Could he love again? Was he being unfair to his children by closing the door to the possibility of a relationship with another woman? With Olivia? It was obvious Kayla and Kyle adored her. Did she feel the same about them? About him?

For the next several minutes, they sat in silence.

Moments later, a sense of peace took hold. Jake hadn't felt like this in years. Was it because he knew Kyle would be okay? Or was Olivia opening his eyes to the opportunity of a new future?

Chapter Twelve

❧

Olivia took a sip of her coffee and unfastened her seat belt. It had been a wonderful week. Thankfully, Kyle had fully recovered from the appendicitis and was back in school on Tuesday. Jake and his friends had completed work on the ramp in Gammy's sunken living room, along with a few other improvements. Olivia couldn't deny that with all the improvements, Gammy's house was probably now safer than her condo in Miami.

"Dr. Olivia!"

Kyle raced across the front lawn, wearing a smile from ear to ear. "Why are you just sitting there? Come inside. Daddy made pancakes."

Olivia's stomach grumbled at the mention of food. She'd gotten up early to take Callie for a long walk. Easing herself into the day wasn't something she was used to, but she had to admit, it felt great. "I hope he puts chocolate chips in them." She exited the vehicle, opened the back door for Callie, and the dog jumped to the ground.

"Sit," Olivia commanded. The puppy sat at her feet and looked up.

"Hey, she's listening." Kyle smiled.

Olivia laughed. It had taken a lot of hard work and determination, but she and Jake had turned the corner with Callie. Jake definitely was a pro.

"Yes, she is. Thanks to your father." Olivia ruffled the top of Kyle's head. "Let's get some pancakes. I'm starved."

Kyle ran ahead with Callie chasing behind.

Olivia smiled as she moved through Jake's house toward the kitchen. Family photos filled the tabletops and the wall going up the staircase. It was exactly what she dreamed of having for herself one day.

Outside the kitchen, she paused. Kayla was chattering nonstop about the day ahead. Jake laughed when she asked if she could get her fingernails painted purple. The banter between father and daughter was endearing. Jake was the type of father a woman would handpick for her children. But he'd closed the door on more children. What if he hadn't? Would things be different for them?

"Dr. Olivia!" Kayla's attention turned to Olivia. She jumped from the chair at the kitchen table and ran across the room. "I'm so glad you're here!" She wrapped her arms around Olivia's waist.

"I'm glad I'm here, too. I heard there are pancakes." Olivia took Kayla's hand and strolled toward the stove, where Jake stood with a spatula in one hand and the handle of the skillet in the other.

"Good morning." Jake smiled.

"Good morning to you." Olivia moved her head closer to the pan. "Those smell delicious."

Jake picked up the open bag of chocolate chips and poured them into the bowl of batter. "There's a slight wait on special orders." He winked.

Olivia's heart fluttered. Was it her imagination, or

was Jake even more handsome this morning? "Word travels fast."

"Before Kyle took off upstairs, he told me you like chocolate chips in your pancakes. That's a favorite of mine too, but I don't make them often. I don't want to get the kids hooked on them."

Olivia crinkled her nose. "You're no fun. That was one of the best memories of my childhood."

"Pancakes?"

Olivia playfully nudged Jake's shoulder. "On Saturday mornings my mother always got her hair done, so my father was in charge of breakfast. He'd make us chocolate chip pancakes. He loved them, too."

"That's a wonderful memory."

Olivia nodded. No matter how much time passed, she still missed her father.

"Kayla, run upstairs and tell your brother breakfast is ready."

"Okay, but we have to eat fast. I want to have Dr. Olivia to myself for the whole day."

Olivia melted. She longed for the same.

Kayla ran out of the room and thundered up the hardwood steps.

"You might need a little extra sugar this morning if you want to keep up with Kayla." Jake poured another handful of chips into the bowl. "From the second her feet hit the floor this morning, all she's talked about is the shopping trip. I can't remember when I've seen her so excited."

"I think we'll have a wonderful time. I found a place to go for lunch where we can eat outside." Olivia had stayed up late last night scouring the internet for the perfect restaurant.

"She'll enjoy that. It's going to be a beautiful day. That's why I wanted you to bring Callie over. Kyle and I plan to take her out and about. It's good for her to continue to get more comfortable being around people in a public setting. She seems to enjoy the attention."

"I think you're right, but she has come a long way from our first solo outing." Olivia had taken Callie to the market, which turned out to be a disaster. After plowing into a few displays, she'd texted Jake for help. "I appreciate that. Some of the public spots in Florida might not be as welcoming to dogs as a small town like Bluebell."

Jake jerked his head toward Olivia. "So you've made your decision about moving Myrna? Does she know this?"

Her shoulders tensed. The last thing Olivia wanted to do was put a damper on her day out with Kayla. She hadn't decided. In fact, each day she spent in Bluebell made the thought of leaving more difficult. "I'm sorry. I shouldn't have brought it up. No definite plans. Let's not discuss that right now. Today is about Kayla…and pancakes."

Jake smiled and turned his attention back to the skillet. "I like the way you think."

"Look, Dr. Olivia! This is my size, and it looks just like the dress you bought for the fashion show." Kayla snatched the garment from the rack and held it under her chin.

The department store buzzed with activity. Olivia scanned the store. She spotted several of what looked to be mothers and daughters spending a lazy Saturday afternoon shopping. Today was a dream come true, except Kayla wasn't her daughter. Was it fair to Kayla to pretend that she was?

"Maybe I should get this dress and we can be twins."

Joy welled up in Olivia's heart. She couldn't resist this vivacious little girl. "I think that's a wonderful idea. Let's go try it on."

A few minutes later, Kayla burst out of the dressing room door and twirled. "It fits me perfectly. Can I get it? Please! I want to look exactly like you and be exactly like you when I grow up."

The possibility of one day seeing Kayla all grown up, walking down the aisle to the man she planned to marry, was a glorious thought. But the truth stared her in the face. She'd be returning to Miami and leaving Jake and his family behind. Reality had followed her like a dark cloud over the past couple of weeks. No. She couldn't ruin Kayla's big day out. "Yes, we should definitely get it. I can't think of anything I'd like more than to be your twin." Olivia winked.

A smile spread across Kayla's face. She raced to Olivia and wrapped her arms around her midsection. "I wish this day could last forever."

Olivia's heart skipped a beat. She bit hard on her lower lip to fight back the tears. She, too, longed to hold on to this day for eternity. "That would be nice, wouldn't it? But remember, the day has just started, so there's a lot more shopping. Then, after lunch, we still have to go to Winston's and get our manicures."

"Oh yeah, I forgot!" Kayla jumped up and down.

"Do another spin and I'll get it on video."

"Yeah! We can send it to Daddy!"

"That's a great idea." Olivia removed her phone from her bag and hit the record button. "Perfect."

Kayla giggled and spun in circles, causing the dress to fan outward. She nearly lost her balance.

Olivia laughed and stopped recording. "Okay, go get changed back into your jeans and sweater and we'll pay for your dress."

"Okay." Kayla skipped back to the dressing room.

Olivia wrapped her arms around her waist. How could she ever say goodbye to this sweet child?

Seconds later, her phone vibrated in her hand. Her eyes narrowed on the screen at the text message. A weight settled on her heart. It was her supervisor. Olivia's mind raced. She hadn't given Lisa an exact date of when she planned to return to work at the hospital. If she responded to the text now, she'd tell her boss she was never coming back. Bluebell was where she belonged. Of course, she couldn't do that. She had to go back. Working as an ER doctor was her life. It was what her father would have wanted.

Olivia tapped the screen. Call me was all it said.

She crammed the device into her bag. Today wasn't the day to think about the stress and long hours that filled her days and nights working in the ER. She was having too much fun pretending to be Kayla's mother. Whether it was right or wrong, Olivia didn't care. At this moment, she was the happiest she'd been in a long time. Correction—ever.

Jake and Kyle strolled along the brick sidewalk in downtown Bluebell. Flower baskets bursting with purple petunias hung from the lampposts lining the street.

"Maybe we should take Callie into the library, Daddy. Miss Myrna goes there a lot."

"You're right. She volunteers there at least once a week." Jake patted his son's shoulder. "Good thinking."

Kyle looked up and smiled. "Do you think Dr. Olivia will change her mind and stay here?"

Lately, that question had caused Jake some restless nights. A part of him couldn't imagine Olivia no longer being a part of Bluebell, but he wanted her to be happy. "I don't know. I guess we'll have to wait and see."

"Can I ask you something?" Kyle chewed his lower lip.

"You know you can always ask me anything. What is it?"

"Is it wrong for me to want Dr. Olivia to be my mommy?"

Kyle's question was a punch in the gut. Jake could no longer deny the fact that he wanted the same. Lately, he envisioned what it would be like to share the daily activities of life with Olivia by his side. Even the possibility of Olivia being the mother of his future children had swirled in his mind. Day by day, his desire was outweighing his fears. How could he fault Kyle for his feelings when he was experiencing the same longing? "Of course it's not wrong."

"That's good because I think about it a lot." Kyle grinned.

"What do you say we pop into The Hummingbird Café and grab a German chocolate doughnut before hitting the library?" Jake definitely needed to change the subject.

Kyle's eyes widened. "Even though I had chocolate chip pancakes for breakfast?"

"Why not? Who says your sister and Dr. Olivia get to have all the fun today? Besides, Callie needs to learn how to be inside a restaurant and not beg for food. Right, Callie?" Jake looked down at the dog.

Callie barked.

"Let's go." Jake tugged on the leash as they headed to the café.

Minutes later, the threesome stepped inside the establishment. Jake removed his cowboy hat. His eyes zeroed in on the chalkboard covering the wall behind the cash register. Cowboy Chili was the special of the day. He loved that stuff.

Sally Raphine, the owner, waved and stepped out from behind the counter. "I had a feeling my special would bring you in today."

"Hi, Miss Sally!" Kyle waved back.

"Hello, Kyle." She reached down and scratched the top of Callie's head. "This must be Myrna's dog, Callie. She told me the puppy is quite the handful, but she sure is cute."

Jake was proud of Callie's progress. "It was slow going at first, but Callie has come a long way."

"That's good to hear. I certainly don't want Myrna being uprooted and moved to Florida." Sally pressed her wrinkled hand to her cheek. "This town wouldn't be the same without her."

Jake couldn't agree more. Myrna was a pillar in Bluebell.

"Should I put in two orders of chili?" Sally asked.

"As much as I'd love a bowl, we just popped in for a couple of to-go doughnuts. We're headed to the library," Jake said.

"Two German chocolates?"

"Thanks, Sally. Take your time." Jake scanned the tables and spotted Dr. Dickerson sitting alone with a cup of coffee. "We'll go say hi to Doc."

"Can I go outside to the ball pit?"

The side courtyard area had several picnic tables for outdoor dining, along with a play area. When they arrived at the café, they'd seen two of Kyle's friends romping among the balls. "Sure, but be careful."

"Thanks!" Kyle took off to the front entrance.

Jake led Callie across the floor. "Hey, Doc. Do you mind if we join you?"

"Please, have a seat, son." Deep crevices surrounded the doctor's eyes and mouth, evidence of a life filled with smiles.

"Sit, Callie." Jake tied the leash to the back of the chair before he took a seat.

The doctor tipped his head toward the dog. "It looks like you've done a good job with her."

"I can't take all the credit. Myrna's granddaughter and I have worked together to train Callie."

"I've seen you two together. You make a good team."

Jake smiled and his face warmed.

"Have you fallen in love with her?"

Jake froze. The doctor was never one to sugarcoat a situation. The chatter inside the café seemed muted, and Jake felt his face flush. He turned away from the doctor, but he couldn't escape the truth. He was in love with Olivia.

"Son, it's okay. I knew Laura all her life. I brought her into this world. She would want you to be happy."

Jake had been denying his feelings for weeks. A part of him felt invigorated to admit the truth to someone. "I know she would." He massaged the back of his neck.

"But how do I move past feeling like I'm betraying her by falling in love with Olivia?"

"God wouldn't have brought Olivia into your life if He didn't know you were ready. He's shown you your future."

Jake brushed the tear that ran down his face.

Doc leaned across the table. "He created us to love. God doesn't want you to live the rest of your life grieving over a loss. He doesn't work like that."

The doctor pushed himself away from the table and rose to his feet. He moved behind Jake's chair and placed his hand on Jake's shoulder for a second. Jake expected the doctor to say something more, but he remained quiet before he turned and strolled out of the café.

Was Doc Dickerson right? Had God brought Olivia to Bluebell to become his wife instead of moving Myrna to Florida? Had those butterflies and feelings of excitement over the past few weeks when he spent time with Olivia been part of God's plan? Jake blinked away the tears and closed his eyes. *I trust You.*

Chapter Thirteen

Olivia tipped her chin to the sun and relaxed her head against the back of the rocking chair. The curved legs slid her forward and backward while a soft breeze blew against her face. Gammy's front porch had become one of her favorite spots to share some quiet time with God. Something she could admit to neglecting back home. These daily moments of solitude had given her time to reflect and had provided her with clarity about what was best for Gammy.

The porch was also a perfect spot to relive every second of her shopping trip with Kayla. Four days had passed, yet she couldn't get the day out of her mind. She hadn't seen Kayla since dropping her off at the house on Saturday evening. Jake and his brother Logan had traveled south to pick up two Labrador puppies, so Kayla and Kyle were staying at Cody's house. Jake was due home today.

She traced her fingers over the top of her laptop. She'd brought it outside to read her work emails. Before last Saturday, she'd checked her emails regularly, but now they seemed like an intrusion—something that would only cause her stress and angst. By logging in to the hospital's secure site, she'd be transported from the idyllic world of Bluebell to a stark, clinical environment filled with fluorescent lighting and antiseptic smells that assaulted her senses. The constant beeping of the monitors served as a reminder of the high stakes involved in her work.

The screen door slammed behind her.

"There you are. I made a fresh pot of coffee. I thought you would like a cup." Gammy passed a steaming mug to Olivia.

The emails could wait. "Thank you. I had a cup of tea earlier, but the caffeine hasn't kicked in enough to motivate me to check my work emails."

Gammy swatted her hand. "You're still on vacation. You shouldn't be checking in with work."

Her time in Bluebell with Gammy, Jake and the twins had opened Olivia's eyes to how her struggle to separate work from her personal life had negatively impacted her marriage. She'd never quite put two and two together. Or perhaps she didn't want to admit it. But the reality was the reason she was single again and childless at thirty-six was because she put work first. "My supervisor texted me the other day and I haven't gotten back to her."

"You've been busy. Besides, like I said, you're on vacation. She shouldn't be bothering you."

Olivia turned off her laptop.

"Oh, I almost forgot to tell you. Jake phoned earlier. He'd picked up the kids from school and was out running errands."

Olivia's pulse quickened. Lately, Jake, like Gammy, was occupying a lot of space in her mind. As much as she wanted to deny it, she'd fallen in love with him. But they were at different stages in life. She wanted children, and he had closed that chapter after he lost his wife.

"Jake wanted to know if we want to meet him and the kids at Charlie's Chuck Wagon in about an hour for dinner. I told him we'd love to. I figured you'd want to see him and the kids since it's been a few days."

Olivia was aware her grandmother wanted nothing more than to see her and Jake become a couple. "I think I can go a couple of days without seeing the Beckett family. Besides, soon I'll be returning to Miami and I won't see them again until I come back to visit you."

Gammy smiled. "Does that mean you're not taking me back to Florida with you?"

How could she do that to Gammy? If there was one thing she'd learned during her time in Bluebell, it was that her grandmother belonged in this town. Everyone loved her. Jake had proved his love and devotion to Gammy. He'd made her house a safer place and continued to train Callie. Olivia was at peace knowing Jake and the people in this town would watch over Gammy. "No, I'm leaving it up to you if you want to come and live with me. But I hope you'll remember my door will always be open for you and for Callie, even if your vision doesn't deteriorate."

"I appreciate that, dear." Gammy took a seat in the rocking chair next to Olivia. "It sounds like you've been doing a lot of thinking lately."

Olivia reached for her grandmother's hand and gave it a squeeze. "That's an understatement."

"I've been praying that you'll reconsider staying in Bluebell, maybe pursue a relationship with Jake. Is that something you've been thinking about?"

"Every day."

"And?"

"You know I can't do that." Her grandmother knew

her better than anyone. Gammy understood why becoming a doctor was important to her.

"I had hoped you'd realize that life isn't all about work. It's about sharing special moments with family and friends. I don't want you to continue to spend your life trying to make up for something that was out of your control. You were a child. You couldn't have saved your father. I know you want to honor his memory and you believe working in the ER will keep you closer to him, but he would want you to have a family of your own and to be happy. I'm worried you're not truly happy with your life right now."

"But if I stay in Bluebell, I'll never have children of my own," Olivia argued. "Jake doesn't want to have more kids. I can't fault him for that after what he went through losing his wife and child. I love Kayla and Kyle and I know I could love them as my own, but I can't give up my desire to have my own children with the man I marry."

Gammy shook her head. "Jake would never ask you to give up your dream. I've seen you two together. I can tell you have feelings for each other, but unfortunately, you're both stubborn. You need to talk to him."

Olivia swallowed past the pain. "What's the point?"

"I've said my piece. If going back to Miami brings you happiness, that's what you should do. All I've ever wanted for you was to be happy. But remember, working in a job that no longer gives you joy won't lead you to the life God has planned for you." Gammy smiled, then stood and made her way back toward the screen door.

Olivia considered her grandmother's words. As a child, she remembered her father talking about "God's plan." But had finding him unconscious on the floor been part of His plan? "I guess I should get cleaned up so we're not late for dinner."

* * *

Forty-five minutes later, Olivia spotted Jake and the kids—despite the dim lighting in the restaurant—sitting at a corner table. The aroma of grilled sirloin teased her taste buds. She was starving after skipping lunch to take Callie on a long walk.

"Dr. Olivia!" Kayla jumped from her chair.

"That child adores you," Gammy whispered in Olivia's ear as Kayla ran across the room.

"It seems like it's been forever since I've seen you. I missed you." Kayla wrapped her arms around Olivia's waist.

"I've missed you, too. Did you have fun with your uncle?"

"Yeah, Uncle Cody is funny." Kayla pulled on Olivia's hand. "I saved a chair for you next to me."

Olivia moved toward the table. Jake smiled broadly as she approached. The sweater she'd carefully selected to wear this evening did nothing to prevent the chill of excitement that radiated through her body when she saw the twinkle in his eyes.

"It's good to see you both." Jake stood and helped Gammy into her chair before turning to Olivia. "Kayla saved a seat for you." He placed his hand on her lower back and guided her to the space beside his daughter. "I thought after dinner we could take a walk around the lake—just the two of us," he whispered in her ear before she sat down.

Olivia had noticed the lit path that circled the lake when she and Gammy arrived. The idea of walking it with Jake hadn't crossed her mind, but it sounded more appealing than that sirloin steak she'd been craving. "I'd like that," she whispered back.

After their meal, the server cleared away the plates. While they waited for dessert, the children went to the jukebox with a handful of quarters.

Gammy cleared her throat. "Well, if you don't tell him, I guess I will."

Olivia wasn't sure what Gammy was referring to, so she complied. "Go right ahead."

"My granddaughter has decided that after all of your renovations and dog training, I'm safe to stay in Bluebell on my own."

Olivia's heart plummeted to the bottom of her stomach. Although it had been her decision, hearing it spoken out loud made it permanent.

Jake clapped his hands. "That's the best news I've heard all week. So you'll be staying on as well?"

Was that a hint of hopefulness Olivia detected in Jake's voice? "No, but I'm sure I'll be back for visits." Would she? Or would she get pulled back into the endless cycle of late-night shifts that left her too exhausted to do anything but sleep? Her phone chimed inside her purse.

"I've been hearing that phone ring all evening, dear. Don't you think you better check?" Gammy suggested.

"I didn't want to be rude."

Jake shrugged his shoulders. "I don't mind. Go ahead."

Olivia grabbed her bag from where it was hanging on the back of her chair and fished out her phone. She tapped the device and opened the text message. Her eyes opened wide and her hand trembled. The room felt as if it were spinning.

"What is it, dear? What's wrong?" Gammy asked.

Jake leaned in closer. "You okay?"

For the second time, Olivia read the incoming text message from her supervisor to make sure she'd read it correctly. Her mind reeled. Since she'd first arrived in Bluebell, all she could think about was how to convince Gammy to move back to Miami. She wanted no attachments with anyone in the community, particularly Jake and his adorable children. Now the last thing she wanted to do was leave, but what choice did she have? She'd lose her job if she didn't return. But it wasn't just a job for Olivia. If she wasn't practicing medicine, she'd lose the only connection to her father she had left. Her chair screeched as she forced herself away from the table and ran toward the front door, ignoring the calls from Gammy and Jake.

Once outside, Olivia raced to the lake. She sprinted down the path until she was out of breath. She stumbled to a bench and collapsed. Why was this happening? Why was she being forced to choose? It wasn't fair. Again, she scanned the screen to triple check, but she hadn't been mistaken. Her supervisor had booked her on the first available flight late tomorrow evening, which meant she would miss the mother-daughter fashion show. Either she would be on that flight or she'd have no job to go home to.

Jake nearly fell on his face when his foot stumbled over a rock. He didn't care. Finding Olivia was all he cared about. The look on her face when she'd read the text message terrified him. Regaining his footing, he picked up his pace and headed farther down the path. Thoughts raced through his mind. Was the message from her ex-husband? Whoever it was from owed Olivia an apology.

Finally, he spotted her sitting on one of several benches circling the lake. It was a good thing because he wasn't sure he could run much farther. Slowing his steps, he approached with caution. "Are you okay?"

"You can't leave!" Myrna's brows furrowed. "Kayla will be heartbroken."

"I explained everything to Jake, Gammy. I don't have a choice. If I don't go back on Thursday night, I won't have a job."

"Would that be the end of the world?"

Olivia looked over her shoulder. "We shouldn't be talking about this now. Jake wants to tell Kayla I'm leaving after they get home."

Myrna released a heavy breath and shook her head. "I don't agree with any of this, but for Kayla's sake, I'm going to stay out of it. I hope you both know what you're doing."

The table remained quiet for the next five minutes until Kyle and Kayla returned.

"What's for dessert?" Kyle asked, breaking the silence.

"I want a piece of chocolate cake," Kayla announced. "You should try it, Dr. Olivia. It's the best."

Jake waited for Olivia to respond, but she simply forced a smile. Myrna tossed him a look of concern.

"What's going on?" Kyle looked at the adults. "Why's everyone acting funny? Did you ask Dr. Olivia on the date?"

Jake flinched and Kyle's eyes widened.

"I'm sorry, Daddy. I forgot it was a secret." Kyle covered his mouth.

Kayla bounced in her seat. "What secret?"

Her brother dropped his hand away from his mouth. "Daddy likes Dr. Olivia. Last night when he tucked me in, he told me he was going to ask her on a date."

"Kyle!" Jake shouted loud enough for the neighboring table to glance their way. "Sorry." He waved a hand.

"Cool!" Kayla voiced her opinion.

Myrna laughed out loud. "I love it."

Olivia's face turned red.

Jake could do nothing but shake his head.

Later that evening, Jake sat hunched at the kitchen table with a cup of coffee between his hands. The pitter-patter of feet vibrated overhead as the children scurried around getting ready for bed. The entire trip home from the restaurant, Kayla had talked about the fashion show. He dreaded telling her that Olivia wouldn't be taking her, but at least she could go with Myrna. After dessert, Myrna had pulled Jake aside and offered to accompany Kayla to the show. Jake appreciated her kind gesture, but he knew in his heart Kayla only wanted Olivia.

Since learning Olivia was leaving, Jake had wrestled with his emotions. Should he have made his feelings toward her known when he'd found her down by the lake? Would that have affected her decision to leave? It was too late now. She planned to leave.

"Daddy, we're ready to be tucked in," Kayla called from the top of the stairs.

Jake sent up a silent prayer, asking for the words to come before he headed upstairs.

After Kyle said his prayers, Jake moved down the hall to Kayla's room. Before entering, he could hear his daughter telling her stuffed bulldog, Rocky, all about her trip to Denver with Olivia and the upcoming fashion show.

"Hey, sweetie. Are you ready to say your prayers?"

Kayla nodded and tucked Rocky under the pink comforter. Midway through her prayers, she yawned before saying "Amen."

Jake kissed the top of her head. "I need to talk to you for a minute about the fashion show."

Kayla's sleepy eyes lit up. "I can't wait!"

"Well, there's been a slight change of plans."

Kayla's brow crinkled.

"You'll still be going, but Miss Myrna will take you instead of Dr. Olivia."

Kayla pushed the comforter aside and popped upright in the bed. "Why? Did something happen to Dr. Olivia? Did she go to Heaven like Mommy did?" Her face turned pale.

Jake placed his hands on her shoulders to settle her down. "No, don't worry. She's fine."

"Then why isn't she taking me? She promised." Tears spilled down her face as she burrowed back under the comforter.

"She really wanted to, but she has to go back to work. Remember, she has a very important job. She helps sick people get well at the hospital, but right now, they don't have enough doctors, so she has to go back to help."

Kayla appeared lifeless in the bed.

Jake gently brushed her hair away from her face. "She'd stay if she could. I know she cares a lot for you."

"Then how could she go? I thought she was going to be my new mommy." She turned onto her side. "Leave me alone," she said and buried her face in the pillow and cried.

Jake reached over and turned off the princess lamp on the nightstand. "Tomorrow will be better, sweetie," he whispered. "I promise."

Chapter Fourteen

Thursday morning, Olivia took a deep breath and tucked the last sweater into her suitcase. She'd been awake since three o'clock. Tossing and turning, she'd spent a restless night in bed, knowing it would be her last sleep in Bluebell.

At first light, she'd peeled herself out from under the down duvet and thrown on a pair of yoga pants, a sweatshirt and tennis shoes to take Callie for a long walk. Once home, Gammy made her applesauce pancakes with warm maple syrup. Olivia would miss her grandmother and Callie after she returned to Miami, but she was confident Gammy belonged in Bluebell.

One thing she wasn't confident about was leaving Jake and the twins. Olivia had picked up the phone to call Jake many times since last night. She wanted to share her heart and tell him she'd fallen in love with him—that she could sacrifice her desire to have children of her own, if it meant she could be with him and his children. But what was the point? After breaking his daughter's heart, he'd probably never want to speak with her again. She couldn't blame him.

"Lunch is ready," Gammy called from downstairs.

Olivia sighed. She placed the last pair of pants into the luggage and zipped it closed. Her time in Bluebell had come to a close. It was time to get back to reality.

Once downstairs, she placed her suitcase next to the front door. Moving to the kitchen, she stopped short just outside the entrance, taking in the sounds of Gammy busying herself as she made their last meal together for a while. The familiar sounds of clanking pots and pans were as soothing as a dollop of honey in a cup of freshly steeped tea.

Olivia's senses were aware of all that surrounded her. She wanted to remember everything about this place, hoping it would provide comfort once she was back home and alone in her condo. The aroma of Gammy's fried chicken caused her stomach to rumble and drew her into the kitchen.

"Are you hungry?" Gammy turned the burner off and moved the skillet onto the trivet. Her normally cheerful smile was noticeably absent.

"I am now. The chicken smells delicious. You shouldn't have gone to all this trouble. I could grab something to eat at the airport."

Gammy swatted her hand. "This is no trouble. It's what I do."

It certainly was. Her grandmother was the most selfless person she'd ever known.

The doorbell rang. Callie took off running to greet the visitor.

"Grab a plate. I'll get the door." Gammy untied her apron and flung it on the counter.

Muted conversation carried through the foyer until Dr. Dickerson entered the kitchen.

"Hello, Olivia." The elderly gentleman nodded and rubbed his right knuckles with his left hand. "My arthritis is acting up. There must be rain in the forecast."

Olivia extended her hand. "I think I heard something about storms. It's good to see you, Doctor. Did you smell the chicken from town?"

He ran his palm in a circular motion over his stomach. "It's my favorite. I always told Myrna she should have opened a restaurant. She'd have customers from all over the state."

"Well, there's plenty for everyone, so please sit down and I'll bring the food to the table." Gammy smiled, happy to be serving a meal.

With the plates filled, Gammy took her seat across from the doctor. "What brings you by, besides my fried chicken?"

Dr. Dickerson picked up his napkin and wiped his mouth. "Well, after months of going back and forth, I'm finally taking your advice, Myrna. I plan to retire next month."

Gammy's eyes lit up. "That's wonderful. I'm sure Doris is thrilled."

"She's already planning our first cruise. She reminded me we haven't taken a vacation in over twenty years."

Olivia admired his dedication to the town. "Congratulations. I'm happy for you and Doris. Did you find someone to take over your practice?" Olivia would hate to see the town without a doctor. When Kyle got ill, she experienced firsthand how stressful it was to travel a long distance when a loved one was sick.

"Actually, that's why I'm here." Dr. Dickerson took a deep breath and continued. "I hope I can convince you to take over the practice. Apart from the necessary licensing requirements, you could step in without missing a beat. I've spoken to many people around town and everyone is in full agreement. You are the best person for the job."

Gammy clapped her hands together. "Wonderful!"

Stunned by the offer, Olivia was tongue-tied. The idea of staying in Bluebell and being a part of such a wonderful community was appealing, but the reality was she belonged in Miami. It was what her father would have wanted for her. Besides, given her feelings toward Jake, living in the same town with him and the twins would be too painful. "I'm flattered by the offer. Truly, I am."

"I detect some reservation." The doctor's smile slipped from his face.

"I'm grateful for my time in Bluebell, but Miami is my home. The ER needs me, especially now with the doctor shortage." Olivia glanced at Gammy, who discreetly wiped a tear from her cheek.

"I can't say that I'm not disappointed, but I respect your commitment to your position and your colleagues," Dr. Dickerson said. "I'm sure the hospital appreciates your dedication."

A casual conversation carried them through the rest of their meal. The excitement over the upcoming retirement that earlier filled the air had faded.

Thirty minutes later, Dr. Dickerson left and Olivia and Gammy cleaned up the kitchen in silence.

"I think I'll head out to pick up my outfits for the fashion show." Myrna approached Olivia with open arms. "It's probably best if I'm not here when you leave. It's too sad."

Olivia moved forward and the women embraced.

"I'm going to miss you bossing me around. You know that, don't you?" Olivia joked.

"It's only because I love you so much."

Olivia took a deep breath. "I love you, too."

"I know you have to do what's best for you. I admire your strength, dear. You're so much like your father." Myrna drew back and narrowed her eyes at Olivia. "I hope you realize how proud he would be of you."

Olivia buried her face in Gammy's shoulder and hugged her tighter. A part of her didn't want to let go or decline the doctor's offer. But she had to face the reality. There was no future for her and Jake.

Following a few seconds of silence, Myrna pulled away and wiped her eyes. "I better go."

Olivia was grateful when Gammy volunteered to take Kayla to the mother-daughter fashion show. Hopefully, her presence would ease Kayla's disappointment. "I don't like the idea of you driving to Denver alone."

"I won't be going by myself, dear. I'm heading over to Ruth's house. She will be driving, so you don't have to worry." She moved across the kitchen to the sink.

Olivia stepped closer to the kitchen sink. "Will you email me photos of the show?"

"Of course."

Olivia hugged her grandmother one more time. "Please drive safe."

"I always do." Gammy grabbed her purse from the pantry and headed out the door.

Moments later, Olivia heard Gammy's car start and drive away.

A chill caused Olivia to shiver as she stood alone in the kitchen. Her eyes scanned the room, taking in every sight and smell to carry back to Florida. She inhaled one last deep breath before heading out to the airport. It was time for Olivia to go home.

* * *

"Maybe you should call her?" Logan opened the crate, and Buddy, the German shepherd puppy, cut loose across the field as if chasing a rabbit.

"Who?" Jake glanced in his brother's direction.

"You're kidding, right? Come on. You've been moping around all day." Logan shook his head and mumbled as he headed toward the barn. "You better go after her, man. God has given you a second chance—don't blow it."

His brother knew him well. Despite his best efforts, Jake hadn't been able to stop thinking about Olivia. Last night, he'd searched her flight information multiple times. Her plane left on time and landed safely. In between checking her flight status, he'd been consoling the kids and trying to explain why Olivia had to go back to Miami. The rest of the evening, he'd questioned whether he'd made the biggest mistake of his life by not telling her he was in love with her and wanted nothing more than to raise a family together.

Jake glanced at his watch as he headed toward the house. A sky of restless clouds drifted overhead. Myrna had phoned this morning to let him know she planned to meet the kids' school bus and help them with their homework, but he wanted to be there when they walked in the door.

Myrna was doing everything in her power to keep their minds occupied and off Olivia. Jake had tried his best to stay upbeat, but he missed Olivia, too. There was a giant hole inside him he couldn't seem to fill. Even working to train his latest service dogs couldn't fill the emptiness. Hopefully, once the mother-daughter fashion show was behind them, Kayla would get past the void left in her life by Olivia's departure. But the question was, would he?

He reached the back patio and his eyes focused on the swing between the Douglas firs. *I'm sure that's a beautiful place to watch the sunset.* Olivia's words played in his head and he kicked his boot into the ground. Because of his stubborn ways, they wouldn't share a sunset together.

He scanned the property and listened to a song sparrow trill in the distance. Olivia was right—there was nothing more the land needed. Except, in Jake's opinion, it needed her presence.

"Daddy! Kayla locked herself in her bedroom and she won't come out," Kyle shouted from somewhere in the house. Jake wiped his boots on the laundry room rug and took a deep breath. *Lord, give me strength.*

He scaled the stairs and found Myrna and Kyle outside Kayla's bedroom door. "What's going on?"

Myrna spoke first. "It seems Missy is at it again." She rolled her eyes.

Jake's busy schedule hadn't given him time to call Missy's parents. Now he wished he'd made it a priority. "Do you know what happened?"

"She's so mean!" Kyle wasted no time in reporting the story. "We were in the lunchroom and she came to our table. She started teasing Kayla about the fashion show."

Of course. That seemed to be the hot topic lately. Jake just wanted the show to be over. "What did she say?"

"She said it wasn't a grandmother-and-granddaughter fashion show, so Kayla and Miss Myrna shouldn't be in it. She said…" Kyle paused and looked down at the floor.

"What is it, son? You can say it." Jake glanced at Myrna.

"She said Miss Myrna was too old to be a model." Kyle turned to Myrna. "Sorry."

Myrna straightened her shoulders. "It's not your fault, Kyle."

Jake didn't have a good feeling about this evening. His instincts told him to keep Kayla home. Why subject her to more ridicule by Missy? But what would that teach his daughter? Jake's father always taught him to never give the power to a bully. The best way for Kayla to handle someone like Missy was to stand up to her. Easy for him to say. "I'll talk to her." He knocked on her door and waited for a response. When she didn't answer, he knocked again. "Kayla, can you open the door?"

"Go away!"

Myrna's and Kyle's eyes darted in Jake's direction.

"Why don't you and Kyle go down to the kitchen? Kyle is probably ready for his snack."

Myrna nodded to Jake. "Let's go, hon. I brought over some fresh chocolate chip brownies."

Jake waited until they were downstairs. He reached up over the door frame and grabbed the key to Kayla's room. Slipping the key into the hole, he slowly turned the knob. "I'm coming in." He paused before entering.

Jake's heart sank when he spotted his daughter sitting at her desk. Kayla gazed at the portrait of her mother he'd had professionally matted and framed for Kayla's birthday last year, after she'd told him it was her favorite photograph of her mother.

He slowly approached the desk and placed his hand on Kayla's shoulder. "Can you tell me what happened, sweetie?"

Kayla sprang from the chair and threw her arms around Jake's waist. Without hesitation, he scooped her up. He couldn't recall when she'd ever held on so tight. She buried her face in his shoulder and cried.

"Oh, baby, I'm so sorry." He carried her across the room and sat down on the edge of her bed. When would it ever get easier? Jake had always considered himself a problem solver. There was nothing he couldn't fix when he put his mind to it. But raising a little girl on his own was more than he could handle. Even with Myrna's help, he felt like he was failing his daughter.

Finally, Kayla's body stopped quivering, and her tears subsided. She lifted her head off his shoulder and looked him in the eye. "I'm sorry I locked my door. I know I'm not supposed to."

"It's okay. I understand you wanted to be alone, but sometimes it's good to talk to someone when you're upset."

Kayla nodded. "That's what Dr. Olivia told me. She said keeping stuff inside makes you feel worse."

Jake missed Olivia's words of wisdom. He missed a lot of things about her. "She was right. So, are you ready to talk?"

Kayla pushed her hair off her face and wiped her eyes. "Do I have to go to the fashion show?"

Jake studied his daughter. "Not if you don't want to."

Frowning, she chewed her lower lip. "Does that make me a scaredy-cat?"

Jake flinched. "Who called you that?"

"Kyle said if I didn't go, Missy would start calling me a scaredy-cat."

"What do you think?"

Kayla's forehead crinkled. "Well, if I go, she can't call me that."

"That's true." Jake nodded.

"What do you think Dr. Olivia would do?" Kayla studied his face.

"I think Dr. Olivia would probably go with Miss Myrna and have the best time that she could. She wouldn't allow Missy or anyone else to steal her joy."

Downstairs, the doorbell chimed.

Kayla hugged Jake and jumped off his lap. "Thanks, Daddy. I think I'll go. I won't let mean ole Missy steal my joy, either!"

"That's my girl. Let's go downstairs and see who's at the door."

Kayla held Jake's hand tightly as they walked down the steps. Halfway down, he looked up and froze.

"Dr. Olivia!" Kayla yelled.

Jake blinked his eyes several times to make sure he wasn't seeing things. He wasn't imagining it. Olivia stood in his foyer wearing a dress exactly like the one hanging in Kayla's closet.

Kayla dropped his hand and raced to Olivia. "I knew you'd come. Daddy said you left, but I knew you'd come back."

Jake wasn't sure what to think. His first instinct was to protect his little girl. He couldn't bear the thought of her being hurt again.

Olivia opened her arms and picked Kayla off the ground. They twirled in a circle, both giggling.

When Olivia placed Kayla on her feet again, her eyes fixated on him.

His pulse raced.

"Hi, Jake." She smiled.

He cautiously moved toward her. His heart pounded in his chest. "What are you doing here?"

Olivia's eyes sparkled with tears. "If it's okay with you, I came to take Kayla to the fashion show."

"What about your job? Aren't you supposed to be there now?"

"I put in my notice this morning and got on the first flight to Denver. I just finished talking with Dr. Dickerson. He's going to start training me next week."

Myrna and Kyle cheered from the corner of the room.

Kyle raced to Jake's side. "Daddy, ask her now!"

Jake could hardly peel his eyes away from Olivia. He looked down at Kyle. "Ask what?"

"Ask Dr. Olivia on the date."

Jake reached for Olivia's hand. He planned to take Olivia on dates for the rest of their lives.

Epilogue

Fourteen months later

"Can I hold Maddie, Mommy?"

The word was sweet music to Olivia's ears. *Mommy.*

"I'll be careful. I promise," Kayla said.

Jake had spread out a blanket earlier for Olivia and their new daughter. He'd gone to grill hamburgers and hot dogs.

"Of course you can, sweetie. Have a seat."

Maddie cooed and squinted into the bright July sun reflecting off the lake. Olivia gave Maddie's sun bonnet a quick tug to protect her eyes.

A month had already passed since they welcomed Maddie into the family. Two days prior to her birth, Olivia had officially adopted Kayla and Kyle. Motherhood was exactly how she'd imagined. Exhausting, but so worth every lost hour of sleep.

"I love being a big sister." Kayla took Maddie and snuggled her in her arms.

"You're a wonderful big sister, and you're a tremendous help to me." Olivia leaned back and relaxed for the first time since the party had started.

Olivia couldn't believe she and Jake were already celebrating their anniversary at the same place they'd exchanged vows one year ago. Mirror Lake held a special place in her heart. It was where Jake brought her on their first date, and it was the spot Jake learned he was going to be a father again.

When he proposed, Jake wanted it to be a big surprise. He'd asked Olivia to come over to his house and watch the sunset on her favorite bench. She'd been back in Bluebell for three weeks and they'd been spending every nonworking moment together. For the first time, she declined his invitation. She'd had a long day of training with Dr. Dickerson and was exhausted.

He showed up at Gammy's house with some story about a rare meteor shower that was happening. Olivia was intrigued and decided to go with him despite her tiredness. To this day, he told the story about how she almost missed her chance to become his wife.

"Hey, how come you get to take a break?" Jake stood over her, blocking the sun. She still couldn't believe this gorgeous man was her husband and the father of her child.

He flopped down onto the blanket next to Olivia. "I thought this was our anniversary party. Why am I stuck doing all the work?" Jake joked. "I thought that big rock on your finger meant we were a team."

Olivia laughed. One thing she loved most about Jake, besides the fact that he was a wonderful father, was his sense of humor. Laughter filled their days. "But you like to be in charge of the grill." She nudged her shoulder against his.

"Daddy, after you finish cooking for everyone, can you take me and Kyle out on the canoe?"

"Sure. I'll have to grab the life jackets from the truck. Where is Kyle?" Jake looked around.

"He and Miss Myrna took Callie for a walk."

Jake nodded and took Olivia's hand. "It's quite a turn-out, huh?"

"Well, that's what happens when you put Gammy in charge of party invitations. The entire town shows up." Olivia wouldn't have it any other way. Their family and friends were a blessing.

"Hey, guys." Logan approached the blanket and removed his black Stetson. "I wanted to wish you both a happy anniversary. It's a fantastic party."

"Thanks, man. I appreciate it."

"Thank you, Logan," Olivia said.

Jake stood and addressed his brother. "We need to find you a nice girl so you can settle down."

Logan laughed. "No, thanks. I'm happy being single."

Olivia didn't believe Jake's brother. She'd have to work on that.

"Daddy, come quick!"

"That's Kyle!" Jake said and took off running.

Olivia took Maddie from Kayla's arms. "Let's go, Kayla."

"He's down by the lake," Jake called out over his shoulder. "He's okay. Gammy is with him."

Olivia, the baby and Kayla joined up with Jake. "What's going on?" Olivia looked down and saw Callie digging frantically in the sand. "What is she after?"

"I don't know. Gammy and I were walking, and Callie just started digging. I kept pulling her leash, but she wouldn't move," Kyle explained.

Jake knelt in the sand. "Would you look at this?" He reached his hand into the hole.

"It's your watch, Daddy! The one I lost!" Kyle yelled.

Olivia couldn't hold back her tears. She watched her husband and son celebrating the discovery of the lost family heirloom and thought *God is good*.

* * * * *

If you liked this story from Jill Weatherholt,
check out her previous Love Inspired books:

Searching for Home
A Dream of Family
A Home for Her Daughter

Available now from Love Inspired!

Find more great reads at www.LoveInspired.com.

Dear Reader,

I hope you enjoyed reading Olivia and Jake's story. Like many of us, they faced difficult circumstances that made it difficult to trust God's plan for their lives.

As I continue to write, I face new challenges, especially during times of uncertainty when distractions can pull me off course. But I've learned I'm not alone on this journey. I'm grateful for the gift and desire to write stories of hope, and as long as I remain faithful to God's plan, I know He won't abandon me. Remembering this brings me peace, and I hope it does the same for you.

I invite you to join me in Bluebell Canyon for the next installment in the series, where you'll meet more lovely residents.

Hearing from readers is the best part of being a published author. I do my best to respond to every email. You can join my newsletter at jillweatherholt.com or drop me a note.

Blessings,
Jill Weatherholt

Get 3 FREE REWARDS!

We'll send you 2 FREE Books plus a FREE Mystery Gift.

FREE
Value Over
$20

Both the **Love Inspired®** and **Love Inspired®** Suspense series feature compelling novels filled with inspirational romance, faith, forgiveness and hope.